Landon

Shay

PART ONE

BRITTAINY C. CHERRY

Published: Brittainy C. Cherry 2019
brittainycherry@gmail.com

Editing:
Editing by C. Marie, Ellie at My Brother's Editor,
Jenny at Editing for Indies, LBEdits
Proofreading: Virginia Tesi Carey, Jenn at Jenn Lockwood Editing
Cover Design: Hang Le

To anyone who's ever felt alone:
Place your hand over your heart.
Do you feel that?
It's still beating for a reason.

This one's for you.

"I love you as certain dark things are to be loved.
in secret, between the shadow and the soul."
—*Pablo Neruda*

Landon
Shay

SENIOR YEAR & JUNIOR YEAR
2003

Chapter One

Landon

INEVER MEANT TO BE A MONSTER, BUT SOMETIMES I WONDERED IF CERTAIN people were born that way, born with a darkness that oozed into their bloodstreams and infected their souls.

My name was living proof that I should've been a better person.

I came from a line of extraordinary men. My mother named me after my uncle, Lance, and my grandfather, Don—two of the greatest men who ever lived. The name Don stood for noble, and Lance meant servant. They lived up to those names, too. They both fought in wars. They sacrificed their lives and their minds for others. They gave fully with arms wide open and allowed people to take and take from their good nature until there was nothing left.

Their names combined should've made me a noble servant to the world, but I was far from it. If you asked most of my classmates what my name stood for, they'd probably say asshole. Rightfully so, too.

I was nothing like my grandfather or uncle. I was an embarrassment to their memories.

I didn't know why so much darkness sat heavily in my chest. I didn't know why I was so angry. I just knew that I was.

I was an ass, even when I didn't want to be. The only people who put up with my jerky ways were my core group of friends and Monica, the girl I was trying so hard to shake from my life.

There wasn't anything noble or servant-like about me. I looked out for myself and the very few people who had enough nerve to still call me their friend.

I hated that about me. I hated that I wasn't a good person. I wasn't even decent. I did a lot of ugly things that probably had both Lance and Grandpa rolling over in their graves.

And why was I this way?

I wished I knew.

My mind was a puzzle, and I hardly knew how the pieces linked up.

I headed to the cafeteria after a pointless morning of pointless classes and grabbed my lunch tray. Senior year, one semester down and one to go before I could rid myself of small town Raine, Illinois.

As I walked toward my table, I grimaced when I saw Monica sitting there. For a second, I considered hanging back until Greyson, Hank, or Eric showed up, but she'd already spotted me and waved me over.

"Landon! Get me a milk—low fat," she commanded, her voice sounding so high-pitched. I hated that sound. She sounded like a banshee, and I swore I'd had nightmares of that girl screaming my name.

I hadn't remembered her voice irking me so much in the past. Then again, for our past interactions, I had always been drunk or stoned. We'd known each other for a long time. Monica and I were neighbors and two kids with kind of messed-up lives. I had my demons, and Monica had her own set of issues.

When our problems got too heavy, we used sex with each other to shut off our brains. There was nothing romantic about the hookups. Honestly, we didn't even like each other that much, which was why it worked for me. I wasn't interested in a girlfriend or anything emotional. I just needed to get laid every now and then to shut up my overthinking mind.

It worked for a while until I decided to go cold turkey on the alcohol and drug front.

Ever since I stopped using, Monica had so much crap to say about the matter. "I liked you more when you were high," she'd stated the last time we banged.

To which I had replied, "I liked you better with your mouth around my cock."

That wasn't even true. I didn't even enjoy sex with Monica. It simply passed the time. She had sex like the girls in pornos, and in theory, that should've been amazing. But in reality, it meant too much slobber, too many hit-and-miss strokes, and every so often, I ended up having to find my own way to a happy ending.

Monica slapped me the night I told her that, and part of me kind of liked the sting. My skin flushed and bubbled up from the sensation. It was a reminder that I was still alive, still able to feel, even though for the most part, I felt like dry ice—frozen solid and painful to whoever tried to hold on to me for too long.

Monica told me she wouldn't screw me again until I was high.

Therefore, whatever disaster we were was officially over—for me, at least.

She hadn't gotten the memo. I'd been trying to shake her from my existence for the past few weeks, but like the dedicated cockroach she was, she kept reappearing in my life, popping up at the worst times.

"Are you high yet? Did you relapse? Want to take a shot off my tits?"

The last thing I wanted to deal with that week was Monica, but I knew if I didn't sit by her, she'd only grow louder.

I plopped my tray down on the table and nodded once toward her.

"What the hell? Where's my milk?" she asked.

"Didn't hear you," I dryly replied.

She reached over, took the milk off my tray with no concern for my thirst, and opened it. She was lucky I didn't have the energy to argue with her. I hadn't been sleeping, and I reserved my anger for things and people who actually mattered to me. That list was short, and her name wasn't on it.

"I've been thinking—you should have a party at your place this weekend," she said, chugging down my milk. On the plus side, it wasn't low fat, so at least she didn't completely get her way.

"You always think that," I replied, diving into my lunch. It was only the first week of school since winter break, and it was nice to see that the cafeteria was still serving us the same crappy food as the months before. If there was one thing I liked in my life, it was consistency.

"Yeah, but you should really have one this weekend, seeing how it's Lance's birthday. We should celebrate his memory."

I felt a small fire starting to burn within me as she spoke of Lance as if she'd known him or she cared. She said it for that exact reason, too—to get to me. To push me. To make me the monster she had recently been missing. In her mind, she couldn't use me to forget her scars if my wounds weren't freshly opened.

It had been almost a year since Lance passed away.

Still, it felt like yesterday.

I gritted my teeth. "Don't push me, Monica."

"Why? Pushing your buttons is my favorite thing to do."

"Don't you have some older dicks to chase?" I exhaled heavily, and she gave me a sinister smile. She liked when I brought up the fact that she messed around with older men. It was how she had tried to teach me a lesson when I didn't want to sleep with her. She'd hook up with some older guy and tell me all about it.

Too bad her plan was idiotic, because I didn't care.

If anything, I felt bad about her lack of self-esteem.

Monica was a classic case of a rich girl with daddy issues. It didn't help that her father was actually a huge dick. When Monica told him one of his business partners felt her up at a holiday party, her father called her a liar. I knew she wasn't lying, though, because I'd seen her go to her bedroom that night and fall apart. People didn't cry like that unless there was some truth to the story. It turned out it wasn't the first time one of her father's partners had messed around with her without permission, yet every time she went to him about it, he called her dramatic and desperate for attention.

So, she became exactly what her father told her she was: dramatic and desperate for attention.

She clamored for attention from the men her dad claimed never wanted her. She had issues with her daddy, so she slept with men his age. She even called them daddy in bed, which was disturbing on so many levels.

Once, she called me daddy in bed, and I stopped screwing her right there. I didn't want to feed her demons; I wanted to help shut my own up for a while.

Truthfully, I was glad she and I weren't messing around anymore.

Monica pushed her tongue into her cheek and cocked an eyebrow. "What? Are you jealous?"

She wished, she hoped, and she prayed.

I wasn't.

"Monica, you do know we aren't together, right? You can do whatever you want with whomever you want. We aren't a thing." I was good at making it perfectly clear to chicks what we were—or more so, what we were not. I never misled them with the idea we'd be anything serious because I didn't do serious. There was only so much free space in my head, and I knew I wasn't relationship material. I didn't have the energy to be someone's someone—just someone's fuck buddy.

Honestly, I wouldn't have even said buddy. I wasn't their friend or confidant, and I never would be.

Monica winked my way like she thought I was the cat and she was the mouse I was trying to chase. I blamed myself, really. The worst thing a broken person could do was hook up with another broken person. Ten times out of ten, it turned into a disaster.

Monica pulled out her cell phone and started texting nonstop, blabbering about something or other as her lips flapped open and shut. She talked about other people and how ugly, stupid, or poor they were. As hot as she was, she was one of the ugliest people I'd ever seen.

Couldn't really judge her on that, though. When I used to be drugged up, I was a bigger dick than I was now. It turned out your level of compassion for others when you're high is extremely low. I said and done a lot of shit I was certain karma would get me for at some point down the line.

"Rumor is there's a party at your place this Saturday," Greyson said as he walked up to the table with Hank and Eric. *Thank God.* Sitting alone with Monica was a nightmare.

"What do you mean?" I asked.

He waved his phone toward me, showing me a text from Monica. *Figures.* I was sure that same message had gone out to a ton of other people, and no matter what, they were going to show up to my house for a party. So, lo and behold, it appeared I was hosting a party.

Happy Birthday, Lance.

I turned my back a little toward Monica, and my eyes widened a bit at Greyson as I whispered, "Dude. She's nuts."

He laughed and ran his hand through his charcoal hair. "I hate to say I told you so, but..." He trailed off and snickered. From day one, Greyson had told me that sleeping with Monica was a bad idea, but I hadn't listened. I was more of a *screw now, consequences later* kind of guy. That quickly came back to bite me in the ass.

Monica tapped me on the back. "Hey, I'm going to go to the girls' room. Watch my stuff."

I shrugged, not wanting to give her any more of my words. Talking to her was almost as exhausting as homework. I'd have preferred to do algebra instead of speaking to her, and I sucked at math equations.

As Monica was walking out of the cafeteria, Shay entered the room, and a knot formed in my gut. Since the year before, that knot in my stomach always appeared whenever Shay Gable entered the room. I wasn't exactly sure what the feeling meant, or if it even meant anything, but dammit, the feeling was there.

Probably gas, I always told myself.

I hated Shay Gable.

If there was only one thing in life I knew for certain, it was that fact.

I'd known her for years now. She was a year younger than me, but her grandmother was my housekeeper, and she used to bring Shay over sometimes when her parents were unable to watch her.

From day one, we never gelled. You know how people have instant friendships? She and I had an instant hateship. I hated her and her goody-two-shoes personality. Ever since we were kids, Shay never misbehaved. She was always getting good grades, always making friends wherever she went. She didn't touch drugs, and she partied sober. She probably said her prayers and kissed her grandma before bed, too.

Little Miss Perfect.

More like Little Miss Fake.

I didn't buy her good-girl act.

Nobody could be that good. Nobody could have so few demons in their closet.

We hung out in the same circles, had the same friends, but we were far from being anything more than enemies. I was comfortable with our hate, too. It felt oddly pleasing. Hating Shay was the most constant thing in my life. Hating her felt like a high I'd always been chasing, and as each year passed, I got more and more high off Shay's dismissal of me. There was something intense about the hate we gave, and the older we grew, the more I craved it.

Shay grew up in ways most girls dreamed of growing. Her body developed as quickly as her mind had. She had curves in every place us dicks hoped curves would exist, eyes that sparkled in every situation, and a dimple so deep you kind of wished she were always smiling. Sometimes, I'd watch her and hate myself for liking what I saw. This year, Shay came back to school looking more grown-up than ever. More curves, more tits, more ass. If I didn't hate her so much, I would've considered screwing her brains out.

Not only was she beautiful, she was smart, too. She was the top of the junior class. Brains and beauty—though I'd never tell her so. For all she knew, my thoughts of her were completely filled with disgust and loathing, but sometimes, I'd watch her when she wasn't looking. Sometimes, I'd listen to her laugh with her girlfriends. I'd study the way she studied people like they were art and she was trying to figure out how they'd been created. She was always jotting things down in notebooks, too, like her life depended on the words on those pages.

I'd only known one person who wrote as many thoughts as Shay did. She must have filled up hundreds of notebooks with how many damn thoughts she scribbled down on the regular.

Monica stopped Shay, likely to invite her to the party.

Why would she invite her? Everyone knew how much Shay and I despised each other. Then again, it was Monica. She kept her head so far up her own ass she didn't notice anyone else's issues. Or then again, maybe she invited Shay solely to spite me. That was one of Monica's favorite pastimes.

Shay stood there with her closest friends, Raine and Tracey. Raine happened to be one of my closest friends, too, seeing how she was dating Hank, who was a good buddy of mine. Raine was the comedic relief of any gathering. If you needed a reason to laugh, she was the person you went to. She often joked that she was named after the town she was born in because her parents were too lazy to come up with something clever on their own. *"Thank goodness I wasn't born in Accident, Maryland,"* she'd always joke. *"That would've made for a hefty therapy bill."*

Then, there was Tracey. She was Jackson High's sugar-pop queen. If you were looking for a girl with team spirit, Tracey was the one to feed it to you along with hearty helpings of glitter and rainbows. Currently, it seemed Tracey was trying to force her brightness down Reggie's throat, and I wasn't sure he had much interest in it. Reggie was the new kid on the block, having transferred in from Kentucky, and most of the girls were smitten by him due to his Southern accent. Honestly? He seemed like a basic douchebag to me who said y'all every now and then. I was a pro at spotting assholes.

Takes one to know one.

Tracey was too innocent for a guy like him. Though she could get a bit annoying and over the top with her rainbow cheer, she was overall an okay person. She meant no harm to anyone, which was exactly why she didn't need a guy like Reggie in her life. He'd eat her alive, then spit her out like they'd never known each other.

That was what us bad boys did: we fed on good girls and tossed them to the side once we were full.

What Reggie needed in his life was a good ole Monica. It was a match made in Hell.

The girls kept chatting, and I knew Monica was probably going on and on about this party I didn't want to have. Shay glanced toward me with an uneasy, disdainful look.

Hello, brown eyes.

If that girl hated anything more than me, it was parties thrown by me, which was why she made it a point never to attend them. The moment we locked eyes, I turned away. We never crossed paths much, but if we did, we exchanged short words with each other. Most of the time, they were rude, too. It was kind of our thing. We both got off on hating each other.

Except that one time nine months ago.

Her grandmother, Maria, had attended Lance's funeral, and Shay had come with her. They came to the reception at my house, and Shay walked in on me during one of my not-so-manly moments.

I wished she hadn't seen me that way: broken, disheveled, raw, real.

I also wished Lance hadn't died, but you know how it goes. Wishes, dreams, hopes—all fiction.

"You sure you want a party?" Greyson asked, lowering his voice and pulling me from my thoughts about Shay. The other guys at the table were talking about basketball and girls, but Greyson seemed unfazed by it all. "With it being Lance's birthday."

No one else really knew about my uncle's birthday, and I was thankful for it. Greyson only knew because he kept track of important things. He was that kind of friend. He had a memory like no other and used it for good. Monica only knew because she collected any information she could somehow use as daggers to stab her victims with. She was the complete opposite of Greyson.

I shrugged. "Rather be with people than alone, I guess." He went to argue, but I shook my head. "It's fine. I could use the company. Plus, I don't see Monica letting up on the idea."

"I could host at my place," he offered, but I declined.

Besides, me throwing a party was one thing; Greyson throwing one was a completely different ball game. My parents would be annoyed to hear about the party but would shrug it off pretty quickly. If Greyson's father found out about him hosting it, he would have a much harsher punishment. If there was anything I knew about Mr. East, it was that he had a violent hand and wasn't afraid to use it on his wife or his son.

He was lucky I'd never witnessed him laying a hand on my friend. That hand would've been chopped off quickly.

A few girls came up to our table, giggling like the damn school-girls they were, and they waved our way. It was no secret that every girl had a crush on Greyson, and quite a few had a crush on me, too. It was funny because Greyson and I were pretty different in almost all ways. Greyson's persona at school was the saintly good student. I was the damn devil, but it turned out, a woman could love the angels in the sunlight and still want to sin at night.

"Rumor has it there's a party at your house this Saturday, Landon," one of the girls said, twirling her hair around her finger. "Can we come?"

"Do I know you?" I asked.

"Not yet, but you can get to know me at your party," she said with a suggestive tone. She stuck her tongue into the side of her cheek and jabbed it in and out for good measure. *Geez.* I was kind of shocked she didn't reach straight into my jeans, yank out my cock, and start slobbering all over it.

It was clear they were younger than us—sophomores, probably. No one was more horny than sophomore girls. It was like one day they went from innocently playing with their Barbies to dramatically making Barbie and Ken bang. I understood why fathers worried about their high school daughters. It was like *Girls Gone Wild: High School Edition.* If I were a dad, I'd lock the kid in the basement until their thirtieth birthday.

I shrugged off her provocative gesture. "If you can find out the address, you can come."

Their eyes lit up with excitement, and they giggled, hurrying off on a quest to find out where I lived. If they would've asked me, I probably would've told them. I was feeling charitable that afternoon.

"So this party is really happening?" Greyson asked.

I bit into my dry chicken patty sandwich and tried to get Lance out of my head and out of my heart. A party would work. It would distract me a bit.

"Yup." I nodded, one hundred percent sure. "It's happening."

I glanced up across the space to see Shay talking to some band geek or something. She was always doing that kind of shit—talking to people in all social classes. People didn't just love her; they *love* loved her.

Shay was Jackson High's royalty, but not the bitchy, asshole kind like Monica and me. People liked Monica and me because we scared them. People loved Shay because she was…Shay, the Princess Diana of high school.

Which was exactly why I hated her. I hated how unapologetically happy she was, hated how she had a way of moving around with so much confidence and joy. Her happiness annoyed the living hell out of me.

She looked like a princess, standing tall with bright chocolate doe eyes and plump lips that always smiled. Her skin was a smooth warm tone, and her hair was the darkest of black with light waves. Her body curved in all the right places, and my mind couldn't help but wonder what she looked like without clothes on. To put it simply, Shay was beautiful. So many dudes called her hot, but I didn't agree. Calling her hot felt idiotic and cheap because she wasn't just hot like some girls at our school. She was a vibrant light. She was the spark that lit up the sky. A fucking star.

As cliché and chick flick as it sounded, every guy wanted her, and every girl wanted to be her.

She was friends with them all, too—every single person. Even if she dated someone, they never ended on bad terms. The split always seemed peaceful. Shay not only looked like a damn princess, but she acted like one, too. Cool, calm, collected. Poised. She never went without saying hi to anyone who approached her. She never excluded anyone from any activity. If she hosted a gathering, she'd invite the nerds, the band geeks, and the football players.

She didn't believe in separation by social class, which kind of made her an anomaly at our school and in life as a whole. It was as if Shay was born with a mind light-years ahead of the rest of us and knew high school status wouldn't mean shit in the scheme of things. She wasn't a piece that fit one puzzle. She was a one-size-fits-all person. She managed to find a spot in everyone's world, and it all seemed so effortless. The geeks at our school talked about Shay the same way the goths did—with love and admiration. She was amazing to everyone.

To everyone *but* me.

I was fine with that, though. Truthfully, the idea of Shay being kind to me was enough to make me want to lose my lunch.

I'd take her hateful looks over her gentle doe eyes any day.

MY FATHER WAS THE KING OF OUR CASTLE, AND I WAS HIS FAVORITE little princess.

Sure, I was his only daughter, which made me his favorite by default, but Mom always made sure to remind me. "Your father's love is big, even though he sometimes doesn't know how to show it."

That was a true fact. My dad wasn't a good man, but he was a good father for the most part, though he never really showed his love in a straightforward way. He showed it in his actions and in his critiques. Once when I was younger, I remembered Mom studying for her nursing degree, and she asked Dad to help her study. He told her flatly that he wouldn't, because she had to learn how to do it on her own, seeing how he wouldn't be there to help her with the exam.

I thought he was being cruel for no good reason.

Mom disagreed. "He's right not to help. He won't be there for the test, therefore I should do it on my own."

She passed the exam without his help, and when she told him the news, he had a diamond necklace awaiting her in the living room as a congratulations gift. "I knew you would pass without my help," he told her. "You're smart without me."

They loved each other. From the outside looking in, it probably appeared that Mom loved him more than he loved her, but I knew better. My father was a complex man. I couldn't even remember the last time I'd heard him say he loved me, but he offered that love in his looks, in his short nods and his tiny smirks. When he was pleased with you, he'd nod twice your way. When he was upset, his ice blue eyes would pierce a hole through your soul. When he was very upset, he'd pierce a hole through a wall. When he was sad, he disappeared.

My parents' love story had years of challenges attached to it. Dad used to get into trouble when he was younger, dealing drugs in their old neighborhood. I knew it was an awkward thing to say, but my father was great at what he did. He was a solid salesman. Mom always said he could sell poop to a person and they'd use it as shampoo. For a while, we lived a pretty lavish lifestyle. It wasn't until he started using the drugs himself that everything began to crumble. The worst thing a drug dealer can ever do is sample the product. As he partook in the drugs, his alcohol usage grew too, and he became even colder than before. Distant. Hard.

Cruel.

There were many nights he'd come home hollering drunk and high, slurring his words. There were other nights he simply wouldn't come home.

The turning point for him was when a buddy of his got shot and killed, and Dad got caught by the cops. He'd ended up in prison for a few years.

He'd been out for a while now, and he'd gone clean from dealing and using drugs and alcohol after he was released.

It had been over a year since he'd come home.

A year, two months, and twenty-one days.

But who was counting?

Mom hated even talking about Dad's former struggles. She glossed over it as if it hadn't even happened. My grandmother, Mima for short, wasn't as closed off to talking about my father's past. She'd moved in with Mom and me when Dad got locked up for dealing. We needed the help around the house, and Mima stepped right in to help cover the bills. Honestly, I was thankful for that. For how cold my father was, my grandmother was the complete opposite. She was warm, open, and giving. Mima's heart was made of gold, and she went out of her way to make sure the ones she loved were taken care of.

When it was just the three girls, the house felt so light, so fun, so free. During that period of time, I slept so much easier, without fear of the unknown with my father. At least when he was locked up, he couldn't get into any more trouble. At least when he was locked up, he couldn't end up dead from a deal gone bad.

It wasn't a secret that my grandmother and father didn't see eye to eye on a lot of things. When he was released, he came back to a home thinking he was just going to be in charge of everything, but Mima had a different point of view. They butted heads on the regular. Mom tried her best to keep our house a place of peace. For the most part, it worked. Mima avoided my father, and my father avoided her.

Except for when we all came together to celebrate important days.

If there was anything my family was good at, it was celebrating important milestones, and Mom's birthday was one of them. She was thirty-two today, and I swore she didn't look a day over eighteen. Often times, people confused Mom and me as siblings—boy, did she love that. I was certain I'd be grateful for those genetics down the line.

My cousin, Eleanor, and her parents, Kevin and Paige, always joined us to celebrate birthdays and holidays. Uncle Kevin was my father's older brother, but I swore he looked five years younger than Dad. Then again, Kevin hadn't lived quite the adventurous, dangerous life Dad had. The wrinkles on Kevin's face weren't formed from stress and struggle—they were from laughter and joy.

Mima set the birthday cake down on the table and began singing 'Happy Birthday' then everyone joined in. Mom grinned ear to ear as we sang out loud, just awfully. She sat next to Dad, and I watched as his hand gently squeezed her knee.

Sometimes, I'd catch Dad staring at Mom with wonderment in his eyes. When I'd call him out on his longing gaze, he'd shake his head, and say, "I don't deserve her. I never have, and I never will. Your mother is a saint, too good for me—too good for this world."

We could both agree on that. I couldn't imagine the things my father had put her through. Mom would never tell me about those things, though. I was certain if I knew all their secrets, I'd end up hating my father, which was probably why Mom never told me. She didn't want to damage my view on the man who'd raised me. But, I knew loving a man like my father wasn't an easy task. It took a strong heart to deal with a man like him, and I knew Mom's heart beat with strength. If there was one constant in my life, it was my mother's love. I never questioned it in any way, shape, or form, and I doubt Dad questioned it, either. She was the definition of ride or die—loyal through and through. She gave her love wholeheartedly, even at the expense of it draining her own soul.

Mima started cutting the cake, and Paige smiled her way. "You'll have to give me the recipe for the cake, Maria. It's to die for."

"Oh no, sweetheart. My recipes will die with me. I one-hundred percent plan to be buried with my cookbook," Mima semi-joked. I had no doubt she'd take that book to her grave. Mom would probably be crazy enough to dig it up, though, just for one more taste of Mima's enchiladas. I wouldn't blame her, either.

Mima's food was like eating a bit of heaven, and I'd be right there with my mother, shovel in my hand, in search of the secret ingredient in her homemade tortillas.

Dad stood up from the table after everyone had their cake in front of them. He cleared his throat. Dad wasn't one for speeches. He was a pretty quiet man. Mom always said he thought all his words to death and by the time they were ready to leave his mouth, they came out mute.

But every year, for every birthday, he gave a toast to Mom—excluding the years when he was away.

"I wanted to raise a glass of champagne," Dad declared, "and sparkling grape juice for the underagers. Camila, you have been a light to this family, to this world, and we are lucky to have another go-round with you. Thank you for standing for this family—for me—through thick and thin. You are my world, my breath, my air, and today we celebrate you. Cheers to another trip around the sun, and to many more to come."

Everyone cheered and drank and laughed. These moments were my favorite ones, the memories being created over laughter and happiness.

"Oh, and of course your gift," Dad said as he walked out of the dining room and then came back with a small box.

Mom sat up a bit. "Kurt, you didn't have to give me anything."

"Of course I did. Open it."

Mom shifted in her seat a little as all eyes were on her. If there was anything she hated, it was attention on her. As she unwrapped the gift and opened it, she gasped. "Oh my gosh, Kurt. This is too much."

"Not for you."

Mom held up a pair of diamond earrings that shimmered and shimmered.

Mima raised an eyebrow. "Those look pretty expensive," she muttered.

Dad shrugged. "Nothing's too expensive for my wife."

"Except when it is and you have a part-time janitor job and a part-time post office job," she shot back.

"How about you worry about your own finances, Maria? Let me deal with mine," Dad hissed her way.

And there it was, the tension that lived in the house. I swore the air grew thicker whenever the two of them fought.

"Well, thank you, honey," Mom said, standing up and hugging Dad. "Though, they do look expensive."

"Don't worry about it. I've been saving up for it for some time. You deserve nice things," he told her.

Mom looked as if her mind was spinning with things to say, but she never spoke her thoughts. Most of the time, she simply overthought them. "Well okay! Let's all eat some cake, drink some more champagne, and keep this celebration going."

The subject of the diamond earrings was put to rest, and I was thankful for that. It probably helped that we had guests that night, otherwise Mima and Dad's argument would've escalated quickly.

Eleanor sat at the table with a book in her hand, and her eyes danced back and forth nonstop.

"I'm glad to see you're not much of an introvert anymore, Ellie," Mima joked, sliding her a piece of cake.

Eleanor shut the book, and her cheeks reddened. "Sorry. I just wanted to finish the chapter before eating."

"I feel like you're always trying to finish a chapter," I said, nudging my cousin.

"Says the girl always trying to finish a script," she replied.

Touché.

The only thing Eleanor and I had in common besides DNA was our love of words and stories, which was enough to make us each other's very best friend.

Having an Eleanor in my life was like having a fresh bouquet delivered to me each day. She was smart, kind, and refreshingly sarcastic. I swore no one could make me laugh more than Eleanor.

The quiet ones always had the best under-the-breath commentary.

"Speaking of scripts," Eleanor said, turning her body my way as she stuffed cake into her mouth. "When do I get to read the one you're working on?"

Eleanor had read all my scripts up to this point—which were a lot of scripts—and she was, without a doubt, my biggest fan. She was also my biggest critic and she gave me feedback that made me a better storyteller.

When I had first given one to Eleanor, I'd made her promise not to talk about the scripts with anyone.

To which she had replied, "Okay, Shay. I'll make sure not to tell Mr. Darcy or Elizabeth Bennet what you're writing about. Though, I can't swear I won't tell Harry, Ron, or Hermione." She joked, referring to the fact that other than me, she didn't have friends, which was too bad. So many people were missing out on the greatness that was Eleanor Gable.

My phone dinged, then it dinged again—followed by about a billion more dings. Mom looked up at me with a knowing grin. "Tracey?"

"Sure is," I replied. The only person who texted nonstop without ever receiving a reply was my close friend, Tracey. We'd grown up together, and it was no secret that Tracey was a bit chatty. She was the head of the cheerleading squad, and the president of student council, and she oozed school spirit. I, too, had a bit of school spirit in my bones, but Tracey was on a whole other level. She lived, breathed, and ate everything high school.

It wasn't shocking that she was one of the most popular girls at our school. She was smart, beautiful, and funny, too. It was just a shame that most of the guys were a bit turned off by her oomph for life.

Tracey: Oh.Em.Gee! Reggie is going to the PARTY @ Land's this SATURDAY! SHAY WE HAVE TO GO

Tracey: Before you say no (which I know UR thinking) I NEED NEED NEED this!

Tracey: I need you to be my wingwoman

Tracey: Three words: Reggie will be there

Tracey: Kk, that was four words, but you get it!

Tracey: PLEASEEEE SHAY! I need you. Reggie is IT for me, and a party at Land's will help him realize it.

Tracey: Say yes?

Tracey: I'll make sure you don't even cross paths with Landon, let alone breathe the same air as him.

Tracey: I'll also buy you a pony or something. Plz?!

I laughed as I read Tracey's overly dramatic comments. She was head over heels for this new student, Reggie. He was the exact type of guy Tracey seemed to always lose her mind over: overly masculine, cocky, handsome in a ridiculous way, and very aware of his good looks. I didn't know much about him other than what Tracey had told me and what I'd witnessed during our brief encounters at school, but I was certain Reggie had what I called AT—Asshole Tendencies. I hadn't gathered enough information to know if he was an FBA—Full-Blown Asshole—but I was slowly but surely collecting data in hopes of protecting my friend from a heartbreak.

If there was one thing I was a professional at, it was reading people. It came with my gift of using real-life people as case studies for my characters' development in my scripts. I could usually see a person and tell if they were a hero, a villain, or a supporting character with just a glance, but some people were a bit harder to grasp from a first meeting. I needed a chance to be around Reggie more to get a real feel for what he was all about.

Tracey: Does your silence mean yes?

Me: I want a blond pony named Marcy.

Tracey: That's why you're my fave human.

Going to a party at Landon's house would be odd. We did pretty good at keeping our hatred for each other strong, and that meant I never went to his place for parties even though he had thrown them frequently throughout the past year. Ever since his uncle passed away, it seemed he had a party every other weekend.

I made it a habit not to attend, but seeing as Tracey was desperate for a shot with Reggie, I knew it was in my friendship duties. My hope was that the party would be big enough that I wouldn't even have to interact with Landon at all.

We ran in the same group of friends, and I pretty much loved them all, but somehow, Landon and I never connected in a positive light. Even when we were kids, he hated me. Once, he called me a chicken because I wouldn't smoke pot at a party. After that, Chicken became his nickname for me. I called him Satan—for obvious reasons.

We'd only ever so slightly connected one time, and that was when Mima took me along to Lance's funeral. The reception after the service was held at his house, and I wandered upon Landon by accident as I looked for the bathroom. He was sitting in his bedroom, sobbing his eyes out on his bed, wearing his suit and tie, unable to breathe.

I didn't know what to do because I wasn't his friend. We were hardly even acquaintances. If anything, I was the villain in his story, as he was the one in mine, but at that moment, he looked so alone, so broken. I might not have liked him much, but I knew the love he had for Lance. It was no secret that Lance was a father figure to him. He was pretty much Landon's father, if you asked me. His actual father was just a man who deposited money into Landon's bank account.

As I watched him cry, I didn't know what to do, so I did the only thing I could think of. I went and I sat beside him. I loosened his tightened tie and held him in my arms as he sobbed uncontrollably in my embrace. He fell completely apart, and I saw every piece of him shatter.

The next day at school, I walked up to him as he was grabbing books from his locker because I wanted to make sure he was okay. He grimaced and slammed his locker shut. His head lowered a bit, and he refused to look me in the eye as he spoke low and controlled. *"This isn't a thing, Chicken—you and me talking. You never cared about my feelings before, so don't pity me now just because Lance is dead. I don't want your charity. Go give your words to someone who gives a shit because I don't, and I won't."*

We didn't talk about his breakdown again. It was almost as if the I'd made that moment up in my mind, and it was only a delusion. I was fine with that. If he wasn't going to bring it up, then neither was I. We went back to our hatred, and I was thankful for the familiarity…though parts of me still thought about it sometimes. I thought about how sad the most popular kid at school was, yet nobody really even noticed.

Maybe it was a temporary sadness, though; the type of sadness that passed with time. Maybe by now, Landon was okay. Either way, he'd made it clear it was none of my business.

I had to come up with a game plan for his party—a few rude remarks in my back pocket, a lot of left turns when he was coming toward me, and a ton of complete avoidance.

"Hey, Eleanor." I nudged her in the shoulder. She'd already slammed her piece of cake down and was now back to reading her book. "Do you want to come to a party with Tracey and me this Saturday?"

"Is it a reading party?" she asked, raising an eyebrow.

"A reading party?"

"You know, where a group of people get together, sit in a circle, and completely ignore one another for hours as they dive headfirst into a novel of their choosing? Does it happen in a library? Will there be bookmarks?"

I laughed. "Well, no."

"Oh. Then that's a hard pass for me." She went right back to reading. I swore one day, I was going to drag her to a ridiculous high school party, and she was going to have an awful time like the rest of us teenagers.

And who knew? Maybe she'd fall in love. Or heck, even fall in *like*. Mom always said the first step of love was falling deeply into like. Then the freefall of love didn't feel so dangerous. Eleanor never put herself in a position to even like someone, though. My cousin wasn't into guys that much unless they were fictional, but I really hoped one day someone would sweep her right off her feet. Then again, that might've just been the storyteller in my heart. I had a thing for happily ever after in all my scripts, and I wished the same for the people I loved, too.

That said, I had a feeling Eleanor would've lived a perfectly content life being locked in a dungeon with five million books surrounding her.

Oh? And how did Eleanor Gable die?

Surrounded by a million happily ever afters and a handful of what-the-hell endings.

While Eleanor dived deeper into her book, I tried to wrap my head around the fact I was going to be attending a party at Landon's. I was going to walk through the front door of the home of a boy I couldn't stand and who couldn't stand me right back.

And I, for one, wasn't ready for that at all.

Chapter Three

Shay

I SPENT MOST OF SATURDAY MORNING TRYING TO CALM TRACEY'S NERVES. If there was anything my friend was good at, it was overthinking every situation tenfold. My mom tried to talk me into staying in and eating Chinese with the family, but I knew Tracey would kill me if I ditched at the last minute.

I would've killed to have an eggroll instead of going to Landon's place, though.

"Oh gosh, I got a belly full of nerves," Tracey spat out as we stood on Landon's front porch.

Me.

On Landon's porch.

Crap.

For a second, I thought about retreating. I considered turning on the heels of my sneakers and waiting for the next party at someone else's house the following week. I hadn't been able to shake this weird feeling in my gut since I decided to attend the party. I knew I was overthinking the whole situation, but the fact that my arms had been wrapped around Landon the last time I'd been inside that house was messing with my head.

The intimate moment of our momentary slip in hatred was so vibrant in my mind, I swore it felt as if it had just happened the day before. I saw his deep blue eyes swimming in the sea of his sadness, I felt his body tremble against my touch, and I felt his pain, so raw and unfiltered. He'd been the complete opposite of how Landon presented himself at school. He always seemed so unbothered by the world as if he was in it but not a part of it. He was cockily cool, calm, and collected as if nothing and nobody could or would ever bother him. That night as I sat on his bed with my arms wrapped around him, I saw his heart, his gentle, pained heart, and it bled just like everyone else's did.

It might've even bled a little bit more than most people.

I looked over at my hopeful friend. Tracey hadn't stopped talking about the party or Reggie since the day she found out there was going to be a party the two of them could attend together. Tracey was convinced she did her best flirting at house parties. She said trying to be flirty at school was too much pressure. She preferred low lighting, and loud music, and tequila.

Tequila mostly.

"I really can't get rid of the nerves," she repeated, snapping me from my thoughts of Landon.

"Why? You're great, and Reggie would be crazy not to notice," I told her as she applied her lipstick, then handed me the tube to do the same to my lips.

"Yeah? Do you think my outfit is too much? I was going for slutty, but not a slut vibe. Like the *yeah, I have boobs, but no you cannot touch them* kind of vibe."

"You could be completely nude, and it still wouldn't give a guy the right to touch you," I explained. "Plus, clothes don't make you a slut. That's just society's messed-up judgments." As the words left my mouth, I swore one day I would become exactly like my mother and grandmother—preaching about a woman's worth, knowing what I did and didn't deserve from a man.

She snickered and rolled her eyes. "Okay, Mother Teresa, but all I'm saying is how do my boobs look?"

I laughed. "If I were Reggie, I'd definitely steal a few glances."

Tracey combed her hair behind her ears before nervously pulling it back out to where it had been originally. She fiddled a lot when she was nervous. "Okay. Okay. He's just a junior. It's not like he's the hottest senior on the block. He's only like four months older than me—that's like nothing, right? There's no need to put this much pressure on the situation, but then again, if I don't put pressure on it then maybe he'll think I don't like him, and well, that's the complete opposite of the idea I want to give him, and, and, and—"

"Tracey," I cut in.

"Yes?"

"Breathe."

She blew out a cloud of hot air. "Okay."

"Just be yourself, and if that's not enough, screw Reggie. There are other guys in this world."

She snickered. "That's easy for you to say. Guys are throwing themselves at you daily, Shay. Not everyone was born freaking flawless."

I didn't respond to her comment, because Tracey always said stuff like that, and it always left me feeling weird. I didn't want to be known just for my looks, but it felt super fake and annoying to say something like that. I knew I was attractive, but for some reason, I was ashamed to admit it even though it wasn't like I'd given myself my looks. It was the least interesting thing about me.

I'd preferred guys be into me for my creativity, my humor, or my intense knowledge of all things *Charmed*, not just because they thought I looked hot.

I was blessed with my mother's genetics. Mima called it our Martinez gift. I swore, my grandmother looked as if she were closer to forty years old as opposed to sixty. We were blessed with youthful-looking skin. Dad always joked that Mom had me all on her own, and there wasn't an ounce of him in me. *"That's definitely my earlobe,"* he'd comment, *"and no lie, that's my left ring finger."*

I had Mom's deep chocolate eyes and her full lips. My hair was curly and charcoal black, and my body had the same curves as my mother's, which guys seemed to like about me. But those very features were also a deterrent for me when it came to liking boys. If one of the first things they mentioned about me had to do with my body, I knew it would never be theirs to have.

"You're more than your body, and only the ones who notice that are al-lowed to have you in that way," Mima always told me, a message I was sure she'd also told Mom when she was a teenager.

Tracey and I walked into the party, and I released the breath I hadn't realized I was holding.

I'd done it. I'd crossed the entrance into Satan's den and lived to tell the story. And, shockingly, I wasn't set on fire. Angels like me weren't supposed to dance in the same ring as the Devil.

A comfort washed over me as I looked around the room and noticed every person was someone I'd call my friend. That made it easier. I could be myself and feel fine knowing my people were around me.

"Look, there he is!" Tracey whisper-shouted, nudging me in the arm. She nodded her head toward the fireplace where Reggie was hanging out with a few of the guys from the football team. He had a beer in his hand and was laughing, probably using that Southern accent of his that made half of the student body lose their damn minds.

"Let's go say hi," I offered, and Tracey tensed up. "Oh, for goodness' sake, Trace, come on. It's not like he bites, and if he does, it will probably feel good," I joked, pulling her forward.

As we approached the group, the manly conversation stopped, and the guys smirked our way.

"Well, well, well, if it isn't trouble," Eric remarked, eyeing me up and down. "And trouble's trouble," he said, whistling low at Tracey and me.

I smiled wide and nudged Eric in the side. "Hey, buddy. I was hoping I'd see you here so I could roll my eyes a bit tonight," I teased. Eric and I had dated for a bit, and by dated, I meant we'd kissed a total of three times before he told me he'd be more into it if I had a penis in my pants. Fair enough. Eric hadn't come out to anyone other than me, though, and his secret was safe. The best thing we'd gotten out of our five-month relationship was a solid friendship.

Yes, we'd dated five months and only kissed three times. Red flags should've gone up a lot sooner for me, but when you have your first boyfriend, you don't really overthink the situation.

"Well, you're in luck," Eric commented, wrapping his arm around my shoulder. "I'm feeling extra annoying tonight."

Tracey stood still, seemingly nervous and feeling out of place. She was drowning in her own self-doubts, and like the good friend I was, I was determined to get her to shore.

"Hey, Reggie, you any good at beer pong?" I asked.

"Only the best," he said cockily, and I swore I saw my friend swoon just from those three words. While he wasn't my cup of tea, I had to shake it off in honor of Tracey.

"Well, Trace here is a reigning champion herself. She's never lost a game."

Reggie turned to Tracey and cocked an eyebrow. Jesus, even his brows were cocky. "Is that so?"

"Well, er, yeah, I guess. I've never lost a game?" Tracey stammered, making it sound like a question. My poor, nervous butterfly. If only she would spread her wings a bit, she'd remember she could fly.

"It's true. You guys should team up and get a tournament going. It could be fun," I suggested.

Reggie shrugged. "Yeah, that could be fun. Let's go grab a drink and get a game going. Your name's Tracey, yeah?"

Her cheeks turned redder than an apple. "Yes, Tracey with an E, not that it matters, because the E is silent when you say it, but my mom thought—"

"Rambling," I coughed into my hand, giving my friend a slight push in her shoulder.

She blushed more and stopped talking. "Yeah, it's Tracey. Let's go get that drink." Before going, she leaned into me, and whispered, "You're so going to get that pony tonight. Also, since Eric is here, you might as well try giving his pony a ride." She smirked and winked, feeling proud of herself.

Oh, Tracey. If only she knew Eric's pony had a no-XX-chromosome-riders policy. Reggie was more likely to get to ride it before I ever would.

They hurried away, and I listened to my friend blabber about everything under the sun as Reggie stole a few glances at her boobs.

"You know he's going to waste her time, right? He's kind of a douche," Eric commented. "I mean, the whole time he was talking to us guys, all he talked about was how much pussy he got back home."

I sighed. "Yeah, I had a feeling, but you know what they say: the heart wants what the heart wants." And Tracey's heart was locked and loaded for her next mistake.

"That's how herpes happens," Eric said, making me giggle.

Speaking of hearts, mine did an odd skipping thing the moment Landon entered the room.

I'd be lying if I said he didn't look handsome. He'd grown up over the years from an annoying boy to an annoying man, and I'd watched it happen from a distance. I wished he would've lived a little longer in the awkward teenager-with-braces phase of his life, but I hadn't been that lucky. Now, he had a perfect smile to go with his perfect blue eyes, messy brown hair, and built body. I swore he'd gone from skinny boy to the Incredible Hulk overnight. His muscles had muscles, and every time I looked at them, it felt like they were flipping me off.

His eyes locked with mine, and he gave me an intense stare, almost as if saying, *You really had the nerve to show up, huh?*

Yes, Landon, I'm here, and you aren't going to bully me out with your stupid looks.

He must've accepted that challenge because he wandered in our direction, red Solo cup in hand and that same damn smirk on his lips.

I hated how he smiled at me. It always seemed so sinister.

I also hated that a small part of me was attracted to said smile. A part of me craved that smile. Sometimes, I'd study Landon from afar, wondering if his lips would curve up. For the most part, he lived with a constant grimace. If he were a Care Bear, he'd definitely be Grumpy Bear.

Landon eased over like the "too cool for school" person he was and settled right between Eric and me. I hated when he stood so close. The hairs on my arms always stood straight up.

"Eric, Chick, it's good to see one of you," Landon commented, taking a sip from his cup. He turned my way and locked eyes with me. "I'm a bit surprised you had the nerve to show up."

I crossed my arms and tried to ignore the chills he always made race up and down my spine. "Trust me, this is the last place I want to be, but I had to be a good friend for Tracey."

"You don't have to make up lies to come to my house, Chick."

"I have no need to lie to you, Satan," I spat back. I hated when he called me Chick. I honestly would've preferred him calling me plain Chicken. Calling me Chick had a much more demeaning feel to it, as if I was just a girl who wasn't worthy of a real name, just some chick he couldn't stand.

Chick.

Chick.

Chick.

Ugh. What a jerk.

He got off on seeing my irritation, too, which was why I worked so hard to keep my emotions in check whenever I was around him. I didn't want to give him any pleasure from my pain. Sure, perhaps my heart beat out of sync when I was near him, but he didn't have to know that.

"Will you two screw already and give the angst a rest?" Eric joked, rolling his eyes.

"That's disgusting." I pretended to gag.

"I'd rather die," Landon argued. "Plus, I'm not interested in your sloppy seconds."

"There's nothing sloppy about my seconds." Eric winked at me, and I smiled. He always made me feel like I belonged, even when people like Landon made me feel the opposite. "I'm off to get a beer. Landon, find me later if you want to play some video games or something. Shay, I would invite you, too, but—"

"He hates your guts like I do," Landon interjected, though I was ninety-nine percent sure that wasn't what had been about to leave Eric's mouth. He probably knew I didn't have much desire to be in the same space as Landon for a long period of time.

Eric gestured toward both of us as he walked away. "Just one fast screw. Penis in, penis out. I'm telling you—get the hatred out in the best way possible."

"Never," we said in unison, and it was one of the few times we were on the same page.

We stood there alone for a moment, giving each other nasty glances, until it became too awkward.

I cleared my throat. "If you'll excuse me, I'm going to go ahead and be anywhere but here."

"Same," he replied, and we went off in completely different directions.

Chapter Four

Landon

I SHOULDN'T HAVE HAD A PARTY.

It didn't take long for regret to settle into my gut as people started swarming into the place, and I didn't even recognize a lot of the faces coming through the door. A bunch of random people decided to crash because they heard there were drugs and booze, and if lucky, some boob and dick touching. Plus, half the people here had probably never even stepped foot into a mansion in their lives.

I'd thought having people around would make it easier to keep my mind off Lance, but the night was proving me wrong. Even though people surrounded me, my memories of the best man who'd ever been in my life continued to consume me.

Forty-five.

He would've been forty-five today.

"Are you sure you don't want to call the cops on your own party, get all these people kicked out, and then play video games?" Greyson asked me as we leaned against the fireplace in the living room while dozens of people pushed through the space, making messes I didn't give a damn about.

"Nah, it's fine." I shrugged, brushing my hand across the back of my neck. He gave me a smile, but it was that fake Greyson smile, the one where he was overthinking shit. I nudged him. "Loosen up, will you? Just get a drink in your system and chill."

"Yeah, all right. I just know that today is—"

I cut him off because I knew what he was going to say, and I had no desire to discuss said topic. "All right, I'll catch you later." I patted my best friend on the back and hurried away, mainly because I didn't want to deal with him questioning if I was okay every few seconds. I was fine, good as ever.

Later that night, like every night I had a party, I ended up in my bedroom. I sat in my room with Greyson, Eric, and Hank. No one else was allowed in my bedroom, and if they stepped foot inside, I made sure to cuss them out and put the fear of Satan into their souls so they'd never come back. Greyson always called me Scrooge after I snapped, and he wasn't wrong. I wasn't polite about kicking them out of my room, but the last thing I needed in my life was some drunk couple screwing on my Italian sheets.

Plus, my bedroom was Ham's safe place, and I didn't need anyone screwing with my dog while they were drunk and high.

Eric and Hank smoked a joint and talked about mindless crap that kept my head from going to any really dark places.

"You guys getting the new *SimCity* game?" Greyson asked, his hands stuffed in his pockets.

"Hell yeah, are you kidding? It looks dope," Hank said, taking a hit from the joint before skipping over Greyson and passing it to Eric. Hank sounded more excited than he needed to be about the game. "I told my parents I've got the theater room for a whole month after it comes out. I'm going to blow through it."

Hank had a deep voice and was a masculine guy. There weren't many people bigger than me, but in shoulder span and biceps, that dude had me beat. Plus, he had more facial hair than any kid our age should've had. Eric called him Ape Man due to the dark hair curling out of the top of his tank top, but Hank didn't think too much of it. We all talked shit about each other; it was how we knew the friendship was real.

But the thing about Hank, his manliness, and his apelike appearance was whenever he got really excited about something, his voice would get high pitched, and he'd sound like Britney Spears. Same when he laughed, too, and Hank was always getting excited or laughing, which made it so damn entertaining. Even on my bad days, all I had to do was get around Hank, and his laughter alone would make me feel better. It made sense that he and Raine were in love. Raine loved to joke, and Hank loved to laugh.

He clapped his hands together. "Dude! It's going to be so dope." He went on and on about the game, as if *SimCity* was the second coming of Jesus.

Eric shrugged. "It looks kind of stupid to me."

That was enough to offend poor Hank to his core, so the two of them went back and forth, arguing about why the other was a dumbass who knew nothing at all about good, quality games.

Every now and then, Greyson would interject his thoughts, but for the most part, he was probably running basketball stats through his brain.

"Okay, okay, then what do you consider a good game?" Hank inquired.

Eric responded without a pause in his breath. "*Super Mario Sunshine.*"

Hank groaned, bending over in horror. "Oh my fucking fuck, that's the gayest shit I've ever heard. I can't believe I shared a joint with you."

Eric flinched ever so lightly at the word gay. I knew enough about people to know when they were uncomfortable. Eric always seemed a bit uneasy with words like gay or fag, but he always laughed it off and shifted the conversations.

I was shocked no one else noticed, but it wasn't anyone's business except his own, I supposed. When he was ready, he'd talk about it. Until then, there would just be awkward laughter and shifting of the conversations. Sometimes I shifted it for him, to alleviate his discomfort.

He never outright thanked me, but he didn't have to. That was what friends did—backed each other up when shit got weird.

"Hey, can I hit that?" a voice said from behind me.

I glanced up to see the Southern charmer standing there with his eyes glued to the joint in Hank's hand. He walked into the room like he owned the place, plucked the joint from Hank's hand, and took a big drag from it.

After he finished, he passed it to Eric and frowned a little. "Shit, I miss Kentucky weed. I swear, y'all's stuff up here is laced with actual weeds or something. It doesn't hit the same. Back home, you'd be messed up for days."

That isn't how weed works, Reggie. He was so full of it. People didn't get messed up on weed for days.

He entered our conversation, turned it completely into his own, and it was a nonstop, one-sided talk about how great damn Kentucky was. The food, the weed, the goddamn sports. Really, I'd never seen a guy get such a hard-on from talking about a state in my life. I wished I could get it up just by thinking about bluegrass music, bourbon, and Kentucky Fried Chicken.

If Kentucky were a cock, Reggie would be the first in line to suck it.

"And what's up with the girls here?" he asked, glancing back and forth between us.

"What do you mean what's up with them?" Hank asked.

"Well, shit. I'm just looking for some random hook-ups. Do you know who would be down for that?"

I looked down at the ground to roll my eyes so hard. This guy was like the poster child of a douchebag. I could hardly handle it. He couldn't be real, could he? He couldn't be that damn transparent. I couldn't believe all the girls at school were throwing themselves at him.

Hank shrugged. "I don't know. The girls are pretty cool here. I've been with Raine for four years now, though, so I don't really think about who to bang," Hank commented.

When Hank made a commitment, he stuck to it. He and Raine would probably end up being one of those couples at a wedding, still on the dance floor after being married for sixty years or some shit.

Hank kept talking, and I kept wishing Reggie would leave. Every time he smoked the joint and talked shit, I wanted to snatch it from his hands and tell him to piss off. Sure, I wasn't smoking anymore, but the supply was from KJ—my former dealer. I knew it was the good stuff. Reggie didn't have a clue what he was talking about.

He went over to pet Ham, and Ham growled at him.

Good boy.

"If you want to know about the best girls in the sack, though, Landon here is the one to go to. He's had more girls than Clinton," Eric commented.

I groaned, not wanting to be dragged into this conversation with Reggie.

"Oh, yeah? Maybe you can help a playa out," Reggie said, nudging me in the arm.

Playa. This white boy from Kentucky, wearing an oversized Biggie Smalls shirt, had actually just said the word playa, and that sealed the deal for me—I couldn't stand the new guy.

I shrugged. "It seemed you had it handled pretty well with a girl a few minutes ago downstairs. I doubt you need help."

"You mean that Stacey girl? Nah, she's a bit too...much for my liking."

"Tracey," I corrected, and I didn't even know why. It wasn't like it mattered to him, but it bothered me that he had the nerve to call her by the wrong name. He was probably the kind of douche who called girls by the wrong name on purpose just to seem cool and aloof.

You know what else bothered me? That he was in my room, smoking my weed.

"Tracey, Stacey, whatever. It's all the same, right?" he joked, elbowing me like we were the best of buddies.

Yeah, okay, playa-playa.

"What's the deal with that Monica bitch?" he asked.

"She's not a bitch," I snapped. What the heck? Was I now standing up for the likes of Monica? This night needed to end.

"Landon and Monica have a...history. I'd stay clear of that one," Hank commented.

"You can do whatever you want. Monica is a free agent," I muttered. I doubted she'd be interested in someone like Reggie, though. He was a bit too young and strait-laced for her. Monica preferred men with children, or at least guys with damage that somewhat matched her own.

Reggie was none of the above.

He rubbed his hands together like a fool needing his next fix. "Come on, man. Give me some tips."

"I really don't know," I said.

"Land is being humble. If you're looking for a guy who can get any girl, it's him," Eric said, and it sounded so cocky even though the words didn't come from my own mouth.

"Except for Shay," Reggie spat out, making me raise an eyebrow.

Wait, what?

"Excuse me?"

"Stacey-Tracey was telling me how the two of you hate each other's guts. Which is crazy, because Shay is fucking hot. Too bad you can't get that."

Fucking hot.

Of course he'd call her fucking hot, because he had a brain the size of a lima bean, but beside that, what the actual hell? Who was he to tell me who I could and couldn't have?

"If I wanted Shay, I'd have her," I stated nonchalantly. The douchebag was making my alpha douchebag side come out.

"Word? You're that much of a baller?" Reggie asked, cocking his other eyebrow.

Every time he used a cliché slang word, I wanted to vomit. "Yeah, word, playa. If I wanted a dime, I could get a dime. You know wassup, dawg," I mocked, using every annoying word I could think of, but he didn't even pick up on it.

Idiot.

Greyson snickered under his breath but didn't add to the conversation. He had a way of staying out of drama of any kind. He had enough shit going on at home, and I understood him not wanting to be involved in anything that wasn't basketball.

"That's wild that you think that, my guy, because the way Stacey-Tracey made it sound, Shay would never give you the time of day," Reggie pushed. I swore he was really trying to get under my skin.

"I could without question. I could even get her to fall in love with me if I wanted to," I declared, and it sounded a lot more asshole-like than I wanted it to, but there I was, sounding like a jerk because I couldn't stand the guy standing next to me, challenging me.

"Uh, hey, you guys…" Eric tried to cut in, but I wasn't interested in being interrupted. This guy really thought he could come into my town, into my house, into *my* bedroom, and sit on *my* Italian sheets, and tell me what I was a wasn't capable of doing.

"Okay, so let's get a nice friendly bet going," Reggie said, standing taller. "I bet you can't get Shay to fall in love with you."

"You guys," Greyson said, clearing his throat. We ignored him, too.

"I one hundred percent can," I said, holding my hand out to him. "Bet." Dammit, now I was out here saying things like "Bet" sounding just as stupid as the Southern charmer.

We shook hands.

"Really, boys, if you want to bet on me falling in love with some-one, maybe you should include me in the bet," Shay said, snapping my stare away from Reggie and to the doorway. Her arms were crossed, and she was sporting her normal level of sass. Her left hip was popped out, and she had an annoyed smirk on her lips.

"Geez, guys, a little warning wouldn't have hurt," I barked at my friends.

Eric tossed his hands up in the air. "Whatever, I quit."

"It was nothing," I argued to Shay, shrugging it all off. "Just stupid guy talk."

"Oh, please, don't go limp so quickly because you got caught, Satan. If you think you could make me fall in love with you, then by all means, do it—but do understand that I want to play now, too."

"Play? What do you mean?" Reggie asked.

"I mean exactly that. I bet I can make Landon fall in love with me first."

Everyone cracked up laughing because they knew how ridiculous the concept of me falling in love was. I didn't love. I hardly liked.

The idea that I'd fall in love with my biggest annoyance was beyond absurd. "Listen, again, it was just stupid guy talk. Drop it, Chick."

"What's the matter, Satan?" she asked, walking up to me, standing nose to nose. "You afraid you might catch feelings for someone you hate?"

That was one thing about Shay that I couldn't argue with—she had bark to her. I would have bet behind the bark was a nice bite, too.

"Never, but I'm not going to waste my time focusing my energy on you."

"Well, who's the chicken now? Cluck, cluck, cluck." She smirked as the guys all snickered under their breaths.

Traitors.

"You really want to play with this fire, Shay?"

"I'd love to see you try to burn me," she replied, still smiling. I'd be lying if I said her alpha side wasn't a tad bit sexy. My jeans grew a bit tighter as she stood close, and I didn't even try to hide the fact that she'd made that happen. Making my cock hard wasn't the challenge, though. Making my heart soft was.

Hank rubbed his hands together. "Now, that's a challenge I can get behind. Two sworn enemies in a battle of love, and the winner—"

"Has bragging rights for the rest of our lives." Shay kept her chocolate eyes locked with mine, not backing down, and hell, I wasn't going to back down either.

"What if no one falls in love?" Hank asked.

"Then, at the end of the school year, the bet is off. We have four and a half months to make it happen," Shay explained.

I stepped in closer to her. "You sure you want to put yourself in this position, Chick?" I asked, cocking an eyebrow. "Because once you love me, every other man you ever date will be an utter disappointment."

"And once you love me, you'll never be able to get me out of your head," she said, stepping even closer. We were so close that her chest almost pressed against mine. At six-feet-two, I towered over her by quite a few inches. Yet she still kept her head held high.

If I hadn't hated her so much, I would've thought it was cute, how she believed in her words, how she was so certain I'd lose the bet. But what she didn't know about me was that there wasn't much room in my life for love. My mind didn't welcome such things. So, this win for me? Easy. Effortless. Pain-free.

"Please." I smirked, lowering my head down toward her face. My lips were centimeters from hers. "I'm going to love every second of owning your body and your heart."

"Whatever." She stood on her tiptoes, and her lips moved in closer. I felt her hot breaths brushing against my skin. "I can make you fall in love with me without you even tasting my lips."

"I can make you love me while still treating you like shit."

"I double-dog dare you, Satan." She held out her hand.

"Bet, Chick."

Bet, bet, bet, bet.

I shook her hand, giving it a bit of a tight grip, and she matched the intensity. It was probably the first time we'd touched since she came into my room a year earlier and held me.

For a second, I thought about holding on for a while longer. My hands were always ice cold while hers felt like the sun.

"Shit." Reggie whistled low before turning to the guys. "Are we sure they aren't already screwing?"

"Honestly, it's hard to tell," Eric commented, but we both ignored them. I was already forming ideas for all the things I could do to make Shay fall in love with me. I was coming up with ways to get under her skin, to drive her crazy, to make myself irresistible. This felt like the task I'd been waiting for, the challenge I needed to keep my mind busy in the upcoming weeks.

Making Shay Gable fall in love with me was going to be a perfect distraction.

People continued getting shitfaced and being louder than they should've been, and I was surprised the neighbors hadn't called the cops already. A few things got broken, and I couldn't wait to tell my parents about the damage because that was my favorite pastime—figuring out what would piss them off enough for them to snap at me. Would it be the good china? The stained carpets? A few expensive vases? Who knew.

I knew it was immature and ridiculous, but I had this twisted need to piss my parents off. More so, my father. When he was pissed off, then he was at least talking to me. Correction: yelling at me.

Sometimes, my screw-ups were enough to bring Mom back to town. She worried about me and my well-being. Dad claimed I was merely seeking attention.

Both were right.

"Let's play spin seven," someone shouted from the living room. A few people groaned while a few others applauded the idea.

I thought the game was a bit childish, but it seemed to be popular at all the parties lately. Spin seven was a mix of spin the bottle and seven minutes in heaven. A group of people sat in a circle, and one person spun the bottle. Whoever it landed on was the person who would be led to the closet for seven minutes.

The infamous chant started each time a couple was chosen and led to the closet. *"Touch a tit, suck a dick, suck a tit, touch a dick."* It was wild how mature us high schoolers were. It was great knowing, someday, we'd be the world's leaders. Though, based on the current politicians, a lot of *suck a dick, touch a tit* was still being played on the regular.

I never really engaged in the game, but when I saw Reggie ask Shay if she was playing, and she shook her head, I took it as a chance to get her to look my way.

"Why aren't you playing, Chick? Too scared?" I asked. Every time she looked at me, she seemed a bit shocked that I had enough nerve to speak to her.

Then she puffed her chest out. "Trust me, I'm not scared. I just don't want to," she argued, shrugging her shoulders.

"Cluck...cluck...cluck..." I whispered for only her to hear, and I knew it was getting under her skin. It always got under her skin when I made the noises.

"I don't see you sitting down in the circle," she said, running her hands through her hair before grabbing the elastic from her wrist and making a messy bun.

Sounded like a dare.

I sat right down and gestured toward the circle.

She rolled her eyes at me. "Whatever, Landon. I don't have anything to prove to you."

My blue eyes stayed attached to her browns as I parted my lips, and mouthed, "Cluck, cluck, cluck."

She wanted to resist. She wanted to shrug it off again and walk away, but that wasn't how things worked between us. When one pushed, the other pushed back harder.

She sat, gave me a wicked "screw you" grin and joined the game.

A few people crashed into the closet for the seven-minute timeslot, and when they came out, they always looked dazed and confused, giggling like the idiotic teenagers they were.

When it was my turn, I reached out to the bottle with no concern about whether or not it would land exactly where I wanted it to go. At fourteen years old, I'd learned how to perfect my spin-seven skills in order to kiss the girl I wanted.

Though, this time, I knew there wasn't going to be a lot of kissing going on. More like yelling.

The bottle spun and spun, around and around. Shay's eyes stayed glued to the glass beer bottle. The moment it started to slow down, I watched her lips part as she quietly muttered, "No, no, no," before it stopped directly in front of her.

The circle began oohing and aahing at the idea that the two sworn enemies were on their way to the closet together for seven minutes straight. They were all here for that show, and I knew the moment we stepped into that closet, the door would be surrounded with people whispering and pressing their ear against it from the outside, trying to catch a snippet of what was going on behind closed doors.

I stood from the circle and gestured toward Shay. "Please," I offered. "Chickens first."

She grimaced, her thick, full eyebrows lowering a hair before she pushed herself up from the floor and headed toward the closet in haste. We both stepped inside and stood nose to nose.

"Okay, friends, you know the rules," Eric said, grabbing the handle of the door. "Seven minutes in heaven—or, in your case, hell. Have fun!" He slammed the door shut, and the moment it happened, Shay whined with irritation.

"I can't believe I'm locked in here with you for seven minutes. I could think of a million things I'd rather be doing," she grumbled, probably with a pout.

"Like what?"

"Oh, I don't know…watching paint dry."

"Well, since we're here, we should probably spend our time wisely," I joked, moving to unbuckle my jeans, knowing it would bother her. I wished I could see the annoyance on her face. I loved when I got under her skin enough to make her nostrils flare.

"Oh my gosh, remove that idea from your mind, Landon, and stop messing with your belt, because there's no way in hell I'm touching you."

"I've thought about it before," I said, my voice low and tame.

"Thought about what?"

"Kissing you."

She huffed sarcastically. "I'm sure that's not true."

"You're right, it's not."

"I know."

It was true, though. It'd happened once—and only once—after Lance's funeral. I had spent a lot of weeks being out of it, using alcohol to cope with the shitstorm raging inside my head, and I was a bit unstable. If my friends hadn't been looking out for me, I would've probably gone overboard. I remembered walking into school one day and seeing Shay standing there at her locker with a few of her friends. She was laughing and tossing her head back in such a genuine way, and I couldn't take my eyes off her.

I kept thinking about how she'd held me weeks prior and stayed with me during the lowest point of my life. She had been there—my enemy—taking care of my scars. And as I'd stared at her in the hallway, I'd thought about thanking her—walking over to her, parting my lips, and giving her my gratitude. I wasn't used to people doing shit for me with no hope of anything in return, and Shay had done it without any expectations.

I remembered looking at her eyes, and then moving down to her slender nose, and then her cheeks, then those juicy lips.

I wondered how those lips would taste if I used mine against them to thank her. I wondered if she tasted like the candy she was always popping into her mouth. I wondered if she dripped of the angelic sin I always claimed her to be. I wondered for a split second…considered it for a blink in time…and then she slammed her locker, walked away, and I sobered up.

Still, I had considered it.

We both went quiet for a few moments before I cleared my throat again. I didn't like silence. Silence and I didn't get along too well. "Just one kiss, Chick. I can keep it a secret."

"You keep secrets the same way you keep girls. AKA, you don't—other than Monica."

"Monica's not mine."

"That doesn't change the fact that she thinks you're hers."

I smirked a little. "You jealous of her?"

"Jealous of her having to deal with a guy like you? Never in my life."

"Whatever you say, Chick."

"I wish you'd stop calling me Chick," she snapped. "I hate it."

"You want a new nickname, sweet cheeks? I can give you a new nickname, sweet cheeks."

She shivered in disgust. Good. There was nothing I enjoyed more than getting on her nerves. "Not that either."

"I'll keep working on it."

"Or you could just call me by my name."

"Nah, Shay's too ugly a name to leave my lips."

"I hate you."

"I hate you more."

"Yeah, but I hate you the most."

I snickered. "You really think you can get a guy like me to fall in love with you?"

"Yes. I'm positive, actually. People are the easiest to read, and that includes you."

"You can't read me, Shay."

"I can, like an open book."

"Okay." I reached into my pocket, pulled out my cell phone, and turned on the flashlight, lighting up the small space. "Read me."

She raised an eyebrow. "You sure you want me to do this? Reading people is kind of my gift, and you might not like what I have to say."

"I never like what you have to say, so this time shouldn't be any different. Go for it."

She rolled her shoulders back and stretched out her arms as if she was about to deadlift me. "Okay. You're fake, Landon."

That was it? That was the big reveal? "What the hell do you mean I'm fake?"

"I mean exactly that. You. Are. Fake. F-A-K-E. Fake. There is nothing real about you. You're a walking lie."

I laughed. No joke, I actually laughed out loud, which didn't happen often for me. It was a deep-rooted, belly laugh.

"What the hell are you talking about?" I questioned. "Everything about me is real. I'm the realist damn person you'll come across in our town."

"No," she disagreed with a shake of her head. "You are the fakest. You're even faker than the new boobs Carly Patrick got for her eighteenth birthday."

"*What?!*" I breathed out, stunned by her words. "I'm not fake, Shay."

"It's not a big deal, Landon." She shrugged her shoulders and went to picking at her nails. "People seem to love your fakeness."

"I'm not fake," I argued again, my blood boiling at this point. "Plus, I've seen Carly's boobs up close and personal. Those are straight in-your-face, nips-don't-flick fake. There is no way in this world I'm more fake than those silicone watermelons. I'm a lot of shitty things, but fake isn't one of them."

"Okay then, can you answer a question for me?"

"Anything."

"How many people know you're sad?"

"The hell kind of question is that?" I barked.

"A very straightforward one," she replied. She seemed so cool, calm, and collected—one of the many things I despised about her. It was as if her life was always so solid. I wished for that kind of stable structure, and seeing that she had it annoyed the living hell out of me.

"How long have you been sad, Landon?"

I glanced at my watch. "About a solid three minutes now, because being trapped inside this closet with you is complete hell."

"Aren't you the one who wanted to come in here with me?"

"Bad call. A lapse in judgment. I forgot how annoying you are."

She smiled. She freaking smiled at me, pleased by my annoyance. "Are you going to answer me about your sadness?"

"Are you going to suck my dick?" I replied.

"Do you always do that?" she asked, tilting her head to the left as she studied my expressions. She was doing that thing she did—reading me. Taking note of my movements and the tightness of my jaw, taking in every inch of me.

Don't let her read your pages, Landon. She couldn't have even handled my prologue.

All my walls were up, and I wasn't going to let her knock them down.

"Do what?" I questioned.

"Use sarcasm to shield your hurting."

"There's nothing hurting here. Look at this life. I have money, ba-dass parties, and girls throwing themselves at me—why would I have anything to hurt about?"

"Maybe because money, girls, and parties don't make a person happy. I see how miserable you are in your eyes."

I grimaced and whisper-hissed, "You don't know shit about me, Shay."

"Then how am I able to get under your skin so easily? If that wasn't true, if you weren't sad, why would my saying that bother you so much?"

"You don't," I calmly replied.

She did.

She was pushing me, making me uncomfortable with the fact that she did seem able to see the parts of me no one else could. Anger was building in my chest, and I needed to defuse it before it became too big.

"Maybe it's best if we shut up for the rest of the time," I told her.

"For the second time in my life, I agree with you."

Shay sat down on the floor of the closet, and I did the same, leaning back against some coats that were hanging. How did seven minutes feel like seventy? Was time moving at all? This was hell.

Then came the silence. The silence that brought out heavy thoughts. Shay could read my mind somehow, and so, when the silence became too much, I cleared my throat and tried to make small talk in hopes of shutting my own brain up. "A chicken and Satan walk into a closet—stop me if you've heard this one."

She laughed a little.

It was quiet and low, and dammit, I'd never heard Shay laugh at anything I'd ever said before, so that was new. What was also new was the small part of me that enjoyed hearing her sound.

"Landon?" she whispered.

"Yeah?"

"Just shut up, all right?"

Yeah, okay.

"One more minute, you horny hatebirds!" Eric called out.

We both stood, and I took a step closer toward her. "I get you not wanting to kiss. That's intimate and personal, but if you want, this is your last chance to touch my cock while no one's looking. I won't stop you."

"No thanks. I'm allergic to peanuts," she said so effortlessly and *loudly*, causing the crowd on the other side of the door to burst into laughter.

Shay smirked again, feeling proud of her little dig at me. That beautiful, annoying smirk I loved to hate.

Shay: 1

Landon: 0

I wasn't worried, though. The game was just getting started. She might've scored one point, but I wasn't going to let it happen again. We were playing on my field, and Shay didn't know what she was up against.

The moment time was up, we opened the door and stepped outside to a crowd. Leading that crowd was Monica, and she had crazy eyes. The last thing I wanted to do was deal with Monica and her crazy. She always had that reaction whenever she saw me talking to another girl even though she was out there screwing a million guys herself.

I rolled my shoulders back and parted my lips to speak, but it didn't matter much at all because *smack*.

Monica's palm landed on my cheek, sending a stinging sensation through my system. God, it'd been almost two months since Monica slapped me last—that had to be a new record.

"Really, Landon? Spin seven with another girl? *With my friend*?!" she yelled breathlessly, her eyes watering over as the crowd kept watching. If there were two things you could always count on, it was Monica's dramatics and the nosy people of our town eavesdropping on her hysterics.

I found it hilarious that based on the amount of shit Monica talked about Shay behind her back, she would call her a friend. I figured she hated Shay even more than I did. It seemed Monica was actually jealous of the hate I gave to Shay, which only deepened her disgust for the girl. Sometimes, I got so annoyed at the crap she'd say about Shay and how low she'd stoop to trash-talk the girl I hated. I'd call her out on it, too, being oddly protective of the girl I wasn't supposed to care anything about. How did one have enough nerve to stand up for their enemy in private but treat them like crap in public? I was that level of asshole.

My mouth opened to speak, but no words came out because she smacked me again.

More chants from the crowd.

Okay, this was getting a little ridiculous.

Monica was getting a bit of a big head from the cheering crowd. She was getting a little too confident in her current state. As she raised her hand to slap me again, I grabbed her wrist, stopping her.

One slap—okay, fine. To be honest, I probably had some karma catching up with me. Two slaps I could let go. I was sure I could've treated our past toxic relationship with more class during some moments. But three slaps?

Now you're just getting greedy, Monica.

I tilted my head and gave her a small smirk and my puppy-dog eyes. "I'm sorry, okay?" I didn't know what I was sorry about, but girls seemed to like to hear guys say that.

"Whatever, Landon. You're a jerk."

I saw her kind of smile, though, as if she enjoyed this interaction. At least someone was enjoying themselves. I was still dealing with a stinging face.

Still alive.

"Don't worry, Monica. Nothing happened. Trust me…"—Shay looked my way and eyed me up and down with disdain in her gaze—"nothing will *ever* happen between us."

She turned and walked away, and for some reason, I felt the impulse to follow her, to tell her why her comment was wrong, and how I was going to grow on her like the bad toxin I was, one she'd have to rid her soul of down the line.

But I stayed in place.

My eyes darted to the crowd hovering around Monica and me. "Get busy or get lost," I hissed, glaring at the circle of people. They hurried away and got back to the party, leaving Monica and me standing there alone.

"You disgust me," she muttered, standing high in heels that were probably killing her feet. "You aren't shit. You know that? You're worthless in this world."

I flinched. "You're drunk."

"It's a party—everyone's drunk...except for you and Little Miss Perfect," she sneered, referring to Shay. *There's the charming girl I've always known you to be.* "I bet she fucks to the theme song from *Mister Rogers' Neighborhood* with her boring ass."

I was hardly listening to her anymore. Most of the time, I let her comments slide because I knew her story. I knew the mess that was her life. I'd seen her wrinkled pages and bent corners. Some pages were torn from her book, hiding the darkest parts of her, and I was the only one who'd ever been able to read them. If she needed a punching bag, I'd take her hits, but that didn't mean it didn't mess me up sometimes, leaving me battered and bruised.

"You should probably head home," I suggested.

"I was planning on it anyway. Your party blows," she said, flipping her hair over her shoulder. "Don't forget to go take a dip in the pool, Landon, in honor of your uncle," she muttered, walking away.

Why would she do that?

Why would she say some bullshit like that just to spite me? To hurt me? To know someone else was suffering other than herself?

I stood there, frozen in place, with the thought of Lance on my mind, and then, like a waterfall, all thoughts of him came rushing back to me. I couldn't breathe as people pushed around me, partying, drinking, not noticing the panic attack consuming me, not noting the pain in my soul, which felt like it was being lit on fire.

I wanted to drown.

I wanted to drown so bad tonight. In vodka. In whiskey. In tequila. In tears.

I looked to my left and found one set of eyes staring at me. As everyone else looked through me, those eyes watched me as if I were a case study, a mouse in a cage being experimented on. A set of beautiful, sad eyes pierced my soul. Shay was the only one who bothered to look my way, and she was doing that same shit she'd done in the closet earlier. She was reading me, digging deep into my psyche and exploring my pages, unwelcomed.

Stop it, Shay.

I forced myself to move and pushed past her, brushing against her shoulder. "If you're not going to blow me then stop staring at me, sunshine," I huffed out.

"Don't call me sunshine," she said.

Then, stop being so damn bright.

I didn't know what time everyone left my place, but I assumed Greyson gave them a nudge to leave at some point after one a.m. When everyone was gone, when all that remained were empty hallways in my trashed house, I headed into the pool area. Our indoor pool was surrounded by glass walls so you could see all of nature yet still swim during the chilly Illinois winters.

"What's the point of having a swimming pool in Illinois if you can't use it all year round?" Mom had said years ago while designing the house.

The pool glistened under the full moon. *Full moon...* Lance's birthday would land on a full moon this year. Part of me wanted to howl at it. Another part of me wanted to cry.

Instead, I walked to the edge of the pool into the pool, fully clothed, and jumped in. I soaked myself from head to toe, and then I went under. I never used the diving board, because it messed with my head too much. I swam deep and stayed under the water as long as I could. I'd jumped into that pool every single night since Lance passed away. I was good at staying under. It was what I'd spent the last few months of my life doing—holding my breath.

Chapter Five

Landon

YOU EVER LIE IN BED WITH NO DESIRE AT ALL TO GET UP?
When morning came, I was tired.

Not only physically, but my mind yawned, too.

I shouldn't have had a party. I shouldn't have made that stupid bet. I should've taken Greyson up on a night of video games and pizza.

I hadn't slept. I'd closed my eyes for a bit but opened them right up when the visions of the past kept knocking on my brain.

When the sun rose, my phone screen was full of messages from people who thought they were my friends, telling me about how amazing the party had been. None of those people were my friends, though. Greyson, Eric, and Hank were the only people I'd ever consider such a thing, and we'd known each other for pretty much all of our lives. Everyone else was just shadows that passed by me day by day. White noise.

I didn't reply to any of the messages, because they weren't really talking to me. They were talking to the person I pretended to be on the regular. They talked to the rich boy who hooked them up with weed and booze. They talked to the rich boy who gave them popularity cred. They talked to the rich boy who changed their social status.

If they'd been talking to the real me, they wouldn't have been impressed by the fact that it took every inch of strength for me to pull myself out of bed each morning. For a while, I wondered if it was this

hard for everyone—getting up each day, dragging oneself out of bed.
There were days when all I wanted to do was bury myself deeper into
the blankets and not emerge from my room until weeks had passed.
I couldn't sleep, but I wanted to sit there in bed, alone with my dark
mind. That was what I wanted to do that Sunday morning: be alone,
stay in bed. Yet, when I saw the messages from my parents, I knew I had
to pull my shit together before Maria came over.

Mom: I got text messages and calls from our neighbors about a
party. Are you okay? Call me when you get this. Love you.

Dad's message was a bit different.

Dad: Get your fucking act together.

Love you too, Papa.

I glanced at the time—it was already 10:01 a.m.

I sat up and called Mom. She answered on the first ring. She always
answered on the first ring. "Hey, Landon."

"Hey, Mom."

"How are you? How are things there? The neighbors seemed concerned." Her voice dripped with worry.

"I'm okay. Things just got a little out of control, that's all. Sorry."

"It's fine as long as you're doing okay."

"A few vases broke," I told her.

"Oh, honey, that's okay…those are just material things. Those can
be replaced. I'm more concerned about you." She got interrupted by
someone in the background and began talking about different kinds of
fabrics. When she came back to our call, she asked me if I needed her to
come home.

I said no.

She was too busy making her dreams come true. I didn't want her
to come home to my nightmares.

"Okay, well, sweetheart, call me before you go to bed tonight, or
whenever you need me. I'm here. I love you. Remember, I'm just one
call away. I love you."

"You too," I said before hanging up.

I headed to the bathroom attached to my bedroom and hopped in the shower. As the water ran against my skin, I didn't think about anything. I didn't have the energy to have many thoughts that morning. I was tired to my core in a way I hadn't known one could be tired. I hadn't known a mind could be so drained when it didn't really do much thinking at all. My bones ached from exhaustion, and my eyes shut as the water slapped against my body.

After I washed up, I got dressed and moved throughout the house, doing my best to straighten things up. I collected all the empty beer cans and vodka bottles and tossed them into garbage bags. Then, I pulled out the mop and vacuum, following that up with scrubbing the disgusting toilets throughout the house.

High school kids were repulsive, especially when it wasn't their own property they were trashing.

That was my least favorite part of having parties—the aftermath. Even though I knew Maria would've come and left the place spotless, she didn't deserve that cleanup. Contrary to how I felt about Shay, I adored her grandmother. It was pretty hard not to love Maria. She was feisty and unapologetic about her strong, bold personality. I was certain that was where Shay got her spitfire from. I didn't know why it worked so well with me from Maria, though. Maybe it had something to do with the nurturing side of her personality, the gentleness and care she gave me when I didn't even deserve it. Or maybe it had to do with the fact that I never knew my grandmother and always wondered what it would have been like to have one.

It probably had something to do with her always showing up with food, though. The food certainly helped.

Sundays were my favorite day of the week, because it meant Maria was coming over to clean the house. She'd been our housekeeper for the past seven years and was one of the better parts of my life.

When Maria came over that Sunday afternoon, she smiled bright my way. She was always smiling, always humming some tune in her head whenever she walked inside.

"You look like poop, Landon," she stated, carrying a dish of food in her hands. "You need to sleep."

"I'm working on it."

"Liar."

My eyes moved to the dish.

Please be lasagna, please be lasagna, please be—

"I made a lasagna for dinner," she said.

Yes!

It was my favorite meal in the history of meals—besides Maria's enchiladas. Maria's food was the highlight of every single week. It was like she baked everything with pounds of her heart and soul, adding an extra touch.

"You've been sleeping this weekend?" she asked.

"Yeah, pretty good."

"More lies. You have bigger bags under your eyes than I do, and I'm like four hundred years old."

"Oh please, Maria. You don't look a day over thirty."

She smiled. "I always liked you, you know that, right?" She handed the dish over to me and instructed me to put it in the refrigerator. "What did you do last night?"

"Just hung out with Greyson. Nothing major. Video games and stuff. Very low-key."

"No party?"

I smiled. I couldn't lie to her again, and she knew it, too.

"How are your grades doing, Landon Scott?"

I swore, Maria was the only one I ever allowed to get away with calling me by my middle name. I actually kind of liked that she used it, too. It felt like it made our relationship somewhat personal, more than client-and-employer status.

"They're good."

"And have you chosen a major for your fall college courses yet?" she asked.

She already knew the answer to that, and she still always asked. I'd gotten into the University of Chicago Law School, per my father's request, and I was supposed to go ahead and follow in his footsteps. I went along with it because what the hell else was I supposed to do? I didn't know what I wanted to be, so it made it a little easier having my father tell me what to become.

College didn't really seem to be something I could completely wrap my head around. I didn't have any idea what I truly wanted to be when I grew up. I didn't have the slightest urge to go after one certain thing, which made it so hard for me. I didn't have a passion. How was I supposed to decide what to do with my life? I could hardly pull myself out of bed each morning. So, I'd just listen to my father and follow after his footsteps. Sure, his life seemed boring and closed-off, but at least he was successful. He must've done something right during that college phase of his life.

"You can go undecided," Maria said gently, as if she could read my thoughts. "You don't have to know everything right this second. You just need to decide on a few topics you think could make you grow the best. You're a smart, talented young man, Landon. You could do anything if you put in the work, and it doesn't have to be law just because your father said it should be."

"You don't think I'd make a good lawyer?" I joked.

"You'd make a good anything. I just want you to be passionate about it."

I kept quiet because I didn't want to spoil the mood by notifying Maria that I wasn't passionate about anything.

I headed to the kitchen to put the food into the fridge.

Before Maria dived deep into her cleaning routine, she peeked her head into the kitchen and nodded in my direction. "How's your heart today?" she asked me, the same question she asked every time she stopped by.

"Still beating."

"Good."

If anyone else had asked me an overly dramatic question like that, I would've flipped them off, but since it came from Maria, I figured she deserved at least some kind of response. I couldn't be rude to that woman even if I tried, probably because I knew she'd whoop my butt and toss holy water at me if I ever spoke back to her.

"And yours?" I asked because I cared, which was shocking. I could count on one hand the number of people I cared about, and Maria held a steady spot on that list. I swore, sometimes, she even darted in and out of the number one spot.

She smiled. "Still beating."

She left and later came to my bedroom, knocking on the door. When she opened it, she had a bra dangling off the end of a broom. "Just a low-key night with Greyson, huh?" She glared.

I laughed. "I guess you could say things got weird after midnight."

She shook her head and muttered something under her breath— probably a prayer for my soul—before going to finish up her work.

A few hours later, I tossed the dinner into the oven, and Maria set the table for two. Sundays with Maria; it was our ritual. Before we ate, she always took my hand into hers and said a prayer.

My eyes stayed open, but she didn't care. She always said one didn't have to close their eyes to receive their blessings.

She talked to me about school, reminded me to not be a dick to people, and gave me advice on just being a good person. I never really said it, but her Sunday dinners meant the world to me. I needed her around, and she was always there. If there was someone you could always count on to show up, it was Maria.

Maria oftentimes went on and on about her family, mostly Shay. For the past few years, I'd tuned out the Shay conversations. I didn't care to know more about the girl I hated and how happy she was, but now that the bet was going on, I wanted to know as much as I could. I knew I could use the information to get her to fall in love with me.

"Shay is getting ready for the school play, so that's all that's been going on in the house. She's amazing, though. Writing and the performing arts are her gifts to this world." Maria beamed as she spoke about her granddaughter. "The arts are in her blood. It's her bread and butter. It was the one good thing her father gave to her—his talent."

"Acting, huh?" I questioned, taking a bite of the lasagna.

So. Good.

"Yes. She's amazing. Truly gifted."

I wanted to know more about Shay, but I knew Maria would get suspicious of me asking too many questions. I knew everything I learned about Shay would help me with the bet we'd made. The more I knew about her, the easier it would be to get her in my bed.

Actor. Writer.

Beautiful, too.

That didn't matter, but it crossed my mind enough to make note of it.

I collected the small clues Maria gave me about her granddaughter, and I put them in my back pocket. I was certain they'd come in handy down the line.

Today I was happy.

I figured I should write it down because it seems like a lot of my days are getting darker.

Harder.

I feel my mind slipping into the darkness again. I'm still taking my meds and working hard to keep my head afloat, but I feel it. I feel myself slipping.

I spend more time with my family because there's something about them that brings me peace.

I'm trying.

I'm trying so hard to not drown.

I don't know what tomorrow will bring, but today I was happy.

Today I am happy.

And that's worthy of being written down.

-L

Chapter Six

Shay

I
T HAD BEEN TWO DAYS SINCE THE PARTY, AND I HADN'T STOPPED THINKING
about Landon and those gloomy eyes of his. As he stood in the
middle of his living room, frozen in place, I knew he was wrapped
deep in a panic attack. I used to have them, too, whenever Dad was
out dealing, or on the nights when he never made it home. I'd become
paralyzed, and each breath would be harder and harder to take. I'd
imagine the worst-case scenario. Him passed out in a ditch. Him getting
involved in a shootout. Him getting killed. Killing others. It felt like the
walls were closing in, and there was no escape at all.

I knew what caused my anxiety, and I couldn't help but wonder
what was the cause behind Landon's. It blew my mind how he could
stand in a room, surrounded by dozens of people who claimed to be his
friends, and no one even noticed his pain.

Except me.

I saw it, and I worried about it, even though it wasn't my place to
worry. I worried so much I reached out to Greyson to find out a little more about it. I was certain he was thrown off by me asking about
Landon, seeing how I'd never cared about the guy in the past, but seeing his sadness, seeing it leaking from his heart and knowing that same
pain, I couldn't look away. I couldn't mentally be okay with having a
stupid bet with Landon if his pieces were already shattered.

At first, I got kind of elated about the idea of the bet. It felt like
a fun challenge, because it was highlighting each of our true talents.

Landon's gift was physical attraction. Over the years, I'd watched him get girls to melt into a puddle by just winking their way. He played the cliché bad-boy role to a T, and those high school girls fell right into his lap—and his bed.

My talent was the complete opposite. While he excelled at physical attraction, I was a master at emotions. I was a storyteller, and as such, I'd spent the past several years of my life learning how to study people. Everyone I encountered became a character to me. I learned their ins and outs. I wrote down their traits in my many notebooks. I studied why they were the way they were, what drove them, what inspired them, what made them tick. I asked them questions. I engaged with them because they all fascinated me so much. I was a people person by nature. It was my gift—seeing people from all sides, all angles. I'd learned early on that there aren't any real villains in life, just heroes who have been beaten down for so long they've forgotten they have the ability to be good.

The challenge of making Landon fall in love with me was fun at first. Making my sworn enemy love me seemed like a decent way to mock Landon for the rest of his life. Plus, someday down the line, I could base a character off him and his complexities.

That was, until I spoke to Greyson and learned the truth about Landon's struggles.

"He's not okay lately, and I don't think he's been sleeping," he told me. "He's the kind of sad you only notice if you look closely enough, and most people don't look. He's one of my best friends, though, and I see it all. Ever since Lance died, he hasn't been okay, and Saturday was Lance's birthday, so I know that triggered some of his issues. I know you two have your own hate and stuff, Shay, but Landon is a good guy. He's just lost, that's all—just like all of us, I suppose."

Those words from Greyson made the game less fun in my mind. It felt cruel, almost, to play a game with someone who was so broken.

I walked over to Landon's locker on Monday at school, and Greyson's words stayed with me as I headed toward him. That morning, I was looking straight at him, uncertain what it was I was going to

see—the sad, broken Landon, or the cold, distant one I usually interacted with.

"Hey, Landon."

He turned my way, a bit thrown off by seeing me standing there. I
had to admit, I was a bit thrown off, too. Never in my life had I thought
I'd be walking up to Landon of all people and saying hi to him.

"Sup?" he asked, pulling out some books from his locker and shov-
ing them into his backpack.

"I wanted to say…we can call off the bet. With everything going
on…" My words faded. His life was messy enough; the last thing he
needed was to keep up with some stupid bet. He had bigger issues to
deal with.

"What do you mean 'with everything going on'?" His voice was
smoky, deep, and still made the hairs on my body stand straight up even
if it was only eight in the morning.

"Well, Greyson told me about it being Lance's birthday this past
weekend, and—"

"What? You afraid of losing?" he said, cutting in, but I'd seen the
small flinch in his body when I had mentioned his uncle.

"No. I just figured you had bigger issues to handle."

"There's nothing in my life that needs to be handled," he said,
closing his locker. He tossed his backpack onto his shoulder. "So don't
try to put that on me. If you want to forfeit the challenge then, by all
means, quit. But I'll be damned if I'm the one to cut it off, because I'm
no chicken."

"Landon, you're still mourning the death of your uncle. You're not
okay."

"You don't have to tell me things I already know," he replied, his
voice dripping in a low smokiness. To my knowledge, Landon didn't
smoke, but his voice was so raspy at times you'd think he did.

"Yeah, but…well, that's a lot on its own. Plus, with the anniversary
of his death coming up in a few weeks…"

His jawline tightened, and he gripped the straps of his backpack
tight. "Greyson talks too much," he hissed.

"I'm glad he told me."

Landon took a step backward. "Look, Chick, I don't want or need your pity. I ain't some charity case, okay? I don't need Little Miss Perfect to fix my life."

"I'm not trying to fix your life, Landon, and I'm not perfect—"

"Yeah, whatever. If you're backing out of the challenge, cool. I didn't expect you to follow through anyway. I knew you wouldn't have it in you, but don't come acting like you're doing me some favor by punking out. I'm still one hundred percent certain I'd win."

I studied him. Not just the words he was saying, but how he was moving. How his fingers fidgeted. How his crooked smile frowned.

Greyson's words floated through my head as I looked at Landon.

He's the kind of sad you only notice if you look closely enough.

His eyes.

His beautiful, sad eyes.

His eyes were heavy and miserable, filled with a story he was too terrified to tell. He kept something to himself. His hurts? His pain, maybe? His truths?

I wanted to know more about those parts of him. I wanted to study the angles he kept hidden from the world. I wanted to know about the boy I hated and why he hated himself even more. I was absolutely certain there was no one who hated Landon as much as he hated himself, and that idea alone made me feel bad for him.

Not pity him...but just...feel bad.

He had to be the most complex character I'd ever crossed as a storyteller, and I'd have been lying if I said I wasn't intrigued by the idea of seeing how his story would unfold.

"Fine. The challenge is still on," I said, rolling my shoulders back.

His body relaxed a little, as if he was pleased with the idea of the bet being on again. It was as if he needed this for some reason.

Seconds later, his body tensed up again, and he shrugged. "Good. See you when you're saying you love me," he said, walking off.

"Not before you say you love me first."

"In your dreams, darling."

"More like my nightmares," I shouted his way. "And don't call me darling!"

He flipped his hand in the air in boredom, putting an end to our conversation as he kept moving away. I stayed beside his locker for a few seconds, coming to the full understanding that I might have taken on more than I could handle trying to get Landon to fall in love with me. I wasn't even sure he knew what love was, let alone what loving me meant.

This challenge was a mistake. We both knew that to be true.

Still, somehow, I wanted it for reasons unknown to me, wanted it more than I should've. Whenever I was near him, I felt this heat in my body that I'd never felt from anyone else. I wanted to know why that was a thing. I wanted to know if he felt it, too.

I wanted to know his story. His ugly, hard novel.

I wanted to read his words, even though they seemed to bleed across the page in the most painful way.

"I'm sorry, let me get this right," Tracey said, standing next to my locker later that afternoon. "You bet Landon you could make him fall in love with you?"

I grabbed my English book. "Yes."

"Landon, as in Landon Harrison?"

"Uh-huh."

"Landon Harrison as in the Landon Harrison who put bubblegum in your hair in middle school?"

"It was chewed-up Laffy Taffy."

"You say that as if it makes it better."

"Yeah, you're right, it doesn't, but it is what it is. Now, I have four months to make him fall in love with me before he makes me want to sleep with him."

Tracey waved her hands in the air in complete confusion at my commentary. "I'm sorry, I'm just confused. You guys hate each other.

It's the only constant thing in my life—your hatred. I think it's so weird that you'd even want to do something like this."

"I know, but I couldn't back down from the challenge. I walked in on him and Reggie placing the bet with each other about me, like some wild monkeys who had their chests puffed out."

"Not my sweet, sweet Reggie!" she cried.

I rolled my eyes. "There's a good chance he's not as sweet as you think he is, Trace."

"That's okay—I like sour candy, too. Speaking of candy..." She held her hand out to me, and I pulled a piece from my pocket. It was a trait I'd definitely picked up from Mima, and I never left home without a pocket full of candy to keep me going through the day.

Tracey grinned, pleased, as she popped the candy into her mouth. "I'm just happy you overheard them. Could you imagine if they tried to play you? A classic *Ten Things I Hate About You* situation."

"That's exactly what I thought, but now I have the upper hand, because I know what's going on. Now, Landon is going to have to deal with the outcome of making a bet on me. He's going to lose so bad." Tracey studied me for a minute with narrowed eyes. "What?" I asked. She narrowed her eyes even more. "*What?!*"

"Sweetheart, I don't know how to say this without sounding like I'm Team Landon, but..."

Her words trailed off, and I cocked an eyebrow. "Just say it."

"You have a sensitive heart."

I laughed. "What? What does that even mean?"

"Oh, sweetie." Tracey frowned, shaking her head. "You write love stories for a living. You're kind to every single person who crosses your path. You once bottle-fed an undernourished kitten before driving it to the vet, and...I don't know, you recycle. I mean, you even put up with Hellica when no one else will," she remarked.

"You mean *Monica*," I corrected.

"I said what I said. She's the definition of evil, and her non-boyfriend boyfriend is your nemesis. Do you really want to get in bed with Hellica's guy? You know she has traits of being a bona fide psychopath to anyone who crosses her. Even if she and Landon have never officially been an item, she still calls dibs on him. There's an unwritten rule that Landon Harrison is off-limits."

"I don't see what that has to do with our bet."

"I just worry that loving is your default setting. If Landon Harrison shows any kind of flaw or weakness or...I don't know, *smiles*, you're going to react to it, and then *bam*! His penis is in your vagina while you're dazed and confused and you're thinking you're in love."

"That's a lie. I can do this." I hoped I could. I prayed I could. Otherwise, I was screwed.

"Okay, well...there's another issue at hand."

"And that is?"

"I think you're going to end up sleeping with Landon Harrison."

"What?! No, I'm not! Also, you don't have to say his full name every time you mention him."

"Uh, yes, I do actually, because it's Landon Harrison—your sworn enemy! You're acting like this is just an everyday situation when, really, you two are walking into the colosseum of fights. You can't lose this battle, Shay. Do you understand me? If you have sex with him, that's you losing your virginity to Landon-freaking-Harrison! That would be a very expensive therapy bill down the line."

I laughed, shut my locker, and started walking away. "It's not that serious, Tracey."

"Um, yes, it is. This is the most important win you'll probably ever have a chance at in your life. If you get Landon Harrison to fall in love with you, you win the win of all wins. You are getting your enemy to bow down at your feet. If that's not epic, I don't know what is. I need you to stay focused these next few months. He's going to try everything to get under your skin. He's going to use his sex appeal to try to pull you in."

"Landon is not sexy," I spat out.

"Listen, Shay, I know you hate the guy, but lying isn't going to help your case. I think all of America can agree that Landon is sexy."

True.

He had a crooked smile with a perfect Cupid's bow and a deep dimple in his left cheek. His eyes were a vibrant blue that reminded me of the lakefront on the clearest summer day, and his body was built like a god. Plus, he always smelled good—you know, when he didn't smell like some other girl's perfume. I wasn't in the business of smelling him often, but sometimes, he'd walk past me, and he'd smell so good I'd want to crawl into the curves of his body just to breathe him in—that is *if* I hadn't hated him so much.

Then there was his voice. It was full and refined. Landon spoke like a man from old Hollywood, very Cary-Grant-like, with a smoothness to all of his words. Even when he seemed completely disconnected from a conversation, his words melted off his tongue like silk.

I could see why girls found him…attractive.

But none of that mattered.

"So, what's your game plan?" Tracey asked.

I wasn't certain how to answer. I didn't have a game plan at all. Truth was, I was planning to stay far away from Landon for the next few months. I wasn't too determined to make him fall in love with me; I was simply determined to make him lose his side of the bet. If it came out as a draw, that felt like a victory to me.

"I don't have a plan."

Tracey frowned. "Well, that's underwhelming."

We turned the corner, and there Landon was, standing at his locker, talking to some girl—probably a sophomore—who was pretty much throwing herself at him.

When he turned his head, he locked eyes with mine. Then, he smirked.

Oh, heck. Did I mention Landon's smirk?

I was certain that smirk got some pregnant on the regular.

"Oh my gosh." Tracey shivered, wrapping her arm around mine and hurrying me past Landon and his current fling. "You're so going to lose this bet."

"Thanks for your belief in me," I huffed.

"I'm sorry, but he's going to use that smirk to win, and it's going to work."

"What do you mean? How do you know it's going to work?"

"Shay, he just had sex with you using only his eyes."

I felt my cheeks heating up as I hugged my books to my chest. "What? No. Shut up, Tracey."

"I'm just saying, it looked like he screwed you with solely his eyeballs. You should go check your panties to make sure you're in the clear."

I swore, my friend was a little too much sometimes. "That's disgusting."

"Oh no, there's nothing disgusting about a good eye-fuck. That's how Reggie gets me through our English lit class."

"You and Reggie have sex with your eyes during English class?"

"Well, it's more of a one-sided thing, but trust me, he'll join in soon enough once he glances my way."

I laughed at my ridiculous friend. "How is the Reggie thing going?" I needed to shift the conversation away from Landon, and I knew bringing up Reggie would do exactly that.

"We're in the playing-hard-to-get stage of it all. He's coming around, though. He gave me a nickname," she said as we stopped by her locker to pick up her English book.

"Oh? What is it?"

She stood still and tall with the biggest smirk on her face. "Stacey."

I blinked.

She rolled her eyes and lightly shoved me. "Okay, so he called me by the wrong name. Tacky, I know, but not everyone can have their sworn enemy eye-screwing them in the hallway."

"We weren't eye-screwing!"

"I bet he's still looking at you right now," she challenged.

"I bet he isn't."

We turned around, and Landon's eyes were, in fact, on me, while the girl's eyes were wide with excitement as they stayed superglued on him. Oh boy, maybe I was a bit bad at this betting thing.

Landon's and my stare locked once more, and a chill raced over my body. Why was he still staring at me? Why did my heart flip when he looked my way?

He parted his lips a little, and his tongue darted out and swept over the bottom one before he bit it and dragged his teeth across it in slow motion. Then, he added in that smirk. The dimple appeared. The Gates of Hell opened up, and I was left speechless.

"Oh my gosh," Tracey whispered, breaking my connection with Landon. "I think I just came for you." She blushed, probably matching the redness of my cheeks, though her skin was much paler than mine, making it so much more obvious. I was thankful for my darkened skin, as it made it so much easier to hide whenever I felt a bit flustered.

And in that moment, Landon had left me a bit distraught.

I didn't have a clue what I'd gotten myself into. I didn't have a clue why I'd asked the Devil to dance with me, but I wasn't going to let him or that dimple get to me. I planned to keep my distance, to avoid him at all costs. I couldn't fall in love with him if I never let him near me.

Every day after school, I walked to Hadley Park. It was a beautiful place with a huge playground and amazing hiking trails. I'd been going to that park since I was a kid. I'd slid down those slides a million times with my parents and Mima. When my father wasn't in his best shape, Mima would get me out of the house, and we'd build sand castles for hours. Then, she'd walk me down one of the trails toward the two biggest willow trees I'd ever seen. It was called the lovers tree. They were twisted together as one with their branches intertwined.

Growing up, I always explored those trails and sat near the two willows. It was still winter in Illinois, therefore all of nature was still fast asleep. The leaves hadn't returned from their slumber, and the flowers weren't yet in bloom, but the bark of the willows still stood strong. And in their trunks sat deep initials. There were dozens of initials carved into the trees. Legend had it that if you carved the initials of yourself and your loved one into the bark, your love story would last forever and always.

Years before, Mima had carved hers and Grandpa's into the trees. Mom and Dad's sat against it, too.

I thought it was the most romantic thing in the whole world—a tree filled with lovers. I wished someday to carve my name into the tree, too, with my future love.

Tracey was right about me. I did have a sensitive heart. I loved the idea of love. I adored the idea of finding someone you'd want to spend the rest of your life with. I craved having that kind of connection with another. I'd written dozens of stories about love, for goodness' sake. Love was something I believed in fully, even though I'd never experienced it on my own. One day, my initials would rest against that tree bark, just not with the likes of someone like Landon.

I had no doubt that I'd win our bet, because I knew Landon wasn't the type of person people loved. Lust, perhaps. But love? Never. He wasn't built that way. He didn't have the ability to let people in the way they needed to be invited into his soul in order for them to love him. His heart was shut off from allowing others to hear how it beat. In my mind, Landon Harrison would never be the hero. He was always the villain of people's stories, including mine.

I knew I'd never carve his initials next to mine, because a person like me could never love a monster like Landon. In fairytales, the beauty fell in love with the beast.

In reality, the beast destroyed beauty.

I wasn't going to let that happen. I wasn't going to fall in love and be left with shattered shards of my soul.

I might have had a sensitive heart, but I refused to let it be sensitive to him.

Chapter Seven

Landon

MY FAVORITE THING ABOUT SHAY WAS HOW EASY IT WAS TO MAKE her blush. She was a good girl, and you saw it all over her face. Getting her to fall for me was going to be effortless. I'd seen girls like her. I'd hooked up with girls like her. Girls like her fell in love heart first, leaving their brains behind. Loving probably came easy to her like the air she breathed.

Her high cheeks always turned the slightest shade of pink whenever I made some kind of inappropriate gesture her way, and I knew it was driving her crazy.

That was why I kept doing it. It amazed me how annoying her was enough to keep me from thinking about the days coming up.

Never in my life had I thought it would have been Shay who kept my mind clear.

Yet, you could count on Mrs. Levi to remind me of how much these next few weeks were going to suck.

Once a week, I was forced to meet with the guidance counselor after lunch. It was supposed to be my free period, but instead, I had to sit with Mrs. Levi like I was damaged goods or something.

I didn't even want to be there, but I knew my parents would give me hell if they heard I ditched. Well, my mother would've. My father wouldn't have cared a lick.

The previous night, Mom had left me a voice message saying she wished she could've been with me, saying how she'd missed me and hated that she had to work so much lately. After Lance passed away, it seemed she was always coming and going.

"Sorry, Land. I wish I was with you. Left my credit card so you can order in food. You can call the chef, too. The number is on the fridge. I'll check in every morning and night. Make sure you're getting enough sleep, too. You need your rest. Also, don't forget to take your pills. I love you so much, honey. We'll chat soon. I love you. Okay. Bye."

She always said 'I love you' twice.

Dad texted me instead of leaving a voice message. His was a much more encouraging message.

Dad: We Harrison men aren't weak. Keep your head up high. Man up.

You got it, Dad.

If there was a bumper sticker for World's Best Father, it definitely wouldn't have been on Ralph Harrison's BMW.

I knew if I ditched my meeting with Mrs. Levi, she'd report it to my parents, and Mom would try to set me up with my previous therapist for after-school sessions. I didn't know about any other high school student, but the last thing I wanted to do after a long day at school was go to some smelly, stuffy office and talk about my feelings to a sixty-year-old man who had probably just banged his secretary during his lunch hour.

I sat in Mrs. Levi's office once again, staring at the pictures of her niece and nephew spread throughout the space.

She was smiling her normal smile with her hands clasped together and resting in her lap. "So, Landon, how was your weekend?"

"Same as always."

"I heard a few mumbles in the hallways about a party you threw…" She started, but her words trailed off as if she didn't want to seem to be nosey when she was, indeed, being nosey.

"Yeah. Just a small thing." Lie number one of our meeting.

"Do you want to talk about how that was?"

Yes, Mrs. Levi. Let me tell you all about the underage drinking and drug usage that went on at my place on Saturday.

"Nah, it's not a big deal. It was a low-key night."

She narrowed her eyes but dropped the subject as she shifted some paperwork around. She seemed tired that morning, but who wasn't? Maybe she had trouble sleeping each night, too. The bags under her eyes kind of matched the deep purplish tones of my own.

"So, your birthday is in a few weeks, huh?"

I cringed a little at the mention of my birthday. I was trying my hardest to forget.

When I remained quiet, she kept talking, because if there was one thing Mrs. Levi wasn't any good at, it was catching a hint.

"Which means it's been one year since your uncle—"

"Died on my birthday? Yes, Mrs. Levi, I'm aware," I snapped. I instantly felt bad for snapping, because it wasn't her fault at all. She was merely doing her job. It just sucked that her job hurt sometimes. It brought up issues I wished to bury deep in my mind. I muttered an apology, and she shook her head.

"No need to apologize. I'd probably feel the same way if an old woman was badgering me about such a heavy topic."

Mrs. Levi wasn't that old. She more so had an old-person personality. I would have bet she knit sweaters and drank apple cider in front of the fireplace on Saturday nights.

I slumped down in my chair, and now my mind was doing that thing again.

Thinking.

I hated when that happened.

My thoughts were back on that day. Every time I blinked, I saw Lance in the darkness of my eyelids. I saw him lying there, floating face down in the pool, the water rippling all around as he stayed still.

"*Lance*," I remembered hollering. "*Lance!*"

Each time the memories came, my throat tightened a little more.

"What do you have planned for your birthday?" Mrs. Levi asked, breaking my mind from spiraling deeper, but her question wasn't going to make me feel any better.

"My mom will be home. I'm not sure what we're doing yet, but she'll be there. My dad will probably find a reason to work or something."

"Do you miss them?"

"Miss who?"

"Your parents."

I shrugged. "It is what it is."

"Yes, but do you miss them?"

"Not my father." I saw him twice a week and felt nothing. If I didn't see him twice a week, I would probably still feel nothing.

"But your mom? You miss her?"

Every single fucking day.

How pathetic. I was a grown-ass guy missing his mommy.

I shrugged. "It's not a big deal."

She brushed the edge of her nose. "Do you think she knows you miss her?"

What a pointless question. "It doesn't matter. It wouldn't make her come home."

"Maybe it would," she offered up.

I didn't offer anything else on that topic. Not worth my breath.

"Don't worry about me." Mom would be back for my birthday. That was all that mattered. She'd be there when I needed her the most.

"I can't help it, Landon. I care about you, which means I worry," Mrs. Levi revealed. It made me uncomfortable. When people cared about me, I felt a pressure to try to not let them down. Then, I always ended up letting them down.

I shifted around in my seat, and she must've picked up on my discomfort, because she moved the conversation forward.

"Well, until then, perhaps we should have no more parties leading up to your birthday, right?"

"Okay."

I had no desire to have any more parties any time soon. I always thought being surrounded by people would help me tune out my sadness. Truth was, it only made it louder. Standing in a crowded room when no one was able to truly see you was the loneliest I'd ever felt.

That night, when Shay looked up and locked eyes with me in the midst of my aching, I felt terrified that she saw me, yet also somewhat…comforted? It was an odd sensation, and I wasn't completely sure how to accept the moment.

When someone saw your pain and didn't look away, it felt like a gift, like they were allowing you to be exactly who you were without shame or judgments.

I just wished that gift was given to me by someone who wasn't Shay Gable.

Mrs. Levi rubbed the side of her neck before straightening out one of the frames on her desk. "Last time we spoke, we talked about finding a hobby for you. How are we doing on finding something to keep you busy? Did you find anything to keep your interest?"

"Well, yeah. Kind of."

Shay.

Shay, Shay, and Shay.

"Good, good. What is it?"

I kept my lips shut.

She raised an eyebrow. "Hopefully it's legal?"

"It is."

A small sigh released between her lips. "Good. That's really good, Landon. But if you need something else, here's an afterschool program I thought you might be interested in." She handed me a pamphlet, and I was officially tagged as damaged goods. Afterschool support groups were the final key to that fact.

"It's a group of teens who have gone through tough situations. They meet up twice a week and just hang out and talk about their issues."

I pushed the brochure back in her direction. "Nah, I'm not really one for therapy sessions, much less group ones."

She pushed it back. "I hear what you're saying, but sometimes, the best thing we can do in life is step outside of our comfort zone."

I didn't argue it and took the brochure. I shoved it into my backpack and sat back in my chair.

The conversation dragged on like the rest of the day. Every time I crossed Shay's path, I made sure to flash her one of my asshole smiles, and she'd get all flustered by it. The next days were a lot of the same, but when Wednesday came around, she smiled back. Her cheeks didn't redden, and she didn't hurry away from me. When I sat at the lunch table before anyone else, Shay walked over and set her tray down directly across from mine.

She didn't look up at me.

She didn't say a word.

She simply sat and opened her paper carton of chocolate milk. One time, I overheard her talking to some girl, saying how she hated regular milk because it seemed a bit too close to a person sucking from an udder, but chocolate milk was different because it had a more-acceptable-for-humans flavor.

I didn't know what she meant by such a weird statement, but it wasn't uncommon for me to not understand the mind of Shay. I'd overheard her say a lot of weird shit before, so the milk comment hadn't been out of the norm.

The next day, she did the same thing—sat right across from me at lunch. Followed by the next day, and the next.

Her oddness was rubbing me the wrong way, and I couldn't stay quiet about it. "What are you doing?"

"Eating lunch." She popped a grape into her mouth and then tore her sandwich in half. "Use your context clues, Sherlock." She smirked.

I almost smiled at her sass level. "I see that, but why are you sitting across from me every single day? You know how annoying it is to sit across from your face each day?"

"What's wrong, Landon?" She raised an eyebrow. "Does my closeness make you uncomfortable?"

"It's going to take a lot more than a little close proximity to scare me off, dollface."

"Don't call me dollface."

"Then don't have one."

She ate her lunch in complete silence after that, staring me straight in the eyes without any kind of blushing or shying away.

Okay, Gable. I see where you're going with this.

She was trying to prove a point—that she could be in the same space as me, face to face, and not back down due to nervousness. She was puffing her chest out and pounding her fists against it.

I am Shay, here me roar.

But still, there was something more to it that I couldn't see, something deeper to her story that she was keeping just for herself. Not being able to crack that open was going to drive me insane.

"Shit," I muttered.

"Something wrong?"

"What's your angle?"

"My angle?"

"Yeah. Why can't I read you, Chick?"

"I don't know," she said, offering a quick shrug before she continued eating, "I'm probably above your reading level."

I smirked.

Oh hell. Shay Gable made me smirk—a genuine smirk—and I was certain she'd noticed it.

I didn't often give real smiles. Most of the time, when I grinned, it was just an act, because that was what people expected you to do. Grin. Laugh. Be happy.

My true smiles were few and far between, yet somehow, Shay managed to get one out of me. I have been lying if I said it didn't feel kind of good, too.

"Whatever, reading is overrated," I stated. That was a lie. Reading was what I did when I couldn't keep my mind in check, which meant I had a full-sized library inside my head.

"I bet you think oxygen is overrated, too, based on the lack of it going to your brain cells." She smiled, and damn, it was beautiful.

She was sassy that afternoon. I wouldn't have ever told her, but her sassiness was kind of sexy.

I reached across the table and snatched up the last of the grapes on her tray before standing up from my seat and walking away.

"Hey! I was going to eat those!" she hollered, irritation coating her words.

"Ask me how much I care," I replied as I kept walking.

"I hate you!" she shouted.

"I hate you more."

"I hate you the most!"

I'd never known hatred could be such a turn-on.

I wasn't sure if I actually had a plan to make her fall in love with me, really. I wasn't sure if she had an idea for the love angle, either, but what I did know was this *thing* between us—whatever the hell it was—felt fun.

Fun.

When was the last time something had felt fun to me?

All the days before had felt like wading through quicksand—slow, exhausting, and hopeless—but now with Shay? I felt entertained, refreshed. It felt good to mess with her, to get in her head. We loved pushing each other's buttons. We loved the way we pissed each other off. We loved the hate we were able to give each other every day we walked into school.

T HE OTHER DAY, LANDON HAD STUFFED MY LOCKER WITH DOZENS OF pieces of paper that had "Do you love me yet?" written on them. I took every single piece, figured out his locker combination, and stuffed them right back into his with the word NO written in bold.

Then, he went into my backpack, took my history extra-credit assignment, and wrote "penis" across it, making it impossible for me to turn it in. In exchange for that, I licked my fingers and stuck them straight into the brownie on his lunch tray.

To my surprise, he didn't seem thrown off by his damaged brownie.

"Thanks, Chick," he commented as he picked up the brownie. "I love my desserts moist."

He bit into it as if he wasn't thrown off by my licks.

The way the word moist rolled off his tongue made me want to vomit. At the same time, it made me cross my legs tighter at the lunch table, and I was certain he saw the redness in my cheeks.

I watched him eat the whole brownie, and then he locked eyes with me as he sucked on each of his fingers.

In.

Slow.

Motion.

Oh my gosh.

Do that again.

Then, he pulled up the bottom of his long-sleeved T-shirt and revealed his toned body. He dabbed the corners of his mouth with his shirt, using it as a napkin as I counted the abs on his torso.

One, two, skip a few…

Landon always wore long-sleeved shirts that were tight enough to highlight his toned arms. If he moved his arms in just the right way, you could swear his biceps were waving at you.

A devilish smirk curved his lips. "If you keep staring, I'll have to charge you."

I clenched my thighs together even tighter as I shifted my stare away from him.

It wasn't fair.

Boys his age weren't supposed to look like that. Landon made it perfectly clear that there was nothing in the world for him to be embarrassed about when it came to his body. No teenager had the right to be as fit and toned as he was—other than Chad Michael Murray.

I cursed the heavens for giving Landon a Chad Michael Murray body.

I stayed seated as long as I could before I grew too flustered and had to stand and leave the table. I could feel his satisfied grin as I walked away, too.

What was supposed to have been a bet about falling in love quickly shifted into the realm of Landon and me falling deeper into our hate. Well, at least that was what was happening for me. I couldn't speak on his behalf, because I didn't care what he thought. I despised him. From the top of my head to the bottom of my feet, I loathed that man.

But still, I didn't know why my heart kept deciding to skip every now and then whenever he pranked me. Or why he'd cross my mind, and my thighs would ache in desire. Or why my stomach swirled whenever he came my way.

Probably gas.

As Landon's and my hate deepened, it seemed Mima's and Dad's did, too. Each day I came home from school, I'd walk into the house to hear the two of them bickering. Mima was always getting on Dad's case about one thing or another. Lately, she refused to let the diamond earring fiasco go. Mom even offered to sell them for extra money, but Mima was stern with her words.

"It's not about the money, Camila. It's about where he got the money. His small jobs are not enough to pay for something like that. Open your eyes," Mima scolded.

"How about you mind your own business, Maria?" Dad would snap.

"My daughter *is* my business," she'd reply.

I knew Mom felt as if she was caught between the two of them—the love of her life and the woman who'd raised her. If there was one thing that was true about my mother, it was the fact that she was a peacekeeper. She didn't like conflict, and she did her best to tiptoe around people in order to not hurt anyone's feelings. All she cared about was making the people she loved happy.

Mima, though? Mima was the complete opposite. While my mother was a mouse, my grandmother was a lion, and she wasn't shy about people hearing her roar. She faced conflict head-on with no remorse. She wasn't afraid to speak her mind, and I figured that came from the struggle of having always been silenced by my grandfather when he was still alive. Once he passed, Mima promised to never bite her tongue for a man again, and she had held on to that promise, too. Unfortunately, that meant my father wasn't saved from her spitfire. She wasn't ever afraid to speak up, even if her words burned Dad.

It was hard for me to listen to them fight, because I loved them all so much.

I just wished, over time, they could find a happy medium.

That was why I did my best to be a good girl. There was already so much tension in my home, and I didn't want to add any more stress to the situation, or add more stress to Mom's already heavily laden shoulders. I was a perfect little princess. I didn't drink. I didn't do drugs. I never, ever skipped school. My grades were all As, and if there was ever extra credit, I was all over it. I was a star student, an easy kid to raise, all because I knew my house was too fragile to withhold any more struggles.

My parents never had to worry about what their daughter was doing—because I was always doing the right thing.

Whenever there was a big argument in the house, I'd escape to my bedroom and close the door behind me. I was certain everyone would clear their heads soon enough, but until then, I'd fall into my own world—my world of fiction.

In many ways, I was my father's daughter. Every bit of creativity I had in my bones, I received from that man. When he wasn't getting in trouble, he was an amazing storyteller, and whenever I felt lost in one of my writing ventures, I knew he was the one to go to for help.

He understood story structures and how characters worked in ways I only dreamed of. It was because of him that I got involved in not only writing but the acting world, too. There was no part of me that had a strong desire to be an actress, but Dad convinced me if I were to step into all aspects of storytelling, I'd be able to understand characters for my scripts even more.

"There's power in looking at things from all angles. That's what the masters do," he'd say.

And all I ever wanted to do was be a master screenwriter like my father—minus his flaws. I had my own flaws to deal with; I didn't need his mixing into them.

For a long time, he was convinced the drugs simply made his mind open more, made him able to see deeper, see clearer, create better stories. In a way, he was right. I had once gotten my hands on some of the scripts he'd written in a drug-induced state. Some of his best masterpieces were written when he was high. The words almost danced off the pages, and the story arcs were passionate and felt like magic.

Then, there were the manic stories. The ones that didn't connect or lead anywhere. The ones that looked like scribbles across the wall. The ones that scared me. When I read my father's messes, I ached with worry and fear for his sanity.

The stories Dad wrote outside of his highs felt more...forced, as if he was trying too hard to get the words right. It would take him months to finish a project while he was sober, compared to the manic state he'd write in while under the influence. He was too hard on himself when he wrote sober. He'd curse his words and call them trash, even though his idea of trash was my definition of glory. During those dark times, he'd fall into a depressed state, which would make him spiral back down the road of bad habits.

Wash, rinse, repeat.

Not only was he not himself when he was high, he also worked like a madman. He wouldn't sleep, hardly ate, and would snap at people whenever his craft was interrupted. Sure, he wrote amazing words when he was wasted, but that didn't make him an amazing man.

Mom supported Dad regardless of what he did, even if she didn't agree with it. Mima called Mom an enabler and often told her that wasn't how a relationship should work, but in the name of love, Mom never listened.

I came from a household of addiction.

My father was addicted to drugs—both using and dealing them—and my mother was addicted to him.

I was surprised an addiction hadn't swallowed me whole yet.

After Dad got out of prison, he'd given up writing. He figured that was his trigger—his creativity. Yet, ever since then, he'd struggled to find his footing, to find something to keep his mind and heart busy.

Mom said he needed a hobby. Mima said he needed a more worthy job.

My father called himself a jack-of-all-trades. He never worked a solid nine-to-five job, because he said he couldn't deal with that level of repetitive tasks. So, he currently juggled three jobs a week. While that kept his mind busy, it didn't feed his soul.

I just needed him to find some form of happiness so he could be the man we all knew he was capable of becoming.

"Knock, knock," a voice said through my closed bedroom door.

"It's unlocked."

Dad turned the knob and stood there in the doorframe with his hands stuffed into the pockets of his jeans. "You okay?"

"Good, just working on my audition that's coming up," I said, leaving out the fact that there was still a knot sitting in my stomach from listening to the three of them argue.

"Oh yeah, you got the school play coming up, right?" he asked, moving into the space and sitting on the edge of my bed.

"Yup. *Romeo and Juliet.*"

He nodded slowly. "'O Romeo, Romeo, wherefore art thou Romeo?' A classic."

Indeed.

"Are you ready for the audition? Do you want me to listen to your piece?" he asked, acting as if there hadn't just been a war zone in the living room a few minutes earlier.

I didn't look like my father. He looked like the cliché all-American boy—blue eyes, blond hair, lopsided smile that always looked more like a frown. His skin was pale, and his hair was buzzed short. The wrinkles around his eyes told his history, along with the way his shoulders were always slouched forward. His face was also sunken in a bit from his past drug and alcohol habits. He looked much older than he should've, but he was here, alive and somewhat well.

If that wasn't a blessing, I didn't know what was.

"Are you and Mima ever going to get along?" I blurted out.

Dad raised an eyebrow, shocked by my question. He shouldn't have been surprised with the amount of arguments those two got into.

"She and I are too much alike. That's why we butt heads so much, but I can't blame her. I've let you all down countless times in the past. Maria is right to be concerned, but I don't plan on screwing up again. Not this time. This time is different, okay?"

I wanted to believe him, but one's belief in a person faded a little more each and every time they broke your trust. It was hard to trust people who'd always lied in the past.

"Promise?" I asked him.

"Promise." He stood up from the bed and moved over to me. He combed my hair behind my ears. "I'm sorry about all the fighting, Shay. Really, I am. Also, I don't blame your grandmother for feeling the way she does—she's just looking to protect you and your mother. That's her job, but I need you to understand that my job is to protect you now, too. I'm here, and I'm healing so I can be a better father and husband. I'm working on myself so I can work on us."

There was a tiny corner in my heart I reserved for my father's words. I didn't let that corner expand too much, because I feared being let down by him. I worried about allowing my heart to break over the first man in my life who was supposed to heal my broken pieces, not create the cracks.

In that tiny corner of my heart, that was where I believed him. That was where I hoped for him. That was where I prayed. I hoped that tiny corner would never get smaller. I hoped someday, somehow, it would grow, making room for more of my father's love.

"Now, come on," he offered, leaning against my desk. "Let me hear this monologue of yours."

If there was one thing my father did well, it was believe in me and my creative skills. That was the only thing I knew was one hundred percent true. His praise was so authentic when it left his lips.

I practiced my chosen dialogue for him for the remainder of the night. He gave me his input, critiquing my pauses and pace and facial expressions. He directed me. He made me laugh. He made me smile. He made me believe in myself, in my talents, in my soul. Then, he gave me his two-nod signal of approval.

And that tiny corner of my heart? It soared.

Chapter Nine

Landon

IF THERE WAS ONE PERSON IN THE WORLD I NEVER WANTED TO BE LIKE when I grew up, it was my father. He was a coldhearted man, which probably helped him in a courtroom. He was driven by two things in life I didn't care anything about: money and praise.

He was a criminal defense attorney and almost too good at his job. The number of criminals he'd gotten off was off-putting. Still, Dad never called them criminals; he called them men and women who were falsely accused.

Sometimes I thought he was so jaded he actually believed the lies he told himself, or maybe he told the lies to help him sleep better at night. I didn't know how a mother like mine could've fallen for a man like him.

"You're late," Dad barked as I walked into RH Law Firm on Wednesday evening. I was ten minutes late, and he was already busting my ass about it.

"Only ten minutes," I muttered. "There was traffic."

"Ten minutes is still late. You'll stay twenty minutes after to make up for it," he huffed.

I wished I looked more like my mother, but I was a younger copy of father dearest. From his brunette hair to his crystal blue eyes, there was no way he could've ever denied being my father.

The resemblance was remarkable, except he wore thousand-dollar suits, and I wore some cheap tie he'd forced me to buy for the internship.

I would've bought a clip-on if I could've found one. Dad would've had a heart attack about it, too.

After he scolded me about being late, I didn't see him again the whole afternoon. He headed into his office and stayed there for the remainder of his night shift. It was like that every single time I came over to work at the firm. My father was a ghost, and I never even saw his shadows. That was okay with me, though. I was definitely a bigger fan of my mother.

She often texted me while I was at the firm, asking me how Dad was doing. Hell if I knew. My father hardly ever let anyone into his psyche. He had walls built so high, higher than mine, which was somewhat of a talent.

Working at the law firm was my least favorite way to keep my mind busy. Time moved slow there, and I felt as if I was on high alert whenever Dad's secretary would go to his office and close the door behind him.

Her name was April, and she was nowhere near as beautiful as my mother.

I didn't tell Mom about Dad's activities, because I didn't have any real proof that my father and April had ever done anything inappropriate, just my doubts about the kind of character my father possessed.

He seemed like the type who would cheat on his wife with his secretary.

Still, not enough evidence to ever tell Mom.

I finished up my pointless tasks at the office and headed out without saying goodbye to Dad. I doubted he even noticed or cared, but he did make sure his assistant stayed with me those extra twenty minutes.

Mom texted me a few times after I got home to check that things had gone okay at the firm. She knew I hated working there and told me I didn't have to if I didn't want to, but knowing my father, he'd come down hard on her if I quit. Mom already had a hard enough time with my father; she didn't need me adding to her stress.

Mom: How was your father? Did he take you to dinner?

Me: Nope. Never does.

Mom: Was April working today?

Me: Yup.

Mom: Did she help your father a lot tonight? Did they seem close?

I knew what she was getting at, and I hated it. I hated how that April chick made Mom doubt herself. Her insecurities were so loud through the messages.

Me: She's not you.

She waited awhile before responding.

Mom: I love you, love you, Land.

Me: You too, Mom. Night.

"What is this thing between the two of you?" Monica hissed, marching up to my locker on Thursday morning. She looked wild in the eyes and pissed off, but then again, it was Monica—she always looked wild in the eyes and pissed off.

"You'll have to be more clear on who you're talking about."

"Little Miss Perfect and you—what's the deal with this bet?"

Oh. Shay. Of course.

I shrugged my shoulders. "It's just for laughs."

"No one's laughing," she muttered. "I don't even know why you would want to spend any of your time thinking about that annoying bitch."

I smirked. "Oh really? Because at my party the other day it seemed like she was one of your closest friends, which prompted you to slap me repeatedly."

"Whatever, I was drunk. Just drop whatever it is that's going on between you two, okay?"

I cocked an eyebrow. "I'm sorry, did I miss the chapter of this messed-up book of ours where you get to tell me what I can and can't do?"

She raised an eyebrow. "You owe me. You promised me you'd be there for me."

I knew exactly the promise I'd made to Monica over a year ago, a promise to look after her whenever I could, and for the most part, I'd kept my end of the bargain. If she was low, I was there for her, but that didn't mean I had to give up the small bit of life I had to give in to her ridiculous requests. Soon enough, we'd both be off to college anyway. She'd have to learn to stand on her own two feet.

Also, I'd made the promise when I was high as fuck. Promises made under the influence should be null and void.

"Listen, I promised to look after you, all right? And I've done that. When you need food, I get you food. When you're fucked up, I help you sober up. But let's be really clear about this: I am not yours to control, Monica. I'm going to do what—and who—I want, when I want."

She pursed her lips and eyed me up and down. "You're really going to do this stupid bet with Shay Gable? Seriously? We hate her guts."

Wrong. *I* hated her. Monica hated the way I hated Shay, as if my hatred was giving too much attention to another girl.

"It's really none of your business what I do."

She pushed her purse up on her shoulder and rolled her eyes. "Whatever, Landon. It's not like she'd ever want to fall in love with someone like you, anyway. A person like her would never fall for trash."

There it was, the insults. Right on time.

Then, she shoved me hard in the chest.

What the hell?

Was she drunk?

High?

It was ten in the morning. How was she already messed up at ten in the morning?

I took a breath and stepped away from her. It was too early to be dealing with her antics. I had hardly shaken off the exhaustion in my body from yet another night of only getting about an hour of sleep.

"Okay, Monica. I think we're done here."

I started walking off, and she shouted toward me. "Yeah that's right—walk away! Walk away from the truth. I just hope you know you're going to lose your stupid bet, because no one could love someone like you. You got those scars to prove just how unlovable you really are."

My hands clenched together at her words, and I hated how she had the power to make my chest instantly light on fire. I didn't respond to her, though. I didn't look back in her direction, but she didn't have to look me in the eyes to know her words burned. She knew how to hit me, where to strike to cause the most pain.

I skipped my next class. I went to the football field—which was covered in snow—without a jacket and stood underneath the bleachers to get away from everything, from everyone.

My chest was tight, and each breath I took in felt frozen like the Illinois air, harsh and intense.

I knew what was happening. I'd had my fair share of panic attacks over the past year. I knew there was no getting around it. Once my body decided it was going to fall apart, all I could do was allow it to crash.

Sometimes, the panics came through me fast, and other times it felt like they lasted for days. I pushed up my sleeves and revealed the scars of my past sadness, the markings of my mind spinning out of control. The first time Monica saw my scars, she called me dramatic. "You didn't even cut the right way to end your life. You just cut for attention," she barked. But, I knew she was wrong. I never wanted people to see my scars. I was ashamed of them. It was why I wore long-sleeved shirts every single day. I wasn't proud of what I did, and it damn sure wasn't for attention. It wasn't for suicide either, though. It was for me to feel something more than empty inside. I was desperate to feel anything, because for the most part, my mind seemed so worn down.

I hadn't cut myself in a while. I was trying my best to find other ways to feel outside of cutting.

My hands trembled, and I held on to the iced-over railing of the bleachers as I lowered my head to try to keep from throwing up. My hands burned from the chilled bar in my grip, but I was thankful for that. I was thankful to feel something, even if it hurt.

Feeling any kind of pain meant I was still alive.

That had to count for something.

I think I was born with a hole in my heart.

It doesn't beat like it's supposed to, and I don't know if that makes it unworthy of love.

What kind of person would want to love a broken heart?

What kind of person would take the time to listen to the heartbeats of something so damaged?

I just hope broken hearts can receive love, too.

I think us broken hearts need love the most.

-L

After my breakdown, I headed back into school, straight for Mrs. Levi's office. We didn't have a meeting scheduled, but I was thankful that there was no one sitting in her office taking up her time.

I didn't know where to go, and honestly, a part of me wanted to man up and just get over myself and my breakdowns, but I wasn't that strong. I didn't know how to move past my own thoughts and be okay.

"Landon." Mrs. Levi looked up from her desk and smiled like always, but her grin had a bit of concern. With good reason. I doubted people came to her office just to talk about the latest high school fashion trends or other mindless topics. "Are you okay?"

I stuffed my hands into my pockets. "Yeah."

That was all I could push out.

She raised an eyebrow, and I looked away from her, somewhat embarrassed by the fact that she could tell I was damaged goods just by looking at me.

"Shouldn't you be in class?" she asked.

"Probably," I replied.

Silence fell over the room, and I glanced up at the photographs of her family upon the wall. They all looked so happy, so connected.

I wondered if she knew how lucky she was.

Dammit.

My mind was doing that emo crap it did on the daily.

"Do you want to sit for a while?" she asked.

"I don't want to talk," I blurted out.

"We don't have to talk at all." She gestured toward the chair across from her. "But please, have a seat."

I sat, and somehow, I think Mrs. Levi heard the silent thank you I was giving her that afternoon. I was thankful to have someone to sit with in silence. Sometimes, sitting in silence with someone who is willing to stay with you helps a heart heal more than talking about one's hurts.

Chapter Ten

Landon

THE FOLLOWING AFTERNOON, HANK, GREYSON, AND ERIC CAME OVER to my place to hang out. They could always tell when my mind was heavy, but they never asked me questions about it. I was thankful for that. I didn't feel like talking much. We all hung out at the pool, talking about pointless topics.

That afternoon, KJ showed up to my house at the request of Hank. My house was the main place for weed pickups, because my parents were gone most of the time. KJ was an older dude in his late forties— about Lance's age. He'd been dealing weed to my friends for a while now, and overall he seemed like a decent person.

Eric smoked a joint on a lounge chair and looked up toward the sky. "You ever play the cloud game?" he asked. The clouds were huge and looked fake, like the clouds on *The Simpsons* intro, all spaced out a little too perfectly. It looked as if an artist had taken an oversized brush and added to the sky canvas.

"Cloud game?" I asked.

He placed his hands behind his head and nodded. "Yeah, where you see the clouds and shout out what they look like."

KJ grinned as he counted the money Hank gave him. "My youngest daughter still goes apeshit for that game. Last summer we'd lay out in the grass for hours just make-believing the things we saw. Turtles. Dogs. Michael Jordan. Shit…" He laughed, shaking his head back and forth. "Those are some of the best times. My older daughter is way past that age, but we used to do it, too. It was great."

KJ always did that, always told stories about his kids whenever he stopped by. I wondered if my parents did the same when they spoke to other people.

Dad probably told horror stories about me.

Mom probably told love stories.

Funny how you could be a different character in different people's storybooks.

"That's good and all, but can I ask why you are sitting in my house, with these teenage boys?" a voice asked, snapping me up from my lounging position.

"Mom, hey." I rose to stand. "What are you doing in town? I thought you'd be in California for a few more days."

"I took an early flight home." She combed her hair behind her ears and looked over to KJ, who was standing there like a puppy being caught misbehaving. "I don't know who you are, and I don't know why you're hanging out with these boys, but perhaps you should go now."

He didn't say a word as he exited stage right.

Hank put on a goofy smile. "Hey, Mrs. H. You're looking beautiful in that trench coat."

Eric stood from the lounge chair. "Is that a new haircut? It looks great on you?"

Greyson grinned. "Are you losing weight? You look like you're losing weight."

Mom smirked a little. "Goodbye, boys." They all started to hurry away, but Mom stopped them. "First, hand over the goods."

"But, Mrs. H! It's for my allergies," Hank joked.

She held her hand out toward him, and he groaned as he placed the weed into the palm of her hand. "Good night, boys."

"'Night, Mrs. H," they all muttered as they left.

Mom walked over to me with an arched eyebrow and a somber look on her face. "Really, Landon? Marijuana?"

She always did that—called it marijuana instead of pot or weed. I didn't know why, but it always made it sound so much worse than it actually was.

Marijuana—the gateway drug.

"I wasn't smoking it," I muttered.

She gave me a *bullshit* look, and that made me feel like shit.

I wasn't smoking it, but she didn't believe me. Truthfully, in the past, I'd given her enough reasons not to believe me. She'd found enough weed in my bedroom throughout the years to think I had my own pot farm somewhere.

My mind was racing with the fact that she was home. Damn…I missed her. I wanted to hug her, but also, I wanted to yell at her for not being around enough. I wanted to call her out on not being much of a parent lately. I wanted to tell her how I wasn't okay, and I needed her more than ever before.

But mostly, I wanted to hug her. So, so badly.

"I'm sorry, Mom," I muttered.

"Yeah." She nodded. "Me too. Come here." She opened her arms, and I fell into her embrace like a damn needy child. She smelled like roses, and I missed that smell. I hovered over her small frame as she embraced me. Even though I was way taller than her, it felt like she was the one holding me up.

I'd almost forgotten how good she was at giving hugs.

"I missed you," she whispered, pulling me in tighter, and I let it happen.

When we let go, I scratched the back of my neck. "What are you doing here?"

"I wanted to check in. I talked to Mrs. Levi, and she seemed a bit concerned."

Oh, that made sense. She was home because an outside person commented on her neglectful parenting skills. She was probably embarrassed that a guidance counselor called her out on such a thing. In my mom's eyes, she probably thought she was doing a solid job. I was alive for the most part, still doing my schoolwork—only because it was a distraction for my brain—and I had managed to not burn the house down.

What more could a parent ask for?

"Let's go get some dinner ordered," Mom said, linking her arm with mine. "Did your father call you? He said he was going to call today."

"Nah, I haven't heard from him."

Mom frowned, but she shouldn't have been surprised by it. My father wasn't too good at checking in on me. It was fine. I didn't need to be checked in on by him.

"I'll have to ask him about that the next time we talk," she said.

"Nah, just leave it. It's not a big deal."

She kept frowning but didn't say anything else as she began walking toward the kitchen. I followed her steps too, like a needy dog, and Ham—the actual needy dog—followed right behind me.

"Okay, what are you thinking? Pizza? Tacos? Tapas?" she asked me, grabbing her cell phone out of her purse.

"Anything's fine."

She glanced at me and smiled. "Pizza it is."

We spent the rest of the night together. We watched shitty movies and *Friends* reruns, and we talked about Mom's clients. I told her about school, and how classes were fine. I didn't mention Shay, because if I did, she would've thought I'd lost my mind, but I thought about Shay every now and then, just passing thoughts. Nothing too heavy; just simple things.

Mom and I didn't talk about Lance, and that was probably because we both couldn't stand bringing him up. Whenever Mom did talk about him, her eyes would water over, and she'd burst into tears over it all. He was her only brother, and losing him had done a number on her heart. She'd once mentioned that it was probably due to the stress of everything that she had the miscarriage, and that broke my cold heart. I couldn't imagine putting that kind of pressure on oneself.

It was an unbelievably shitty situation, but Mom wasn't to be blamed for it. I'd told her that time and time again, but she didn't believe me. That was why I kept so much of my crap to myself instead of unloading it on her shoulders. Her baggage was already heavy enough—she didn't need me weighing her down any more.

We both went to our beds around midnight. She told me she loved me, and I believed every syllable of the words. I never in my life doubted my mother's love. I just knew it came in spurts. Whenever it showed up, like a famished child, I swallowed her love whole, using it to nourish my sick soul.

Mom stayed in town for two more days before she had to fly out to Florida for work. During those two days, she didn't let me out of her sight. She even had me skip school on Friday so we could spend the whole day together. We shopped, explored, and even drove down to Chicago to replace a lamp that was broken from the party I had. I figured Mom would've wanted to meet up with Dad while she was in town for lunch or dinner or something, but she never brought it up. I couldn't think of the last time the two of them had been in the same space with each other, but it seemed to work for them. Some love stories didn't need constant watering. They made their relationship work in their own way.

Mom tried the cooking thing, too.

She made pancakes that tasted like baking soda, a burnt lasagna, and an extremely hideous coconut cake—my three favorite foods, completely butchered at the hand of my mother.

Maria would've been horrified. Shit, I was horrified, but she was there, trying—failing miserably at the cooking thing, but trying nonetheless.

Those nights, I knew she was right down the hall, just two doors away from me.

I knew her heartbeats were under the same roof as mine, beating the same rhythms as mine. I knew I wasn't alone, and for the first time in a while, I was able to sleep.

I felt high with her being home—the kind of high pot couldn't get a person.

Saturday morning, she was leaving, so I woke up early to cook her breakfast. I couldn't really take any more burnt meals, and I figured it would be a nice gesture. Maria had taught me quite a few things in the kitchen throughout the past year.

Every time I made them and flipped the pancakes without messing them up, I felt like she was right there with me, patting me on the back, and saying *job well done*.

As I cooked the pancakes, Mom dragged her suitcases into the kitchen. She had one more suitcase than when she arrived, and I would've questioned why, seeing how she'd be home in less than two weeks for my birthday, but I'd learned from an early age to never question why a woman carried so much shit with them when they traveled. Once, on a family weekend getaway, Mom had brought five swimsuits. Five swimsuits for three days.

Somehow, she'd managed to wear every single one, too.

Some she had worn twice.

"Why does it smell like real food in here?" she questioned. "Mmm..." She walked over to the countertop, picked up a few pieces of the sliced bananas I'd prepped, tossing them into her mouth with the chopped walnuts. "Since when do you cook?"

Since you left me home alone to fend for myself.

I didn't want to be a dick, though, not with her leaving soon. The last thing I ever wanted to do was make her feel like shit for being a shitty parent sometimes, even though, honestly speaking, she was a shitty parent sometimes.

I was sure I was a shitty son sometimes, too, but she never gave me hell about that.

That was part of being human—being shitty on accident sometimes. It was part of the human DNA.

"I've picked up a few tricks here and there," I muttered. I left out the fact that Maria had taught me because I didn't want Mom to feel like there was a woman being a better mother to me than she was. She was sensitive about that kind of stuff.

"Well, it smells amazing—and not burnt."

"It's my lucky day, I guess. I've burned my fair share of things."

"You must get that from me," she joked, walking over to kiss me on the cheek.

I volunteered to drive her to the airport, but she told me if I went with her, saying goodbye would be too hard. I understood, I supposed.

I was feeling emotional enough to beg her to stay a little longer, and I didn't want to be the dramatic dick asking their mommy to stay with them. Besides, she'd be back home soon enough for my birthday. It wouldn't be too awful having her gone for a few days, because she'd turn around to come right back home to me.

"Can I have a hug?" she asked, and I obeyed.

She held me tight and pulled back to stare at me longingly with tears building up in her eyes. Then she hugged me again. I hated when she cried. It always made me feel hopeless.

"Come on, Ma, don't get emotional. I'll see you in a bit. Plus, you're going to make me burn the pancakes."

"Yes, sorry. It's just..." Her eyes darted away, and her small frame shook a little.

"It's just what?"

She shook her sadness away and smiled. "It's nothing. I'm going to go put my hair up and wash my face. I'll be right back for breakfast."

She placed her purse on top of one of her suitcases.

As I was flipping her pancakes, her purse fell over, knocking all her girl crap across the floor. I put the spatula down and went to pick up a tampon I wished I hadn't seen. The idea of your mom using tampons was an oddly disturbing thing. Moms weren't supposed to have periods and crap. That was gross to think about.

I picked up the rest of her crap, too; lipsticks, change, pens, plane tickets.

My eyes darted across the roundtrip tickets, and I felt a knot in my gut.

She was flying to Paris?

Why hadn't she mentioned that over the past few days?

I thought she'd be heading back to California or something.

Then, I saw the return date.

Five weeks out.

Two weeks past my birthday.

What the actual fuck?!

She was supposed to be there for me. She was supposed to come home during the shittiest time of my damn life to be there for me. She was supposed to hold me up while I was drowning. But instead, she was going to be sitting in France, eating macarons with some hotshot celebrity, and dressing them for some premiere show.

Now, it was clear to me. Her tearful moment seconds ago wasn't because she was sad to be leaving me; it was because she was abandoning me.

I loved my mother so fucking much, but I hated her right then and there.

She'd lied to me. Well, she'd withheld the truth from me, which was pretty much worse than a lie in my book.

I pushed everything back into her purse and tried to control my emotions. I wanted to snap. I wanted to shout and cuss and tell her what a terrible mother she'd been by choosing work over me, but I didn't.

I went back to cooking the pancakes and waited, because I knew she had to tell me. She wouldn't actually leave the house without telling me her plans of going to a foreign country for several weeks. She wouldn't have the nerve to do such a selfish thing.

We sat at the dining room table, and I watched her stuff the food into her mouth. She went on and on about what an amazing cook I was and how I should consider culinary school in the future. She talked about her job—except for the parts where she mentioned her travels. She told me what celebrities were like; she discussed what the latest fashion trends were going to be for the summer; and she never mentioned Paris. Not once.

As she gathered her things to head to the airport, the anger I'd been holding in for so long shifted to despair, to sadness, to loneliness.

"Come give me a hug," she ordered. Once again, I obeyed.

I wished I were stronger. I wished I had the balls to stand up to my mother and tell her how much her actions broke my already shattered heart, but I didn't do it. I didn't say a damn thing, because she was my mother, and I loved her.

Love was a sickness. I didn't understand why people craved it. It always left me feeling empty inside.

We released our embrace, and she walked toward the taxi she'd called to come pick her up.

As she climbed inside, I stood on the front porch with my hands stuffed deep in my pockets.

"Hey, Ma," I called out. She looked up toward me and waited. "I was wondering when you were going to tell me about Paris—before you touched down or after?"

Her eyes widened with shock, and her lips slightly parted. "How did you…?"

"Your tickets fell out of your purse."

A small tremble took over her tiny frame, and she shook her head. "Land, I swear, I was going to tell you. I just… I knew it would upset you with your birthday coming up and all. I was just given a huge opportunity to work with some amazing clients for a European tour they are doing for their upcoming film. You won't believe—"

My cold heart? It iced over even more. "It's fine," I forced out. "It's not a big deal."

"Sweetheart…" she murmured, stepping one foot toward me.

"You better get going before you miss your flight."

Or you could stay and pick me. Stay for me.

Please, Mom. Just…

Pick me…

She took a step backward. She didn't pick me.

I was an idiot for thinking she would.

She grabbed the handle of her suitcase. "I'm so sorry, Landon. I truly am. There's so much you don't know, so much you don't understand…and I want to explain it all to you. I do, but this job opportunity is something I can't pass up right now. I will explain more when I get a chance, but—"

"Don't bother," I hissed, turning around and walking into the house. "Safe travels."

She didn't follow after me.

The house was empty again, and I headed to my bedroom where I lay in my bed. My hands formed fists, and I pounded them against my forehead.

"Fuck!" I hollered, and it woke the sleeping Ham in the corner.

"Fuck!" I pounded harder, trying to push the tears back, trying to stop being a little bitch about being alone.

Ham got up from his sleeping position and stretched out his body before wobbling over to me and climbing into the bed. He pushed himself under my arms, and I nudged him away. Every time I pushed him away, he kept coming back. Again, and again, and again.

"Ham! Go away!" I shouted, annoyed with the stupid dog.

But he didn't care. He just kept wagging his stupid, short Corgi tail, and he wiggled his way into my arms again. Finally, I surrendered and let him be. I wrapped my grip around him, and I refused to let myself cry.

We stayed there for a while.

It was quiet again. The walls echoed memories of yesterday, and sleep refused to come that night.

The next afternoon, I pulled myself out of bed when my doorbell rang. I glanced over to my clock, well aware that it was Maria, coming to clean.

As I opened the door, she gave me her bright smile, but it quickly faded the moment her eyes fell on me. A frown found her lips.

I must've looked as bad as I felt.

"How's your heart today, Landon?" she asked me.

Shit. Shit. Shit.

My eyes watered over at her words, and I shut them so the emotion wouldn't fall down my cheeks. I needed to be a man. I needed to man up.

But Maria's question hit me hard that morning after a hard, hard night.

I didn't answer because I knew if words left my mouth, they'd crack, and I'd fall apart.

She didn't say another word. She simply stepped forward and

wrapped me in a hug. She held on tight, and I allowed her to do so. Truth was, without her, I would've fallen.

She lay her head against my chest and didn't let me go. I wrapped my arms around her and hugged her back.

"It's still there, Landon," Maria swore. "Your heart—I still hear it beating. You're good. You're okay. You're all right."

That broke me even more.

She began to pray for me, and I didn't know why. All the prayers she offered up were clearly being unheard. Maybe God's answering machine was full, and he wasn't accepting any more messages. Maybe he was busy taking someone else's calls at the time Maria prayed. Or maybe, just maybe, there wasn't a god at all. Maybe Maria was praying to a wish, a hope, a dream.

She'd prayed for Lance, too.

Obviously, that hadn't worked out too great.

Still, she prayed.

Still, I let her.

And even though I didn't know how it was possible, my ugly, damaged heart still continued to beat.

Chapter Eleven

Shay

DAYS PASSED WITHOUT ANY INTERACTIONS WITH LANDON. HE'D missed a few days of school, and when he came back, he was distant—and not just from me, from everyone. He descended the hallways like a fallen angel. Dark, moody, wounded, shattered in ways I hadn't known people could be shattered. Had he rested at all over the past few days? Gosh, it was exhausting just looking his way. I wanted to fall asleep for him.

I took a step toward him, but recoiled. I wanted to ask him what was wrong, but also, I knew that wasn't who we were. We didn't check in on each other. We didn't care about our emotions. We were just playing a game. Nothing more, nothing less.

Curiosity rocked me as I scribbled about his disconnection in my notebook. Each time I had a character in mind, I filled up a notebook with information about them. With the way things were going with Landon, I was already on my third notebook.

I felt foolish waiting for Landon to take notice of me again. I'd become used to his snarky comments, crude remarks, and childish pranks, and now that they were missing in action, a knot formed in my gut.

Was he over it?

Over me?

Over our bet?

Because I wasn't. I still wanted to play, wanted to watch him, wanted to explore.

Just when I thought all hope was lost, a deep voice whispered behind me as I grabbed my books from my locker.

"Those jeans make your ass look huge."

My heart pounded against my rib cage, and chills raced over my body, and I hoped he didn't see my shivers.

I smirked, shaking my head, knowing Landon was the one the rude remarks were coming from. "Yeah? Well, your ears make you look like Dumbo," I replied, trying to act cool as a cucumber even though my hormones were at a ghost pepper level of heat.

Of course, my comment about Landon's ears was a lie. Everything about Landon's body was perfectly proportioned, and if there was a flaw, I hadn't yet found it.

I turned around to face him, pressing my back against the lockers behind me as he hovered over me. I was reminded of how tall he was when he was inches away, and I had to tilt my head up to make eye contact. He looked tired, like always. A bit sad, too—like always.

"I got a nice Dumbo-sized member down below, too, if you want to see," he joked, placing his left hand against the locker, looking slick as ever. I tried my best to ignore the increased heart rate I was experiencing in response to his flirtation.

"Sounds like elephantiasis. You should really get that checked out." He smiled.

I hated it because Landon's smile made me want to smile, too. It looked so good on him. He should've done it more often.

He placed his right hand on the other locker, boxing me in. "So, when are we going out?"

"Out?"

"Yeah, like on a date."

I laughed. "You don't date people, Landon, and you definitely don't date me."

"Listen, if you want to skip straight ahead to the banging part, by all means…" he offered.

I rolled my eyes and bent down to slip under his arm. I started off toward my next class, and he hurried beside me.

"Okay, no banging, but I'm serious—when are we hanging out? How am I supposed to make this bet come to a conclusion if we don't see each other outside of school?"

"Well, isn't that a shame? Looks like you're going to lose your little bet."

"So, you're going to play hard to get?"

"No." I shook my head. "I'm not playing at all. I *am* hard to get. I'm busy, Landon, and I refuse to change my life to let someone I despise into it."

"How do you plan to win the bet if you never see me, though? How can you make me fall in love with you if we never talk?"

"I couldn't care less about you falling in love with me. As far as I'm concerned, if you lose, that's a win for me."

"So, you're throwing the game by avoiding me?"

"Yup. Pretty much."

He smiled again, and this time, it was a bit sinister. "Sorry to burst your bubble, but the bet's not going to go down like that."

"Oh? And how do you plan to get around this issue?"

"I don't know yet, but don't worry, I love a good challenge. I'll figure it out."

"You do that, Landon. I'll be waiting." I started walking off, and he called after me one last time.

"Chick."

"Yeah?"

"The ass comment?" His eyes danced across my body, moving up, down, and all around. "It wasn't an insult."

My heart...

It skipped. It flipped. It vomited.

"Satan?"

"Yeah?"

"My Dumbo comment?" I combed my hair behind my ears. "It was an insult."

I turned away as his lips curved up one more time.

That made three.

Three smiles from Landon all in the span of five minutes. Three smiles. Three breathtakingly beautiful smiles.

"Guess who's going out with Reggie this weekend?" Tracey gleamed, bouncing over to my locker. She pointed her thumbs to her chest. "This girl."

I frowned a little, kind of disappointed in that fact. After a few weeks of observing Reggie, I knew he was not the best person in the world. I was secretly hoping Tracey's infatuation with him would've disappeared sooner rather than later.

"Oh?" I said, not sure what else I could've pushed out.

"What's that?"

"What's what?"

"That tone in the way you said, 'Oh'?" She cocked an eyebrow. "Aren't you happy for me?"

"I am. It's just…Reggie's kind of a jerk, Tracey."

"What?" She snickered. "No, he's not. Why would you say that?"

"Well, I've seen him bullying people. I've seen the way he talks down to them and judges them. I mean, he couldn't even remember your name for the longest. I just want you to be careful, that's all. I don't want you to get hurt."

She tensed up completely, and I felt her energy shift. "What the hell, Shay? Why can't you just be happy for me? You know these kinds of things don't happen for me often."

"I think you can do better, that's all."

"Well, history is telling me a different story. I can't believe this is the way you're acting, after all the times I had your back no matter what, especially with your new situation."

"What situation?"

"Landon. If you want to talk about jerks, don't you think you should start with him? And you're the one falling for him."

I huffed. "I'm not falling for Landon."

"Yes, you are. I see the way you look at him in the hallways. You have no poker face."

"Okay, but this has nothing to do with Reggie. I don't think you know enough about him to be interested in dating him."

"And what do you know about Landon other than the fact that he's treated you like crap since elementary school?" she shot back, growing defensive.

I tossed my hands up. "Okay, okay. I'm sorry. I don't want you to get hurt, that's all. I'm being too protective."

"Yeah, well, don't. I know what I'm doing, and I'm happy, so don't try to rain on my parade," she scolded me, before turning away and walking off.

Later that afternoon, I saw Reggie all cuddled up with a sophomore girl.

Tracey was so far out of that jerk's league, it was shocking, but she didn't know it, which made the situation that much worse.

Chapter Twelve

Landon

"HOW'S MAKING SHAY FALL IN LOVE WITH YOU GOING, LAND?" Raine asked as she lay on a pineapple-shaped floatie in my swimming pool. Raine had been Hank's girlfriend for the past forever years, and she sometimes crashed my hangout days with the guys because she swore sunbathing at my house was the best. My pool got the best angles of the sunlight, she claimed, even though the sun didn't actually come into the pool area—glass walls and all.

Whatever.

I didn't mind Raine crashing guy time, because she was pretty much one of the guys, anyway. We even had a group nickname: The Fantastic Four (+Raine). She and Hank were glued to each other, and if it had been anyone else, I would've called their clinginess disgusting, but with them, it seemed more like a destiny thing.

I'd never seen two people more meant to be together. They were the kind of thing corny romantic comedies were modeled after.

"I don't have to make Shay fall in love with me. I just have to get her to sleep with me, and she'll think she's in love," I said, sitting back and reading one of the comic books Eric had brought with him. He'd recently gotten into collecting them because his dad had given him some as a birthday gift the year before, and ever since, it was his new favorite pastime. I figured it was because it gave him and his father something to bond over. I didn't blame him for wanting that connection with his dad.

It was the same reason I drove down to Chicago to sift through paperwork for my dad's law firm. It was my pathetic attempt to feel close to the guy who was a professional at keeping his distance. Driving to his firm was my attempt to close that gap between us.

"Uh, yeah, sorry, Landon, but you do," Eric agreed. "Shay isn't one to just sleep with someone without emotions attached to it. Emotion should be her middle name, actually."

"I don't know how to make people fall in love with me." As far as I was concerned, I had been deemed unlovable a long time ago.

"Just let your walls down, Beast," Raine shot my way. "And then Beauty will let you in. Open yourself up to her."

Open myself up to Shay?

Doubtful.

I hardly opened myself up to Ham, and he couldn't break my heart or tell my secrets even if he wanted to. Dogs were loyal even to jerks who didn't deserve their devotion.

"Nah, not my style," I told her. I looked over to Eric. "How did you get her to fall for you?"

"Trust me…" He snickered and kept flipping through his comic. "You don't want her to love you the way she loved me."

I didn't want her to love me at all, but if that was the only way to win the bet…

"Just give me some tips and crap to help get in her good graces."

"Oh no." Eric tossed his hands in the air. "Nope. I'm not getting in the middle of this mess. I'm Switzerland."

I glanced to Grey, and he shook his head. "I love the Swiss Alps. Sorry, buddy."

Crap.

I cocked an eyebrow at Hank, and he laughed. "Did I ever tell you my favorite cheese is Swiss?" he joked.

"What happened to bros before hoes?" I spat out.

"Hey, watch it!" Raine hollered, tossing water toward me. "Your sexist ways are showing. Besides, I think we can all agree that Shay isn't a ho. But…" Raine wrinkled up her nose. "She's always been into writing. She writes screenplays and stuff. I'm sure you've seen her with one of her millions of notebooks."

"Raine! Come on!" Hank sighed, splashing water toward his girlfriend. "We're Switzerland! We don't get involved in other people's drama."

"I never said I was Switzerland. I'm more like America, just kind of sticking my nose in other people's business. Plus, I think it's kind of romantic." She swooned. I swore, she swooned, and I didn't even know what she was swooning over.

"What's romantic about it?" I asked.

"Well, it's obvious the two of you are going to fall in love at the end of this. Therefore, like every good romance movie, you need a fairy godmother to help push you toward each other."

Hank groaned, slapping his forehead, knowing his girlfriend was being dramatic as always. "You are no fairy godmother," he said.

"And you don't like Swiss cheese," she shot back.

Hank flipped her off.

She flipped him off back.

"Love you, honey buns." He winked.

"Love you, too, my Swedish Fish," she replied.

No doubt about it, I was going to get love diabetes from being around those two. They were always that dramatic with their love. They were snappy and rude and corny and fun.

If I ever fell in love, I'd want it to be something like theirs. It wasn't always rainbows and butterflies for them, but it was real, and it was theirs.

"What else, Raine?" I asked.

"Recently, she's been obsessing about her upcoming Shakespeare audition," she told me.

Shakespeare, huh? Interesting. I knew my fair share of Shakespeare, though I wasn't a pro. Lance had a collection of Shakespeare plays, and over the past few months, when I wasn't able to sleep, I'd go into the coach house and thumb through some of his books out of boredom. If you needed a sleep aid, Shakespeare's plays worked like a dream.

"Do you want a basket to catch all your word vomit, Raine, or are we done being nosey Nancys?" Hank asked.

"Nosey Nancy, over and out." She saluted and then lay back on her floatie.

She'd given me enough to keep me going, though. This was the second mention of Shakespeare—the first being from Maria—so that had to be pretty important. I was going to take that Shakespeare knowledge and run with it.

When Thursday came around, KJ showed up and dropped off the weed for the guys. He'd decided it was best not to stick around too long, seeing how Mom had caught him the last time, and he hadn't wanted any trouble.

As we made our exchange, my mind was on Shay, thinking up a million ways I could get near her. The other day, Reggie had come up to me mocking me about how I hadn't been able to get Shay to fall in love with me yet, going on and on about how he could've already banged her and had her loving on him if he wanted to.

I wanted to punch him in the face and tell him he would never be good enough for Shay, but I kept quiet. I didn't feel the need to waste my breath on a pointless person. I'd have bet Kentucky was missing their favorite clown boy.

Still, he was right. I hadn't figured out a way to get close to Shay. We'd never really had true interactive moments outside of spitting rude comments toward each other in the hallways. I needed to be in the same space as her for longer than five minutes in order to close this bet down.

But how?

"All right, I think we're all settled. I'll catch you around, kid."

"Wait, can I ask you something?"

"Shoot."

"Have you been dealing to Monica? She's seemed a bit out of it lately, and I know she normally buys from you. I mean, I know she's always out of it, but she seems extra burned out, more than weed. What have you been giving her?"

KJ sighed and whistled low. "Sorry, Landon. That's doctor-patient confidentiality right there. I can't give out that information."

I huffed. "You're not a doctor."

"But I do make people feel better." He smirked. "Sorry, buddy. If she wanted you to know, I'm sure she would tell you. She's a grown woman. She can take care of herself."

She wasn't a grown woman, though, and she couldn't take care of herself. I'd seen her low points when she wasn't feeding herself or showing up for class, when I had to make her food and do her homework just so she could pass. For a long time, I'd worked as her anchor, but now she was floating away on her own. She was hardly eighteen, and she was on a path to destruction, a path KJ was helping her travel down.

"Look, all I'm saying is she has a lot of shit going on in her life. She doesn't need whatever you're giving her to add to that chaos," I explained as calmly as I could.

"And like I said, she's a grown woman. She can handle it."

"Stop selling to her, KJ," I spat out, the words rolling off my tongue with disgust.

KJ laughed and shook his head. "You're not her parent or guardian."

"You don't even care, do you? You don't care that you're killing her?"

"I'm not stuffing the pills down her throat, Landon. That's on her."

I stood up and my hands made fists. "You need to get the hell out of my house."

"Monica was right." He kept snickering, tossing his hands up in defeat. "You're less fun when you're sober. Listen, I'll pull back with her, all right? I'm not out here trying to kill nobody. Take it easy. Life's not that serious."

He swore he'd pull back, but I didn't know him well enough to know if I could believe him. All I had to go on was the hope that he'd do the right thing down the line.

Chapter Thirteen

Shay

MONICA SMITH WASN'T MY FRIEND.

I knew what a friend was, and I knew what an enemy was. What I didn't know was what exactly Monica was to me. A frenemy, perhaps. An enemy who smiled as if we were close? An acquaintance who'd betray me down the road?

There had been a time when we were close friends, though, a time when I didn't doubt our connection. We hung out all the time as kids, with Tracey and Raine. We'd go pretty much everywhere together, and we were into the same kinds of things. There wasn't a weekend that the girls weren't sleeping over at my house, and that included Monica.

The shift in the friendship happened when Monica and I both auditioned for the middle school's performance of *Cinderella*. Monica was so excited about playing Cinderella, but when I was given that role and she was cast as one of the wicked stepsisters, she seemed to somewhat resent me. She quit the show and never auditioned for anything else again.

She claimed theater was for losers who didn't have good enough lives to be themselves, so they had to act like someone else.

She also said she couldn't be seen in my neighborhood anymore. "This is where poor people live, and my father said it's not safe for me to be over here," she commented. I knew that was a lie, though. I'd been to her mansion enough times to know her father hardly noticed she was alive.

Over the years, while the friendship between Tracey, Raine, and me stayed intact, Monica became her own Cruella De Vil. It was as if her personality shifted overnight.

Monica was a perfect example of the girl who had social status, beauty, and wealth. She oozed popularity and despised anything and everyone who wasn't as popular, rich, and stunning as her.

Therefore, she pretty much hated everyone.

She was the queen bee of our high school, and she wasn't afraid to call people out as peasants. I reserved my hate for Landon, but sometimes, the way Monica treated people truly rubbed me the wrong way.

If Landon was fake, I was certain he'd learned his skills from the fakest girl of them all.

"Hey, Shay." Monica turned in her desk to face me. She sat in front of me in World History, but she never went out of her way to talk to me. Normally, she was too busy texting nonstop to engage with the outside world. I always wondered who she was talking to, seeing how she seemed so bored by everyone in high school—everyone except Landon, of course.

"Hey."

She eyed me up and down, from the top of my head to the bottom of my shoes.

I hated how she looked at people. She stared at them as if she was telling a joke and their mediocre life was the punchline. Then, she'd giggle quietly to herself before making eye contact once more with a menacing smirk.

"So, what's the deal with you and Landon?" she asked with crossed arms. The gum in her mouth kept popping in the most dramatic fashion. Her lips were painted red, like always, and she smiled at me, but it didn't really feel much like a genuine smile. It felt like a threat.

"What do you mean?"

"It seems like ever since you guys had that spin seven situation, the two of you have been…I don't know. It looks like something's going on there. I saw you guys hanging out by your locker a few days ago. You seemed…close."

"Well, there's nothing going on." I glanced at the clock on the wall, waiting desperately for class to begin. I much preferred learning about the fall of the Roman Empire than talking to Monica about Landon.

Monica didn't blink as she stared my way. I wondered if she ever blinked. Her eyes were always so alert and zoned in on her prey, as if she was ready to attack at any moment.

She combed her hair behind her ear. "I thought you said nothing happened in the closet."

"Nothing did happen. Like I said, there's nothing going on between Landon and me."

"You don't have to lie, Shay." She laughed, flipping her hair over her shoulder. "I've moved on from him, and I'm hardly even thinking about him anymore."

Well, if that didn't sound like a bald-faced lie, I didn't know what did.

She pulled out her tube of lipstick and applied more. "I just want to make sure you're okay, because I know you've struggled a bit with your dad in the past."

I raised an eyebrow. "What's that supposed to mean?"

"You know..." She lowered her voice and leaned in. "With his jail time for drugs."

A knot formed in my gut, and I couldn't help but wonder how she knew that. Then again, she was Monica. She knew things. She knew *all* things.

I cleared my throat. "What does that have to do with anything?"

"Well, because it's Landon. Listen, it's not my place to say"—that had never stopped her before—"but it's no secret that he has a history of partying. Over the past few months, he's developed a bit of a drug problem. That's why I broke up with him. I couldn't handle him spiraling."

I raised an eyebrow as the knot in my stomach tightened. There were some things in life I could handle, but drugs weren't one of them. It was a hard limit. "Oh? He hasn't really shown any signs of that..." My words trailed off, and I shut my mouth. I didn't see any reason to push the conversation, because at the end of the day, it didn't matter.

I didn't want to get half-truths from Monica. I knew who she was, the vindictive creature she'd been in the past. Trusting her was like trusting politicians—it always ended in a bigger scandal than anyone wanted.

When she didn't get her way, she acted out. She threw fits, made scenes. The last thing I wanted to do was get wrapped up in her and Landon's world.

"Like I said before, Monica…Landon and I aren't a thing." *And even if we were, you'd be the last to know.*

"Okay, good. I just wanted to let you know. Us girls have to look out for each other."

Yeah, Monica. You're real Spice Girls "Girl Power" over there.

The bell rang, giving me a break from the conversation from hell.

Monica smiled brightly and with a touch of evil in it. "But I guess we're in the clear, seeing how there's nothing going on between the two of you." She turned around, and before the teacher started speaking, she looked over her shoulder and whispered, "Plus, he has a small dick."

Well, okay. Mark that down as something I hadn't needed to know.

Chapter Fourteen

Landon

"ARE YOU ON DRUGS?" SHAY BLURTED OUT AS SHE SAT DOWN across from me in the cafeteria.

I snickered. "I ask myself that each day."

"I'm serious, Landon. Are you on drugs?" She didn't have to tell me she was serious; her eyes said that all on their own. She was tensed up, her body looking rock hard as she stared me in the eyes.

"What the hell are you talking about?" I asked.

"Just tell me, because if you are, I don't want to do this. I don't want to play this game if you're just drunk and high all the time. I don't want anything to do with any of that stuff, okay?"

Her voice cracked with despair as she spoke my way. I didn't have a clue where her intense emotions were even coming from, seeing how we had recently been joking with each other about my Dumbo ears.

Seeing how serious she was feeling made me sit up a bit straighter. The only thing I looked forward to lately was being able to bother Shay a little to keep my head clear. So, based on her reaction, I knew right now wasn't the time to be a sarcastic ass to her.

"No," I said flatly.

"Don't lie to me, Land. *Please.*" The last word melted off her tongue with pain.

What was that, Chick? A small glimpse into your imperfections?

"I swear, Shay. I used to, but I stopped a while ago, after Lance…" I shut my eyes for a slight second and took a breath. When I reopened them, I stared straight into her eyes. "You read people, right? That's what you do? Look into my eyes and tell me if I'm a boy who's lying to you. Tell me what you see."

She narrowed her stare and didn't look away. She drank me in as I swallowed her whole, and we sat there for a few seconds before blinking and looking away. "Sorry," she muttered, standing from the table.

"Where did this come from?"

"Earlier, Monica said something about—"

Monica. Of course. I should've known. "That should've been your first warning sign."

Shay shifted around in place. "Are you two still a thing?"

"We never really were."

"Tell that to her," she huffed, combing her hands through her hair.

"Trust me, I have. Listen, I'm not using, and I'm not going to be using anything. As long as we're doing this bet, I can promise you I won't do anything like that, all right? I swear. I know a promise from your sworn enemy doesn't mean shit, but there it is."

"It means something," she whispered, timid as ever. She turned away from the table and muttered an apology—one I didn't need. If Monica had gotten to her, I completely understood. She had a way of poisoning a person's thoughts with such few words.

"So, I guess the game is still on," I said, throwing a carrot her way.

She caught it and bit into it as she shrugged her shoulders and began to walk away. "Catch me if you can."

Don't worry, Shay Gable. I will.

I spent the next few days thinking about the clues Maria and Raine had given me over the course of our interactions. Anything they mentioned about Shay I plugged into my brain. There was one thing that stood out the most that I figured could come in handy, one thing she would've never imagined I'd use to get close to her—which meant, by all means, I had to use it.

On Wednesday afternoon, I pulled out the ammo I had in my possession, and Shay's reaction was priceless.

"Are you kidding me right now?" Shay gasped as I entered the auditorium for the *Romeo and Juliet* auditions. We hadn't really interacted in a few days, because she'd been busy, and I had too.

Did you know this Shakespeare dude talked in circles? Half the time, I didn't even know what the hell he was even saying. Thank goodness for SparkNotes. I was thankful there were enough nerds in the world to translate the meaning behind the old guy's words.

When I'd stumbled across his most public insults on my internet search, that was when the fun began. For example: *"Thou sodden-witted lord! Thou hast no more brain than I have in mine elbows."*

I'd have to use that one on Reggie when I got a chance.

Then again, he'd probably reply, "What, dawg? Man, I miss KFC."

Shay's jaw sat on the floor, and she shook her head in disbelief. "What are you doing here?"

I walked down the aisle of the theater and then sat in the row behind her, two seats over. "I had some free time on my hands and thought I might audition for the show."

"Yeah right. You don't act."

"My whole life is an act, sweet pea."

"Don't call me sweet pea."

"You didn't like dollface, and you said you're not keen on Chick, so I'm testing out new nicknames for you."

"Well, I don't like sweet pea. Keep trying."

I smiled, and she hated it. I loved when she got flustered around me. Lately, she'd been pretty good at keeping it nose to nose, batting my advances back like a perfectly matched game of tennis, but me showing up in her theater world? She hadn't seen that coming.

"Really, Landon—what are you doing here?"

"Really, Shay—I'm auditioning."

She grimaced and fidgeted with the piece of paper in her hand. "This is part of your game. You're trying to get close to me."

"You shouldn't be so vain. Me auditioning for this show has nothing to do with me trying to be around you. I'll have you know I am a huge Shakespeare fan. That guy? He knew his shit."

She huffed and rolled her eyes. "Oh, please. You couldn't name five Shakespeare plays if your life depended on it."

"*Othello, Hamlet, Romeo and Juliet, A Midsummer Night's Dream, Macbeth.*"

You could learn a lot about Shakespeare when you didn't sleep at night.

"What, did you SparkNotes it or something?"

Yes, princess.

Princess.

I'd have to try that nickname. I was sure she'd hate it.

Sure, I'd used SparkNotes, but that wasn't the only reason I knew a bit about Shakespeare, though I didn't feel the need to let her in on all the details of my knowledge.

I leaned forward and placed my hands on her shoulders. "No offense, Shay, but you're acting like a very big shrew that needs to be tamed right now."

She swatted my hands away. "I don't know how you know all this stuff, but it's annoying and you're annoying."

"What can I say? I'm a very smart man. Wait till you see what I know tomorrow."

She bit her bottom lip and narrowed her eyes my way. "Seriously, Landon, what are you doing here?"

"I told you, I'm auditioning for the show. I read up a bit on this *Romeo and Juliet* thing, and I think I've got what it takes to take on the Romeo role."

She huffed, rolling her eyes. "In your dreams."

"That's the thing about my dreams, buttercup—they always come true." I winked her way, and she made gagging sounds.

"Buttercup is a no-go. I'm not a Powerpuff Girl."

"Fair enough."

"Whatever. I know you're just trying to get under my skin by showing up here, but it doesn't matter. You'd actually have to get a part in the show to be around me, and I doubt that's going to happen. You probably couldn't act your way out of a plastic bag if you had to."

"Why in the hell would I ever have to act my way out of a plastic bag? What does that even mean? Also, who has plastic bags that can just fit actors inside of them?"

She rolled her eyes hard, clenching her audition piece in her hand. "Can you just go away? I'm trying to get in my zone before my audition, and you're really making me slip out of character."

"Right, right—method actor. You're in character. Good, me too. Don't mind me. I'll be sitting right here, a row behind you, practicing my lines."

I could see the tension in her shoulders as I sat behind her. I affected her. I didn't know if it was in a good way or a bad way, but she physically responded to me being nearby. I could almost feel the heat radiating from her body.

Mr. Thymes, the head of the theater department, was calling people up to the stage one by one. To be honest, I didn't think I'd ever stepped foot into the theater, and everyone was looking at me as if I was some strange alien of sorts.

I didn't blame them.

Landon Harrison in the theater? Hell must've frozen over.

"Shay, you're up," Mr. Thymes called out, and she hopped up from her seat. Before walking to the stage, she closed her eyes and muttered something, holding on to the cross necklace around her neck. Maria had the same kind around hers. I wondered if believing in God came easy to Shay.

The battle of God was more like a war for me. I wanted to believe in him, but he'd given me so many reasons not to do so.

When she made it to the stage, the whole room went quiet. The second Shay began her audition, it was as if she became something completely new. She immersed herself in the character, in being Juliet, from head to toe. She moved across the stage as if she were a brand-new person. She talked with such powerful softness to her words. I didn't have a damn clue what she was saying exactly, but I believed it.

She was beautiful, and anyone else who was auditioning for Juliet should've packed their bags and left, because she was easily the right one for the role, and I was determined to be her star-crossed lover.

Everyone clapped for her, and she deserved the applause. I probably clapped the loudest, and when she walked over to sit back down, I leaned forward and whispered against her ear with my hot breath. "You're meant to be Juliet."

She shivered from my heat and took a deep breath. "But you're not my Romeo. You'll *never* be my Romeo."

"Landon," Mr. Thymes called out. "You're up."

I stood and looked toward Shay. "Aren't you going to tell me to break a leg?" I asked.

"Go ahead." She nodded. "Break two."

Cold, Chick.

I liked it.

W ELP, I DIDN'T SEE THAT COMING.

Landon got on that stage and blew his audition piece out of the water. He was exponentially more engaging than the other guys who auditioned for the role. He made it look easy, effortless. It was as if he'd been acting his whole life.

Even Mr. Thymes jumped to his feet and started clapping.

"Bravo, Mr. Harrison, bravo!" he shouted. "I think we just found our Romeo!"

For the love of all things righteous, this wasn't fair. Landon couldn't be an amazing actor without even trying. I'd have bet he'd picked out his audition piece the night before. It wasn't right. You couldn't be that good-looking, that rich, that popular, *and* that talented. I wondered which demon he'd sold his soul to in order to become the person he was.

When Landon came to sit back down, he leaned forward near me once again. "What was that about me not being your Romeo?" he mocked.

"Bite me, jerk."

"Of course." He leaned in closer, his lips gently touching the edge of my ear. "Just tell me where."

"I know you think you somehow managed to figure out a way to hang out with me outside of school, but the joke's on you—I haven't even gotten the role of Juliet yet. You could end up spending your time with some other girl."

"Come on, Freckles," he whispered, shaking his head. "You were made to be Juliet. There's no one better."

I kind of liked Freckles. Most people didn't even notice I had freckles. You had to look pretty close to notice them.

I didn't tell him I liked the nickname, though. I didn't want him to have that pleasure.

I narrowed my eyes. "Truth or game?" I asked.

"What?"

"Is that the truth or is it just part of the game to try to get me to fall in love with you by being sweet and crap?"

"What do you think?" he questioned. His eyes locked with mine, and there seemed to be such sincerity in his stare. Then again, he could've just been trying to get in my head and mess with my thoughts.

If so, it was working.

Gosh, it was working. Every now and then, he'd say rude comments, but then he'd slip in a few nice gentle words, and my heart would start to melt like butter. For a second, I almost fell for it, almost succumbed to his cheesy kindness.

But you know what you get from a melting-butter heart?

Clogged arteries.

That was what Landon did to me—he clogged my freaking arteries.

Mr. Thymes waited a week to announce the cast. Each day that passed felt like a ticking bomb, and I was certain it wasn't going to go in my favor. To my surprise, it all worked out. Even though I felt as if my audition hadn't been strong enough, Landon was spot-on about me being his Juliet, and even though it killed me inside, he was the perfect Romeo.

After I found out, I hurried home with joy racing through my veins. I knew it was stupid, but being Juliet was a dream come true for me. I'd been giving it my all, and the first person I wanted to share the news with was the man who'd helped me perfect my audition piece.

"Dad! Dad!" I shouted, rushing into the house and tossing my backpack to the floor. After searching the whole house, I hurried downstairs to his writing cave, where he was sitting at his computer, typing frantically.

"Dad..." I paused and raised an eyebrow. "Are you writing again?"

He turned around to look at me and gave me a dopey smile as he ran his hands over his head. "Yeah, I am."

"I thought you gave it up, since...you know..."

You seemed unable to write without a joint in your hand and whiskey in your cup.

"I know, but I felt inspired, and when an artist is inspired, we have to create. You know this better than anyone."

True. An artist without art lives a very lonely life.

"Well, I don't want to take up too much of your time, but I got it!" I shrieked, unable to hold in my excitement. "I got the part of Juliet!"

"Of course you did," he said, his voice not getting excited, because Dad didn't get excited about things. "There was no way you wouldn't have. You did the work, put in the time, and it paid off."

"I couldn't have done it without you. Thanks for helping me perfect the monologue."

He gave me two nods.

He was proud of me.

He didn't say it, but I saw it.

My feelings were still soaring from excitement as I raced over to him to give him a thank you hug, and as I wrapped him in my embrace, he turned his head slightly away from me, but it was too late.

I'd smelled it.

The whiskey on his breath.

My heart dropped in an instant, and I took a few steps back. I gave him a big smile and tried to push away the tears that wanted to fall from my eyes. "I'm gonna let you get back to your work, but I just wanted to tell you the good news."

"I'm looking forward to seeing you on stage again. You're going to nail it."

Whiskey. Whiskey. Whiskey.

Had I made up the smell? Was I delusional? Had he gone back to his old ways?

"Thanks. Okay, good night. I'll see you in the morning."

I hurried up to my bedroom, closed the door, and shut off the lights. I climbed into bed and pulled the covers over my head, and the tears began to flow all on their own.

Dad was tapping into his old habits again… I'd smelled it, at least I thought I had. Soon enough, Mom and Mima would notice. Soon enough, there would be fighting. There would be yelling. There would be hatred.

There would be tears. There would be drama. There would be pain.

So. Much. Pain.

I was so tired of how history kept repeating itself every few months. I was so tired of being tired. I hated that a part of me believed Dad would change his ways after being locked up, but it seemed he wasn't a different man after prison. Maybe people didn't change. Maybe that was a truth that only existed in fairytales.

I lay in bed and mourned my father who was still alive. I mourned the man I was hoping he could someday be. I mourned my dreams of who he could've become. I mourned the loss of my trust in him. Maybe someday, Mom would start mourning him, too.

The following days, I convinced myself I hadn't smelled what I'd thought I smelled. Mom and Mima hadn't said anything about it, and there hadn't been as much arguing at the house lately, so I didn't want to bring on drama that didn't need to exist.

Maybe I was wrong, too. Maybe I'd made a mistake. I hadn't actually seen him drinking, after all. I hadn't seen the toxins going into his body. There wasn't a bottle sitting on his desk, he wasn't slurring his words, and he had been coherent when I'd spoken to him. Those were all really good signs.

So, instead of focusing on what I had no control over, I focused on what I did: *Romeo and Juliet* and Landon Harrison.

Each day we rehearsed, Landon's talent became even more apparent. It floored me how effortless he made it all look, too, and how dedicated he was. At first, I'd thought he would drop out of the show the moment he saw how much work it actually took to bring a performance together, but Landon didn't shy away from the challenge—he embraced it.

When he wasn't on stage, he was sitting in the auditorium, combing through the script of the play he'd already nailed down. He had his lines memorized by week one. By week two, the blocking was nailed down completely. But still, he studied as if there was something he could learn, something he could unlock from his chamber of talent.

Part of me hated how easily it came to him.

A bigger part was secretly turned on by his skills.

I was a girl who appreciated seeing raw talent. Raw talent—like my father's—always amazed me. It didn't work that way for me, though. I had to fight tooth and nail for every ounce of skill I had.

No one knew the hours I'd stayed up trying to perfect my audition piece. No one knew how I moved furniture around in my bedroom to recreate the setup of the stage so I could rehearse my blocking and movements. No one knew the number of hours I stood in front of a mirror and honed facial expressions.

No one knew the number of nights I cried because I felt like I was failing when I was giving it my all and it still wasn't good enough.

We rehearsed for two hours after school each day of the week, and Landon made sure to always sit close by me. When he wasn't near, I could feel his perfect stare gazing my way. If he wasn't studying his script, he was studying me—his second favorite hobby. He knew he got under my skin, but sometimes, I'd catch him looking at me with such a gentleness in his stare that I almost thought he'd forgotten we were playing a game.

Good.

As long as we were going to be forced to be around each other, I might as well win the bet, too.

I had to remind myself daily that none of the butterflies that found me whenever Landon was around were real. I had to have pep talks about how the fluttering of my heart was just heartburn. I had to convince myself that anything I felt was just passing hormones.

I knew deep down that I could never fall for Landon.

He wasn't the kind of guy who would catch the girl.

Especially me.

Me and my sensitive heart.

"I need ammo, Raine," I told my friend, barging up to her and Tracey where they were talking at Raine's locker after school. Tracey was probably going on and on about Reggie, seeing how she was the only person on the planet who hadn't faced the reality that he was a complete douchebag. I'd watched him in the hallways, had studied the way he treated people who were deemed lesser than him in the way of looks.

He bullied Billy Peters for the clothing he wore. He tripped Jovah Thomas during gym class and called him a fat Teletubbie. He also told Wren Miller that eating disorders were okay if they were used on a body like hers.

I told Tracey all of these things, and she refused to believe it. *"It's just his humor, Shay. You just don't get it,"* she'd told me.

I supposed I didn't find bullies hilarious.

I didn't push the topic any further, because each day it seemed she was growing more and more protective of the guy. I didn't want to ruin my friendship over something as mundane as Reggie. I simply prayed Tracey would figure out what he was really about before she got her heart broken.

As I walked up to the girls, Tracey made a quick excuse to leave. I'd have to find time to talk to her and make sure she wasn't upset with me about voicing my opinion about Reggie. But first...

"Ammo? Why, are you going hunting?" Raine joked, tossing her schoolbooks into her backpack. "I'm pretty sure Hank can lend you some of his camo to blend into the woods."

"No, I'm serious. I need you to give me some ammunition to use against Landon. I need information to use against him."

Raine's green eyes widened with nerves, and she shook her head. "Oh, no. Hank said I'm not allowed to meddle in other people's business anymore, ever since I helped my nonna order a vibrator through a television commercial because she said my grandfather wasn't the stallion he used to be."

I cocked an eyebrow. "But you owe me."

"Owe you? For what?"

"Oh, I don't know—telling a boy I was auditioning for the school play and then having said boy also audition and get a part in the show."

Raine's eyes lit up. "Oh my gosh! He got a part?! I'm so proud of him!" she exclaimed. "I mean, I know you hate his guts, but it's no secret Landon is like a little brother to me."

"He's older than you, Raine."

"Yes,"—she placed her hand over her heart with a gleam in her eyes—"but his childish ways make him seem so young."

"Well, seeing how you helped him out, it means you need to help me out, too."

She cringed. "I can't, Shay. Hank would kill me if I got involved again. He gave me the silent treatment for a solid five minutes after I helped Landon, and I don't know if I can handle that again."

"Fine." I frowned, crossing my arms. "I guess that's okay."

"Don't do that," Raine said, waving her finger my way.

"Don't do what?"

"Pout. You know I can't take it, seeing my friends sad."

"Well, I guess you just like Landon a little more than you like me," I argued. "Seeing how you helped him out and not me. I thought we lived by the motto *chicks before dicks*, but I guess not…"

"Ugh." She groaned, slapping her hand against her forehead. "*Fiiine.* You twisted my arm. But this doesn't get back to Hank—or any of the guys. They are worse than us and tell each other everything."

"You have my word."

"Okay. Landon loves his dog Ham. Like, loves him. You should take them to a dog park to get on his good side."

"What? No. I don't want to know what he loves. I want to know what he hates!"

"Why?"

"So I can annoy him the way he annoys me."

"Wait, don't you want him to fall in love with you to win the bet?"

"Yes."

"And you want to do that by torturing him?"

"Uh-huh."

Raine raised an eyebrow and shook her head. "I don't think you understand how love works."

Maybe she was right. Maybe I didn't know how love worked, but I did know Landon had entered my world, my space, and was making himself far too comfortable in it. The theater was supposed to be my safe haven, and he was currently leaving his fingerprints all over it with that annoyingly handsome grin of his, so screw love.

I wanted to annoy him the same way he annoyed me.

"Please, Raine?" I asked.

She released a weighted sigh and groaned. "Fine. He's terrified of reptiles."

"Reptiles?"

"Yes, reptiles. All kinds. Snakes, lizards, turtles—oh! And bugs! He hates bugs. Once I saw him physically run into a building trying to get away from a fly. Like, *bam*! Straight into a brick wall. And don't even get me started on spiders."

I smirked.

This was perfect.

"Thanks," I said, patting her on the back. "You've done your country good."

"From here on out, I'm moving to Switzerland. Oh, and just for future warning, if your grandmother asks you for help buying a vibrator from a 1-800 number, don't do it. It makes holiday dinner conversation very uncomfortable."

Duly noted.

"Also, what's the deal with you and Tracey? Are you guys fighting?" Raine asked.

"Not that I know of...but I'm guessing she's mad I mentioned how Reggie doesn't seem like a good guy."

"Well, I'm glad someone did. He's a total jerk. Have you noticed whenever he's with Tracey, he's checking out other girls behind her back? He's a total creep."

"Yeah, but Tracey is head over heels for the guy."

Raine puffed out a breath. "More like shit over ankles. What a messy situation. If Hank ever treated me the way Reggie has been treating Tracey, I'd cut off his balls and make French onion soup."

I laughed. "Why French onion?"

"Because balls smell like onions, and Hank is seventy percent French. If I'm going to castrate my boyfriend, I'm going to at least respect his heritage."

I laughed at my crazy friend and wrapped an arm around her shoulders. "You're such a good girlfriend."

She smirked. "I know, right? The lucky bastard doesn't deserve me."

No one does, Raine.

"So, since you and Tracey are in a rut, how about an old-school sleepover at my house sooner than later? We can do facials and gossip, and I can be Dr. Phil and help you two fix the dramatic state of your friendship."

I narrowed my eyes. "I thought you were out of the business of meddling in other people's stuff?"

"What can I say?" She shrugged her shoulders and gave me an angelic grin. "Old habits die hard."

Chapter Sixteen

Landon

"LET'S GO ON A DATE THIS SATURDAY."

I had to rub the tiredness out of my eyes in order to make sure it was Shay who was talking to me after theater rehearsal. She seemed to go well out of her way to avoid interacting with me during the school day and now during our rehearsals. Truly, the only time she'd given me the time of day was when I was Romeo and she was Juliet. She was a hard book to crack open, that was for sure. That didn't mean I was going to stop trying.

I was walking out of the school building when she came jogging up to me. I cocked an eyebrow at her words.

"A date?" I asked.

"Yes, a date. You and me. Let's do this."

"I thought I didn't date people, especially not you," I spat out.

She rolled her eyes, and that dimple in her right cheek shone so bright in the darkness of the afternoon. "Do you remember everything that was ever said to you?"

"It's a gift, a curse," I muttered.

"So…this Saturday?" She wiggled her eyebrows in anticipation.

I narrowed my eyes and gave her a stern glare. "You really want to go out this Saturday?"

"Yes."

"With me?"

"Yes."

"Why?"

She laughed. "To make you fall in love with me. Duh."

She was up to something, because she had the goofiest grin known to mankind on her lips. She looked like a damn five-year-old holding the secret that she didn't brush her teeth before going to bed or something.

"What are you hiding up your sleeve, Gable?" I asked.

She widened her eyes in surprise then rolled up the sleeves on her coat jacket, revealing her arms. "Just skin."

I studied her smooth, tan color for a second before moving my eyes back to hers. I brushed my thumb across my nose. "What did you have in mind?"

"It's a surprise. Don't worry, I'll pick you up and drive us there. One in the afternoon. Be ready." She began walking away from me, and then she spun around, holding the straps of her backpack. "Oh, and Satan?"

"Yeah?"

"You did really great today during rehearsal. I hate to say it, but no one could do what you do. You're that good. Have a good night." She turned back around, walking to her car, and something happened to my heart in my chest. It tightened? It skipped? It beat in overdrive? I wasn't exactly sure. I wasn't used to my heart doing anything other than following its mundane pattern. Then, along came Shay Gable, and she went ahead and messed up my rhythmic patterns, all because of a nice compliment.

Was she being sarcastic? Was her comment genuine? Was she screwing with my head?

Open your damn book for me to read, Shay.

I stared at her—and her sweet ass—as she walked away, my heart still trying to figure out what had happened.

Had my heart skipped a beat over my sworn enemy?

What. The. Hell. Was. That?

What. The. Hell. Is. That?!

I sat in Shay's car as we pulled up to the location of our date. I should've known there would be some kind of dramatic crap when Shay asked me out on a date. I just didn't think it would have been this.

Of Reps and Men was the clever name of the building sitting in front of us, a place of hell where messed-up humans went to mess around with creatures they had no business messing around with. Through the window, I saw a guy holding a snake around his shoulder blades.

Like a freaking psychopath.

"What the hell is this?" I barked out, my skin beginning to itch from the thought of walking inside that place.

"It's like a petting zoo for reptiles and things. I thought it could be fun." Her tone was so matter of fact, and I swore she could see the fear dripping down my forehead. "A little birdie told me you loved reptiles."

"A little bir—" I stopped my words and groaned. "I'm going to kill Raine."

"Oh, come on. She owed me after she told you about the auditions for the play. It's only fair that I get a fact about you, too."

"Well, good for you. You know I hate reptiles. Awesome." I slow-clapped. "But there's no way in hell I'm stepping foot inside of that place."

"What's the matter, Satan?" she cooed, pursing her lips together. "Scared?"

"No. I'm just not an idiot who finds enjoyment in playing with creatures that aren't meant to be played with. That's not a damn black poodle in there; it's a boa constrictor, an animal that can physically squeeze a person to death if it pleased."

She smiled. "Sounds exciting. Come on, let's go."

She opened her car door, climbed out, and I stayed exactly where I was. There was no way in hell, heaven, or any other made-up location that I was going to unbuckle my seatbelt and climb out of that car.

Shay laughed when she saw me. "Are you telling me the bad boy of small town Raine, Illinois, is really deathly afraid of a little spider?"

"Those are tarantulas! There is nothing little about a freaking tarantula, Shay!"

She giggled. "You're sweating."

"I'm not," I replied, knowing it was a lie. The backs of my knees were sweating, my toes were sweating, and my balls were pretty much sitting in a puddle of my damn nerves.

"You are. I'm just a bit amazed, I guess. In an odd turn of events, it turns out I'm not the chicken in this hateful relationship, after all—you are."

"I'm no chicken," I barked.

She leaned in toward me and puckered her lips together before saying, "Cluck, cluck, cluck..."

The hairs on my forearms stood straight up at her clucking.

She drove me mad, but—so annoyingly—she still kind of turned me on.

Okay, Chick.

Game on.

I unbuckled the seatbelt, climbed out of the car, and slammed her door shut. "You really want to do this? Fine, but don't come complaining to me when you need a tetanus shot in your ass because you decided you wanted to pet a damn tiger-striped spider."

She smiled and walked in front of me toward the building. It seemed like lately, she was swaying her hips even more than normal in an attempt to hypnotize me.

It was working, too—right up until we walked inside the building and I felt an instant need to turn around and run. But I knew I couldn't punk out in front of Shay. That was exactly what she wanted me to do.

"Laffy Taffy?" she offered, holding a piece of candy out toward me. I went to grab it, and she paused. "Just don't chew it up and put it in my hair again."

"I remember your hairdo from back then. Trust me, I was doing you a favor." I snatched the candy from her hand, ripped the package open, tossed it into my mouth then chewed it quickly and swallowed it whole.

Her mouth gaped open. *"What was that?!"*

"What was what?"

"The animalistic way you ate that candy. You don't stuff the whole Laffy Taffy into your mouth like that. You savor it. What you did was very beastlike."

"Well, I'm sorry, Beauty. Please, show me how to eat a piece of Laffy Taffy properly."

She pulled out another piece of candy from her purse and opened it slowly, peeling back the wrapper from the yellow candy. "Banana is the best flavor, so I like to take my time with it," she explained. "And then, you nibble at it, taking small bites so it's not gone in an instant. You don't rush the process. You take your time."

"You're insane. Just shove it into your mouth and eat it."

"No. You have to take your time with it. The best things in life are worth taking your time with, like Laffy Taffy."

"Just swallow it, Chick. I'm sure you have some experience with that," I joked.

She rolled her eyes and playfully shoved me in the arm. I liked that. I like when she touched me even if it was followed by the words, "You're such a pig."

"Yeah, but I'm sure you like bacon."

She smiled, that dimple deepened, and she nibbled at her Laffy Taffy like a gerbil.

"Come on. Let's go meet some friends," she said, walking up to the front desk. Before we were able to go into the back area with the animals, we had to sign waivers.

Red flag number one.

We were also led into the room with all the creatures and were told to never reach for the animal on our own due to their temperaments.

Red flag number two.

Then, we were told to take off all jewelry due to some animals grabbing onto certain items.

Red flag number freaking three.

"This is a terrible idea." I grimaced.

Shay kept nibbling at her banana Laffy Taffy. "You're being dramatic. This is going to be great."

I snatched the Laffy Taffy from her hand, balled it up, and popped it into my mouth.

Without any hesitation, she reached into her purse, unwrapped another piece of candy, and began nibbling again.

Nibble, nibble, nibble. Bite, bite, bite.

It seemed she was Willy Wonka, and her purse was the chocolate factory with unlimited supplies.

Our tour guide for the afternoon was Oscar, and he seemed a bit too excited to wrap a snake around my neck. "Don't worry," he said, patting me on the back as we headed toward the snake cages. "They don't bite, and if they do, you'll probably be dead so quick you wouldn't even feel a thing."

It was meant to be a joke, but I didn't laugh.

I was too busy being tensed up.

Oscar grabbed one of the creatures, and without thought, I took a step back. Shay laughed at my retreat, but she didn't step any closer to the creature herself. She seemed as nervous as I was. *Good. Equal playing field.* She was acting all confident up until we were finally in the room with the creatures. Now, she was more wide-eyed and concerned as she slowly chewed her candy.

"Ladies first," I offered, gesturing toward Charlie—the garter snake.

Shay took a deep breath, balled up her Laffy Taffy, and shoved it into her mouth, swallowing it whole.

Thatta girl.

She was quiet as she walked over to the snake. I watched as she flinched a few times as Oscar moved the creature in her direction, but she allowed it to be placed in her hands. She shivered and wiggled, I guess from the odd feeling of the thing.

My mind couldn't even wrap my head around what it felt like. I was still eyeing the exit.

After a few different snakes, and me passing on holding them, Shay started clucking again. She even added in the chicken arm movements, flapping her arms.

"Fine," I groaned. "Give me the snake."

The last one we met was Greta, and she was a freaking giant monster of a ball python.

Oscar had me hold my hands out.

"Shaking won't help the situation," he warned.

"Listen, this is the best you're going to get out of me, so just put the snake in my palms, okay?"

I snapped at the dude and I felt semi-bad about it, too. My nerves were getting the best of me. Sweat was dripping down my forehead, and my vision was blurring over. But still, I wasn't going to punk out—not with Shay watching. That would've given her too much joy.

He lowered the snake into the palms of my hands, and within seconds, everything went black.

"Landon…hey, Landon. Wake up, get up," a voice said as my head stirred. I opened my left eye to see Shay's face hovering over mine. "Oh, thank goodness. I thought I killed you," she exclaimed.

I pushed up on my hands to come to a sitting position. I rubbed my arm up and down. "What just happened?"

"Well, it didn't just happen. You blacked out for five minutes," she explained. "I was already planning out your funeral, but then, like the Satan you are, you rose from the ashes."

I groaned and went to stand up. As I stood, I got extremely dizzy. I began stumbling, but Shay caught my arm, making me balance a bit more.

"Easy," she said, her voice low and almost sounding like she cared. "You should probably get checked out. You fell face first."

"I'm fine. Perhaps we should leave the reptiles alone, though."

"Oh…" Shay nodded slowly and raised an eyebrow. "Yeah, we're not really allowed back in this place, seeing how, when you fell, you tossed Greta into another cage, and…yeah, we're not welcome back."

"Oh, man. That's too bad. I was really hoping to come back and spend money on this crap."

"It's not your lucky day, I guess."

I studied her lips as she spoke to me. The longer I stared, the more focus I was able to retrieve. My head was still foggy, but I knew a few more seconds of staring at Shay would clear it right up.

"We should probably get you home, so you can ice your forehead," she commented. I ran my fingers across it, and there was a big knot. Great. I had Pinocchio's nose growing out of my forehead.

I didn't argue with the idea of going home. The sooner I was away from those animals, the better.

We drove in silence, and every now and then, Shay would find herself in a giggling fit.

"What is it?"

"Nothing, nothing…" More giggling. "It's just…when you went down, you looked like a tree that was being cut down in the forest. Stiff and awkward, face down. It looked like something out of a movie. *Timberrrrrr*," she called out.

"Well, I'm glad I could entertain you."

"You really did." She nodded. "Your butt in those jeans as you went falling forward…" She began giggling again. I wanted to call her out on talking about my butt, but her laughing was annoyingly adorable, and I didn't want to interrupt that sound. I hadn't known you could love a sound you hated.

"Thanks for an awful first date," I told her as we parked in front of my house.

She smiled bright. "Anytime! Have a terrible night."

"Yeah, yeah, you too." I climbed out of her car and slammed the door shut. I began walking toward my front door but turned around when I heard Shay calling my name. "Yes?"

"That comment about your butt?" Her grin spread wide as her dimple deepened. "It wasn't an insult."

I almost smirked at her, but instead, I nodded once and walked toward my house, shaking my goods from left to right. That's right, I was shaking my ass for Shay Gable after completely blacking out due to a snake in my hands.

And a part of me wasn't even mad about it.

"Oh, no, no, no," Raine exclaimed, shaking her head as I stood on her front porch that night. "I'm not getting involved again," she told me, crossing her arms. She knew I was there for more information on Shay, and by her stance, it appeared she had no desire to give it to me.

"I blacked out from a snake in my hands, Raine!" I argued, rubbing the huge knot on my head.

"Yeah, I heard." She smirked a little then began giggling. "*Timberrrrr.*"

Of course Shay had already told Raine about what had happened. I shouldn't have been surprised. Even though I was close friends with Raine, I knew she and Shay were just as close—if not closer. Girl code and all.

"Come on, Raine. You have to give me something."

"Sorry, I can't. Hank said he was going to ban me from watching rom-coms with him if I got involved with you guys anymore, and my favorite pastime is watching him cringe while we watch rom-coms."

I sighed. "I can't win this bet if I don't have anything to use against Little Miss Perfect," I said.

"Perfect?" Raine arched an eyebrow. "You think Shay's perfect?"

"Of course. Her life is too perfect. She doesn't have anything wrong with her, no flaws. Me, on the other hand? I have too many, and she can see them. She can somehow see me, and it's not fair."

"That's Shay for you—the master of reading people. So, maybe you need to do that...maybe you have to read her back."

"Trust me, I've tried. Her pages are clean."

"Oh, Landon..." Raine shook her head. "Nobody's pages are clean. Everyone has ink that stains. I know for a fact Shay has her own struggles, too."

I gave her a wolfish grin. "Oh yeah? Like what?"

She parted her lips to speak but then caught herself and pointed a stern finger my way. "Nope. Nope. I'm Switzerland. I'm fondue. I'm Swiss cheese. You're going to have to figure it out on your own without my help."

"How do I do that?"

"Just look at her, Landon, and I mean really look. Try to figure out her love language."

"Her what language?"

"For the love of...ugh. One second." She marched into her house and then came back to the porch with a book in her hand. She shoved it toward me.

I looked down and read the title: *The Five Love Languages* by Gary Chapman.

"What the hell is this?" I asked.

"This is the key to making Shay fall in love with you. It's a book that makes you understand the different ways people love. It saved mine and Hank's relationship a few years ago. You see, I thought he was being all sexist and old school and stuff when he was always trying to pay for our dates, and I'm all, 'Psh, please. I am an independent woman, and I can pay for myself.' And we got into a heated fight over it, and it was actually kind of cute. The night of the fight, he was wearing that button-down flannel I hate, the one with the—"

"Can we fast-forward to the point of all this?" I cut in, knowing Raine could turn a short story into a full novel with her roundabout way of talking.

"Oh. Right. What was I getting at? Oh yeah! The languages. There are five love languages: receiving gifts, acts of service, quality time, words of affirmation, and physical touch. Each person has a love language. Mine is quality time—rom-coms with Hank for example—and Hank's is acts of service, which is why he always changes my oil and carries my books at school and stuff, or buying me dinner. That's how he shows his love. Now, all you have to do is read this book and then read Shay. Shay's story is there, you just have to do some digging to unlock it. And who knows? Maybe at the end of the day, you'll realize you two have more in common than you think. Maybe you have the same love language."

Hard to believe, but whatever. I knew Raine wasn't going to give me any more details outside of a cheesy book—not with her rom-coms on the line—so I had no reason to stay any longer.

I thanked her for the little details she had offered me.

She frowned. "Landon, maybe a good starting point is you showing her the parts of you that you keep hidden from the world. Maybe that will help her show you her own shadows, too."

"Yeah, all right." Not a fucking chance.

"Just read the book. I swear, it will help." She gave me a stern look. "But that's not me getting involved. Again I'm smelly, Swiss cheese over here. You and Shay are none of my business."

"Message received, Raine. I won't ask you for anything else about her. I swear."

"Good. Good night."

"Night."

I walked down her driveway, and she shouted my way. "Landon! Landon! One more thing!"

"What?"

She bit her bottom lip and groaned, slapping her palm to her face. "Shay loves peonies!"

"*Penises?*" I echoed. Okay, those were the kind of details I could work with.

She groaned even louder. "No, you sick jerk. I said peonies. They are her favorite flower, but you didn't hear that from me!"

How the hell were peonies and a book about love languages going to help me make Shay fall in love with me? Hell if I knew, but my dumb ass started reading the book the minute I made it home.

I WISHED I COULD'VE ENJOYED THE TRIUMPH OF TORTURING LANDON FOR A longer period of time, but when I made it home, my house was a warzone once again. The fighting lasted straight into the next school week, and I was exhausted.

I was struggling through my rehearsal that afternoon after suffering from a morning of arguments in my house. The yelling had come back, and no matter what, it seemed my father couldn't do anything right in my grandmother's eyes. With good reason.

It seemed I hadn't imagined the stench of whiskey lingering on his breath.

I was exhausted from all the anger swimming throughout my home, and it was affecting my sleep patterns. I couldn't think of the last time I'd had a decent night's sleep, truly. Most of the time, whenever I laid my head down, I wondered if Dad was okay or not.

My lack of sleep led to me stumbling over my lines during rehearsals and lagging behind. I felt how clouded my brain was, and I was having the hardest time clearing the fog. By the end of rehearsal, I was kicking myself for messing up so many times. I'd have to rehearse on my own at home to make up for the crappy rehearsal.

"You kicked ass today," Landon said as I packed up my bags to head out for the night. He said the words, but he was completely wrong. I'd missed my marks. I'd hiccupped over words. I'd forgotten my lines, and yet still, there he was, telling me how well I'd done. I couldn't help but think he was being his nasty self when the words left his mouth. I wasn't really in the mood to play our back-and-forth game at the moment, though.

I was mostly in the mood to tear up and cry.

"You don't have to mock me, Landon. I know I messed up all night."

He cocked an eyebrow and tilted his head, but he didn't say anything. He simply paused his steps and stared at me, looking completely baffled.

"What?" I asked.

"Nothing." He shook his head. "Just wondering if you've always been your harshest critic or if this is a new development."

"It's not easy for me."

"What's not easy for you?"

"*This.*" I gestured toward the theater space. "This doesn't come easy to me, not like it does for you. Most people can't just pick up a book and memorize the lines like it's the easiest action known to mankind." Landon had been off book faster than anyone else. Sure, I wasn't convinced he knew exactly what he was saying, but the words danced off his tongue in the most magical fashion that made you believe he was, indeed, Romeo.

"You make it look easy, though," he commented, his voice low. "You get on that stage and own every inch of it. You demand people's attention. You ooze confidence. Watching you onstage is like watching live art being made. It's addictive, all-consuming, and you do it in a way that looks so effortless." He combed his hand through his hair then stuffed it into the pocket of his jeans. The biceps in his arms were showcased nicely as he rocked back and forth. "It doesn't matter if it comes easy or not. It matters how it looks, and it looks perfect."

I wanted to think of something snarky to say. I wanted to shoot something sassy his way, but I was too emotionally exhausted to do so. Plus, his words made my heart skip, and I couldn't be snarky with skipping heartbeats.

"What's up your ass today?" he asked me.

"Nothing."

"Bullshit. You're off. Why?"

"If I was off, which I'm not, you'd be the last one I'd talk to about my issues, Landon."

"Why's that?"

"Because I know you don't really care. I know everything that happens between us is just part of the stupid game."

He dropped his head a tad, and his shoulders rounded forward before he looked up at me with those blue eyes, irises that swam in a gentle sea. "You're having a shitty day, and you're right, you probably can't trust anything that leaves my mouth. I'm known for being cold and heartless, but I get having off days. I've been having nothing but off weeks—off *months*—lately. So, I get feeling like shit. Therefore, I'd never use your bad days against you, Shay. Not for this game; not for this life."

I wanted to thank him for that, but I didn't have time to do so.

He turned around on the heels of his sneakers and murmured, "I hope it gets better, though. 'Night."

"Good night," I muttered, and I wasn't even sure he heard me.

On my way home that night, I tried my best to push out the thought that I'd be spending the next few weeks in Landon's presence. Although, lately, I'd choose spending time with him over my own family.

When I got home, it was clear it wasn't a good night for my family.

As I walked up the front porch, I heard Mima hollering with anger. When she was extremely angry, she went from speaking English to Spanglish, and then, when she was at her breaking point, full-on Spanish.

I cracked the front door open and stood there listening before entering the house. I knew they'd stop talking about what was going on when I walked in, and I hated not knowing all the details.

"You can't keep making excuses for him, Camila! I smelled it on his breath when he walked in today. He rushed to shower and wash up because he knows I know. How are you going to sit here and act like everything's sunshine and rainbows when your husband has fallen off *again* and lied—*again*?"

"Mom, I don't need this right now. I know this is a mess. You think I don't see that he's broken and falling apart? Don't you think I know he's losing his way?"

"Of course I know you know that, Camila, but what I don't think you know is that you don't have to keep picking up his broken pieces. He's bringing his demons into this house over and over again."

"Having you snap at him over little things isn't helping. You're adding to the drama of it all."

"It's not my fault he's a liar. This isn't my fault, and I'd wish you'd stop making up excuses for him. What are you teaching your daughter about relationships?"

They went back and forth about Mima wanting Mom to leave Dad, about her abandoning him, and truthfully, I understood where Mima was coming from. How many chances could you give someone before time was up? How many times could my mother be forced to sacrifice her own wellbeing at the expense of his?

It was becoming an embarrassing show to watch, and ever so slowly, I was becoming so disappointed in who my mom was becoming. I always pictured her being the strongest woman I knew, and she was that person…except for when it came to her love for my father.

We had been so much happier when he was behind bars.

I crept back outside, not wanting to go in.

If Dad was inside, I wanted nothing to do with him. He'd lied to me. He'd looked me straight in the eyes not that long ago and promised that he wasn't going to be getting into any trouble anymore. But that was what liars did best—they lied. I hated how he'd let us down time and time again. I hated that Mom defended him time and time again.

I hated the loop that we were stuck on.

I pulled out my phone and sent a quick text message to Eleanor.

Me: Sleepover?

Eleanor: Always.

I headed over to my cousin's house, which was always the safe landing place when my father pushed himself over the edge. Whenever

I came over to spend the night, it was a clear sign to my aunt and uncle that my father had slipped up.

Aunt Paige opened the door, and the moment she laid eyes on me, she knowingly said, "I'm sorry, Shay." She looked tired, but she didn't give me much of a chance to study her appearance before she pulled me into a tight hug. Paige had a way of giving the best hugs each and every time I came over.

She didn't even know what she was apologizing for, other than the fact that all my unplanned sleepovers at her house meant there was a war going on at my residence.

I lazily grinned. "It's okay."

"It's not," Uncle Kevin said firmly, walking into the living room. "It's not okay."

It felt good to hear that, to hear that it wasn't okay.

If only my family could've realized that fact. The fighting drove me mad. Watching Mima and Dad go at it on the regular was really wearing on me. Sometimes, it didn't even seem as if they were fighting about anything of importance. If there was a spoon left in the sink, they'd go to war over who had left it there, and, like the peacekeeper she was, Mom always took the blame, which would spiral into yet another argument from Mima about how Mom was being an enabler, not a team player.

"Your love is what keeps him from doing right," Mima would tell my mother. "Why should he do the right thing when you always forgive his wrongs?"

So often I thought Mima was right.

So often I prayed she was wrong.

Coming to my cousin's house always felt peaceful. I wasn't sure they ever fought, and if they did, it was probably over what TV show to watch or something. I'd never seen three people fit so perfectly together. Eleanor's family was pretty much perfect. They were those smiling people you see in the picture frame before you put the real photograph in.

Picture perfect.

My family was an episode of *The Real World*. You could walk in and see what happened when people stopped being polite and started getting real.

I headed to Eleanor's bedroom, and she already had a blowup bed pumped up with air. She lay on it with a book in her hand. I would've fought her about her taking the air mattress over her actual bed, but whenever I stayed over, she refused to let me take the uncomfortable bed.

"You're already feeling down. Your back doesn't have to feel down, too," she'd tell me.

Eleanor's room was filled with bookshelves from floor to ceiling. There were dozens and dozens of novels sitting on those shelves, and if it were anyone else, I would've assumed so many of those books went unread, but knowing my cousin, she'd probably read through all of them more than once.

I plopped down on her bed, where she'd already laid out a set of pajamas for me. My lips released the most dramatic sigh in the history of sighs.

Eleanor looked up from her book then closed it.

I knew that didn't seem like a big deal to a lot of people, but for Eleanor to close her book to have human interaction was a big deal. My shy introvert of a cousin only closed her book for those she loved the most.

"What were they fighting about?" she asked, sitting up and crossing her legs to face me.

"Beats me. I just heard the yelling and turned around to leave."

"Seems to be happening a lot more than normal lately," she commented, and I didn't reply because a reply wasn't needed.

Yes, it'd been happening a lot more lately.

Yes, I hated it every single second of every single day.

"Do you think your dad is…" Eleanor's words trailed off because she knew how sometimes words could hurt even when they weren't intended to sting. She didn't want to finish her thought, but I knew what she was asking—was my father dealing again?

No, I prayed.

Yes, I found more likely.

"I don't know," I answered, speaking truthfully.

The last time my dad and I had spoken about it, he'd promised he wasn't, but a promise from a former liar was the hardest truth to believe. Dad used to lie about everything to cover up his missteps. It usually worked for such a long time, too, up until he either blacked out drunk, overdosed, or Mom caught him in his web of lies.

Once, she followed him to a house where he was dealing.

I'd sat in the back of her car.

I was ten years old.

What a time to be alive.

"I hope he's not," Eleanor said.

I gave her a sad, tight smile, because her words made my eyes water over. I was so tired of crying over the man who was supposed to be my hero.

"I just wish my family could be more like yours." I wiggled my nose to keep the sniffles away. "You guys are perfect."

Eleanor's gaze shifted to the ground, and she grew a bit somber. "We're not perfect. We have struggles, too. Really hard struggles."

"Yeah, I get that. It's human to struggle, but you all struggle together...as one." They all played for the same team; they all wanted the same thing in life—happiness. My family was split up into different divisions. Sure, we all wanted happiness, but we all thought it came from different avenues.

"We can talk about something else," she offered, feeling the heaviness of the room.

"Please," I choked out. I'd talk about anything—anything that wasn't my family's wounds, which were being deepened with each passing day.

Eleanor jumped up from her sitting position and moved over to her desk. She picked up a stack of papers and came back over to join me on her bed. Then, she plopped the paperwork on my lap with a big thump.

"What is this?" I asked.

"It's the script you sent me."

I arched an eyebrow. "Ellie, I sent this to you at like ten last night." When I couldn't sleep, I wrote. When I wrote, I sent my pages over to Eleanor. The night before, I'd finally completed a manuscript I'd been working on for over three years, and I had sent it to my cousin for her painfully honest feedback.

"Yeah, I know, and you're the reason I slept through my alarm clock, by the way. I read through it three times, Shay. I read it over and over again to look for where I could give you notes on improvements, on your character developments, on the story arc, but there's one major problem."

I swallowed hard. "What's that?"

"It's already perfect."

My heart started racing at a pace I couldn't keep up with. "Don't just butter me up because I'm having a crappy day, Eleanor."

"I'm not. Shay, this is a masterpiece. All you have to do now is share it with the world somehow."

My heart hiccupped as realization set in that the one person I wanted to share it with was the person who might've fallen back off the wagon. I couldn't share my blood, sweat, and tears with my father if he wasn't doing right.

Clean-cut father deserved to share my passions with me. Liar father did not.

"How would I even begin to share this?" I asked her.

"Come look," she said, hurrying over to her desktop. She sat down, opened a web page, and started scrolling. "I did some research, and there are all these contests you can enter to have professionals read your manuscript. You can even send them in to some colleges for grants or scholarships. I know you've been wavering back and forth on getting a degree in film and creative writing, because realistically, for the average person, it's a crappy idea, but you aren't average, Shay. You're extraordinary."

"You're only saying that because I'm your favorite cousin."

"You're my only cousin," she remarked as she nudged me in the arm. "But really, I get not wanting to risk the financial side of things. So, maybe apply for scholarships to see what you can get. That could ease up the stress of losing a crap ton of money to an art degree."

I scrunched up my nose. "Maybe."

Eleanor was always pushing me to go for more, to chase my dreams, to become the best human I could be. I had her email me the website with the applications and said I'd look into it more when I had time.

I didn't know what my future would be, but it felt good to have someone in my corner who believed in me.

We talked about everything under the sun until both of our eyes grew heavy, and as I lay down in the darkness of the room, Eleanor called out to me.

"I know we don't talk about boys, because, whatever...but what's the deal with you and Landon?" she asked, her question making my stomach swirl. Eleanor never really engaged in high school drama, and she was highly skilled at keeping to herself. Outside of me, she didn't really care much about anything that went on within the halls of our high school. So, the fact that she'd even noticed something between Landon and me was baffling.

Were we that obvious with whatever tango it was that we danced?

"What do you mean?"

"I heard about the bet you two have going on. It's high school people talk. Sure, they weren't talking to me, but I overheard."

"Oh." It was all I could think to say.

"Are you okay? Are you falling for him?"

"No, not at all." Just a few heart skips every now and then, nothing I didn't have under control.

"But you could," Eleanor offered up. "You have a loving kind of heart. You could love monsters if they could be loved."

I snickered. "Tracey called it a sensitive heart."

"Yes, that's it. I don't mean it in a bad way. All I mean is, I think you feel things more than most people do. You love harder and deeper, and I just worry if Landon hurts you—"

"He won't," I cut in. "I won't let him."

"But what if he does? What if you fall for him and he breaks your heart?"

"I don't know," I confessed. I didn't have a clue what I'd do if Landon caused cracks that would slice into my soul. Each day that passed, I worried a little more and more about that possibility.

"Just be careful." Eleanor yawned before rolling onto her side and hugging her pillow. "I don't want to kick a popular guy's ass, but I will if I have to."

What would happen if Landon did manage to make me fall in love with him? What would happen if he then broke my heart?

I played with those thoughts for a while before coming up with my final thoughts on the subject.

My lips parted slightly, and I felt the tremble of my body as I spoke my newest truth. "If he breaks my heart, I hope the cracks tell a good story."

Eleanor was half asleep as she responded, muttering so low, "If he breaks your heart, I'll break his spine."

Eleanor Gable, my savior, my hero.

She fell asleep before me, her snores low and gentle.

I stayed up, thinking about Landon and how he so effortlessly kept crossing my mind. I stayed up, thinking about my dad, wondering if he'd fallen off the wagon again. I stayed up thinking about two men who shouldn't have been keeping me up at night.

Around midnight, my phone dinged, and I opened it to see a text message from an unknown number.

Unknown: We should rehearse the kiss.

I read the words over and over again, confused. Just as I was about to put my phone down, it dinged again.

Unknown: Isn't that a big part of this stuff? Romeo kissing Juliet.

Landon. Of course.

Me: How did you get my number?

Landon: I have ways of finding out things I want to know.

Raine.

Obviously.

Landon: So what do you say? The kiss? You skip over it every day at rehearsal, so if you want to practice on our own, I'm fine with that.

Me: I'm good, actually.

Landon: You can show me just how good you are. With your tongue, your lips, your hips, your lips…

Me: You said lips twice.

Landon: Two different sets of lips, Chick.

Jesus, take the wheel.

My stomach flipped and turned as I read his words over and over again. A slight tingle found its way between my thighs, and I tried my best to ignore it.

Me: You're so vulgar.

Landon: And you're so perfectly neat.

Me: Shouldn't you be sleeping?

Landon: Shouldn't you?

Touché.

Landon: I can come pick you up now if you want. We can practice at my place.

Me: Probably not a good idea.

Landon: Some of the best ideas are the bad ones. Obviously, neither of us can sleep tonight. What do you have to lose?

Me: My mind apparently.

Landon: We don't even have to rehearse. I was only half kidding about the kissing thing, anyway, trying to get under your skin. We can just talk. Or not. We could just sit in the same room, not saying shit at all.

I glanced over to my sleeping cousin and swallowed hard. WWED—what would Eleanor do? Well, for starters, she'd tell me to go to sleep. She'd say a tired brain isn't a good brain to make decisions with. She'd talk about how terrible Landon was and his history of being an awful person.

She'd tell me I was too good for him. She'd tell me to not give in to the advances. She'd tell me to stand strong and tell him no. But wise

Eleanor wasn't available in that moment. She was sound asleep with not a care in the world. She didn't have the ability to tell me anything, so I listened to my heart instead of my head.

My stupid, sensitive heart.

I texted him the address, and then I held my breath.

Chapter Eighteen

Landon

I'D READ THE LOVE LANGUAGE BOOK TWICE ALREADY.

Even highlighted some crap in it.

Ever since, I'd been doing my best to look at Shay in a way I hadn't before, and to my surprise, I was seeing parts of her that reminded me a bit of myself.

I'd have to thank Raine for sliding me Shay's number, even though she'd said she hadn't meant to text me the seven digits. Raine couldn't help herself from wanting to play the fairy godmother to the beauty and the beast.

Shay was timid when I picked her up from the address she'd texted me. I hadn't ever seen her as quiet as she was when she climbed into my car. We drove ten minutes without her saying a word. Normally, within seconds, she was throwing some kind of insult my way, but that night, she was mute.

I wanted to ask her if she was all right, but based on the fact that she was sitting in a car with a boy she could hardly stand well after midnight, it was clear that she wasn't.

I wondered what the storm inside her head looked like. I wondered if her thunder rumbled as loud as mine, if her lightning struck her soul repeatedly, if she drowned in her own thoughts.

As I pulled up to my house, I put the car in park and went to open the driver's door.

"No," she whispered, her voice low.

"What?"

"I don't want to get out. I don't want to go into your house."

Now I was confused. I didn't know much about how girls' minds worked, but I knew it was a shitshow inside their heads, so confusion was always going to be likely.

"Then, why did you…" I started.

She shrugged. "I didn't want to be alone with my thoughts tonight, that's all."

"Oh." I raised an eyebrow. "You can be not alone inside my house."

"No. I can't."

"Why not?"

"Because I've been thinking about kissing you."

I smirked a little. "Oh?"

"Don't let it go to your head, dork. I just mean, at some point, we have to kiss for the show, and it's just been on my mind a lot. Just for show purposes, of course. If I go inside your house, I'll keep thinking about kissing you because I'll think you're thinking about kissing me, and I can't be thinking about kissing you inside of your house, because in that house is your bedroom, which contains your bed, and I don't want to be just another girl you're kissing in your bed, even if it is solely for bettering our performances."

Well, that was an earful.

She lowered her head. "You can take me back if you want to. I know this isn't what you signed up for tonight."

"It's fine," I muttered. "I didn't really feel like being alone tonight, either."

"What are we doing, Landon? This bet, this stupid challenge between us, this back-and-forth pettiness—what is this? Why are we even bothering with something so dumb? A challenge that was forged by Reggie, who probably hasn't even thought about it since the drunken night he brought it up…what is this?" She sighed, begging for an answer to her question.

"I don't know," I told her. Truthfully, I didn't know what to think about us. All I knew was that when I thought about her, my thoughts didn't feel so heavy. "It's weird, right?"

"Yeah, it is."

"It's just…" I sat back in my seat and clutched the steering wheel in my hands as I closed my eyes. "If I'm thinking about you and this stupid bet, it gives me less time to think about me and the shitstorm that is my life."

"Same," she confessed. When I opened my eyes, her head was tilted my way. Those deep brown eyes burned holes into my soul with such ease. Her eyes were my favorite part of her, too. They told full-length stories without any words.

That was my favorite part of watching her perform on stage. Her eyes always showed the truest forms of her emotions, and that night, they were saying something so heartbreaking.

"You're sad tonight," I whispered.

"Yes," she replied.

I combed a fallen piece of hair behind her ear. I wasn't certain I was even allowed to touch her, but I did, and she let it happen. I placed my head against the headrest and kept my stare locked with hers.

"Can I ask you a question?" she asked.

"I won't stop you."

"Why do you hate me? Why have you hated me all these years?"

"Easy—because you always seemed so happy, and I envied you. I envied how people loved you, and how your life is this picture-perfect thing. My life has been hard for longer than I remember, and you walk in and you're all rainbows and crap. I'd kill for that."

She snickered a bit. "That's it? That's why you hate me?"

"Pretty much. You have everything I've ever wanted…a stable life."

She laughed even harder. "If only you knew why that was so funny."

"You can tell me. I like to laugh."

"Since when?"

"Since now."

She bit her bottom lip and shrugged. "No one has a perfect life. Some people are just better at keeping their secrets hidden. You said

I'm all rainbows, but you do know you can't get the rainbow without the rain, right? My life isn't easy—far from it, really. I've just been really good at wearing a mask at school."

I smiled. "And you say you're not a good actor. You've had me fooled."

"Well, good. I think...I don't know. Sometimes I wish I could let people in so my mind didn't have to spin all by itself. Just to have someone to say, 'That sucks and I'm sorry. Here's a hug.' You know what I mean? I don't need anyone to try to fix me or anything—I'm strong enough to fix myself. I just wish I had someone to get comfort from every now and then. But I'm okay. Really, I'm good. Overall, my life is good."

"You don't have to do that," I promised.

"Do what?"

"Say you're okay when you're not."

Her head lowered and shook back and forth. "People don't like me when I'm sad."

"How do you know? You never let them close enough to see your tears."

Her lips parted, but no words came out. For the first time in my life, I saw Shay. I saw the girl behind the mask, the one who felt so much and hid those feelings from the world because she felt as if they were too much of a burden to impose on others. I saw her cracks, and they were so beautiful that it almost made my frozen heart beat again.

I'd never known sadness could be so hauntingly beautiful.

"Tell me your secrets, and I'll tell you mine," I whispered her way, the words rolling from my tongue and piercing her ears. She shut her eyes for a second, and when she reopened them, they were flooded with emotions, but she didn't dare let a tear fall down her cheek.

It was still too much to let someone in that close.

"My dad's a liar. He's been that way as long as I can remember, and tonight my grandmother called him out on his lies again. I went home after rehearsal and heard the shouting in my house, so I left and went to my cousin's. That's where you picked me up from."

"That sucks. I'm really sorry." I hoped she believed me, too.

"My mom will just keep allowing his lies, too. She loves him too much. He could tell her the sun is purple and she wouldn't even ask him for any proof. She'd just blindly believe him."

"Maybe this time will be different."

"Maybe. Probably not." She glanced down at the car's manual stick and trailed her finger up and down it in a slow motion. Then she made small circles, round and round against the metal rod. "You ever feel like you're running in circles? You have your past behind you, and you're trying to beat it, to be better than it, but then situations keep coming and tossing you backward. Every step you take forward, you fall two steps back. It feels like no matter how much you fight for your future, your past keeps pulling you under."

"I know that feeling all too well."

"I want my parents to do something different, even if it's just for a day. I want them to stop this cycle. I want Dad to quit with the lies for good. I want Mom to leave him if he doesn't change his ways. I want her to know her worth. I want something to stick. I want the change to really matter. I want to stop living in a house that suffocates me and leaves me jaded." She didn't give me time to respond to her comment. She palmed the hair out of her face as she sat up and crossed her legs in the passenger seat. "So, tell me your secret," she said, and I didn't even try to keep it to myself. I wanted to know all of her secrets, and I wanted to tell her all of mine. Why though? Why did I feel such a pull to a girl I'd spent so much time hating?

"You know how you have down days like today?" I asked.

"Yes."

"That's every day for me."

I'd never told anyone that before. I'd never confessed how heavy my heart sat in my chest, how hard it was to breathe every single day, but she had opened up to me in the middle of the night, and I figured why the hell not open up to her, too. That night we were on an even playing field. She was sad, and I was, too.

I was suffering partly from insomnia, partly from too much

loneliness, and mostly from keeping it all to myself. I'd never thought Shay would be the one I'd be opening up to, yet there I was—opening up to her and asking her not to judge.

She didn't, though. You could see when a person was judging you, could see their disapproving stares, but Shay was there with only honesty in her eyes. I hadn't known how much I craved her honesty until she gave it so willingly.

"What makes you feel down?" she asked me.

"I don't know," I confessed, and the words echoed in my head. I sounded a lot more like my uncle than I wanted to. So often I thought some of his dark shadows had embedded themselves inside of me. Maybe it ran in my genes—the sad trait.

Either way, I felt as if I was fighting a daily battle against depression.

Depression.

Why did that word feel so heavy?

Why did it make me feel like such a failure?

I was fighting to avoid being swallowed alive by my own mind, and it was an exhausting task to face. I wished they taught us about depression in school. I wished we were given tips and tricks to avoid falling too deep into the dark. Instead, we learned algebra equations. I couldn't wait for that to come in handy in my life.

"Are you depressed?" she asked. She asked the question as if it wasn't a loaded gun pointing straight at my face.

"No," I lied. I'd always lie about that, too. People looked at you different if they thought you were depressed, especially when your life looked a certain way, when it seemed you didn't have anything to be sad about at all. I knew after I found out about Lance's depression, I looked at him different. It wasn't even on purpose, but when a person you love is broken, you see the cracks every time they are around you, and you just wish you had the tools to fix those breaks.

"You always lie about that?"

"No," I said truthfully. "Never had to lie about it because no one ever asked."

"You're going to get sick of being around me. I ask a lot of straightforward questions. I don't sugarcoat things."

"Good. I don't want to get diabetes. Plus, I don't sugarcoat anything either. I don't have the energy to do so."

She stared at me for a while, tilting her head back and forth, taking mental notes on me. Then, she parted her lips. "I should get back to my cousin's house before they notice I'm gone."

"Yeah, of course."

I wanted her to stay a little bit longer. We wouldn't even have to talk. We could just sit in silence and it would be good enough for me. But, she wasn't mine to keep.

She was still sad, worrying about her dad, and she had every right to be sad, too. Lance had struggled with a drinking problem and it was the ultimate cause of his death, so I knew how serious it could be.

I didn't try to tell her to stop being sad. I just allowed her to feel what she had to feel.

On the drive, we passed a park, and Shay called out quickly. "Can we stop here real quick?"

I raised an eyebrow. "Why?"

"I want to see something."

I pulled the car over and parked, and we both climbed out. Now it was my turn to trust where she led me. We walked through the woods, down the pathway, and it seemed like Shay was on a mission to find a certain thing.

When we came to an opening where two huge willow trees sat, she walked over to it, running her fingers along the bark. The two trees were connected, twisted into each other as if they were meant to be together as one. The closer I grew to the tree, the more I noticed the carvings in its bark.

"It's called the lovers tree," Shay said, still searching. "The story is that if a couple comes here and carves their names into the trunk of the tree, their love story will last forever. My family has been doing it for decades and decades."

"That's corny," I muttered. But kind of cool, too.

"I love it," she replied. "Well, *loved* it." She stopped when she found a set of initials.

CAM & KJG

Before I could ask about the pairing, Shay reached into her pocket, pulled out a set of keys, and started scratching at the letters.

"Whoa, whoa, whoa, slow down," I shouted, grabbing her by the waist and pulling her back, but even though she was small, she was strong. She ripped out of my hold and went back to slashing at the bark.

I grabbed her again, this time tighter, and spun her around to face away from the tree. "What the hell are you doing, Chick? You can't be out here destroying people's happily ever afters."

"No, I have to. The legend says the initials mean their love will last forever, not that they will be happy, and my parents aren't happy. They're trapped in this messed-up loop, and I have to stop it."

My cold heart broke for her. She was shaking repeatedly as she tried to get back to the tree, but I wouldn't let her go. I couldn't. She was falling apart in my grip, tears washing down her cheeks as she lost herself in me.

"This tree isn't a gift, it's a curse, and my mom will never be able to let go of my dad if she's still attached to this thing. Just like my grandmother was attached to my grandfather, just like my great-grandparents. This tree is cursed. I need to get their names off it," she cried.

"Shay," I whispered, my voice cracking as I watched her fall apart. "Shay, listen to me. Crossing out letters on some tree isn't going to change who your parents are."

"But maybe it will. Maybe this tree is part of some kind of curse or something, maybe...maybe...maybe..." She dropped her keys and began sobbing into my arms. I couldn't think of anything to say. I couldn't think of how to make her feel better, so I stood there and held her as she fell apart.

For so long, I'd hated her because I thought she was Little Miss Perfect. I'd hated her happiness. I'd hated her because I had scars and she had none, and now I felt like a damn idiot for ever thinking such a thing. It turned out everyone in the world had scars. Everyone had cracks and cuts that bled into their soul each night. Some people were simply better at hiding them.

She pulled on my shirt and cried, losing herself against my white long-sleeved T-shirt, and I held her like I was planning on never letting her go. As she lay there in my arms, my heart melted a little for her, for her hurts, for her pain and suffering. When she was finished falling apart, she pulled away, a bit embarrassed. She wiped her nose with the back of her hand and sniffled repeatedly, turning away from me.

"Sorry," she muttered, wiping at her eyes. "I'm snotty and a complete mess."

Her eyes were red and puffy, and tears were still falling from her eyes, and she was right—she looked like a complete wreck. Broken, raw, and—

"Beautiful," I truthfully told her. "You look beautiful." Honestly, I wasn't sure Shay had ever looked so beautiful and real. Her pain had the kind of beauty that made you want to protect her from the world. I wanted to hold her again, soothe her, and let her know her emotions were what made her real.

"We should get going." She sniffled some more with her rosy cheeks and her exhausted eyes.

"Yeah, we should."

I bent down to pick up her keys, and before handing them back over to Shay, I walked over to the tree and scratched out the rest of the initials of her parents. If said tree was a curse, I wanted to end it for her. I wanted to break the spell of jaded love that affected her family line. I wanted to free her so that somewhere down the line, she could have a real love.

She released a weighted sigh and took the keys from my hand. Her fingers brushed against my palm, and a part of my soul I hadn't known existed lit up. What was that? What was that feeling, and how had she unlocked it?

"Thank you, Landon," she whispered.

"Always," I replied.

I think I meant that, too.

I think I meant always.

We drove back to her cousin's house, and as I put the car in park, I turned to say good night to her, and that was when I found her lips.

Her lips.

Pressed against…

Mine.

Her hands rested against my cheeks as she pulled me in toward her. She tasted like salty tears and peach Chapstick, and oddly enough, that was my new favorite taste. At first I didn't kiss her back. At first I stayed frozen, thinking if I moved, the moment would disappear and I'd never be able to return to it.

"Landon," she whispered, her eyes closed as her forehead rested against mine. I loved that. I loved when she said my name. Not Satan. Not asshole. But Landon.

I loved when those two syllables rolled off her tongue.

It made me feel seen. I didn't know the last time someone had been able to see me so clearly.

"Yeah?" I breathed out, my breaths brushing against her lips, her full, plump lips.

"Kiss me back," she ordered, and so I did.

My lips.

Pressed against…

Hers.

I kissed her gently at first, trying to ignore the way my jeans were tightening as my cock registered the fact that I was kissing a girl—and not just any girl, *the* girl. I was kissing Shay Gable, and every time our lips touched, she stole a piece of me.

I kissed her harder, deeper, next, parting her lips slightly to slide my tongue into her mouth. I wanted to kiss her so hard her moans were all that would feed me for the rest of my existence. I wanted to tangle my tongue with hers, wanted to allow my hands to wander across her body, feeling every inch of her being. I wanted her.

I wanted her so bad it hurt.

But then, she stopped.

She pulled back, her skin flushed and her cheeks rosy as ever. She combed her fingers through her hair and gave me a wary smile. "There," she whispered, slowly rubbing her thumb along her bottom lip before she nervously bit that same lip.

Geez, Chick.

Bite it again.

"There's your kiss, Romeo," she said, opening her door and climbing out.

"Thank you, Juliet," I said breathlessly. At least I thought I spoke. My mind was so fogged, I didn't know which way was up. I readjusted my crotch region and leaned in her direction. "You think we should keep practicing? For the show. I want to put on the best performance possible."

She laughed, and that sound made me harder.

Note to self, don't wear jeans when around Shay. Sweatpants from here on out.

"Good night, Landon." She shut the car door.

Landon.

Say it again.

She began to walk away, and I was still leaning in her direction like a desperate puppy dog craving its owner's attention. I hurriedly rolled down the passenger window and called her way. *"Good night, good night! Parting is such sweet sorrow,"* I shouted.

She looked back my way, and her lips spread wide as her hands landed against her chest. *"That I shall say good night till it be morrow."*

We quoted *Romeo and Juliet*. I began the line, and she finished it.

What…

The fuck…

Was that?

And who…

The fuck…

Was I?

I was having a hard time recognizing myself, but there I was sitting in my car, at half-past two in the morning, quoting Shakespeare to the girl I'd once hated. Hated—past tense. Truth was I couldn't have told you the last time I had hated that girl. Maybe when she'd sat with me in my bedroom a year earlier, maybe never. All I knew was my lips tingled from the fact that hers had been against them, and I loved her taste.

I waited to make sure she made it back inside the house, and then I plopped backward into the driver's seat. My hands fell onto my chest, and I felt my heart rapidly beating against my rib cage.

She did that to me.

She made my heart turn back on.

Her kiss gave me life.

There I sat like a drugged fool, grinning ear to ear because I'd quoted Shakespeare to a girl and she had quoted him back.

Maybe it was all part of the game. Maybe she was just getting in my head to make me feel things toward her. Maybe this was all fake, but in the moment I didn't care, because it felt so real, felt so good.

Screw you, Shay Gable.

Screw her for making me feel again.

"**G**OOD MORNING." AUNT PAIGE SMILED AS I WALKED INTO THE kitchen to brew a pot of coffee. To my surprise, she had already brewed some. Normally in my house, I was the first one up and at it. I always had a cup of coffee before Mom rolled out of bed to join me, but it seemed Paige was an early riser just like me.

"Morning." I grabbed a mug and poured myself a cup.

"You need creamer?"

"Nah, I drink it black like my dad."

She shivered at the thought. "Not me. I like a splash of coffee in my cream," she joked.

Aunt Paige was beautiful. She was an artist, and you'd always find a paintbrush sitting behind her ear. Her clothes were invariably covered in paint, and she had the kind of smile that could light up any room.

A bandana always sat on her head, too, and when you looked at her, it was as if you were looking at a piece of artwork.

Eleanor looked so much like her mother, it was unnerving. The same way I looked like Mom, I supposed. It seemed my uncle and father didn't have strong enough genes to swallow their kids up. The women in our family seemed to do most of the work with the genetics.

Paige tightened the bandana on her head and looked my way. "So, how was your joy ride last night?" My eyes widened as the words left her lips, and she just gave me the sweetest smile. "Don't worry. I won't tell your parents, but I want to make sure you're not getting yourself into any trouble, Shay. I love you and care about you so much that I just worry about you getting hurt. So, are you okay?"

I nodded. "I'm good."

She gave me a lopsided smile. "You remind me of myself when I was a kid, a bit of a rebel spirit. Want a bit of advice from an old fart?" she offered.

"Sure."

"Make sure he's worth it."

"How do you know I was out with a boy?" I asked.

She snickered. "Because there's always a boy with late-night escapes. Lead with your heart, but take your brain with you." She moved over and kissed my forehead. "I'm going to go wake Eleanor. I'm sure she'll sleep through her alarm again if I let her."

"Okay. Thanks, Aunt Paige." Her words danced in my head and in my heart.

As she rounded the corner, she glanced back my way. "Oh, and Shay?"

"Yes?"

"I know this is a lot to ask, but...if you ever get the chance to take Eleanor on a joy ride with you, can you do that for me? I know she's an introvert, but I want her to live, too. I don't want her life to be so wrapped up in books that she forgets to live herself." Her eyes watered over with so much emotion that it made me nervous.

"Is everything okay?" I asked softly.

She let out a small laugh, but it felt a little broken. "Yes. Even when things don't look okay, the universe has a way of making it all work out in the end. Just promise me you'll look after Eleanor?"

"I promise."

A tear fell down her cheek and she wiped it away, nodding. "Thank you."

I didn't push the conversation any more, because it was clear she didn't want to dive any deeper into the subject. I knew I could keep that promise to my aunt. I'd look out for Eleanor the same way she'd always looked out for me. Forever and always.

When I got to school that morning, I opened my locker and gasped when I saw it was filled with peonies and dozens of banana Laffy Taffys. There was a sticky note sitting against the metal locker, and I pulled it off and read it.

Here's some flowers and candy to make up for your crappy night. I was going to get you penises, but went with peonies instead.
-Satan
P.S. Do you know how hard it is to find peonies during this time of the year? It's almost impossible.
Almost.

I glanced down the hallway toward Landon's locker. He was of course standing with some girl, who was trying to be all over him. He wasn't paying her any mind, though, seeing how his eyes were locked on me.

I pulled out the flowers and breathed them in. They were perfect. So, so perfect.

I placed them back into the locker, pulled out a Laffy Taffy, and began nibbling at it as I looked back over to Landon.

His eyes?

Still on me.

I smiled.

He almost smiled back. The right side of his lips kind of curved up, and to me, that was a win.

When lunchtime came, I sat across from him. "How did you get all the banana-flavored Laffy Taffy?" I asked, curious.

He shrugged. "They sold a pack of them that way at the store. It wasn't a big deal."

It felt like a big deal to me. "That was really sweet."

"It's whatever." He was being the moody, dark Landon he normally was, but again, that right side of his lips curved up. "You in love with me yet?" he asked.

"No. Not at all. You love me yet?"

His stare fell to my lips. "Not a chance."

"You still hate me?" I whispered, my eyes moving to his mouth…that same mouth I'd tasted…that same mouth that had tasted me.

"Yes."

"Good, because I hate you, too."

"Good," he echoed.

"Good," I replied.

Chills raced up and down my spine as we ate our meals in silence while all of our friends joined up and had conversation around us.

Good.

We went our separate ways after lunch, and for some reason I found the need to break into Landon's locker during sixth period to leave him a thank you note for the candy and peonies. As I opened it, I saw grocery bags filled with Laffy Taffy—all the flavors but banana. He'd bought jumbo packs of candy and sifted through them to pick out my favorite flavor.

Who knew it could happen?

Who knew a heart could skip for the Devil himself?

Everything changed once Landon and I kissed—at least for me it did. It was as if the wall we'd spent years building was finally coming down, brick by brick. After the night we shared together, after the night I showed him my scars and he showed me his, I was hooked. The candy and flowers were what pushed me overboard.

I wanted to be close to him, because I liked how he sped up my heartbeats. I wanted to be near him, because I liked how he grimaced. I liked how he smiled even more.

I'd text him to rehearse our lines, and we'd end each night kissing, nothing more than our lips. Sometimes his hands would try to wander, but I'd always slap them away. Once I let him grab my ass cheeks, though.

I liked that…a little *too* much, which was why I went back to guiding his hands to my waistline.

He never pushed for more than I gave him, though. It was as if any kind of touch was enough for him. Me, on the other hand? I craved more. Quietly, I thought about what it would be like to kiss him, to touch him, to have him lead me to his bed. But, in the back corner of my mind, I kept thinking about the bet, not to mention Eleanor reminded me of said bet all the time.

"Don't let him play you," she would say. "That's how he's getting to you—by being too sweet. Flowers and candy? That's basic boy 101. At least that's how it is in the books I read."

I knew there was a chance she was right, and maybe I was letting my guard down a little too prematurely, but I couldn't help it. My heart craved him, even if my brain told me not to do so. I tried my best to listen to Paige's advice, but hearts were stubborn. They beat faster for certain people without the brain's permission.

We still had our sharp tongues. We still hurled insults toward each other on a daily basis, but they felt so lighthearted, so flirty and fun.

Sometimes he'd smile at me, and I'd be smiling all day from his smirk alone.

I wrote down everything about him in my notebook. Before the bet had even started, I'd already filled a notebook with my thoughts on Landon. I'd started it the night of his uncle's funeral. I couldn't get him off my mind after that, and every now and then, I'd add my thoughts on the type of person Landon was. In the beginning, the words were not the kindest. In the beginning, I wrote with hatred and annoyance. I spelled out my anger toward him through my written words. Even after the bet began, my words stayed on edge. But lately the narrative had shifted. The story of the boy I'd once hated was shifting into something new every time he showed me a part of him he hid from the rest of the world. He was one of the most complex characters I'd ever had the honor of studying, and if we kept down this road, it would be my heart that was going to fall first and hard, not his.

Plus, he'd become my outlet from my home drama. Tension was

building up in my family, and now the arguments seemed much more common between Mom and Mima. Those two had never fought when Dad was locked up. They loved each other so much whenever he wasn't in the picture. I hated that he was creating a crack in a bond that was so strong while he was gone.

When I needed a break, I went to Landon and lost myself in him, in us—whatever we were. He always welcomed me in, too. No matter the time or the last-minuteness of me reaching out to him, he always told me to come over. I was thankful for that, for his willingness to let me in.

I told him it was simply so we could rehearse. I think he knew it was more than that. I think he was learning to read me the same way I was reading him. He never asked me for details. If anyone knew how important it was to escape from life sometimes, it was Landon.

That Saturday was no different. He was there when I needed him to be.

"We should really be rehearsing." I giggled in between short kisses. I'd finally managed to enter his house to work on our scenes together, but I forbid myself from going to his bedroom, or his closets. Closets at Landon's house had a history of getting hot and heavy.

"We are rehearsing," he muttered against my lips as he placed his hands beneath my butt cheeks and pulled me into his lap.

I wrapped my arms around him and shook my head as I gently sucked on his bottom lip. "I mean we should be rehearsing our lines."

"These are our lines," he mumbled, sliding his tongue into my mouth and forcing a moan to escape me as I felt the hardness in his sweatpants. I definitely shouldn't have been sitting in his lap, because as he grew, my desire to grind against him grew, too.

I slid off, moving to the left side of the couch, feeling a bit bashful about it all. It wasn't the first time I'd felt Landon's happy member since we'd started making out on the regular, but it still always made me blush. I pulled my shirt up to my mouth and chewed on the collar, trying to hide my nerves.

"You do that a lot, you know—chew when you're nervous," he told me, running his hands through his hair.

"You do that a lot." I nodded toward him. "Run your hands through your hair when you're turned on."

"Well, you keep turning me on." He smirked, grabbing me again and placing me back onto his lap. He rocked his hips upward ever so slightly, pressing himself against my jeans. My thighs began to quiver, and my heartbeats intensified instantly. Oh my gosh, he was dry-humping me...at least I thought that was what was happening. I'd never been in the dry-humping phase, seeing how Eric and I hardly made it to first base.

"You're just so easy to turn on," I pushed out, my head feeling dizzy. I wondered if this was what it felt like to be high—dazed, confused, fan-freaking-tastic.

A slight moan escaped my lips as he pressed his hips up and kept them there. I closed my eyes in bliss as he began rubbing back and forth against my jeans. My forehead fell to his and my eyes fluttered shut.

"Yes..." I whispered, which made him grind even more. My fingers landed on his shoulder blades and I dug in ever so slightly as he moved his lips to my neck and began sucking. "Yes..." I muttered once more, loving it more and more as he continued doing it.

He groaned against my skin as his voice went deep and smoky. "Let me taste," he begged, grunting against my neck.

My mind was clouded, I could hardly breathe, and oh my gosh, how did this feel so good?

"I...I've never..." I'd never had a boy go down on me before, and even though I wanted it, I heard Eleanor in the back of my head. *This is a part of it...this is part of the game.* "No," I said hurriedly, leaping out of his lap. "No, no, no."

I stood up and shook my hands and kicked my legs around.

He sat up straighter and cocked an eyebrow, though that wasn't the only thing he was cocking up, that was for sure. His gold member was trying its best to burst right out of those sweatpants.

Also, boys shouldn't be allowed to wear sweatpants around us girls. It makes it almost impossible to think straight.

"What is it?" he asked.

I started pacing back and forth. "This is just part of the bet. I got caught up in the moment, but this is the bet."

He laughed, shaking his head. "Shay, this isn't the bet. This is just you and me right now."

"And what are we exactly?"

"I don't know, we're just us. Look, you're overthinking it."

"I'm not. I mean, I am, but I don't know how not to. If the bet wasn't hanging over my head, I would just be free willy about it and all, but the bet does exist, whether I like it or not. And I can't just hook up with you, okay? I can't."

"Okay."

He said it so effortlessly that I was completely thrown off once more. "Wait, what?"

"I said okay. We don't have to hook up or make out. Listen, I get that we have a game going on, and I get that you're on red alert, but if I'm honest, real honest, I just like being around you. Do I want to screw your brains out? Yes, obviously. But am I okay waiting until you're ready? Of course. Especially since you're a virgin."

"What?" I stood up straight. "Who said I'm a virgin?"

He snickered and pointed toward me. "That face right there. I wasn't sure, but I wondered just based on how you tense up sometimes when we're making out when my hands wander."

I felt embarrassed, exposed...like a child. He could tell I was a virgin, which obviously meant I was doing something wrong. But what? How?

"Stop that," he told me.

"Stop what?"

"Overthinking and chewing on your collar."

I dropped the shirt I hadn't even noticed was in my mouth. "I just feel stupid, that's all."

"Why?"

"Because it's clear I'm inexperienced, and you're not."

"Chick." He stood up and moved over to me. He placed his finger beneath my chin and raised my head to make sure our eyes were locked for his next words. "Kissing you feels like kissing heaven. You're far from inexperienced. You being a virgin doesn't change the fact that you're the best kiss I've ever had. I could kiss you all day and not get sick of it. But you being a virgin? That's a big deal, and I won't take that from you until you're willing to give it away. Okay?"

I shyly nodded. "Okay."

"Also, just for future reference"—he moved his mouth to my ear, and his hot breath had every hair on my body standing straight up— "there are a million ways I can fuck you and keep you a virgin."

My cheeks heated up. "I'll keep that in mind."

He finally cleared his throat. "Okay, well, I'm going to run to the bathroom really fast and handle this, uh, issue in my pants. Then we can just talk and—*fuck*..." His voice faded as he realized my hand had slid into his sweatpants. My fingers wrapped around his hardness, and I began stroking it up and down slowly. My heart was pounding in my chest, and part of me worried Landon would hear it, but when I looked at him, his eyes were shut and there was a smile glued to his face. It was clear he wasn't thinking about my wild heartbeats at all, because he had his own experience taking place.

I wasn't completely sure what I was doing. Everything I knew about hand jobs, I'd learned from Raine, Tracey, and *Cosmopolitan*. Heck, everything I knew about sex came from Raine, Tracey, and *Cosmopolitan*.

As I stroked up and down, Landon seemed to like it, seemed pleased, which made me pleased. We moved back to the couch when I noticed his legs about to buckle, and as he sat down, I got on my knees and kept stroking, nice and slow.

"More pressure," he said as he exhaled between groans of pleasure. "You can hold it tighter, Shay. I promise you won't break it."

I did as he said, and his smile grew even more.

I pulled my hand out of his pants for a moment, slid my tongue along my palm, and slid it back in for more strokes.

Cosmo hand jobs 101: Make him sweat, make it wet.

"Yes...yes...and the head...rub the head..." He sighed, obviously enjoying every second of it.

Odd kink, but okay.

I cocked an eyebrow, and even though I didn't understand completely, I did as he requested. I began rubbing his head with my free hand, tangling my fingers in his hair as I kept stroking at his privates.

Within seconds, Landon burst out laughing, making me lean back, a little puzzled. "Not my *head* head, Shay. My *dick* head. The tip of my cock."

Oh.

Well, that was shockingly embarrassing.

I yanked my hand out of his pants, horrified, and covered my face with my hand. Then I realized I'd been stroking Landon's penis with said hand and now I had penis face, and he was probably staring at me and my penis face and—

Ohmygosh this is where I die.

The complete horror that sat in my gut was nauseating, and I thought about darting out of his front door, transferring schools by Monday, and never seeing Landon and his stupid penis again.

Bet's off, Landon. Moving to Europe. Adios mi enemigo!

"It's okay." He laughed.

"It's not," I coughed out through my penis fingers that were still hiding my surely red face.

"No, trust me, it is. These things happen when you're figuring this stuff out."

"I doubt anything like this has ever happened to you."

"Trust me, it has."

I spread my fingers against my face and narrowed my eyes as I peeked his way. "Tell me."

He sighed and ran his hand through his hair, which I'd gone ahead and messed up for him. "Okay. The first time I ever went down on a girl, I was going at it like a madman, licking, slurping, having a damn feast, and when I asked if she was enjoying it, she replied, 'Uh, that's the back door, not the front.'"

"Oh my gosh…" My hands dropped to the ground, along with my jaw. "*You ate a girl's butthole?!*"

"You don't have to sound so entertained by it," he spat out, but I couldn't help it. The fit of giggles wouldn't stop escaping me. He wrinkled his nose. "Stop laughing," he ordered, but I couldn't.

The squeals kept flying out of my mouth at a rapid speed, and I bent over into a howling fit at the idea of young, naïve Landon licking a girl's butthole.

"Stop," he ordered again, but with a slight smirk on his face. I couldn't have stopped if I'd wanted to; it was all too perfect and wrong.

The more I laughed, the bigger his smirk grew. Then, he leaped toward me, tackling my body. "Fine, if you want to laugh so much, let me help." He began tickling me, making me burst into more laughter. I was rolling back and forth, trying to break away from him, but he kept tickling me nonstop. "Surrender!" he commanded.

"Okay, okay, I surrender!"

"Say Landon is the best and Shay was wrong for laughing at him."

"Landon is the best and Shay was wrong for laughing at him," I echoed.

"Okay then." He stopped tickling me, and I instantly missed his fingers running along my skin.

Our breaths were both heavy and tired from the wrestling. He boxed me in with his body and lowered his face so it was inches from mine. I pressed my hands to his chest and felt his heart beating. It was wild, erratic, untamed—like mine.

"Kiss me," I whispered.

He did as I said.

"Again."

Another kiss.

And again, and again, and again…

We molded together, and his crotch pressed against me. The air that had been laced with laughter was now filled with desire. The stiffness in his pants came back, and I was thankful for that fact.

If at first you don't succeed, try, try again.

"Couch," I whispered.

He moved without needing me to say anything else. As he sat down, I returned to my kneeling position.

His eyes stayed locked with mine. "You don't have to do this, Shay," he promised, and I knew that.

But I wanted to do it. I wanted to please him and his head, and this time I was going to give the right head the pleasure.

I started slow again, and the way he grew in my grip turned me on more than I'd known it could. I picked up speed, and my thumb circled the top of him.

"Yes, that, oh my gosh, yeah..." he moaned. "Geez, Shay...right... *oh fuck...*"

Each time he groaned in pleasure, I felt myself getting more and more turned on. I began thrusting my hips in sync with the motion of my hand. Up and down, up and down, up and...

"Babe..." I liked the sound of that. He'd never called me babe before. "Shay, right there..." I liked it even more when he moaned my name as if I controlled his mind and heart with my touches. "I'm going to...Shay, I'm going to...pull away," he warned, but I didn't.

I kept stroking, up and down, up and down, harder, harder...my hips grinding against the air as my hand ground against his rod.

"*Fuckkkkk,*" he groaned as his body tensed up and he released himself into my hand. I kept stroking, feeling elated and hot, and horny, and proud.

It felt so good to make him feel that way, too.

I pulled my hand out of his sweats and slowly licked my fingers as he watched. It was salty and disgusting, but I tried my best to play it off.

He laughed. "You don't have to do that," he promised. "You can just wash it off. Trust me, you did enough. Geez..." he muttered, collapsing against the couch. "That was everything. You. Are. Everything."

I went to the bathroom to clean myself up, and before I washed my hands, I stood in front of the mirror and finished licking my fingers clean.

I found that I did actually like it. I liked how he tasted on my tongue.

When I was done, I headed out to the living room, where I found Landon wearing a different set of sweatpants. He smirked my way.

"Truth or dare?" he asked me as I plopped down on the couch beside him.

"Truth."

"I truth you to take off your pants."

I laughed and threw a pillow at him.

He shrugged and tossed his hands up in defeat. "I had to try."

Fair enough.

I shifted around in place and crossed my arms. "Can I make a change to the rules of our game?"

He arched an eyebrow. "What are you thinking?"

"We have to make it real. Only our truths, no lies. No more pranks. No trying to make each other swoon or trying to get under each other's skin just in an attempt to win the game. I need you to be you—the realest version of you, and I'll be the realest version of me. Then, if one of us falls in love, that's game. That's how we'll determine a winner, by being real."

He grimaced and rubbed his chin repeatedly. "Only truths?"

"Only truths."

A sigh rolled through him, and he lowered his head a bit before looking up and locking his stare with mine. "I think that's an unfair playing field."

"Why do you say that?"

"Because my truths aren't really something worth loving."

Oh, Landon.

Just those words alone made my heart ache.

"I think that's for me to decide, not you," I said. At first, he hesitated. He wasn't sure if he was willing to show me his dark sides, to open up in a way I was certain he'd never opened up before. But there I was, holding out an olive branch, giving him a chance to be real for the first time in forever.

"Come on, Landon," I whispered, giving him a small smile. "What's the worst that can happen?"

His brow knitted, but then he gave me a small smirk. It was so tiny that I almost missed it, but luckily, I was studying him from all angles.

"I'm not good at talking about my feelings, really. I kind of close up," he confessed.

"Okay." I walked over to my backpack and pulled out a spare notebook and a pen. "If you can't talk about them, then write them down in here and let me read your thoughts."

"Do you always have spare notebooks lying around?"

I laughed. "Doesn't everyone?" I took the pen and wrote a question on the first page for Landon to answer. "Here. Just reply to the question whenever you feel like it and leave it in my locker. You can write a question, too, and you can ask me anything. We don't even have to discuss whatever we write out loud. We can just read each other's truths and go from there. Deal?" I held my hand out for him to confirm our agreement.

He shook my hand. "Deal."

As we touched, a spark raced through my system, and I probably held on to his hand a second too long…or he held on to mine too long. Either way, we were holding each other, and we didn't let go too fast.

I liked the way it felt when his skin touched my skin.

When the feeling became too big, I dropped his hand. "I should probably be getting home actually. It's pretty late."

"Wow, a hit-it-and-quit-it kind of thing. I feel used, Chick."

"Well maybe someday I'll let you use me back," I shot back, and a part of me was shocked that the words even left my mouth. "Walk me to my car?"

"Of course."

We walked out and he opened my car door for me like the gentleman I'd never thought him to be, and I thanked him. "Oh wait, one last question," I said.

"What is it?"

I pushed my tongue in my cheek and wiggled my nose. "Was there any leftover tissue in her butt from wiping, and if so, did you accidentally swallow it?"

He shook his head, laughing. "I hate you so much."

"I hate you, too."

"Yeah, well, I hate you the most," he promised before he leaned in and kissed my forehead.

It felt so much more intimate than anything we'd done before. Forehead kisses had officially become my favorite thing he had given to me.

"Drive safe, Chick," he said before stepping away. As I drove home, the butterflies in my stomach remained, and every time I thought about my hand wrapped around his hardness, every time I envisioned his face as I brought him to completion, my whole body would heat up all over again.

When I arrived home, I felt as if I were floating on air. My heart was soaring from my interaction with Landon, but all of that came to a crashing halt when the reality of my life at home slammed back into me.

It was quiet, calm as a river moving downstream. I couldn't think of the last time it felt that tranquil at my house, but it wasn't a peaceful calmness. It was terrifying.

"What's going on?" I asked as I walked into the living room.

Mima stood there with her coat on and three suitcases at her side. There were also a few boxes stacked up beside the suitcases.

Mom looked up from the dining room table and stood up. She walked toward me, and I noticed the puffiness of her eyes right away. "Shay...we'd thought you'd be back a little bit later, but—"

"What's going on?" I repeated, cutting her off.

Mima smiled my way, the saddest smile I'd ever seen. I hadn't had a clue that Mima had the ability to give sad smiles. That was enough to break my heart.

"We've all decided it might be best if I move into my own place. I'm going to be staying in a small apartment down the way."

What? No. "You can't leave. This is your home. We are your home," I choked out, feeling my body began to tremble. Mima couldn't leave us. She was the key to the strength of our household. She was the anchor that kept us grounded, and without her there…

We'll collapse.

"Mima, no. Put your stuff away. This is silly," I argued, moving over to her suitcases. "This is your home. You can't go."

"Shay—" Mom cut in, but I snapped at her.

"Is this because of Dad?" I barked, my chest feeling as if it were on fire. "Is this because of him? If so, he should be the one to go. I smelled it, too, Mom. I smelled the alcohol on his breath. I bet you did too, didn't you? And did he ever explain how he could afford those earrings? Mom, he lied. He lied to us, not Mima. He should be gone, not her," I said, my voice shaky with anger. How was this happening? How was my grandmother the one being pushed out when my father was the liar?

This isn't right.

"Shay, please understand," Mom said, her eyes watering over. "This wasn't an easy decision."

"It's not a decision at all, because she's not leaving. Tell her, Mima," I begged, shifting my stare to my grandmother. Her eyes were watery too, which broke my heart even more. Mima was strong. She didn't cry. She didn't break. She was our strength.

She sniffled and stood up straight. "It's for the best, Shannon Sofia."

Shannon Sofia.

She'd used my whole name, which meant her words were written in stone.

She was really going to do it. She was going to walk out the front door and leave because of my drunken father and his lies.

How was this right? How was this fair?

"She's been there for us when he couldn't be, Mom. How can you do this?"

Mom began crying and left the room as if it was too much for her to handle. If it was too much, why was she allowing it to happen?

"I'll go with you, Mima," I promised. She shouldn't have to be alone. She shouldn't have to walk out that front door on her own.

"No. You'll stay here. It's what's right. You need to be here at home."

"This isn't a home without you. You are my home," I whispered as the tears began falling down my cheeks. I rushed over to her and wrapped my arms tightly around her body. "Please, Mima. Please don't leave me here with him. I can't do this anymore. I can't watch him pull her down and break her again."

She held me so tight.

So. Very. Tight.

"Sé valiente, mi amor," she whispered. *Be brave, my love.* "Sé fuerte." *Be strong.* "Sé amable." *Be kind.* "Y quédate." *And stay.* "Be here for your mother. She needs you, Shay. More than you'll ever know, she needs you. Don't make this harder for her."

"I don't understand. Why is she like this? Why is she so weak for him? I hate him. I hate him so much, but I hate her more for loving him. I hate them both for taking you away from me."

"No, no, no," she scolded, placing her hands on my shoulders. "Don't ever speak so ill of your mother. She has been through more wars than you'll ever know. You have no clue the things she's done to protect you, to be there for you."

"The best thing she could do for me is to leave my father."

"Oh, honey…" Her voice dropped and she shook her head. "I'm sorry this is so hard on you. It's hard on me, too. It's sitting heavy on my heart."

It was becoming hard to breathe, and my heart was twisting into a knot more and more as reality set in. She was going to go. She was going to leave me. I pulled her in for another hug. "Mima…" I sobbed against her blouse. She didn't cry, though. Mima never fell apart; she simply held others together. "Please let me go with you, Mima. Please. I can't do this without you."

"You're not without me, Shay. I won't be far, but your mother? She can't do this without you being here. That's the truest truth. Be easy on her heart. Be easy on her soul—it's broken and raw. You're the only daylight she has right now. So please…stay."

I cried into her arms for a while before she asked me to load up the car. Before she drove away, she pulled me into a hug once more and kissed my forehead.

Who knew forehead kisses could both heal and hurt?

I stayed on the sidewalk until her car rounded the corner.

Dad wasn't even home. He was probably off in some bar, drinking or out dealing with people he shouldn't have been messing around with, with no concern about what his actions were doing to our family. Each negative choice he made ripped the strands of our family unit, and yet he kept doing it, not thinking about us, not thinking of anything but himself.

I barged back into the house, heartbroken and furious. I had to get through to my mother. I needed her to wake up from this nightmare love story she'd been living in for far too long. As I entered the house, ready to snap at her, I paused my steps as I headed in her direction. She was in the bathroom with the door shut, and I listened as she sobbed uncontrollably. Her breaths were weighted and tired. When I turned the doorknob and opened the door, I found her sitting on the side of the tub with her hands covering her face.

I was still angry, hurt, confused. I still planned to let her know how I felt. I still planned on voicing my thoughts and making it clear that her choices were affecting everything and everyone around us, not just herself…but I couldn't in that moment.

She was already low, and I couldn't push her any lower.

Sé valiente, sé fuerte, sé amable, y quédate.

I moved into the bathroom. I sat down on the edge of the bathtub with her. I wrapped my arms around her.

And I stayed.

Chapter Twenty

Shay

I COULDN'T SLEEP THAT NIGHT. THE ALARM CLOCK SAT ON MY DRESSER, the red lights displaying the time, mocking me and my exhaustion. Dad hadn't come home. Mom was still crying in her bedroom, and Mima wasn't here. The house felt emptied of its light, and it made it impossible for me to sleep.

I glanced at the alarm clock once more.

12:09pm

Too late to call him, I told myself. Plus, why would I even try? If I woke him up, I'd feel bad for interrupting his sleep, seeing how I knew he struggled to fall asleep on his own. But, if he was up…if the night was keeping him awake, I wanted to hear his voice on the other end of the line.

I dialed Landon's number. As it rang, my heart sat in my throat, and I tried my best to swallow it down.

"You okay?" were the first words to leave his mouth as he answered. His voice had its normal smokiness without any hint of just waking up.

My heart, which still sat in my throat, began racing even more. I placed my collar into my mouth and chewed on it lightly. "Why would those be your first words?"

"Because it's past midnight, and most calls past midnight are with upsetting news or booty calls. If this is a booty call then, by all means…"

I could imagine the smirk on his face.

"It's not a booty call."

"Damn. So back to my original question...you okay?"

"Define okay." I laughed, grinding my teeth against the fabric. "My grandmother moved out today. Or, well, my mother pretty much kicked her out after one too many arguments about my father."

"What?" His voice was alert. "Where is she? Is she okay? Where will she stay?"

I'd almost forgotten how much a part of Landon's life Mima had been. The concern in his voice made me wish he was there with me so we could worry about my grandmother together.

"Is she okay?" he asked again.

"She has an apartment she's renting for the time being. It's hard to tell if she's okay, really. She has a hard shell and acts like nothing gets to her, even though I know it does. She doesn't show weakness ever, and when she's broken, I don't think I'd even notice. She's been our family's rock from day one. I don't know who she leans on when she's hurting, because we've all spent so much time leaning on her. I just worry she's struggling with all of this and she'll never admit it. She doesn't show her emotions like that."

"The people who show the least emotions are normally the ones who hurt the most," he stated.

My chest tightened. "Personal experience?"

"Something like that." The tone of his voice made it clear he didn't want to dive deeper into the subject. "Maria means a lot to me. Even though she's my housekeeper, she's been there for me through some of the hardest days."

"Housekeeper?" I asked, confused.

"Yeah. She comes over every Sunday. She has for the past forever years."

"Landon, my grandmother hasn't been a housekeeper for years. She opened her yoga studio about four years ago..." My heart skipped as I thought about Mima and what she always said she was doing on Sunday afternoons. "She said her Sundays were meant for a dear friend of hers."

Landon went quiet on the line. I imagined his bushy brows pushed together, and the confusion swirling in his mind as the silence stretched across the call. "She isn't a housekeeper anymore?"

"No. Not for a long time now."

More silence. "I don't get it…" he confessed. "I don't get how she's such a good person."

"Yeah, neither do I."

"Is that why you can't sleep? Because you're worried about Maria?"

"Yes." I shifted around in my bed. "Why are you up?"

"Kind of what I do."

"You need sleep, Landon."

"I know, but just because you need something doesn't mean it comes easily."

True.

"I can stay on the phone with you until you fall asleep if that helps."

"I don't know if it will, but it's worth a try. And Chick?"

"Yes?"

"Stop chewing on your shirt."

I dropped the fabric from between my lips and shifted around a bit. "What should we talk about?"

"Anything you want…everything."

So, that was exactly what we did. We talked about stupid things. Favorite things. Sports.

I didn't have much to say about sports, but he shared his favorite teams. Even though he was from Illinois, he loved the Green Bay Packers. Even though he should've repped the orange and blue, his sports colors were green and yellow.

I called him a traitor, even though I knew nothing about football. He called me beautiful just because.

His favorite candy was Reese's Cups. His favorite soda was Mountain Dew. If he could visit any state, he'd want to go to California. He was afraid of snakes and loved dogs.

His favorite movie was *Home Alone*. "I love the part when he plays the movie clip and it says, 'Merry Christmas, ya filthy animal.' I swear, when I was ten, I said that to anyone and everyone for a year straight.

I still think it's the funniest shit," he explained, snickering to himself. I loved his laugh the most.

I gave him facts about me, too. How my goal in life was to see one of my screenplays made into a film or television series. How I dreamed of achieving the EGOT—an Emmy, a Grammy, an Oscar, and a Tony. Sure, it seemed like a farfetched dream, but if Audrey Hepburn could do it, maybe I could, too.

Even though I was nowhere near as talented as Audrey.

I told him she was my favorite actress. Her romantic comedies were some of my favorites and the reason I'd fallen in love with writing romances. I told him my favorite writers, too.

I told him so many things others probably found boring, but he listened and asked me questions about my dreams, my wishes, and my hopes.

"You can do it all, Chick. You *will* do it all," he promised. "You're too damn stubborn not to."

That wasn't a lie. Even if I didn't do it all, I was going to fight like hell to get as close to my dreams as possible.

"What about you?" I asked. "What do you want to do?"

"I hate that question," he muttered. "It always feels loaded."

"Loaded with what?"

"Pressure." He grumbled a little through the receiver and then cleared his throat. "Everyone has an idea of what they want to do. Hank and Raine want to open that bakery and café shop crap. Eric wants to do engineering. Grey is a shoo-in for taking over his family's whiskey company. Reggie has it locked down to be a homeless dick begging people for money so he can get a ticket back home to Kentucky. Everyone has their stuff figured out, while I'm walking around lost as fuck like John Travolta in *Pulp Fiction*." He paused. "That's another favorite movie. *Home Alone* then *Pulp Fiction*."

"I've never seen that movie."

"Ah, and to think you were just starting to grow on me."

I snickered. "You've been growing on me, too, actually."

"Is that so?"

"Yes. Like a disgusting fungus between my toes."

He laughed out loud, and my stomach fluttered with butterflies from the sound. I liked that. I liked that I made him laugh.

"You don't have to have it all figured out right now, Landon. So many people go to school undecided. Some people take a year off to figure out what they really want to do. Some people don't go to school at all. None of those are wrong choices. None of those choices are better than others."

"Yeah, I guess. I just wish my dad understood that."

"I'm beginning to think parents aren't meant to understand us kids."

"And we aren't meant to understand them," he added.

Never a truer statement. I wondered if parents even remembered what it felt like to be young, and confused, and completely without direction.

Then again, Mom had looked to be all those things that evening.

Maybe parents were still kids with old, tired hearts, and every time they beat, they cracked a little more.

My phone dinged and I received a message from Tracey. She and Raine had been texting me all night about a party at Reggie's house—which was the last thing I wanted to be a part of.

Tracey: You were right about Reggie. He's an asshole and I'm done with him forever.

The relief I felt when I read those words was overwhelming. For a split second, I wondered what brought about her revelation. Then, I realized it didn't really matter. As long as he was out of the picture, I was happy.

"It seems Tracey is officially over the Reggie infatuation," I yawned into the phone receiver.

"Good. He's a fucking asshole. And that means a lot coming from an asshole like me."

"You're not an asshole, Landon," I yawned again, "You're a like a teddy bear hiding in a grizzly bear outfit."

He snickered. "You're yawning," Landon noted. "Go to sleep."

I rubbed my eyes, trying to get the sleepiness to fade. "I'm still here. I'm good."

I yawned again.

"Hang up," he said.

"Not until you're asleep."

"You'll be asleep before me."

"But stay on the line until you fall asleep, too."

"Okay."

I yawned once more, my eyes feeling heavy. "Promise?"

"Promise."

I didn't know if he was a boy who broke his promises, but I was hoping he wasn't.

As I was falling asleep, I gently spoke. "You could be an actor, Land. You know that, right? You're so good at it. You could be the greatest actor in the world."

"That's sleepiness talking. You're delusional." He yawned next. *Perfect.* "Good night, Chicken. I hate you."

He'd called me Chicken, and I hadn't known I could love a nickname that grew from hate. "I hate you, too, Satan."

"Yeah, but I hate you the most."

Chapter Twenty-One

Landon

SHAY FELL ASLEEP BEFORE ME, BUT I KEPT MY PROMISE TO HER AND stayed on the phone until I was sleeping too—and I actually did fall asleep. I wasn't sure if it was the sound of her breathing or the fact that I had a feeling she'd somehow find out if I did hang up on her, but I slept.

I went to sleep with the moon and woke to the sun.

I woke up refreshed, which was something I hadn't done in such a long, long time.

When the doorbell rang that afternoon, I hurried downstairs to answer it, knowing it could only be one person. I swung the door open and there Maria was, sporting her classic Maria smile.

"Afternoon, Landon." She grinned ear to ear, walking in with a food dish in her hand. Meatloaf—at least it smelled like meatloaf. She handed it over to me and eyed me up and down. "You look well-rested—that's good. You slept."

"Yeah, I did." *Thanks to your granddaughter and her magic powers over me.* "The place isn't that messy today, if you want to just hang out and watch television or something."

"I don't get paid to watch television, Landon Scott."

I wasn't certain she was getting paid at all.

"I won't tell if you don't." I smirked, nudging her in the side. "Plus, I made your favorite cookies—oatmeal raisin with pecans."

She raised an eyebrow. "You baked for me?"

"Yeah. So, what do you say? How about a day off?"

She darted her eyes away from me, and I figured it was to hide her emotions. Maria was far too proud to ever show her struggles, and I knew this. So, I wasn't going to push her into opening up to me. I planned to make her day as comfortable as I could, bringing her a little bit of joy during a crappy season of her life.

"You won't tell your parents?" she asked, her voice low with concern.

"I won't. We can hang out in the living room and watch TV. I have the DVDs of *Friends*."

"I've never seen that show," she admitted.

What was with Shay's family and not seeing great entertainment?

"Well, today's your lucky day. Come on."

We sat in the living room all day watching episode after episode of *Friends*. Every now and then Maria would laugh at the show, but most of the time she shook her head and grumbled, "Dios mío!" with annoyance at the characters.

She didn't even make us eat at the dining room table for dinner. We ate the meatloaf, mashed potatoes, and one too many cookies with ice cream on the coffee table as we watched.

"You're a lot like that Joey character," Maria remarked, nodding toward the screen. "A dorky, handsome guy."

I snickered and raised an eyebrow, giving her a slight nod. "How you doin'?" I quoted.

Of course, Maria didn't pick up on Joey's infamous line, and she shrugged her shoulders. "I'm doing fine, but this show is awful."

That made me laugh even more.

I'd never had a grandmother figure, but I figured this was what it would feel like if I did. It would be a collection of random moments that added up to big things, big memories. That was what Maria had been to me over the past several years. She'd been these small moments that built up into something important to me. There weren't many important things in my life, but she was one of them.

Top five at least.

Her granddaughter was climbing her way up that ladder, too.

After the night ended, Maria collected her things and headed to the front door. "Thank you for tonight, Landon. I know you may not know this, but I needed today. I needed a day off."

"I'm glad I could help." I brushed my hand through my hair before stuffing my hands into the pockets of my jeans. "Hey, Maria?"

"Yes?"

"How's your heart today?"

She gave me a small smile and her eyes watered over, and to my surprise, a small tear danced down her cheek. "Still beating."

I hugged her without asking permission, because Maria wasn't the type of person who needed warning that a hug was coming her way.

She simply always hugged back.

On Monday, it was apparent that Monica and Reggie were a new pairing, which was odd because I was pretty sure Tracey and he had just ended their fling like, forty-eight hours ago. A lot can change over a weekend with teenagers. The hormones move so fast and it was hard to keep up with who was loving who each week. Monica made sure to have herself wrapped all around the wannabe Eminem, and every chance she got, she'd flash me a wicked smirk that read, *Jealous?*

Not really, Mon.

Every time I saw her, she was looking worse. I wanted to check in on her, wanted to make sure she was eating and at least trying to sleep, but as time moved on, I realized I wasn't the person she wanted me to be. Therefore, it was probably best to keep my distance.

Still, it rubbed me the wrong way seeing her with Reggie. It turned out that asshole wasn't worthy of any girl's time. Including Monica. I shot her a message, telling her he had issues and was an abusive dick, but she told me to mind my own business.

As I looked away from the odd pairing, I turned and walked over to Eric, who was standing at his locker.

"Did you hear? Monica and Reggie appear to be a thing," I mentioned, patting him on the back.

"Yeah, they were all over each other at the party this weekend," Eric said, his voice low. He hadn't turned to face me, and he seemed less than his chipper self. If anyone was a morning person, it was Eric. He'd walk in singing songs from *The Sound of Music* at seven in the morning like that wasn't the most annoying thing in the world.

"What's up with you? You seem less than awake. Party too hard?" I asked.

He finally turned to face me, revealing a black eye. I raised an eyebrow at him, giving him a 'what the fuck' expression. Over the weekend, the guys (+Raine) had been texting me nonstop about a party at Reggie's house, telling me to come out and kick it, but I'd ignored them all, because if I had to choose between hanging out with Shay and going to Southern Charmer's party, I was always going to go with Shay.

Hell, if I had to choose between Shay and anyone lately, I'd probably still go with Shay.

"What the hell happened to you?" I spat out, looking him up and down.

He grimaced and shook his head. "It's nothing. It's not a big deal," he muttered.

"Dude, half your face is black and blue. This doesn't look like it's nothing."

"Just drop it, will you, Land?!" he snapped.

Yup, that's right—Eric, cool as a cucumber Eric, snapped.

Not only had he snapped, he'd snapped at me.

Just then, Reggie walked past us with his arm wrapped around Monica, and he looked in Eric's direction and shook his head with a look of disgust on his face. "Fucking faggot," he muttered.

My body tensed up and I puffed out my chest. "What did you just say?" I barked, making Reggie look my way.

"Not you, Landon. Cool your jets," he said.

"Did he do this to you, Eric?" I whispered. Eric's frown conveyed that it had been Reggie. The blood in my veins began boiling as anger built up in my body. There was only a handful of things I actually cared about, a handful of people I'd give my life for. It just so happened Reggie had chosen to lay a hand on one of those people, and that wasn't okay.

I clenched my jaw as I walked toward Reggie. "What did you say?" I demanded again.

"I said faggot," he repeated, gesturing toward Eric. "This asshole had the nerve to show up to my house then the next thing I know, he's drunk, and I find him kissing some random dude in my bedroom. It's fucking sick. The world doesn't need fucked-up people like—"

No more words from the homophobic asshole.

I shut him up with my fist. Ninety-nine percent of my reasoning for slamming my knuckles into Reggie's jawline was for Eric, but that one percent was selfishly for myself. I'd been wanting to slug that guy from day one.

Reggie stumbled backward like a giant awkward gorilla. He ran his hand against his lip, wiping blood away. "You shit." He growled before charging toward me, but I had my fist already prepared to slam into his face again. He body shoved me against the lockers, then we both went tumbling around like apes on the ground. He got a few hits in, but then I flipped him over and started hammering my fist into his face. Black and blue, the same way he'd done to my friend—I was going to hit him until he was black and blue.

A crowd formed around us, and it took a few teachers to pull us off of each other.

"Reggie! Landon! Principal's office. *Now!*" Mr. Thymes hollered.

We were both dragged away by teachers, and Mr. Thymes looked at me as if he was so disappointed in me for using my fists. But hell, I was sure Romeo had thrown a few punches in his time.

I wiped the corner of my eye, which was stinging. Reggie had clipped me good with his fist, and blood was dripping down my cheek. I looked up and saw my favorite pair of brown eyes staring my way. She looked terrified as she hugged her textbooks to her chest. I wasn't sure if she was scared by the fight as a whole or by me. I knew how I could get. I knew how I lost myself in my rage. I didn't want her to see that side of me. I didn't want her to judge me for my shadows.

But then, I watched her lips. They parted slightly and mouthed, "Are you okay?"

She was concerned about me. Even though I was broken and bruised, even though I looked like an untamed beast, Beauty still saw me and wondered about my wellbeing.

I nodded once.

Yes, Chick.

I'm okay.

Principal Keefe was an older man with a Santa Claus beard and a Santa Claus gut. It had been a while since I'd spent time in his office due to fights. After Lance passed, I didn't feel the need to get my aggression out in that way. Still, Principal Keefe didn't seem surprised in the slightest by my arrival to his office. It was almost as if he'd expected it to happen at some point.

"For a minute, I thought we were past this stage, Mr. Harrison," he muttered, his voice low and tame.

Yeah, yeah, me too, Principal Keefe.

Reggie sat next to me, his face already changing colors, and at least I had the benefit of watching that happen. He looked uncomfortable.

Good.

He didn't deserve any kind of comfort whatsoever.

Even though he was obviously the loser of our fight, he still had a slick tongue on him. As Principal Keefe stood up to go get some paperwork, he left us in his office.

Reggie brushed his hand beneath his nose and mumbled under his breath. "You're acting like a real dick just because I'm fucking your bitch."

My hands clenched, but I didn't react. I didn't want to give him the satisfaction of getting under my skin again. Plus, Shay would want me to do better, be better. I wanted to do better, too. I wanted to be better. Therefore, I wasn't going to feed into his taunting—at least I didn't plan to until he kept talking.

"That's right, I'm fucking your old bitch, and I can't wait to fuck your new one, too. That mouth of Shay's? That sweet hole on her face looks like a great one to fill with my cock. I bet the good girl will even say please and thank you after accepting my load," he mocked, and well, that was a wrap on his life.

We were wrestling again in the principal's office, and by wrestling, I meant I had him pinned down and my fists were slamming repeatedly into his face.

"Landon! What in the world?!" Principal Keefe hollered, coming back into his office with widened eyes. He hurried to pull me off Reggie, and Reggie scrambled to stand up straight.

"See, Principal Keefe? He attacked me again," Reggie lied, crying like a little bitch. "I didn't have anything to do with him. It's clear he has anger issues and is just mad that I'm dating his ex-girlfriend. I'm not one to fight, ever. This isn't me. I have too much respect for you and your student body to do such a thing."

I swore, if Reggie could have stuck his head up Keefe's ass any more, he have been eating his shit.

Principal Keefe was buying it, too. Maybe because he was so used to me being the one to stir up shit. Maybe because he didn't have a history with the likes of Reggie, but he had a long one with the likes of me. He knew I was trouble, that was a fact. What he didn't know was Kentucky was even worse than me.

"Just keep your hands to yourselves, boys," Principal Keefe instructed sternly, but his stare fell solely on me. "I am going to get another ice pack for you, Reggie. Landon?"

"Yes?"

"Don't move."

Roger that.

Reggie's parents arrived with concerned Southern voices, worried that their "honey bear" had been in a fight.

"It's not like him at all!" his mother announced, clearly completely unaware of who her child was. "Never in his life would my Reggie throw a punch. He's a good boy. He must have been provoked," she said, eyeing me up and down.

I didn't say a word to her or give her any dirty looks. Soon enough she'd find out about the boy she was raising. No one could keep their shadows hidden forever, not even the Southern Charmer.

"He had a party at your house this weekend," I muttered to his parents as they were walking out of the office. "Check your liquor cabinets."

Reggie's eyes widened with shock that I'd ratted him out. Yeah, it was a low blow and completely uncalled for, but what could I say? I was feeling extra petty that day because he'd had the nerve to put his hands on my friend.

They kept me in the principal's office until my dad could get there. Mom was still over in Europe living her best life. She'd been leaving me daily voice messages, but I ever didn't call her back. I figured she knew she deserved the silent treatment.

I did, however, text her letting her know I was alive. I didn't want her to worry too much, even though she pissed me off.

Dad was going to be so mad at me. I knew he'd already be annoyed that he had to drive back into town from Chicago during a workday to deal with my dramatics, and when he walked in, I saw the irritation all over his face. My father never said much with his words but he said everything with his jagged facial expressions.

Principal Keefe explained that it was unclear how the fight had begun, saying all he knew was that it had ended with teachers getting involved. "Now, normally, we'd have to look at a short suspension, but since Landon is the lead in the school play that's premiering soon…" Principal Keefe's words trailed off, and he shifted some papers around. Our school was known for two things: basketball and the arts. The idea of the theater department losing their dear Romeo for a few days was a bit too much for Principal Keefe's heart. "Also, we think him having the afterschool activity has been good for him. Even though he had this slipup, we are hoping it is a one-time offense. He and Reggie have also been advised to keep their distance from each other."

No problem there on my end.

Dad looked surprised to hear about me being in the show. I'd never shown any interest in the performing arts, and well, we didn't ever talk about it. His brow knitted, and he apologized on my behalf for me being completely reckless.

We walked out of the office, and Dad grumbled to himself.

I slung my backpack onto my shoulder and shrugged slightly. "I'm sorry they had to call you out here. It wasn't even that serious."

"You bashed a person's face in, Landon. That's serious."

"Yeah, but—"

He pinched the bridge of his nose and shook his head. "I can't do this right now. I can't handle your antics. And what is this about a school play?"

"I just..." I took a deep breath and gripped my backpack strap. "I really like it, Dad, this theater thing. I've been thinking about going to school for acting in the fall."

He huffed and shook his head. "Yeah, all right, Landon."

"I'm serious, Dad. It's something I'm really interested in, and UOC has a pretty good theater department and—"

He cut me off. "I forbid you."

"What?"

"I said I forbid you. I am not going to pay for an idiotic major just for you to waste your time and my money. I forbid it. You're going into law, like we've already determined."

"We didn't determine it. You did. Dad, I—"

He wasn't listening. He never listened. My words were pointless.

At least Mom would've listened. She always listened.

He glanced at his watch. "I don't have time for this. I need to get back to Chicago and try to play catchup for today, which means I'll probably have to go in this Saturday too. And just a heads-up, I'll probably be busy the following weekend, too."

"The following weekend?" I stood up, alert. "But that's my birthday weekend. I figured you'd be home, seeing how Mom won't."

"Yeah, I thought the same—until you went around swinging your fists like a wild man. You say you're serious about this theater crap, but you can't even act mature enough to stop using your fist to solve your problems. The only kind of acting you need to do is acting your age. You're not a kid anymore. Stop acting like one. We'll talk about this later."

We wouldn't, though. It would be brushed under the rug like every argument we'd ever had. Dad would fall back into his work world, and I'd fall back into my mind, and we'd deal with our issues on our own.

I missed Mom.

He walked off, leaving me standing there like a dumbass, fully in my feelings about him not being there for me on my birthday. I needed him. I needed him more than ever that day, and he wasn't going to be there for me.

Perfect.

I started walking toward the exit after Dad left. My mind was already too messed up about my birthday, and there was no way I was going to sit through American History and talk about dead dudes when I had my own mind haunting me on the daily.

"Where are you going?" a voice said as I pushed the door open. I turned to see Shay standing there with the same concerned look she'd had when Mr. Thymes was dragging me away.

"I don't know. Just anywhere but here," I pushed out. I didn't feel like talking. I didn't feel like being around people, especially Shay. I didn't want her to see me at one of my lows. Lord knew she'd already seen that enough.

"Okay," she replied, walking over and pushing the door open.

I cocked an eyebrow. "What are you doing?"

"I'm leaving with you."

She said it so matter-of-factly, as if it was common sense. If I was leaving, of course she was going, too. Obviously.

"No, you're not. You aren't the type of person to ditch school."

"Well, that's changing today. Come on, we can go to my place. No one's home right now, and I can help clean up your face."

"Look, Shay, I don't want to be dramatic—"

"Then don't."

"What?"

"Don't be dramatic. Just let me do this today, Landon. I'm sure you were going to go home to your empty house and sit around on your own and be sad, and sure, you can do that later, but right now you shouldn't be alone. So, come on."

She began walking toward my car, and she gave me no choice.

Besides, a part of me knew that wherever she led, I wanted to follow.

We went to my car, and I even handed her the keys to drive. My mind wasn't able to focus enough on the road, and I knew the keys would be safest in her grip.

That was until she got behind the wheel and started jerking it back and forth like a psychopath.

"Geez, Chick, I can do without the heart attack."

"Well, you should drive an automatic car like a regular person, not a stick."

I sat up in my seat as my eyes widened in horror. "You don't know how to drive stick?!" I blurted out.

"No." She shrugged. "I figured it couldn't be that different."

Jerk. Stop. Jerk. Ohmygoshwearegoingtodie.

"Pull the car over!"

"But—"

"Shannon Sofia! Pull the car over now!" I hollered, making her eyes shoot out of her face, and she quickly pulled over.

"Okay, okay, sheesh. You're sounding so much like my grandmother right now. I'm getting out!"

"Good."

We switched seats, and I tried my best to clear my thoughts to focus on getting us to Shay's safely.

"How did you know my middle name?" she asked softly, looking my way.

I rubbed my thumb against my nose and tried to think of a way to not sound like a complete nerd. "When you used to come over to my place with your grandmother as a kid, she yelled it at you once. It's just something that stuck in my head."

Along with every detail about her since the first day I saw her.

I could feel her eyes on me, and I wished I could read her mind. I wished I knew how her thoughts worked. I wished I could read her the way she was so effortlessly good at reading me.

When we got to her house, she led me straight to her bedroom, not even giving me time to look around, and sat me down on the bed. "Let me get a warm rag for your eye. I'll be right back," she said.

I looked around her room, and her walls were covered in movie script pages and posters of actors and actresses. She had a bookshelf filled with notebooks, and I'd have bet she'd fill every single one out to the very last page.

Words came easy to her. I didn't have enough thoughts to fill up one notebook, let alone dozens.

Shay came back with the warm towel and placed it against my face. I cringed a little but welcomed the warmth.

"You used to fight a lot before," she whispered, gently dabbing my cheek. "When you were younger."

"Yeah."

"People probably always thought you were this beast or something, but you only fought people who bullied others...at least that's what I noticed."

"You noticed my fights?"

"I noticed your everything," she confessed, and that frozen heart of mine thawed a bit. That happened a lot when she was around.

"Eric told me what you did for him today. That was very brave of you."

"It was stupid. I could've lost my spot in the school play. I could've jeopardized graduating."

"Yeah, it was stupid, but stupid things can still be brave things. Eric doesn't really talk about it, about his sexuality."

"Is that why you two broke up?"

She nodded. "I've known for a while. Did you know?"

I shrugged. "I kind of assumed but never brought it up. It was none of my business, and it didn't change the fact that he was one of the most important people in my life. He can love anyone he wants and that isn't going to change how I feel about the guy."

"Wow." She exhaled slowly and sat back on her heels. She stared at me with those eyes again, and my heart? A puddle.

"A penny for your thoughts?" I asked out loud. Mom used to always say that to me when I was a kid.

"I just...you just..." She sighed. "You're nothing like the person I've spent years building you up to be in my head."

"I think the same about you more and more each day."

"If you had to choose one word to describe me, what word would you choose?" she asked, and that was the easiest question ever.

"Good."

She raised an eyebrow. "Good? That's it?"

"Yes. Good. You're good to everyone on so many levels, even people who don't deserve it, like me. You take the time to look deeper into people and see things from different sides. You're patient, too. That would be my second word for you. You don't rush people to be what you think they should be. You just let them exist."

"Wow..." She held her hand to her chest. "That's the nicest thing an enemy has ever said to me," she joked.

I snickered.

Not your enemy, Chick. Never your enemy.

"What about me? What's my word?" I asked.

"Good," she repeated.

"Copycat."

"Maybe, but it's true."

I rolled my shoulders back. "I've been called a lot of things before, but good hasn't been one of them." I glanced over to her bookcase, which was filled with her notebooks. "Are all of those used?"

"Yes. They are all my character portfolios I make of people I know. It helps me craft characters for my stories."

I raised an eyebrow. "Are there any about me?"

She blushed. "Maybe a few."

"Can I read them?"

She laughed. "Definitely not. Can I ask you something?"

"Shoot."

"Why did we hate each other?"

I shrugged. "I don't know. Maybe because we were too stupid to face the truth."

"And what's the truth?" She inched closer to me, moving her lips gently against mine. Her inhales became mine, and my exhales belonged to her.

My lips parted and I swept them against hers. "The truth is—"

She cut me off by kissing me hard. Her tongue slid into my mouth and I placed my hands beneath her ass and lifted her up into my arms. She wrapped herself around me, and our kiss deepened. I swore I could spend forever against her lips and never get sick of her taste.

Some of my favorite moments in the world were when her lips were pressed against mine. Her kisses often tasted like the lemon candies she was always popping into her mouth, or like Sour Patch Kids, or Skittles.

My God, I loved her sweet kisses. I loved the way her tongue swept against my bottom lip before she parted her mouth so I could get a deeper taste. I loved the way her hands fell to my chest as mine cruised down her lower back. I loved how she moaned ever so lightly against my lips. I loved the way her spine curved in my direction. I loved how I fucked her with my tongue, and she'd fuck me just as hard.

I pulled back and looked at her. I wanted more. I wanted to taste her, explore her. I wanted to feed on her body and her soul.

"Can I...?" I nervously asked like a damn inexperienced fool, but I didn't even care. If I was going to be a fool, it was going to be for her.

"Yes." She nodded, moving from my lap to lying on her bed.

I loved undressing her, watching as her eyes dilated from anticipation. I loved how she craved me taking control, but dammit I loved it even more when she ruled me. I loved how she trembled at my touch but her eyes told me to keep going. I loved how my hands trembled against her skin but my heart told me to keep going…

Keep feeling…

I loved when I parted her legs and went down on her and she moaned in pleasure. I loved when I began to rise up to kiss her lips and she told me no, and then I lowered back down to finish my favorite meal course. I loved when she arched her hips up as my tongue fucked her clit. I loved how she'd tell me to go harder and deeper as my tongue lapped repeatedly against her core. I loved her taste. The wetness felt like a reward I received from her being pleased by my job well done.

Then, I became addicted to when her moans grew more and more, making me finger fuck her harder and deeper, my tongue rolling in and out of her, sucking against her clit, teasing every single piece of her as her hands stayed tangled in my hair.

"Oh…my…Land…wait…yes…go…slow…ohmygosh…" she cried out.

I loved when she begged.

"More, more, more…."

I loved that. I loved it so much. I loved…

I…

Loved…

"What's going on here?" a voice said, breaking us from our dazed trance. I shot my head up to see a grown woman staring my way.

"Mom, hey," Shay hollered, grabbing a blanket and wrapping it around her body. "Oh my gosh, I—you—we—" Her words were jumbled, and I stood up quickly, stunned to see Shay's mother standing in front of us…in Shay's room…seconds after my head was between her daughter's legs.

Nothing about this situation looked good at all.

"What are you doing here?" Shay nervously asked, holding the blanket tightly around her waist.

Holy shit, Shay's mother just walked in on me eating her daughter out.

I wanted to die a slow, painful death, and the redness in Shay's face told me she felt pretty much the same way.

Her mom raised a sharp eyebrow. "Came home from work for lunch. What are you doing here? You should be in school!"

"Sorry, Mrs. Gable. This is my fault and I—" I tried to explain, but she gestured toward the front door.

"Leave."

I did as she said. What other choice did I have? Try to explain to her why my head was placed nicely between her daughter's thighs during the middle of a school day?

I headed home, and I texted Shay when I got back to my place.

Me: You good?

No response. I texted her a dozen more times that night with no responses coming my way. The next day at school, she walked up to me, holding the straps of her backpack, and she smiled.

"Grounded?" I asked.

"Grounded," she replied.

"Cell taken away?"

"Yup, and internet access."

That made sense.

"No regrets?" I asked, lowering my brows.

Her lips turned into a bigger smile and her adorable cheeks were rosy. "No regrets."

Eric texted me late one afternoon, telling me he was sorry for what went down with Reggie. He said he was ashamed, too, which I thought was sad. He hadn't had shit to be ashamed of.

Eric: I'm not gay or anything, you know…I mean, I'm just trying my best to figure everything out.

Me: Whatever you are is good enough for me.

Eric: Thanks, Land.

Me: I'll kick anyone's ass for you, E. Just say the word, and I'll trample them.

I missed my afternoon dates with Shay, though I supposed it made sense that she was only allowed to go to and from school each day. If I had been her parents, I would have banned her from any human interaction for the next thirty years. I was lucky enough I even got to see her during the school day and at rehearsal.

That Tuesday, there was a knock at my front door, and I hurried to answer it, stupidly hoping it was Shay. To my disappointment, there stood Monica. She was the last person I wanted to see, but like a bad habit, Monica had a way of popping up at the worst times.

"What do you want?" I asked her, opening my front door.

"To get high with you," she muttered, already stoned out of her mind.

"I don't have time for this, Monica," I sternly stated, going to shut the door.

She placed her foot in the doorway, stopping it.

"Monica, really. I'm busy."

"With that bitch?" she hissed.

My jaw tightened. "Don't call her that."

"Oh, I see. Now you're protecting her instead of me?"

I rolled my eyes and shut the door. She wasn't in the right state of mind for a conversation of any kind. What had happened to KJ not dealing to her anymore?

"Has she seen them?!" Monica shouted on my front porch. "Have you gotten so close that you've shown her your ugly fucking scars?! Has she seen what you've done to yourself?!"

Her words vibrated against my skin as I flung the front door open again. I grabbed her by the arm and pulled her inside, slamming the door shut behind her. "What the fuck, Monica?!" I hissed, my heart pounding faster and faster against my chest.

"Let me go," she whined, yanking her arm out of my grip.

"What the hell is wrong with you? Who do you think you are coming over here shouting like a madwoman?"

"I wouldn't be shouting like a madwoman if you didn't make me so mad!" she cried, her body trembling.

She was shivering like a damn fool, and it was clear she was very high. I arched an eyebrow. "What are you on?" I asked.

"Nothing," she slurred, her words coated with depression.

Dammit, Monica.

I hated this girl. I hated her addiction, and I hated how much of myself I saw in her broken eyes.

"Tell me, Mon," I ordered.

"I did tell you. I'm on nothing. What? You think you're the only asshole who can get clean?"

"Did you get something from KJ?" The last time I'd seen him, I'd asked him to stop dealing to Monica. I had begged the guy to let her be, told him how she slipped deeper and deeper each and every time. He'd sworn he'd stop but promises from a drug dealer are like promises from Santa Claus—fiction.

My anger toward Monica for barging in on me, on my life, on the life I was trying to heal had shifted. The anger became true concern, genuine worry. I was worried about the thorn in my ass.

I crossed my arms. "When was the last time you ate?"

"Shut up, Land."

"Answer me."

She shrugged. "Don't know."

I sighed, pointed toward the dining room. "Sit."

"Oh, so now you want me to stay? Screw you, Landon. I can open my phone and find a shit ton of men who will want me to stay, who will want me to touch them, to want them, to spread my legs for—"

"*Sit the hell down, Monica!*" I barked. My patience was being tested, and every time she talked about what other men did to her, it pissed me off—not because I wanted her, but because I knew they didn't. They used her, abused her, then tossed her to the side.

Just like Reggie would end up doing.

She gave me a sly smirk, curtseyed, and then sat down at the dining room table.

I went into the kitchen and slapped together a peanut butter and jelly sandwich, grabbed a glass of milk, and set it down in front of her.

I sat across from her at the table, as far away as possible.

"Eat," I said.

She rolled her eyes and flipped me off. Then, she picked up the sandwich and took a bite.

With each bite she took, a part of me sighed with relief.

There'd been many nights I had sat there with her, eating PB&Js, drunk, high, and wasted out of my mind. I didn't miss those nights.

I didn't miss that cold feeling of despair, that emptiness.

Even when we ate the sandwiches together, I always felt alone whenever I was with Monica. Maybe her loneliness made me drown even more.

"Was it over me?" she questioned.

"Was what over you?"

"The fight with Reggie. Did you fight him because of me?"

The question was so heavy, and the desperation in her eyes was clear as day. She wanted us to fight over her. She wanted to be the reason men lost their minds. I'd never met a woman who craved being wanted so much. It was sad to see. I didn't answer for two reasons. One, it would've hurt her already damaged heart if I told her the truthful no, and two, I knew my silence would be enough of an answer.

Her eyes watered over for a split second before she returned to her sinister stare. Every now and then, you could see flashes of the hurt girl Monica was. You could see it in her eyes, but she never showed it long enough for most people to notice.

"So, did you?" she asked.

"Did I what?"

"Show her your scars."

"We're not talking about that."

She snickered, shaking her head. "It's because she'll never accept you. She'll never accept all your scars. She'll never love you for who you really are, Landon. She'll never love—"

"Stop," I whispered, pounding my hand against the table.

She pounded her hands against the table as well. "No. No. No. No!"

"Monica!"

"Landon!"

"You need to—"

"Why her?!" she screamed, tossing her hands up in the air in frustration.

"What?"

"Why…" Her voice cracked. "Her?" Her eyes watered and her body shook, and I knew it wasn't from whatever drug was invading her body. Her emotions were taking over, overwhelming her to the point that they had no other escape but to leak from her tear ducts. "Why not me? Why couldn't you fall in love with me?"

"Monica, don't do this. You know why that's never going to be a thing. You and I are toxic."

"Yeah, like *Romeo and Juliet*. Don't you see? I want to be your Juliet. I'm meant to be your Juliet, not her. She doesn't deserve you."

Lies.

I didn't deserve Shay. I didn't deserve her, and yet I couldn't stop craving her.

I didn't reply to Monica, because she was high and emotional. It was a pointless conversation. I just wished she would finish her sandwich and head home. I was tired of this ride Monica had been taking me on for the past few years. It was giving me motion sickness.

"So that's it, huh? You're just going to give me the silent treatment?" she hissed. "You're just going to ignore me? Well, screw you, Harrison!" She picked up the plate and threw it across the room, making it shatter against the wall.

There she was, angry Monica. Shocking.

"Okay," I muttered, standing up from my chair. "It's time for you to go now." I moved over to lift her from her chair, and she swatted my hand away.

"I don't need your help," she seethed, standing—and stumbling—on her own. "I don't need anyone's help."

She started walking toward the front door, and I followed, though not too closely.

As she stepped out on the porch, she turned to look at me. "Just to be clear, Landon, I wasn't your toxicity. I wasn't your poison. You were born sick like your fucked-up uncle, and anyone who comes near you gets infected with your disease. So, fuck you for judging me when you're the one who made me this way!" she cried.

I didn't say a word. She was too far gone for common sense.

She shoved my chest. "Eventually, you're going to snap. You're going to show your true colors. You're going to rage, and I hope your stupid Juliet witnesses it all—your lowest lows, the ones you put me through nonstop, you asshole. Your time is almost up. Tick tock, jerk."

She shoved me again, and I allowed it. She was hurting and angry and lost, and I understood all of those things. If I was forced to be her punching bag, I'd take her hits.

"Fight back," she demanded as she kept hitting me, kept pushing me, kept begging me. She was asking me to snap, to fall back into the darkness with her, to paint her shadows with my companionship, but I couldn't do it anymore. I couldn't dance our old dance, couldn't be who she wanted me to be anymore. I was changing, because Shay believed in my growth. She believed in me.

And I was starting to do the same.

"Fight, Landon!"

"No." My voice was controlled and solid.

She hit me a few more times, but I didn't crumble. I didn't fight back. I didn't break with her.

"Fine!" She finally stepped away and started down the steps. "Have fun with your stupid play and your stupid Juliet and your stupid make-believe fairy tale. But, spoiler alert, Romeo!" she shouted, her hands still gesturing all over dramatically. *"You both fucking die in the end!"*

She stomped away, back to her house, still cursing me and still up in flames.

I waited on the porch for her to get safely inside.

Later that night, when Monica's mom pulled the car into the driveway, I walked over to speak with her. Mrs. Cole wasn't the biggest fan of me, and to be fair, I wasn't a fan of hers either. She was a nasty woman who I'd witness belittle Monica's looks on the regular. Every crash diet Monica ever had, was due to her mother's orders. It must've been easy for Mrs. Cole to judge other people's bodies, seeing how hers was nearly all made at a plastic surgery clinic in Mexico.

"Mrs. Cole. Can I talk to you for a minute?" I asked.

She looked at me, seemingly already bothered by the fact I was speaking her way. Her eyes moved up and down as she studied me. Her gaze flicked upward. "What is it, boy?"

She knew my name. She just preferred to never use it.

"I wanted to let you know that I think your daughter may need some help. She's been getting into a bit of trouble, and she's struggling. I wanted to give you a heads up to see if—"

"Aren't you the one who used to smoke pot and get drunk with my Monica?" she barked, holding her purse tight to her side.

"Well, yes, but—"

"No buts needed. My daughter is fine, as long as you keep your toxic self away from her. I know you, Harrison boy. I've heard stories about your dark, dark soul. Keep away from my daughter, do you hear me? You're no good for her."

Was she even hearing what I was saying?

"Look, hate me all you want, but Monica is sick, and she needs her parents—"

"She has her parents. Don't come here telling me how to raise my daughter. She is fine. Now get off my driveway before I call the cops. If I see you anywhere near Monica again, trust me, there will be consequences."

She wouldn't listen to me. She couldn't get her head out of her own ass to realize that there was a big issue at hand. She couldn't deal with the possibility that she was slipping as a mother.

I left her place, then sent KJ a text message to cuss him out for selling to the most unstable teenage girl alive.

I walked back into my house. In the living room sat a huge grandfather clock that was ticking loudly. Monica was right about one thing: the ticking in my mind was growing louder and louder with each passing day as my birthday approached. I was working hard to avoid the explosion, though.

That night, I couldn't sleep, so I finally built up enough nerve to open the notebook Shay had given me to reveal my truths.

I read her question at the top of the page and felt a bit nervous about writing down my answer for her. Her handwriting was beautiful. The letters curved against one another and the ink danced across the lined notebook.

What makes you sad?

I didn't overthink my answer. I didn't wring my brain out trying to not sound a certain way, trying to not come off as a complete loser. I wrote my truths. Every single word held a piece of me, and the next day, I placed it in her locker.

Chapter Twenty-Two

Shay

THE NEXT DAY AT SCHOOL, I FOUND THE NOTEBOOK IN MY LOCKER. I quickly grabbed it and flipped to the first page where he'd written out his thoughts to me. I read his words over and over, wanting to drink in all the things that made Landon the person he was, and each time I read them, I felt myself falling a little more and more.

Chick,

What makes me sad? That seems like a loaded question, and one I'm not even sure how to attack it right off the bat. So, this may just be a lot of rambling, but whatever. This is what you wanted, right? My random messed-up thoughts.

The Bulls make me sad, and so does the crappy season they played this year. It makes me sad that I didn't get to experience the greatness that was Michael Jordan on the court, and I am left to only old videos of him playing. I didn't believe there was magic in sports until I watched those clips of him playing.

Ham makes me sad when he chews the heels of my Nike shoes. He only chews the left shoe, too, never the right. The least he could do is make the shoes evenly screwed up. The little bastard. If I didn't love that dog so much, I'd hate his freaking guts.

But then again, I'm guessing these aren't the kind of answers you were looking for. You seem like the kind of girl who wants deeper thoughts.

So, here goes.

Being alone makes me sad, and for a while I thought I'd get used to it. I've been alone for so long, and I thought the sad part of it all would disappear, but it stays. Every night, I sit in bed and loneliness swallows me whole. I struggle with sleeping and overthinking. It's a buzzkill, and I hate it.

Some day I hope I can get past it. Some day I hope I can fall asleep and be happy.

The whole being sad thing is exhausting. I'm tired. All the time. Have you ever been so young but felt so old? That's the kind of tired I am. I'm the ninety-years-old kind of tired, the kind of tired where everything aches right down to my bones.

This sounds real emo and I am seconds away from ripping this whole notebook apart and ditching this whole idea, so I am going to close it now and shut the hell up.

-Satan

I went to my next class, holding the notebook close to my chest, and instead of listening to the teacher, I read Landon's words over and over again, taking it all in, taking him all in. Then, I returned the notebook to his locker so he could respond to the other questions I left for him. From that point on, we exchanged that notebook back and forth. Reading his replies felt like a special passageway into Landon's heart, and based on the heaviness of his replies, I knew it meant a lot for him to share such a part of himself with me. I hoped writing was helping him, too, the same way words helped me. Getting one's thoughts down on paper can make the emotions easier to deal with sometimes. It's as if the written word is a great escape from being swallowed alive by one's own mind.

What's your favorite time of the year?

Chick,

I love the fall. There's something magical about watching the leaves shift colors and float down to the ground. It's like the trees are dying, only to come back to life in a few months. People seem happier around the fall, too. I haven't really figured out why, but maybe it's because they know the best holidays are right around the corner. Halloween, Thanksgiving, Christmas…it's like the tri-fecta of happiness.

Is it stupid that I love holidays? Mom never travels during the trifecta, so it's nice to have her around. She takes that holiday shit seriously—especially Christmas. It's like she's Mrs. Claus and she expects me to eat every cookie known to mankind. The only problem with that is my mother is a terrible baker. She thinks baking soda and baking powder are the same thing, which is beyond problematic. Still, I eat her nasty cookies because she has the biggest look of pride about the crap.

We sit in front of the table, watch crappy Hallmark movies that are all cliché, but between this notebook and me, I actually kind of like the corny shit, and we fall asleep under the Christmas tree lights.

My mom's missing my birthday this year.

Still a little sad about that. And by a little, I mean a lot.

For a long time, I felt like she was one of the only people who would never let me down when I needed her the most. But that's the thing about people, I guess—sometimes they end up letting you down.

Hopefully next holiday season she'll be around, though.

And I'll still eat her shitty cookies.

-Satan

What's your idea of a perfect day/date with a person?

Chick,

Sex. Smoking-hot, break-the-headboard kind of sex.
Is that the answer you were looking for?

If headboard breaking sex isn't involved, I guess my next idea of a perfect day would be sitting on the sofa, eating pizza, and watching a marathon of Friends. If someone likes the same television show as you, I think that means they are your soulmate.
-Satan

P.S. If you want my first idea of a perfect day to come true, you know where I live. My headboard is quite sturdy, but with enough determination, we could make dreams come true.

Blank page. Freestyle your thoughts.

Chick,

It's three in the morning, and I can't sleep tonight.
There's a thunderstorm pounding against the windows and the sound of the thunder is making my head hurt. I hate storms. I hate the way it sounds like it's drowning me. Of course, that could just be due to the fact that tomorrow is my birthday. I hate birthdays. Not all birthdays, but just my own. I feel like my birthday had been cursed from this point on, seeing how Lance died on that day. I kind of understand my mom running off to Paris. It must all be too hard for her. How can you celebrate a life without mourning a death? I want to hate her for not being here tomorrow, for choosing work over me, but an odd part of me gets it. I don't know how I'd feel about celebrating a birthday knowing that was the day my brother took his life.

I like to pretend I'd be different, though. I liked to think I'd tell my son or daughter that the world was a better place because they were there. I'd like to think I'd give them words of encouragement to push them into the direction of never blaming themselves. I'd like to think I'd love them the loudest because I knew they'd somewhat hate themselves.

But what do I know? It's hard to walk in someone else's shoes when they don't fit your feet. Maybe my parents are just doing the best they can. Maybe they are just trying to get through each day without falling apart.

I want to hate my uncle, too, for taking his life on my birthday. Though, I don't think he even knew it was my birthday. By the time he took his life, his mental state was so far gone.

My goal for tomorrow is to just get through it. Nothing more, nothing less. And then I'll wait another 365 days to do the same exact thing.

I wish I was born on leap year. Then I'd only have to go through this crap every four years.

Anyway, the highlight of this night was that you crossed my mind a lot. That has to count for something, right?

-Satan

We had rules about our notebook. We were never supposed to talk about what Landon had written inside. He wasn't supposed to spill his truths out in a verbal fashion, and I kept my word on that the best I could. Yet, that Friday when I read the words Landon had written in his notebook, I found my way to him. He was standing in the cafeteria, seconds away from picking up his lunch tray, and I darted toward him.

Without any words, I wrapped my arms around his frame and pulled him into the tightest hug known to mankind. Everyone in the cafeteria was watching, I was sure. Everyone was staring as Shay Gable wrapped her arms around her sworn enemy. Everyone looked on as Landon Harrison wrapped his arms around me, too.

He hugged me back.

Oh my gosh, he was hugging me back, and that made me tug on his body even harder. There was no way to tell where his heartbeats began and where mine ended. It was as if they were beating as one, as if we were two willows tangled up with each other.

For his birthday, he smelled like smoky oak and dressed like darkness.

My favorite version of him—the realest one.

"Happy birthday," I whispered, my head resting on his chest. I wasn't even sure he heard me. The words were so quiet as they rolled off my tongue.

He pulled me in closer, kissed the top of my head, and then rested his chin there. "Thank you, Chick," he said softly, his words cracking as if they were hard to get out.

"Always, Satan," I replied.

I think I meant that, too.

I think I meant always.

Chapter Twenty-Three

Landon

IT HAD BEEN THREE HUNDRED AND SIXTY-FIVE DAYS.

The Earth had orbited the sun over the past three hundred and sixty-five days.

The moon had risen over each of those three hundred and sixty-five days.

People had laughed, cried, and celebrated all sorts of occasions.

And Lance had missed all of it.

He'd missed the sunrises, the sunsets, the thunderstorms, and the clear days.

He'd missed my birthday.

My birthday.

I was eighteen years old.

Young and stupid but feeling old as shit.

I couldn't remember the last time I'd slept longer than thirty minutes—except for when Shay forced me to sleep. The past week had been a struggle, seeing how she didn't have her cell phone to call me late at night.

My head hurt from the lack of sleep, and no matter what I did, the circles under my eyes were still there, heavy and deep.

The hug she gave me in the cafeteria was more needed than she even knew. I was standing in the cafeteria while my mind was shouting at me, and I couldn't move. Then, along came Shay with her embrace. Maybe she knew, though. Maybe she had become such a professional at reading me that whenever I was about to break, she knew to be there for me.

I found the notebook back in my locker by sixth hour with her next question for me: *What makes you happy?*

I left the page blank.

After the school day, the fantastic Four (+Raine) tried to talk me into hanging out at Hank's house to celebrate my birthday, but I lied and told them I had plans with my dad. I didn't feel like being surrounded by people that night. My mind was too loud, and I didn't want to be the dramatic buzzkill for my friends.

I tried my best to not think about the fact that my parents weren't there. Mom called first thing in the morning, which was late at night in Paris. Then she called again and again.

"*I love you and I love you,*" she repeated each time. "*I'm so sorry, honey, I promise I'll explain soon. Happy birthday. Please call me. Please text. Please. Okay, I love you, Landon. I'll be home soon. I love you.*" I didn't answer her calls, didn't feel like hearing her excuses for why she wasn't around, but I sent her a text, because fuck me, I was pathetic and didn't want her to worry too much about me that day.

Me: I'm okay. Hope you're okay, too.

I would have bet that text made her cry. Mom was always so easy to make cry.

Dad hadn't called at all. He didn't even have to wish me a 'happy' birthday, because it was hard to be happy on a day like today, but a simple 'birthday' greeting would've meant the world to me.

I went home, hung with Ham, and played video games as long as I could. I heard things being tossed at my window, but my shades were drawn. I knew it was Monica trying to get my attention, but I didn't have the energy to give her any of me that afternoon. I didn't have the energy to give her any of me ever again.

When my doorbell rang around six p.m., I grumbled as I went to answer it. I was one hundred percent certain it was Monica coming to cuss me out for not answering her window call, but to my surprise, there stood Shay with a big box in her hands.

"Hey you." She smiled wide, and I was falling.

I was falling so deeply in love with her, and this bet of ours was going to come to a crashing end due to me losing.

"What are you doing here?" I asked, raising an eyebrow. "Aren't you grounded?"

"Yes, but I snuck out."

"Chick…" I sighed, feeling a knot in my gut. She wasn't the type of girl to sneak out. She wasn't the type of girl to break rules, or to skip school, or to lie. And now, she was doing all of those things.

Why did I feel like my badness was rubbing off on her a little too much?

"Are you going to invite me in?" she asked, still smiling. "Or am I just going to have to stand here like a dork with this box in my hands?"

I stepped to the side.

She walked right in, heading toward the kitchen.

"What's in the box?" I asked.

"A surprise for later," she said, opening the fridge and sliding it inside. "No peeking." She then turned around and I was still falling, falling, falling… "I figured we could hang out tonight and we should order pizza and watch *Friends*."

A perfect day with a perfect girl.

I am falling in love with you…

"For sure."

The nerves in my stomach were so loud, and I swore I would've been surprised if she didn't hear my heart beating wildly.

We sat on the living room couch, and I was so damn thankful that she appreciated the gem that was *Friends* more than her grandmother. Every time she laughed at something Joey said, I'd capture her smile in my mind. Every time she chewed on her T-shirt whenever Ross and Rachel were on the screen together, I'd capture her beautiful eyes.

"You always stare at people when they aren't looking?" she joked, peeling a pepperoni off her pizza.

"Only you. Only ever you."

She turned to me, seemingly surprised by my words. She placed her pizza down, wiped her hands on a napkin, and moved in closer to me. Her finger traced my lips as her eyes studied them as they parted. Then, she placed her forehead against mine and closed her eyes.

Her mind was moving, yet still, I couldn't hear it.

"A penny for your thoughts," I whispered. "A nickel for your time...a quarter for your heart..." I inhaled deeply. "A dollar to make you mine."

"What are we doing, Landon?" she asked, her voice so low and shaky.

"I don't know."

"Is this still a game?"

"I don't know..." That was true. I didn't know if we were still doing this because of the bet, or if this was becoming something real for the both of us. I didn't know if she was beginning to feel things the way I felt them, too. I didn't know if she was falling, falling, falling...

"It scares me a little," she confessed. "Whatever's happening in my heart when I'm around you...it scares me."

"It scares me too, but I know one thing for certain," I said, placing my fingers beneath her chin and lifting it so we were looking into each other's eyes.

"What's that?"

"I am going to love loving you as much as I loved hating you."

She kissed me, and the last sleeping part of my soul finally woke up as she fell against my lips.

I tasted her heaven as I fed her my sins.

"Can we go to your room?" she asked, and I tensed up a little.

"No good comes from us being in each other's bedrooms, Chick, and if I take you up there, I'll want to—"

"Break your headboard?" She smirked.

I chuckled. "Exactly. And—"

She cut me off again, this time placing her mouth against mine. Then she whispered her words against my lips. "Can we go to your room?" she repeated, giving me small kisses afterward.

I felt myself getting hard from her words, and I wrapped her in my arms. "Are you sure?" I asked.

"Yes," she promised.

I lifted her up into my arms and headed upstairs to my bedroom. When we reached the room, I hurried and got Ham out of there, closing the door behind me. The bonus to living a life like the one I lived? I knew no one was going to barge in on us that night.

I placed her on my bed, and I stood in front of her. She looked up at me with doe eyes wide with wonder, and I watched as she studied my body, her eyes scanning up and down.

"Nervous?" I asked.

"Yes," she replied.

"You still want to?"

She grasped the hem of her shirt and pulled it over her head, tossing it to the side of the room. "Yes."

Why the hell was I wearing jeans around her again? My bulge was going to explode out of my pants any second now. She went to move my shirt up, and I paused, tensing up. "Wait, Chick…" I hesitated. I shut my eyes. I took in a sharp inhale, and she stopped.

"What is it?"

"I, um…" I turned away from her and my hands formed fists. I could hear Monica in my head, shouting at me. *Has she seen your scars?* "It's just…"

"Hey. It's okay. You can talk to me," she said, her voice so reassuring.

I nodded once, knowing she meant it, but I knew words wouldn't fix it. It wasn't something that had to be said; it was something that needed to be shown.

I kept my back turned to her, lifted the edges of my shirt, and pulled it over my head. I revealed the markings that raced up and down my arms. Cuts from my past panics. Cuts from my messed-up brain. Cuts from my pained heart.

Her gasp was loud and clear. "Oh my gosh, Landon. What happened to you?!" she said, moving over toward me to examine the marks to my skin. Each mark stood for a time I lost myself. Each mark showed my pain and struggles against my skin.

My scars were healed, but still they were redder than the other parts of my skin. They raced in different directions. Sideways, up and down, slices of me exposed for her to see.

I closed my eyes, knowing they probably terrified her. Each day I showered, my fingers would brush against the memories of my mind.

She probably thought I was the worst kind of damaged goods, unworthy of love, unworthy of anything and anyone. Who could love someone with a mind as heavy as mine? Who could want someone with such ugly markings of their pain resting against their skin?

"My, um..." I took a breath, still unable to voice it—my truth. "Look, I get if you don't want to hook up after seeing this, after seeing how fucked up I am in my head, but I figured I should show you before just freaking you out and taking off my shirt and—"

A chill raced down my spine as her fingers moved across the markings on my forearms. My shoulders rounded forward, and she traced the markings. My head lowered and I shut my eyes. I'd never felt so weak, so exposed...so real.

"You're sad?" she whispered.

"Yes."

"How sad?"

"Very sad."

"How often?"

I swallowed hard. "All the time." That truth was the hardest to tell. "My uncle was sad, too. He kept his hurting to himself. I saw it sometimes. I saw it, and I didn't do anything about it. Not that I could. But, I should've tried harder. If I'd tried harder, maybe he wouldn't have..." I took a breath. I lowered my head. "I found his journals after he passed away. He had a lot of dark thoughts. He was so lonely...but the scariest thing about reading his words was how much they matched my own mind, and that scares me. It scares me how much of my uncle I see inside of myself."

"You're not him, Landon," she whispered, and I nodded slowly.

"Yeah...but what if I'm worse? What if my pieces are so messed up that I won't ever be able to pull myself up? What if I end up like him?"

"You won't."

"How do you know?"

"Because I won't let that happen."

I shut my eyes. I tried to push back my emotions. I tried to understand why she hadn't yet run away from the mess that was me.

"Can I ask you something that I asked you before?" she whispered, her voice low, controlled, perfect.

"Yes."

"Are you depressed?"

The tears rolled down my cheeks, and I didn't even try to wipe them away. I nodded slowly, feeling as if there was a bomb inside my chest that was seconds away from exploding. "Yes."

"Okay." She sighed and moved in closer. "Okay."

That was all she said. She didn't run. She didn't tell me my depression was wrong. She didn't shy away.

That was exactly what I needed.

I just needed someone to stay.

Her mouth fell against the scars and she gave them small kisses. She made sure to kiss every single one, before moving to my cheeks and kissing my tears away.

"You are more than the story these scars tell, Landon. You are more than your uncle. You are more than your depression. You are kind." She kissed my chest. "You are strong." She kissed my neck. "You are intelligent." She kissed my palms. "You are talented." She kissed my thumbs. "You are beautiful." She kissed the corners of my eyes. "And this world needs you. I know those are just words, and you might not even believe them, but I am going to tell you them every single day, just as a reminder when you need it."

She kept telling me things about myself as she kissed every piece of me. For every scar, she gave five more compliments, which she called my truths. For every pained memory, she promised me a better one for the future. She kissed my scars and called them beautiful.

"Landon?" she said softly, pressing her body against mine.

"Yes?"

"Can I have you tonight?"

Yes...yes...a thousand times yes.

"Yes, but the real question is: can I have you?"

"All of me," she promised. "All of me is yours." She nodded, so sure, and her sureness made my eyes want to water over with emotion all over again. I didn't allow them to, though, because now my mind was on the best birthday gift I was ever going to receive: her.

I turned off the light, still uncomfortable with her seeing my scars. The only light that shone was a flood of moonlight coming through the windows.

First, I finished undressing her, and she hurried to take off my jeans. The freedom my cock felt when they were off was unbelievable. She studied my hard-on, in amazement, almost, as if still unsure what to do with it. Her finger trailed along the fabric of my boxers, and I shivered at her touch, shutting my eyes.

"For you," I muttered. "Only ever you."

She went to take off my boxers and began to lower herself to her knees, but I stopped her. "No," I ordered, turning her around and laying her down on my bed. "You first."

I got down on my knees, spread her legs, and returned to my newest favorite pastime—making Shay's knees quiver in pleasure.

She twisted her hands in the sheets as I tongued her, moaning as I sucked her, crying out in desire as I pleased her. Each time she thrust her hips up toward my face, I worked harder at her clit. Each time she tried to pull away, I pinned her down a little more. I wasn't going to stop until she exploded against my tongue in a way she didn't know bodies could release. I wanted to taste all of her against my mouth. I wanted to drown in her and not come up for air.

"Landon!" she screamed my name into my pillow as her body released what I'd been craving, and I greedily licked her clean as my cock sat hard throbbing between my legs. "Oh my gosh, Landon, that was... that was..." Her words faded and I smirked.

"Good?" I asked.

"So. Freaking. Good." Her breaths were heavy and she pulled me up to her mouth. I hovered over her body, my eyes dancing across her frame, and I loved every inch I was able to see.

She pressed her forehead against mine. "Now, I want you, all of you, inside of me."

I hesitated for a moment, knowing what a big deal this was for her. "Are you sure?"

"Yes, but..." She paused her slight movements in the bedsheets and looked up at me with an intense, emotional stare. There was a gentle fear that sat uncomfortably in her brown eyes. Her vulnerabilities were loud and clear as she lay naked in my bed. I knew that had to be scary for her—allowing me to see her in such a state. I had a feeling not many people saw that side of her personality.

"Can you do something for me?" she whispered as she placed her hands against my bare chest.

"Yes. Anything."

She lowered my lips to hers and slipped her soft syllables straight into my mind. "Go slow."

I didn't know if she meant go slow with her body or with her heart.

So I took my time with both.

We became one in that moment, our hearts beating in the same way. When I entered her, she cried out, and I tried my best to take it easy, to take my time, to give her all of me at a pace that worked for all of her.

I loved it. I loved how she felt. I loved how she moaned.

I...loved...her.

I couldn't say it then. If I knew anything, it was that you couldn't tell a girl you loved her during the first time you had sex. Rule 101 of not being a douchebag.

But I loved her. I knew I did. How could I not?

Maybe I always had, even when I hated her. Loving Shay came as easy as the wind. It pushed through my system and left me completely breathless.

I was making love to her, and she didn't even know it...she didn't know my feelings for her, she didn't know how she woke up the sleeping parts of me. She hadn't known how her existence made me better.

So, I made sure she felt it. With every thrust, kiss, and moan, I fed her my love. I filled her up inside, hoping she knew, hoping she'd feel it, hoping she'd feel my feelings for her. Based on the way she opened her eyes and looked my way? Based on the way she caressed my cheek? The way she whispered my name?

I think she felt it, too.

I think she felt the love.

When we finished, we collapsed against each other, completely raw, and exposed, and real.

So very real.

"That...was..." She breathed out.

"Amazing." I finished.

We didn't say anything for a while. We lay in bed with nothing but the sound of our heavy breaths and wild heartbeats.

"We should get dressed," she finally said, shivering a little. "I'm getting a little cold, plus we still have our movie marathon to do."

I agreed, even though a part of me wanted to lie beside her for the rest of forever.

We went back to the living room and watched more episodes of *Friends* before turning on *Home Alone* and *Pulp Fiction*, followed by *Breakfast at Tiffany's* and *Sabrina*. Two movies for me, two movies for her.

We laughed, too, which was something I thought I'd never be able to do on my birthday, but Shay had a way about her. She was able to make me laugh even when I thought it was impossible. Somehow, she managed to return my wild heart to a calmness only she'd ever been able to provoke. She made the darkest days feel like the sun.

It was well past midnight, and I knew she should've been heading home. I knew she was going to be in a shit ton of trouble with her parents come morning, but I was going to be selfish. I was going to ask her for something I probably didn't have the right to ask her for.

"Shay?"

"Yes?"

"Stay with me tonight?" I choked on the words yet still got them out of my soul. I wasn't above begging her to stay with me. I wasn't above falling to my knees and requesting she stay by my side. All I knew was, whenever she was near me, I felt a little bit better. I felt a little less alone.

She didn't bat an eye at my request. She didn't shake her head in dismissal. She simply stood, held her hands out toward me, and pulled me to stand. "Let's go to bed."

We didn't say another word that night. But when we reached my bedroom, I pulled her into a kiss. I pressed my lips against hers and whispered a lie. "I hate you."

She smiled against my lips. "I hate you, too."

"Okay, now kiss me and take off your clothes."

She did as I said, and I hurried and stripped down, too.

I went to shut off the lights, and she placed a hand on my hand, shaking her head. "No, Landon...please..." She stood on her tiptoes and kissed my lips as she whispered, "I want to see you. I want to see all of you. Love me with the lights on."

Our bodies rocked against each other, and I took my time with her once again. I did as she'd requested earlier, going slow. I'd never had sex like that before. I'd never had it with emotions, with feelings, with truths.

She now knew the parts of me I'd kept hidden for so long, and still...

She stayed.

That night, I fell asleep with her in my arms, and I knew there was no part of me that deserved her. But still.

She stayed.

She was gone when I woke up, and it made sense.

I'd slept past noon. It was the best night's sleep I'd had in years.

I walked down to the living room, and everything was spotless from the night before. The pizza boxes and the snacks we'd had were all tossed into the trash cans.

On the refrigerator was a note: *Open me.*

I pulled the fridge open, and there was the big box Shay had brought, sitting on the middle shelf. I pulled it out and opened it to find eight perfectly frosted cupcakes, each one with a letter written on it.

I HATE YOU

A note was next to that, and I read it over and over again.

Happy Birthday, ya filthy animal.
-Chick
P.S. Don't worry, I still hate you, but every birthday boy deserves a cupcake.

I picked up a cupcake and took a big bite.

Damn. It tasted absolutely amazing.

Fuck, Chick.

I hate you, too.

Chapter Twenty-Four

Shay

MOM AND DAD SAT IN FRONT OF ME ON THE LIVING ROOM COUCH. They stared my way as if they didn't even know who I was anymore, but to be fair, I stared at them the same way. I missed Mima being at the house when I got home. I missed having her laughter, her warmth, and her wisdom so nearby.

"You're grounded," Mom said, her eyes burning with emotion.

"Tell me something I don't know," I muttered, crossing my arms.

"Don't talk to your mother like that," Dad snapped, pointing my way. "You've been acting out, and it's not okay. So, from now on, we are putting our foot down. You don't sneak out anymore, Shannon Sofia. You do not speak back to us with that attitude. You don't bring boys back to our household, and you definitely do not stay out until morning. Do you understand me? Do you hear what I'm saying?"

I didn't say a word, and my silence seemed to piss him off.

He stood up and approached me. "I said, do you hear me?"

I gritted my teeth together. "Loud and clear."

"Why are you doing this, Shay? You've never acted out before. You've always been a good girl," Mom said.

"Yes, tell us why. It makes no sense that you're acting out. We don't understand why you're making things more difficult for this household," Dad added in, and that made my skin crawl.

I huffed. "You're kidding, right? I'm the one making this house difficult?"

"I don't like the tone, Shannon Sofia," Dad hissed, his hands gripping into fists.

"Yeah, well. I don't like that you're a liar."

"Listen, you guys," Mom started, but I cut her off.

I sat up straighter. "Are we going to have a family meeting about you dealing again?" I shot at my father. "Or are we going to pretend that that's not a thing?"

"Shay!" Mom snapped at me.

"What? I don't see why we skirt around the subject. Isn't that why Mima moved out? Or why you kicked her out? For speaking the truth. If we are going to scold people for acting out, maybe we should start with Dad's behavior."

That pushed him over the edge. His clenched fists tightened, and he shot up from his seat. "You have a lot of nerve, little girl," he barked, flashes of anger in his eyes. He took a step toward me, and Mom leaped up to stand, stepping in front of him to block his advances.

She placed her hands on his shoulders. "Stop, Kurt," she ordered.

He grimaced and his eyes pierced into me for a second before he took a step back. "Go to your room," he ordered. "And don't fucking think about leaving it until we say so."

I hated him. I hated how he pushed Mima away. I hated Mom for allowing it. I hated that our house felt nothing like a home anymore. It felt more like a prison cell, and I wanted to break free.

I did as they said. I went to my room, and I lay in my bed, with no regrets of being there for Landon. He'd needed somebody last night, and I was glad I had been there for him when he needed me the most.

When Monday came, the first and only thing on my mind was Landon. My second thought was Monica, who I found creeping through my locker.

"What are you doing?" I barked.

She took a step back and slammed the locker shut. "Oops, wrong locker," she hissed, giving me a tight grin.

"Why do I feel like that's a lie? What were you doing going through my stuff?"

"Chill, Shay. It's not like you have anything of interest in that thing." She pulled out a tube of lipstick and started applying it. "I saw you were hanging out with Landon for his birthday. That's cute. What did you two do? Play Checkers? Chutes and Ladders?"

"That's none of your business."

She tilted her head and studied me. "Did he show you his scars?"

"Like I said...that's none of your business."

"Ohh," she cooed, tapping her manicured nail against her lips. "He did, and let me guess, you slept with him, too. Poor, broken Landon needed a good lay for his birthday, and easy Shay was right there to give it to him."

"What's your problem with me, Monica? What have I ever done to you?"

"That's easy—you took something that was mine, and I want it back."

"Landon isn't yours."

She huffed. "He's more mine than he'll ever be yours. I get it, Shay. You want to believe Landon isn't the same shithead he was last year, want to think he has a new lease on life, but face the facts. He's a monster, just like his uncle, and I wouldn't be surprised if he ended up six feet under, too."

"You're disgusting," I told her.

"Yeah." She flipped her hair again. "I guess I am, but at least I'm not pretending to be something I'm not like Landon is. It's all an act, Chick, and soon enough, the game you two are playing will come crashing to an end. Enjoy him while you can. Soon enough he'll come back to me. He always does."

I hated that she called me Chick, as if she had a right to use the nickname Landon had created for me. I hated that she felt as if she had a right to something that was so clearly mine and Landon's. I hated that she pushed it off her tongue like venom to sting me.

I hated her.

Even though I had my opinions about Landon, I knew I'd never truly hated him, not to my core. I knew there was something genuine there, something somewhat flirtatious, but the truth behind the hate was pretty loose. A strong dislike, perhaps.

But Monica?

Oh my gosh, I hated her. I hated her in a real, deep-rooted way, more so than I'd ever hated anyone before—other than my own father. Monica wasn't just cruel; she was pure evil. She did things to hurt people simply for her enjoyment. She went after people just because she could. She destroyed lives because she was bored. I hated the smugness of her personality, too, and how she seemed so confident she could get away with just about anything because of who she was and the money and status she came from. It bothered me to my core that she was so confident in her ability to wreck lives, in her ability to break people.

But she wasn't going to get away with threatening me or trying to scare me.

For the longest time, I'd stayed out of her way and hadn't pushed back because I knew how she was. I knew the ugliness that lived beneath her manicured nails and fake eyelashes. I knew the beast in her soul and how it attacked.

Now, I wasn't afraid to unleash her beast, because it turned out I had a monster inside me, too, at least I did when it came to the things I cared about the most, and Landon was now one of those things.

"Aren't you a little old to be messing with people? Landon doesn't want you anymore, Monica, and I know you don't want him either. I'm not even sure you ever did. Why don't you just leave him alone? Leave us alone. You're going off to college next year anyway. Why can't you just let people be? We're not bothering you, so why do you have to bother us?"

"Because I don't like you, Gable. Okay? I don't like your goody-two-shoes personality, and for the longest time, Landon hated it too. Besides, just because I don't want him, doesn't mean I'd let some mutt have my leftovers. So I'm going to give you this fair warning: stay away from Landon, Shay, or you will regret it."

"You don't scare me. There's nothing you can do to me. I'm not some kind of puppet in your world that you can manipulate, Monica. If I want to talk to Landon, I will. There is nothing you can do to hurt me."

"Oh, Chick," she hissed, leaning in close. "You have no clue how bad I could burn you. Don't push me. I will destroy your whole life in one fell swoop."

"Why are you like this, Monica?"

"Because I can be," she stated. She arched a brow. "Maybe you and I should make a bet of our own. What do you think about that? I bet you I can ruin your life before opening night of your stupid show."

"I'd like to see you try."

"Game on, Shay. Don't expect me to play like Landon where I show you sympathy because he thinks more with his dick than his brain. Your life is officially in my hands. The countdown is on. Get ready to burn."

She walked off, and I dashed to my locker, opened it up, and searched for whatever it was Monica had been trying to find...but it seemed nothing was missing. Everything was in its place, and I was left dazed and confused.

I jumped out of my skin when I felt a hand land on my lower back.

"Hey," Landon said, tossing his hands up in surrender. "You're a bit jumpy."

"Sorry. Just tired."

"Did you get in a lot of trouble over the weekend with your parents?"

"Oh, you have no clue, but it was worth it. No regrets."

He smiled, and oh gosh, I loved when he did that. Then he glanced down the hallway and raised an eyebrow. "What were you talking about with Monica?"

"Oh, nothing," I said, closing my locker and securing it. "Nothing of importance anyway." He looked at me with concern, but I shrugged it off. "Walk me to class?"

"Of course."

As we walked together, he made me laugh, and just like that, Monica was nothing but a fleeting thought in my mind.

Chapter Twenty-Five

Landon

"WHAT IS THIS?" I ASKED MONICA AS SHE STOOD ON MY FRONT porch with notebooks in her grip.

"It's everything you need to know about your pretty, pretty princess. Or, more like everything she knows about *you*."

She held them out toward me, and I began flipping through them, reading words that were obviously written by Shay.

Words about me...words that were very negative about me. She called me closed-off, mean, a monster. She said I pushed people away, and I kept things to myself. She called me fake and said I lived a life of lies.

She said she hated me.

She wrote that a lot.

I hate Landon Harrison.

Underlined, highlighted, and written dozens of time.

But everything was dated before the bet happened. She was writing about me before I let her in, and I didn't have a problem with that. From Shay's point of view at that time, everything was spot on.

I *was* a monster. I *was* mean. I *was* fake. I *did* live a life of lies.

Yet all of that changed after we made the bet. That was before she opened my eyes, and melted my heart. Everything she'd written in those notebooks had shifted, because Shay allowed me to be real for the first time ever in my life.

"Where's the rest of it?" I asked.

"What?"

I flipped to the end of one of the notebooks and showed the edge, remainders of the pages that had been ripped out. "Where are the rest of the pages?"

She shifted in place. "What does it matter? Didn't you read the shit she said about you? She thinks you're awful."

"*Thought*," I corrected. "She thought I was awful, and she was right. What was the lie in her words?"

Monica parted her lips to speak but nothing came out.

I cleared my throat and shrugged my left shoulder. "We need to stop this, Monica. Whatever this is, it needs to end. We're never going back to what we were before, okay? And please, leave Shay alone. If anything, she's making my life better."

"You're really going to do it, aren't you?" Monica asked. "You're really going to choose Shay?"

"I'll choose her if she chooses me."

In that moment, I saw something in Monica I hadn't seen in a long time. She wasn't angry. She wasn't vicious. She was sad—maybe even sadder than me.

Her lips parted as a whisper escaped her. "Then who's going to choose me?"

I didn't know how to answer that.

I didn't know what to do to make her happy. Truth was, people had to find their own way to happiness. It was an independent journey, and I was still trying to figure it out for myself.

"I think you need to start choosing yourself."

She wrapped her arms around her body, and tears rolled down her cheeks. "Just remember when I crash, it's your fault because you refused to catch me. You're going to ruin her," she promised. "Just like you ruined me."

"I didn't ruin you, Monica. Life broke you, not me. A bit of advice?" I offered.

"Advice from Landon Harrison. This should be comical."

I crossed my arms and nodded once. "Talk to someone about what happened to you. Someone who can help you. A therapist, a counselor, hell, even Mrs. Levi. She helped me more than she knows. Just stop keeping all this shit locked up in your head. That's how it morphs into something even heavier. Talk about it. Find someone you trust, and let them in. It just can't be me anymore. We're no good for each other, but you deserve help. You deserve more than this bullshit life."

Her lips parted, but no words came out. She wiped her eyes, turned on her heels, and walked away.

She left that afternoon, and for the first time, I finally felt as if the two of us were finished with our final chapter. It was clear to her that I wasn't going to revisit the past toxic life that we used to share.

When you stopped allowing toxins into your system, it meant getting rid of certain types of people in your life, too. Addictions didn't only come in the form of alcohol or narcotics. Some of the worst addictions in one's life could be the people allowed into it. I'd learned to be very selective about who I allowed into my world. It turned out, you didn't need a big circle of people to be content. You simply needed the right people.

The days passed by fast, and before I knew it, we were a few weeks out from the end of the year, which meant, it was almost showtime for Romeo and Juliet. The week before the play's opening weekend, we had a parents' night event where they came out to watch the performance. We used our parents as a test run before putting on the show. I didn't even bother telling my parents to come. I was still butt-hurt about them both missing my birthday, and seeing how they'd been lately, I doubted they would've shown up.

Needless to say, everyone else was extremely excited about having an audience. I supposed I was happy about it too. We'd been performing for Mr. Thymes for so long now that it felt a bit stale. I headed to the theater to get ready for the performance as everyone else was chatting and excited backstage.

Shay hurried over to me, and she had the biggest smile on her face. "Hey! How are you?"

"Nervous as ever," I replied.

She grinned even bigger. "Good. My parents are up front, and my dad wanted to meet Romeo before the show if you're up for it." She grimaced a little. "He knows about you being in my bedroom but don't be scared. He's nothing more than a liar, and we don't really care what he thinks anymore."

"Yeah, for sure."

We walked up to the front of the auditorium, and when we made it to Shay's parents, my heart completely sank in my chest.

"Mom, Dad, this is Landon," Shay said, introducing us.

I was going to vomit. I was going to vomit all over the freaking theater.

My eyes stayed on them, and I couldn't have looked away if I wanted to. Well, I could have looked away from Camila, but not Shay's father.

Her father's name was Kurt.

KJ for short, I assumed.

I saw it in his eyes, the panic that fell over him, the sweat that beaded along his forehead. I would have bet his hands were clammy and a million thoughts were shooting through his head the same way they were flying through mine.

No, really.

What the actual fuck?

He cleared his throat. "Landon, right?" He held his hand out toward me—his sweaty, nasty, guilty hand. "I'm Kurt, Shay's father."

No fucking shit, asshole.

I gripped his hand tightly and shook it.

"I hope you two have a great show tonight." He stepped back and crossed his arms. "I hear you've been working really hard."

I didn't say a word because my mind was on speed. I thought of every conversation I'd ever had with the man in front of me, tracing back every single word of his dialogue, and one fact stood out strongly to me.

It was the one thing he spoke about almost every time I saw him with my friends.

His daughters.

Daughters—plural. More than one.

As far as Shay was concerned, she was his one and only, and now there I stood, knowing the fact that her father, the man she looked up to more than anything, was a lying scumbag living a double life.

I felt nauseous. I wanted to shout from the rooftop what I knew. I wanted to express how messed up the whole situation that was unfolding in front of me was. I wanted to rip KJ's eyes out for ruining the kind of good thing so many people would've killed for, for ruining his family.

Family.

I would've fucking killed for a family unit.

Shay smiled and stepped forward. "We should probably get backstage and get ready for the show," she suggested, nodding in my direction.

My eyes were still glued on KJ, who was smiling brightly as if he hadn't just been caught in the biggest lie of the century.

"Landon?" Shay said softly, lightly shaking my shoulder, knocking me out of my trance.

I shook my head. "Yeah?"

"We should go get ready?" She said it like a question, tilting her head with concern in her eyes. Concern...Shay was always concerned for everyone around her, always so caring, always so giving...

How had she, the kindest, most giving person in the world, come from such a monster?

I scratched the back of my neck and took a step backward. "Yeah, sure. Okay."

I mumbled a goodbye to Shay's parents and wandered off toward the dressing rooms. Shay hurried behind me and grabbed my arm.

"Hey, you okay?" She said it with those sincere eyes that always shone in her face.

"Yeah, sorry, just a little out of it."

"Is it because you just met my dad? I know he can be a bit intimi-dating, but—"

I shook my head. "No, it's not that. Just first performance nerves."

She stretched her lips into a grin. "Oh my gosh, of course. I'm so stupid. It's your first time performing in front of an audience. I get that nervous energy, but you have to use it to fuel your show. Okay? Use that energy to launch your first scene. Feed into it and let it help you put on your best show possible." She leaned in and kissed my cheek before grabbing my hand and squeezing. "You got this, Landon. You're going to be amazing. I have to go get ready, but break a leg tonight."

"You too. Go ahead..." I smirked a little and nodded. "Break two." I winked, and her cheeks went rosy.

She walked away, taking her light with her as she left, leaving me sitting in the dark with information I didn't have a clue how to deal with. I didn't know how to process what I'd seen, what I knew.

KJ, the asshole who fed teenagers drugs, was Shay's father.

KJ, the asshole who had another daughter, which meant Shay had a sister she had no idea existed.

Even if Shay didn't know it, her worst nightmare had come to life, and I was the only one who possessed that information.

The show went on, as shows always did. I delivered all my lines, hit my cues, and when it came time for me to kiss Shay, my lips fell against hers. The parents howled and applauded at the end of the performance and brought flowers for their kids to celebrate the show. All I could think was how I needed to get out of there. How I needed to skip past greeting anyone and head home where I could collect my thoughts.

When Shay stopped my hasty exit by grabbing my arm in the hall-way, I knew I couldn't keep running.

"Hey, you were amazing tonight." She smiled and stepped forward. "Mima came to the show, and we are going to get ice cream. You're more than welcome to come if you want."

I scratched the back of my neck and took a step backward. "Nah, I think I'm going to call it a night. I want to brush up on some of the scenes before opening night."

"Are you kidding?" Shay laughed. "You can't get much better than that. It was a perfect performance."

I shrugged. "You know what they say about artists—"

"We are our worst critics," KJ finished, walking up behind his daughter.

I wanted to punch him square in the face.

"Yeah. Well, it was nice seeing you all." *Except for you, asshole.* "Shay, I'll see you back at school on Monday." I walked off quickly before she could reply. I didn't look back until I was a few feet away from my car. I stared at Shay and her family walking out of the auditorium with the brightest smiles on their faces. Shay was very chatty, and her father was taking in all of her words like he wasn't this double-life-living scum.

I thought my father was bad news, but compared to KJ, Ralph Harrison was looking like a damn saint.

"Landon." A voice called my way, and I tensed up as I heard it. I turned around to see Mom standing there with a bouquet of flowers in her hands. I wasn't certain I could've been any more confused about life that day, but there I was, confused about fucking life.

"What are you doing here? Shouldn't you be in Rome or something?" I snapped, still obviously hurt by her abandonment at my birthday.

"I landed earlier today, and Mrs. Levi told me about parent's night. The show...you..." Her eyes watered as her hands grew shaky. She looked broken-down. Sad, even. And even though I was working really hard to hate her, I still wanted to walk over and wrap her in my arms to make sure she was okay.

Damn.

I wondered when that would go away. I wondered when I'd stop being a mama's boy and be strong enough to hate her.

Never.

I'd never hate my mother.

"You were amazing," she said. "You were absolutely astonishing on that stage, Land. What you did was beyond words. I didn't know you had that in you, but then again it makes sense. I always knew you'd be good at whatever you decided to do. I'm so proud of you."

I didn't say anything because my mind was still spinning. I still wanted to hug her like the fool I was, I still wanted to hate her, but currently I was so happy to hear that she was proud of me.

"You missed my birthday," I shot at her, and I hoped the bitterness of my tone hit her heart.

"Yes…I know."

"I needed…" I shut my eyes and took deep inhales. "I needed you, and you weren't there."

I never admitted to needing anything or anyone, because I thought it would've made me weak. Yet there I was—weak, broken, and still in need of that fucking hug.

"I needed you, Mom, and you still got on that plane and left. Didn't you know? Didn't you know I needed you?"

"I did," she said. She lowered her head and stared at the parking lot pavement.

"That's it? That's all you can give me? Because honestly, I'm going to need a lot more than that."

"Landon…your father and I…he…we're…" She swallowed hard and looked back up to me. "Your father is leaving me."

Wait…what?

She nervously shifted around in her shoes. "We've been struggling for some time now, ever since Lance passed away. We fought a lot over my brother's death, and he blamed me for your struggles for allowing Lance to stay with us all those years."

"That's bullshit."

"Sometimes I wonder if he's right. Sometimes I wonder about the mistakes I've made raising you around my brother, knowing of his mental struggles."

"Lance was a good man, Mom. He taught me a lot of good. Life was better with him around. With you both around."

A weighted sigh slipped through her lips. "It's good to hear that, Landon. You have no clue. But, your father isn't in love with me anymore and doesn't wish to continue in this marriage. He said he doesn't feel as if we are a right fit, therefore he's leaving me. It's been in the works for a while now. I've been struggling, trying to find my footing. When I married your father, I thought it would be forever. So, when he gave me a prenup, I signed it without a moment's thought. But...he's taking everything, Landon. He's leaving me with nothing. That's why I was in Hawaii, meeting with Katie's divorce lawyer. Then, the girls were helping use their connections to land me stylist jobs. That's why I started back working. I needed some kind of income."

"He's taking everything?"

"Yes. Every cent. That's why I was so curious about if he was messing around with April, because of a clause in the prenup. If he cheated, I would've at least not lost everything. I would've received income which I could've used toward your college funds."

I arched an eyebrow. "Toward my college?"

"Yes. I know how much you don't want to go into law next fall, but your father is determined that you do for his own selfish reasons. I don't want that for you, though. I've lived under your father's shadow for so long, I don't want that for you. I want to be able to provide for you and give you the income to help with you going into the major of your choice. That's why when these jobs came up, I had to take them. I knew I couldn't lose out on such a big lump sum of money that could've been used to help you."

She was thinking of me. After all these weeks I'd spent being upset with her, it turned out she was thinking of me the whole time. She wasn't abandoning me—she was fighting for me. She wasn't going on these luxury trips around the world, she was hustling hard to provide for me.

"Why didn't you tell me?"

"The lawyer said it would be best to get all my ducks in a row before bringing you into it. They didn't want your involvement pushing your father to be more vicious than he already plans to be. I wanted to tell you sooner, Land. I hated keeping this from you. I hated holding this all in for so long, but…" Her body began shaking in the chilled air, and I took off my coat and wrapped it around her.

I didn't know what to say, so I said the only thing that really came to mind. "I'm sorry Dad's a dick."

She laughed and started crying. "It's okay."

Without any more thought, I hugged her, and like always, I melted into her arms. "I'm sorry," I said again, this time for her hurting. She cried into my shoulder, and I held her even tighter.

She pulled back a little, nervously laughing as she wiped away her tears. "I didn't plan on crying, I swear."

"You always cry."

"Not always," she snickered. "I got your flowers," she said, handing me the now smooshed up bouquet from our hug. "They looked better before, I swear. I'm not sure if you're supposed to give male actors flowers, but I'm your mother, so you're getting flowers."

I smirked. "Thanks."

"Do you want to go home and watch some bad movies and stuff our faces?" she asked.

"One hundred percent."

For the time being, I put KJ to the back of my mind. I knew I'd have to deal with that sooner than later, but for now, Mom was home, and I didn't want to waste a minute of my time with her.

"I can cook us something," she offered.

"No offense, Mom, but please stay away from the kitchen for the remainder of your life."

She smiled. "Fair enough."

We got home, ordered in some food, and trashed the living room. We didn't even turn on the television, we talked for hours.

"So, this acting thing," Mom said, smiling from ear to ear. "You're into it?"

"I mean, yeah. I told Dad I was thinking of picking up a theater major next fall, but he shut down that idea."

"Your father doesn't get to control your choices. That's why I've been working so hard—to give you that freedom."

"I don't want to put all that stress on you. That's too much for you to do for me."

"Landon." She shook her head and placed her hands on my shoulders. "Everything I do, is for you. If you want to go into the acting program at your college, then we are going to get you into the acting program at your college. No ifs, ands, or buts."

I nodded once. "I don't even know if I'm good enough—"

"You're good enough," she cut in, "you've always been good enough to do anything." She tossed a French fry into her mouth. "On another topic... Is there anything there between Miss Juliet, or is that all acting?"

I laughed. "Is it that obvious?"

"Only to a mother's eyes. The way you look at her... What's the story there?"

Oh, if only she knew.

"It's complicated. We've been doing really good. She's been good for me, Mom, but recently I've found something out that could change her life forever. I'm not sure what to do with the information, either. I know it will hurt her, but I also know that keeping it from her is wrong."

"The key to a good relationship is communication, Landon. Your father and I never really had that. We never talked, not really. Maybe about things on the surface, but never anything of true meaning. Maybe if we would've, our relationship would be stronger. Or perhaps it would've ended much sooner. All I know is that you can't build something strong without having hard conversations every now and then. Do you care about this girl?"

"I love her," I said with confidence.

"*Love*." Mom breathed out, placing her hand over her heart. "My baby boy is in love."

"Don't cry about it," I joked.

"I'll try not to. If you love her, then be one hundred percent honest with her. That's what I would've wanted. That's what all girls want. Honesty."

I knew she was right. It just sucked building up the nerve to tell Shay something that I knew was going to break her heart.

"Thanks, Mom."

"Always. I love you, I love you," she said.

"Why do you always do that?" I asked. "Why do you always say "I love you" twice?"

She smiled. "Once for your heart. Twice to leave an imprint."

I nodded. "I love you times two." Her eyes watered over and I laughed. "Stop crying so much, Mom."

"I'm sorry. That was really sweet, and you have no clue how much I needed to hear that."

"I'll do my best to make sure I say it more."

"Thanks, Land."

"How are you doing, though? With everything going on with Dad?" I shifted around in my seat and took a question from Maria's handbook. "How's your heart?"

She started crying again, shaking her head. "Broken. It's been broken for some time now…with everything that happened with Lance, and the miscarriage, and now this divorce, it just feels like I can't get my footing. I can't stop drowning," she confessed, covering her face with her hands. "I'm sorry. This is too much for you. You don't have to carry my burdens. I'm okay. I'm fine."

"You can talk to me, Mom," I offered.

"I know, honey." She wiped her eyes and stood up. She moved over to me and kissed my forehead. "I just need rest, that's all. We'll talk in the morning. Good night."

She headed to her bedroom and closed the door behind her.

I cleaned up the mess we made, and as I was heading toward my bedroom, I walked past Mom's where I heard her crying inside. She sounded as if every single part of her was breaking that very night.

Instead of sitting outside of her bedroom like I used to, I turned the knob. I walked into her room, climbed into bed with her, and wrapped my arms around her.

"Landon, I'm okay. I'm okay," she whimpered, but I shushed her.

She didn't have to pretend to be okay with me. She didn't have to lie and say everything was fine when it was clear she was in the middle of one of the hardest storms of her life.

Her breaking down didn't mean she wasn't strong. Sometimes the strongest thing a person could ever do was fall apart. It took real strength to become that vulnerable.

"It's okay, Mom. Fall apart. Don't worry. I got you."

She cried into me for the remainder of the night, and I refused to let her go.

Chapter Twenty-Six

Landon

AFTER THE WEEKEND, MOM HEADED OUT FOR ANOTHER JOB opportunity. She kept going on and on about feeling bad for leaving me again, but I told her she was leaving for us, for our future. Plus, I promised to call her every night to talk. That seemed to bring her some comfort.

I still hadn't told Shay what I'd learned about KJ, seeing how I spent the whole weekend making sure Mom was okay, but I knew I'd have to tell her after school that afternoon. I couldn't keep something that big from her. Even though it was going to crush her, I knew she had every right to know.

"Landon, hey." KJ away from the wall as he stood on my front porch Monday morning as I was getting ready to head out to school. I knew at some point he'd rear his ugly head at my place. How could he not? He couldn't ignore seeing me after that evening.

I didn't say a word. I didn't owe a man like him a greeting.

He brushed his hands over his face before stuffing them into his pockets. He looked nothing like his daughter. Well, nothing like Shay at least. Who knew what his other kid looked like? She could've been his spitting image. That would've sucked for her, though. Her father looked like an asshole.

"Listen—" he started, but I cut him off.

"You have two daughters," I said. "Does Shay know that?"

He stood tall. Almost emotionless. It was eerily creepy how calm he appeared. "There are things in this life that you're too young to understand."

"That sounds like a bullshit response from a bullshit human."

"You think I wanted this to happen? I never thought in a million years you'd be in the same show as my daughter. I never thought—"

"That you'd get caught."

"You can't say anything," he warned.

"Excuse me?"

"You can't. Landon, if my family finds out about this, it will ruin us. Why would you want to hurt Shay like that?"

"You need to leave," I sneered, my voice low and controlled. "We don't have anything else to say to each other."

He brushed his hand against the back of his neck and shook his head. "Just give me a week to tell them. Give me that time to break the news."

I didn't say a word, because he didn't deserve my words. Plus, I knew he was lying, because that was what he did best.

As he turned to walk away, he paused and looked back to me. "Are you in love with my daughter?"

The words rolled from his tongue as if he was pained by even having to ask them. I didn't answer, though. Again, my words weren't made for him.

He sighed. "If you care anything about her, you won't get any more involved. She's a good kid. She's the best kid."

"I hope your other daughter doesn't hear you saying that," I spat out.

Still, he showed hardly any emotions on his face. He simply appeared hardened. "I see you, Landon. I see you and the fucked-up life that you live, and I don't want my daughter around that kind of mess."

"Funny, coming from you."

"No, I get it. I'm a monster. I am not a good person, and I have fucked up my family more than I can say. That's why I'm saying you should stay away. Shay already has a monster in her life. She doesn't need two."

"Yeah, well, too bad you don't have the right to tell me what to do."

"You think you're better than me? Better than my demons? I've watched you; I see your broken pieces in your eyes. You're never going to stop fighting the demon that lives in your soul. I don't need you bringing that crap around my daughter. Before she started hanging around you, she was good. She was well behaved and obedient."

"She's not a damn puppy."

"Yes, but before you, she was house trained. She never spoke back. Never skipped school, never lied, never snuck out of the house. You're doing that to her. You're making her someone she isn't."

I stood tall with my arms crossed tight. My mind was running wild from his words, and I tried my hardest not to move, because if I moved, I'd punch him out.

"Thanks for the talk."

"I'm not kidding, Landon. Stay away from my daughter."

"Okay." I nodded, sliding my hands into my jean's pockets. "But, remind me quick. Which daughter are we speaking about?"

"You really don't want to push me, kid. I've been on this Earth a lot longer than you; I've been a monster longer. I know how to hurt people. To make them suffer. Don't cross me. Trust me, you'll regret it."

His lips sealed shut and he didn't say another word. He walked to his car, climbed inside, and drove off. Then, I headed to school to tell his daughter the truth.

I waited until after theater rehearsal to tell Shay about her father. I didn't want to do it during the day, because I wasn't certain how she'd react, and I didn't want to throw her off before rehearsal.

As time ticked by, the knot in my stomach grew bigger and bigger.

"Opening night is going to be so good," Shay said as she packed up her things in the auditorium. "You get better every single night, which is kind of annoying," she joked.

"You're amazing," I said somberly, feeling completely guilty for what I was about to tell her. "Do you know that? Do you know that you're an amazing person?"

Her cheeks reddened a bit. "Don't do that."

"Do what?"

"Make it so easy to fall for you. Do you want to go get some food or something?" she asked.

"Aren't you still grounded?"

"Yes, but it doesn't matter. I'll just tell them rehearsal went late."

She was planning on lying to them. That fact alone made my skin crawl. Maybe KJ wasn't wrong. Maybe I was a bad move for his daughter. Maybe while she was making me better, I was making her worst.

"Don't do that, Chick," I murmured.

"Do what?"

"Become a liar."

She arched an eyebrow at me. "Are you okay?"

Everyone else had already gathered their things to head home, leaving the two of us alone in the theater space. I stuffed my hands into my pockets. "Yeah, there's just something big I have to tell you and it's making me nervous."

She stood up straighter. "What is it?" She stepped closer to me, concern in her eyes. "How's your heart?"

I snickered. "You're sounding a lot like your grandmother."

"Landon," she said sternly, placing her hand against my chest, "how's your heart?"

Chills raced through me. "Still beating."

"Good," she muttered, nodding slowly, "good."

I shifted around in my shoes. "Look, I don't know how to say this, so I'm going to blurt it out because if I keep it in anymore, I'm going to explode so—"

"I love you," she said, cutting me off.

Every thought I'd been thinking left me right in that moment. Every negative feeling in my head evaporated into thin air. My stare fell to her lips, and for a second, I thought I'd imagined it. I thought I was so delusional from the past few days that I'd officially lost my mind. She must've picked up on the baffled look in my eyes, because she stepped closer to me and took my hands into hers.

"Sorry," she whispered. "I just wanted to say it before you. I'm fine with losing the bet, because I love you." She paused and narrowed her eyes. "That's what you were going to say, right? That you love me?"

I grimaced, and she flicked slightly.

Her cheeks turned red and she dropped her head. "Oh..."

Shit.

I saw the emotional spilling out of her eyes. "No, that's not it. But—"

"It's okay, Landon, because I love you," she repeated. "I love you, I love you, I love you. And I know this means I've lost the bet. I know this means you win, and I don't even care because I love you, and loving you makes me feel like a winner. I just wanted to tell you that, because I couldn't keep it in much longer. You don't even have to say it back. I don't care. Because I don't think you tell people you love them just so you can hear it back. I think you tell people you love them because it feels like a rocket in your soul. The love becomes so powerful that it shoots through you until you're finally forced to express it through words. So yeah," She laughed nervously and shrugged her shoulders. "This is awkward, but I love you, Landon Harrison. I love you in the light and in the dark. I love you like a whisper and like a shout. I love your good days and your bad days, and I...love...you. All of you. Every single piece..." She began fiddling with her fingers, and her T-shirt collar moved between her lips, "And every single scar."

I moved in closer to her and placed my forehead against hers. I closed my eyes and swallowed hard, breathing her in.

"Why would you love someone like me?" I asked.

"Because it's impossible not to."

I opened my eyes and looked into hers. I wanted to say it back, I wanted to tell her how I loved her first. How I felt it first. How I lost the bet way back when on my birthday, but it wasn't the right time.

First, I needed to tell her the hardest truth she'd ever have to hear. "Shay...there's something you should know about your father."

She pulled back a little and her brown eyes locked with mine. "What is it? Did he..." She stood up straight. "Did he say something to you? Did he offend you? Did he—"

"He lied. He's been lying to you, to your mother, about so many things."

"What are you talking about?" she choked out, her voice shaky with confusion.

"Shay, he, um..." Why were the words now freezing up in my throat? Maybe because I saw her nerves. Maybe because I knew how much she loved her father, even if she wished she hadn't. Maybe because I knew what I said next was going to break her heart. "He's a dealer. He's been dealing shit to kids at our school."

Her face shifted a bit, but the lack of surprise in her eyes kind of shocked me. "I know. That's why Mima got so fed up with him. He used to deal in the past...but we thought he stopped. We'd thought he'd pulled his life together. We'd thought he'd got solid jobs and was on the up and up. But...he lied. Because that's what he does. He lies. And still, my mom keeps choosing him."

I raised an eyebrow. "And she knows?"

"Yeah. We all know."

"No, I mean..." I swallowed hard. "She knows about his other daughter?"

She laughed.

No shit, she laughed. Really hard, too.

"Wait, what?" she said between giggles. She looked at me and her laughter began to dissipate as she saw the seriousness in my stare. "Wait. What?"

It was clear she hadn't known about all of his dark, dark secrets. "Shay, he has another daughter."

"That's ridiculous. My father is a lot of terrible things, but he's not...he doesn't have..." her words faded. "I'm his only..." She sniffled a bit and stood straighter. "What's the punchline, Landon? What's the joke?"

"It's not a joke. He used to deal to me, Shay. He always talked a lot about his family. About his two daughters..."

"No," she spat out. "No. I'm his only child."

"Shay..."

"Stop it, Landon. This isn't funny anymore," she scolded, her eyes watering over.

"I'm not trying to be funny, Shay. He has another daughter."

"Stop," she snapped, shutting her eyes. "Stop it right now. I don't know why you're doing this."

"I'm doing this because you deserve to have someone who tells you the truth. No lies, only truths, remember?"

She parted her mouth, but nothing came out. She took steps away from me and she stared my way as if I were a complete stranger. Someone she didn't know. Someone she couldn't trust.

I was doing the right thing. I was being real with her and I was telling her the truth.

"I can't do this right now," she said, walking away from me.

"Shay, wait!" I called after her, but she didn't turn around. She didn't look back. She broke out into a run, and not once did she look back at me.

I didn't even get to tell her that I loved her, too.

Chapter Twenty-Seven

Shay

MY HEART HADN'T STOPPED BEATING ERRATICALLY SINCE I HAD LEFT Landon standing alone in the theater. His words replayed over and over again in my mind, like a nightmare I couldn't wake up from.

Another daughter.

A whole other person.

A human being that held part of my DNA.

How could that have been? How could he have hidden something so massive?

When I walked into my house, my parents were sitting on the couch as if they were a completely normal pairing. As if our house wasn't swarming with lies upon lies. They were laughing as they watched some show together, cuddled up as if they were made from the same heartbeats.

It made me sick.

I stepped right in front of the television, blocking their view and halting their laughter.

Mom sat up first. "Shay? What are you doing?"

"Is it true?" I barked, crossing my arms as my stare pierced into my father.

"Is what true?" Mom asked.

Dad tensed up as he sat up straighter. He clasped his hands together and released a weighted sigh.

Oh my gosh. It's true.

The swirling in my gut intensified as I stumbled backward. "You're a monster."

"Shay, perhaps we should talk alone in the other room," Dad suggested, but it felt more like a threat.

"So, she doesn't know?"

"Know? Know what?" Mom stood from the couch, and her stare moved back and forth between my father and me. "What's going on?"

"Shannon Sofia," Dad warned, his voice low and smoky. But I didn't care. I wasn't afraid of him. He didn't hold the same grip on me as he held on my mother.

"He has another daughter," I spat out, the words burning my throat.

Mom huffed and shook her head. "What?"

"He has another kid."

"No, he doesn't," Mom argued, still shaking her head. "That's ridiculous. Tell her, Kurt. Tell her that's ridiculous," she urged.

He didn't though. He stayed quiet as Mom's face drained of all color.

"Oh my gosh," she muttered. Her eyes glassed over as her hand moved to cover her mouth. "Oh my gosh..."

Dad shifted around in his shoes and lowered his head. It was clear he couldn't lie his way out of this one, but I wouldn't have put it pass him to try. "It was years ago, Camila. When I was using. I made a mistake and slept with another woman. A few months later she showed up with a kid, claiming it was mine. I didn't believe her, of course. Then, we took a DNA test and..." He looked up to Mom with tears in his eyes, and I wanted to slap him for the crocodile tears.

A little too late for the fake emotions, Father.

"I fucked up, Cam, but she means nothing to me. All I do is provide money to the kid, that's it. It's nothing personal."

"Is that what you tell them about me?" I barked his way. "That it's nothing personal? Or have they not yet discovered what kind of man you are?"

"You need to watch your tone, little girl."

"I don't need to do anything you say," I replied. "You are not my father. You are nothing to me. Mom, let's go," I said, turning toward her. She was frozen in place, tears streaming down her face.

She kept staring at my father with such a look of shock. "I can't leave, Shay. Not yet. There's still so much that's not clear. Things that still aren't adding up."

"What do you mean? Everything is added. He lied to you—*again*. He betrayed you—*again*. He had another daughter behind your back and only confessed to it when he realized he had no other choice because he got caught."

"How did you even find out?" she asked.

"Landon told me. He found out, and he told me the truth."

"And you just believed him?" she questioned. Those words made my mind spin.

"What? Mom. Dad just confessed! He told you straight out what happened, and now you're questioning Landon? Are you kidding me?"

"Camila, please," Dad begged, "just stay and let me try to explain."

"There's nothing to explain. I'm going to go pack a bag. You should do the same, Mom."

I hurried to my room and packed up a suitcase. I didn't know what I needed or what I should've left behind. I simply tossed as much as I could into the suitcase and hoped like hell that Mima would help me pick up the rest of the stuff another day.

As I pulled the suitcase out of my room, I saw Mom standing still as Dad sat on his knees in front of her, begging her to stay. He looked pathetic and still very much like a manipulative liar. He was throwing heavy emotions at Mom in an attempt to gaslight her into thinking she was in the wrong if she walked away from his toxins.

I raised an eyebrow at my mother. "Come on, Mom. Let's go."

She looked at me and back toward Dad, still so unsure about what her next actions were going to be. I knew there was so much to my parents' story that I hadn't ever read. So much history and pain raced through Mom's heart on a daily basis. I wanted to blame her for being weak. I wanted to call her out on not choosing herself ever in her life, but she was hurting. She'd been beaten down for so many years that she didn't know what it felt like to not be in such an agonizing pain.

In a way, suffering felt normal to her. She was used to it. If only she knew there was a whole life waiting for her outside of the castle's prison. If only she knew that she could walk away and begin again.

"Mom," I stated once more, "look at me." She turned my way, and I smiled at her. Everything I knew about love, I'd learned from my mother. She was the first person in this world to give love so unconditionally to me. She was the one who first made me laugh, made me smile, made me live. And her heart was currently broken. She was so sad and scared, and I was certain she felt so alone, so it was my job to reminder her that she wasn't.

I walked over to her and took her hands into mine, stepping right in front of my father, and blocking his viewpoint from her.

She was hurt, just like Landon. Lost, confused, and so unsure. So, I knew I had to say to her the same truths I had spoken to him. "Mom... you are more than the story that this man wrote for you. You are more than my father. You are smart. You are funny. You are strong." My eyes watered over as I felt the trembling in her hands. "You are loyal. You are breathtaking. You are beautiful. And this is not the end of your story; it's only the beginning. But it begins now. With you and me, walking out of that front door. You can do this. You don't have to walk alone. I got you."

"Don't listen to her, Camila. She doesn't know you like I do," Dad barked as he stood. His crocodile tears were now gone, and his cold stare returned once more. "I am your home. I am your truth. You can't leave me."

Her hands were still shaking, but I didn't let go. I wouldn't walk out of that house without her. I wouldn't leave her side in the middle of a war. I simply held on tighter.

"Mom, it's okay to leave him. It's okay for you to turn your back on him. You deserve more, and you won't be alone. But please, come with me. I'll be it..." My voice cracked as tears began to fall down my cheeks. "I'll be your willow tree."

That was when she fell apart, but I was there to keep holding her up.

"Can we go home now?" I asked her.

"This is her home," Dad argued, but I knew he wouldn't understand. Truth was, my father never really had a home in his whole life. Home wasn't a building; it was a feeling of warmth. Kurt Gable lived in coldness his whole life.

I ignored him. "Mom?"

"Yes," she finally whispered, the word so small and delicate. "Let's go home."

"Do you want to pack some things?" I asked.

"No." She shook her head and squeezed my hand. "I have everything I need right here."

We walked out of the house with Dad shouting toward us. "You're making a huge mistake! You'll come back to me, Camila! You always come back! I am all you'll ever have! You need me."

His words were harsh and filled with lies. He was belittling and mean, but my mom? She kept walking. She kept standing, even though he tried his best to shatter her spirit. She kept going. Each step making her stronger. Each step moving her toward a better tomorrow.

And that tiny corner of my heart reserved for my father? It completely dissolved.

When we arrived at my grandmother's apartment, she opened the door in her nightgown and raised a curious eyebrow. Then, her stare moved to the suitcase and to her daughter.

"It's okay." She smiled a sad smile and wrapped her arms around Mom, who finally completely began to crumble and sob into Mima's arms. Mima parted her lips as she held onto her daughter. Her blood. Her first love. She whispered softly into her hair, "It's okay."

Mom and I stayed in Mima's guest room that night. I showered and got ready for bed first. When Mom came into the room, she smiled my way. Her smile was sad, but at least she still was able to curve her lips up.

Her hair was dripping wet from the shower she'd taken, and she wrapped it in a towel. She moved over to join me on the bed and sat on the edge of the mattress. "You must think I'm stupid and weak," she timidly stated.

"Never."

"I've tried to leave before, you know. Millions of times. Yet, somehow, he'd always find a way to pull me back in. He'd beat down my self-esteem so much that I'd be left feeling like I was worthless. I know it sounds stupid to believe the words from someone like your father, but I was so young when I met him. I was young and confused, and he was there during the hardest time of my life. I owe him for the greatest part of me, and he loved to hold that over my head...he loved to remind me that, without him, there wouldn't have been a you."

"Just because he's part of my DNA doesn't mean that he gets to hold that over you, Mom."

"No, but you don't understand...Shay..." She swallowed hard. "I was seventeen years old when I had you. I was a very troubled kid. I ran away from home for a long time and got involved with drugs. That's how I met your father. That's how we fell in love."

"I never knew that."

She nodded. "Yes. When I found out I was pregnant, I was strung out. I was in no shape to have a child. I was high on the regular, hardly eating, and my mind was so far gone, I didn't think I could do it..." Tears danced down her cheeks as she gripped the edge of the mattress. "I didn't think I could get clean. I was just a kid, for goodness' sake. I didn't know what I was doing, but your dad was there. He helped me through the withdrawals. He held my hand through the hardest time of my life, which brought me you. So, in a way, I always felt like I'd owed him for that, and it was something he held over my head time and time again."

"He abused you."

"No. He never laid a hand on me," she disagreed.

"Mom." I shook my head. "He abused you. He hurt you emotionally and mentally. He fed you lies for decades, and that's not your fault. I would have believed all the things you did if I was fed those lies on a daily basis. You're not weak because you stayed so long. You're strong because you did. But know that I'm here now because of you. Because you raised me, not him. You were a mother and father to me whenever he wasn't around. You're my hero, and it's going to be okay."

She smiled and nudged me in the shoulder. "How did you get so smart?"

"I blame the two women who raised me."

Mima peeked her head into the room and raised an eyebrow. "Are you two hungry and done crying like silly gooses? I just whipped up some food."

"Starving," Mom and I echoed at the same time.

We stood up and headed toward the dining room. As we sat at the table, my phone dinged.

Landon: How's your heart?

I smiled at his words.

Me: Still beating.

Chapter Twenty-Eight

Landon

FOR THE PAST FORTY-EIGHT HOURS, I'D BEEN IN TOUCH WITH SHAY constantly texting her, calling her, and making sure she was remembering to breathe. She hadn't been at school for two days, and honestly, I couldn't blame her. Her life was turned upside down. It made sense that she and her mother needed time to regroup.

Me: How's your heart today?

Shay: Still beating.

Good.

On Wednesday afternoon, I was surprised when my doorbell rang, and Shay's mother was standing on my front porch. She was wrapped up in a long, brown trench coat with sunglasses on, and her hair was pulled up into a messy bun.

"Mrs. Gable, hey."

She flinched a little as I said her last name, as if it were tainted.

She removed her sunglasses then crossed her arms and hugged her body tight. "Please, call me Camila."

"Okay. How can I help you?"

Her eyes had purplish bags beneath them as if she'd spent the past few nights crying. Again, I couldn't blame her. Her whole life had been transformed in a matter of moments. All because of one man's selfish choices.

"I wanted to say thank you. For what you did, for telling Shay the truth about Kurt. You can imagine that the past few days of our lives have been a living hell, but Shay and I have moved out, and I am in the process of filing for divorce…" Her words faded away, and she sniffled a bit, wiping her hand beneath her nose.

I saw so much of Shay within her mother. Her same brown eyes, her same dark hair, the same frown lines around her lips. I wanted to hug her and give her comfort, but it didn't seem right. In a way, I was to blame for the hurting she was experiencing. I was the cause of her current suffering. If she was in need of comfort, I doubted she wanted it from me, which made me come back to the first thought on my mind: what was she doing here?

She shifted back and forth in her tennis shoes and ran her hands against her forearms.

I cocked an eyebrow. "Why do I feel like you have something more to say?"

"Well, because I do. I haven't figured out how to word it correctly."

"Spit it out in any way, shape, or form, and we'll go from there."

She took a deep inhalation. "I need you to stay away from my daughter."

Well, okay.

Didn't see that coming.

"Wait, what?"

"I'm sorry, Landon, I really am, but I see it in you. I see the damage in your eyes, in your heart, and I don't want my daughter going through anything so heavy. Not after this. Not after everything she's been through. Her heart needs a break."

I gritted my teeth together, feeling sick to my stomach. "You don't think I'm good for her heart?" How was that possible? I did the right thing. I didn't keep secrets and crap the way Camila's husband had. I'd been upfront and completely honest about the situation at hand. I did the right thing.

But still, in Camila's eyes, I was not good enough for Shay.

"It's not that, sweetheart," she promised. Calling someone sweetheart while telling them to stay away from your daughter felt like a new kind of insult. "I just, I can tell you're troubled. You've been through a lot of personal traumas—no fault of your own—but Shay doesn't need that kind of energy in her life."

"The same way she didn't need your energy of not believing her and Maria about your fucked-up husband for years?" I spat out. I didn't mean to sound so harsh, and I definitely didn't mean to cuss at her, but my chest was hurting. My mind was a mess. I did the right thing. I told her what her husband was doing. I didn't lie. Yet, somehow, I was the troubled one.

"I see why you're upset. You care about my daughter. Just like I do. But if you really care, you'll let her go, Landon. You're off to college in a few months anyway, right? And Shay needs to focus on her future."

"I can be her future."

"No." She shook her head. "You have to be her past. She deserves a fresh start. A new beginning. Please," she pleaded, "I'm begging you to leave her alone. In the future, you'll thank yourself for not placing your heavy bags against her shoulders."

"You should leave now," I said, feeling my chest aching from her words. I stood as tall as I could, and she frowned as she put her sun-glasses back on.

"I'm sure you think I'm an evil lady, and maybe I am. Maybe my mind is so messed up that I still don't know right from wrong. But tell me…would you want your daughter dating a boy like you?"

"You don't know me."

"No…but I know your kind—damaged. Please, Landon. I'm beg-ging you. Don't damage my daughter the way my husband damaged me."

She walked away, leaving me alone with my thoughts, which was never a good thing.

I wondered how many times a person could hear they were dam-aged before those words planted themselves against one's mind.

First Monica, then KJ, and lastly, Camila.

I hadn't been able to sleep after talking to Shay's mom. The next morning, I woke up, dragging my feet, feeling like a zombie who'd spent the whole night overthinking every single thing about myself.

Each flaw that I held was sitting at the surface of my mind, replaying itself over and over again in my thoughts. Even though Shay's father was a complete waste of space, he told me I wasn't good enough for his daughter, and Shay's mom said the same exact thing. When two parents thought you weren't good enough for their kid, that hit you hard.

Maybe they were right. Maybe I wasn't any good for their daughter. Before me, Shay wasn't acting out. Yet, the moment we began the bet, a wildness released from her soul. I wasn't sure it was due to me, though. Maybe it was due to the fact that she'd been a caged bird for so long, and she was finally allowed to fly, but the gut-wrenching feeling was still there within me.

I couldn't stop my mind from telling me how I was too fucked-up in the head for someone like Shay. I couldn't stop my thoughts from drowning in self-doubt.

"You're shit," it told me. *"Someone like her could never love someone as broken as you,"* it taunted. *"She just said she loved you to end the bet, not because she really cares."* That was the thing about anxiety and depression: there was nothing logical about it. When my brain started to spin the webs of self-doubts, it spun fast, spinning me round and round into its webs of lies. The panic in my chest made it hard to focus on my surroundings. When I got to school, I went to stop by Mrs. Levi's office to have her smile and feed me some mumbo jumbo about self worth and how I wasn't a complete failure, but she was in a meeting with another student.

As I walked away from her office, I heard Shay calling my name from behind, but instead of turning to face her, I kept my pace up. I wasn't in the right frame of mind to talk to her. I wasn't in the right frame of mind to talk to anyone.

I headed to the football field and went straight to the bleachers. I gripped the railings, put my head down, shut my eyes, and tried my best to shut up the noises inside my head.

Sometimes it worked. That time, it didn't.

I skipped most of the school day, only showing up for theater rehearsals. As I walked into the auditorium, Shay was right there with worry in her eyes.

"Hey. Where have you been?" she asked.

"Just skipped school, that's all."

"Why? What's going on?"

"I don't need a reason to skip school; I just did."

She arched an eyebrow. "Landon."

"Yeah?"

"What's wrong?"

Me. I'm what's wrong. "Nothing, it's all good. Let's just get this rehearsal over with, all right? I don't feel like talking." I started walking away, feeling like shit for shutting her out, but I'd spent the last eight hours coming up with every single reason why I wasn't good enough for her.

The list was long, detailed, and damn accurate.

What could Shay give me if we were together?

Happiness. Joy. So much fucking laughter. A feeling of home. A safe place to fall. Hope. Love. Her mind, body, and soul. Her light.

And what could I give her if we were together?

My scars. My panic attacks. My heaviness. My mood swings. My pain. My depression. My darkness.

It didn't seem like equal playing fields, that was for damn sure. She'd give me the world, and I'd take it away from her. Everyone was right—she was completely out of my league.

"Land, wait." She wrapped her fingers around my forearm, and I shut my eyes. Her warmth. Her touches. She'd give me that, too. "Talk to me."

"Let it go, Shay, all right? Let it go and let me go."

Her fingers released from my arm, and chills raced through me. The moment she let me go, I missed her touch.

She kept staring at me, reading me, breaking me down piece by piece.

Stop it, Shay… Stop reading these pages. The ink is still wet, and the words ain't pretty.

"You're struggling," she commented. "Don't shut me out. Please, Landon. Let me in. Whatever it is, I can handle it. I'm here. I can help you."

She was being that perfect person that I'd fallen in love with. She was standing there with care and concern. Her brown eyes were wide with love. She didn't even have to tell me about her love. I saw it in the way that she looked at me. Shay Gable looked my way as if I was a prize. As if she saw something in me that I'd yet to discover. I fucking loved how she looked at me. I hated that I'd never be able to live up to those expectations.

"Drop it," I warned one last time. "Let's just get this shit over with, all right?"

I hated myself for being so cold toward her. I hated how my mind was all messed up. I hated...myself.

Shit.

I hated myself.

We ran through the show, and when it came time for Juliet to take her life, for the first time during our rehearsals, Juliet cried real tears. They fell against me as she delivered her final lines, emotions pouring out of her as she spoke.

I opened my eyes to watch her, to see her reddened eyes.

I did that to her. I broke her heart, and we hadn't even really been dating yet. What kind of damage could I have done to her over time?

"Bravo, bravo!" Mr. Thymes applauded after Shay's tearful performance. He placed his hand over his chest, and his eyes stayed wide in amazement. "And that is why Shay is our Juliet, folks. Shay, what you just did on this stage was breathtakingly raw. What did you tap into to unlock that?"

She gave him a wary smile and shrugged her left shoulder. "Pain?"

Mr. Thymes clapped his hands together in awe. "Pain. Yes, I felt it. Good, good. Keep that up for the shows this weekend. Hold on to that pain. And Landon?"

"Yes, sir?"

"Keep your eyes closed during her death scene. Romeo wouldn't be staring at Juliet while she's killing herself."

"Noted."

"Outside of that, you two should be very proud of yourselves. The chemistry between the two of you is nothing like I've seen before. I can rest easy tonight knowing the show will be a wild success due to the two of you. Goodnight."

I packed up my things and hurried out of the theater, hoping to avoid Shay talking to me, but unfortunately, she was quick.

"Landon, wait." She met me at my car. As I was opening the door, she placed her hand on it and shut it before she stepped in front of it.

I grimaced. "Move, Shay."

"No. Not until you tell me what's going on. Why are you acting so weird? What happened today?"

"I'd rather not do this. Move."

"No. Landon, you're hurting, and I see it. Let me know how I can help."

"You can't. I don't want your help."

Her eyes watered over, and she placed her hand against my chest. "What did I do wrong?"

What did she do wrong?

She was blaming herself, even though there was nothing she could've ever done wrong—

besides falling for a guy like me.

I was watching as it happened, as my coldness began to break her heart. She might've been able to read me from day one, but over the past few months, I'd learned how to read her right back. I was hurting her, cutting into her heart and leaving her there to bleed.

I needed to end it now, before we fell even deeper for one another.

"Look, I didn't want to tell you right away because of all the personal shit you're going through, but since you're being so dramatic about it, I'll tell you now. I won."

"Won? Won what?"

"The bet." I gave her an asshole smirk, and my heart died while I did it. "Don't tell me you actually thought I was falling in love with you? Come on, Chick. This was never real. It was a game—nothing more, nothing less."

She went to take a step backward from shock but bumped into my car. "What are you talking about?"

"This thing between us, it wasn't real. It was never real. I was bored, and the bet was a good way to pass some time. But it's over now, and I don't want anything to do with you. After this show's over, we don't ever have to cross paths again."

"No," she whispered, shaking her head. "No. We were real. This is real. I don't know what happened to you, Landon. I don't know why you're talking like this, but I know you. I know your heart and how it beats. I know your truths. Remember? Only truths. No lies."

My damaged heart was shattering second by second. "It's all been lies. Nothing was real about this."

"You..." She shut her eyes. "You showed me your scars, though. You showed me everything."

"Making Chicks Fall in Love With You 101. Tell them sad crap and make up a sob story. It works every time."

Her lips parted, and her eyes stayed glassed over, but she didn't say another word. She tossed her backpack strap higher on her shoulder and walked away.

Later that night, I received a message from her.

Shay: I don't know what today was about. I don't know why you shut me out, or why you're pushing me away, but I just want to let you know that I'm thinking about you. I want you to know that you are good, and worthy, and loved. I won't stop telling you that, Landon. Even if you push me away, I'll still keep telling you that this world needs you here. When you're ready to talk, I'm here.

Fuck, Chick.

It baffled me how someone so good could exist and want me.

I didn't reply back.

Even though every part of me wanted to tell her I loved her in hopes of hearing she loved me, too.

She didn't stop writing me each morning and night. During the school day and rehearsals, she'd still walk up to me and check to make sure I was okay. She'd ask me how my heart was, even though I refused to answer her. She was determined to make me not feel alone, and dammit, it was working. But I couldn't have her, and she couldn't have me—not in the way she wanted, at least. She deserved a full type of love, and mine was broken into pieces.

So, I knew I had to do the unthinkable. I had to cross a line that I couldn't come back from.

I had to break her heart completely to keep her from loving me anymore.

So, I sent out a massive text to people.

Me: Opening Night party at my house tonight. Bring booze and your worst behavior.

It amazed me how instantly I regretted having a party every single time.

The opening night performance was amazing. Mr. Thymes seemed overjoyed. Shay cried. I kept my eyes closed. And the crowd gave us a standing ovation.

It would've been great if I could've celebrated the success with Shay. If I could've taken her back to my house and showed her body the way I loved her. If I could've laughed with her while we watched Friends. If I could've just loved her every day for the rest of my life.

Yeah, that would've been great. But it wasn't realistic.

People crowded my house, drinking, gossiping, and talking about shit I didn't care about.

I noticed Shay the moment she walked in with Raine and Tracey. It blew my mind how quickly I could spot her in a crowded room. It was as if I was drawn to her energy, her light. *Her.*

She chatted with people, giving them her grand smile and bubbly personality. She shined in groups of people, being able to talk to anyone about anything. It was one of the very things I had learned to love about her. Her charm. Her wit. Her everything.

She was such a light in the world, and I was about to break her.

She glanced my way, and the smile against her lips faded into a wary frown. She tilted her head in confusion at me. Then, her lips parted, and she mouthed, "Hi, Satan."

I gave her an accidental half smile. It was hard not to smile when you looked her way.

Hello, brown eyes.

I tore my stare away from her and moved on to something less pleasing to my eye: the rest of the world.

"Spin seven, spin seven!" a few people chanted. It looked like a group of sophomores. Maybe juniors. Either way, I was game to play.

I sat down in the circle, and right as I was about to spin the bottle, a voice pierced me.

"What are you doing?" Shay asked, making me turn to see her.

"Playing a game," I dryly replied.

She raised an eyebrow, then she sat down in the circle, joining the game.

Why was she being so strong? Why was she still putting up with my bullshit?

There were a few giggling girls sitting next to her, drinking whatever cheap liquor sat in their plastic cups. They were annoying as fuck. The complete opposite of Shay. The complete opposite of everything I had ever wanted.

I was up first.

I grabbed the bottle and spun it, watching it go around and around. Shay's eyes stayed glued on the bottle while mine stayed glued on her.

"Oh my gosh!" a girl giggled as the bottle landed on her. Her friends joined in on the childish laughter as Shay's eyes shut. A small sigh released from her lips.

I stood and nodded toward the girl. "All right. Let's get this over with."

She hurried to stand, still chuckling and blushing like a newbie to the whole spin seven world.

We walked into the closet, and the door shut behind us.

"Oh my gosh, I can't believe I'm about to make out with Landon

Harrison! Like *the* Landon Harrison." She gasped, more excited than she should've been. She talked about me as if I were some ancient arti-fact—often studied but never touched.

"What year are you?"

"I'm a sophomore. A junior in a few months, though!" she added, as if that made me more interested in her. It didn't. I didn't care who she was, I didn't care where she was from. I just needed to know she'd follow through with my plan.

"So..." She curled her hair with her finger, and dammit, I wished she was Shay. "Do you use tongue, or—"

"I'm not going to make out with you," I cut in.

"Oh?"

"Nothing against you. You're beautiful, but my heart kind of be-longs to someone else."

"Then, why are you even playing this game?"

"It's complicated. I do need your help, though. When we walk out of here, I need you to act like we hooked up. And really sell it, too. Then, it's a win-win for us both. You get to say you hooked up with me to your friends."

"And what do you get?" she asked.

"Not really your business, but trust me, I get what I need."

She arched an eyebrow. "You don't even know my name, do you?"

"I don't."

"Why would I want to help a guy who doesn't even care to know my name?"

"I didn't say I didn't care. I simply said I didn't know it. So, tell me."

"Jessie."

"Okay, Jessie, nice to meet you. You seem like a top notch girl. Do we have a deal or what? We're kind of on the clock here."

She bit her bottom lip. "Okay, deal. But! I get to say we used tongue."

"By all means."

Before we walked out of the closet, Jessie pinched her cheeks to make herself look flustered. She walked out of the closet and gave an award-winning speech about how my tongue was shoved down her throat.

Shay stood in front of the closet with her face was drained of all color.

"Are you serious, Landon?" she asked, stunned by what had taken place.

I stuffed my hands into my pockets and shrugged. "Like I said, we were just a bet. Nothing more, nothing less."

I saw it happen, too. The moment she let me go. Her eyes that were, seconds ago, filled with emotion were now ice cold. She stood taller and rolled her shoulders back. "Okay. You wanted me to stop caring about you? Congratulations, Landon. You win."

I hated myself more than ever. Especially since I was going to push her further and further away. "I know I won, Sunshine. That was the whole point of the bet."

"Don't call me Sunshine," she hissed.

Then stop being so bright.

"Look, are we done here? I got what I wanted from you already, so I'd really like to—"

Slap.

Shay's hand flew against my cheek, and her voice cracked. "Fuck you, Landon." Instant guilt found its way to her eyes. She pulled her hand back, still a bit shocked that she actually had enough nerve to place her hand against my face. Her voice dropped, and she lowered her head. "I'm sorry," she whispered, taking a few steps back.

She turned and hurried away, leaving me standing there with a crowd. If you ever wanted a woman to stop messing around with you, all you had to do was humiliate her in front of a crowd. There was no coming back from that kind of destruction.

"Move on and fuck off," I muttered.

"Landon, what the hell was that?" Raine asked, walking over to me stunned. "Why the heck would you do that to Shay?"

"I'm not in the mood to talk, Raine," I mumbled, turning away from her. She grabbed my arm and pulled me toward her.

"No. Landon. I don't understand…what you and Shay have…it's real. It's the realest thing I've seen since Hank and myself, so I don't understand why you're pushing her away."

"Drop it, Raine."

"I won't. You're both my friends, and I don't—"

"Raine, for once in your goddamn life, can you go ahead and mind your own business?" I snapped at her. She took a few steps backward, stunned by the stinging of my words.

She shook her head. "This isn't you, Landon. I don't know what's going on, but this isn't the real you. But for now, I'm going to go check on Shay."

"Raine?"

"Yeah?"

"Make sure she's okay?" I asked, my voice cracking as the words left my lips.

She frowned. "I will. Then, I'm coming back to check on you to make sure you're okay, too, Land. Shay's not the only friend I have in this situation. Even though you're an asshole, I still love your dumb ass."

She hurried off to track down Shay, and I was happy to know someone was looking after her. A hand landed on my shoulder, and I turned around to see Greyson standing there.

He raised an eyebrow. "You okay?"

"Not really."

"You want all of these people out of your house?"

"Yup."

He nodded once and set off to handle it.

It wasn't long before everyone left my place. Greyson was good at kicking people out. I had to thank him for that later. As I stepped into my bedroom, there were four people sitting there, staring my way.

The Fantastic Four (+Raine).

"What are you guys doing here?" I asked.

"When you said to get rid of everyone, we knew you didn't mean the cool people," Hank commented.

I scratched the back of my neck. "Listen, I kind of want to be alone tonight."

"We know." Eric nodded, patting a spot next to him on the bed. "That's why we're not leaving. We're your friends, Landon, and we can tell when heavy shit is going on in your head. So, even if you want to be alone tonight, you're not allowed to be alone. Because you're not alone."

I sighed. "I don't deserve you guys."

"I know." Raine walked over and nudged me in the arm. "Now shut up and let me beat you at *Mario Kart*." She grabbed a controller and handed it over to me.

I took it from her hands. "Hey, Raine? How is she?"

She grew somber. "Heartbroken. Confused. Devastated. How are you?"

Heartbroken.

Confused.

Devastated.

I shrugged. "I'm okay."

She smiled a sad grin. "Liar."

Shay stopped talking to me after my party. The only words she gave me were Juliet's words to Romeo. Outside of that, it was radio silence. I couldn't blame her. I wouldn't talk to me after that, either.

I was an asshole who hurt her due to my own insecurities. It was better that we weren't together, though. At least, that was what my brain kept telling me over and over again.

The school year came to an end with me receiving a cap and gown. I still didn't know what was going to come of my life in the upcoming months, but I knew I didn't want to do the law school thing. Dad was still adamant about me going into law, while Mom was pushing hard for Dad to let me make my own choices.

"You need to stop babying him, Carol. He's not a child anymore, and he needs to have a real career," Dad said.

"It is a real career, even if you don't agree with it," Mom shot back his way.

Those conversations went on for weeks during the beginning of the summer.

I didn't really care much either way. My mind wasn't on college. I couldn't think of what major I wanted to go into, what classes I wanted to take, because the only thing crossing my mind was Shay.

I missed her.

I missed her so much, and I hated myself every time I thought about what I did and how I pushed her away. I figured the only way I'd be able to clear my head from thoughts of her was returning to my old habits of alcohol.

It started with one sip at a random party. A couple of guys were taking shots, so I took one with them. The second I tasted the alcohol, I instantly felt like a failure. Maybe Monica was right. Maybe people didn't really change for the better, and I'd always be this messed-up person full of scars inside and out.

The alcohol burned my throat as it went down, and I hated every second of it, but I kept drinking it because I thought it'd help drown out the memories of Shay. Unfortunately, it didn't. The thoughts of her only intensified.

I ran into her twice on two different occasions. One was a party at Hank's. It was a pretty mellow hangout, and I drank one drink too many. When Shay walked in, I was already shitfaced and made an utter ass of myself in front of her cousin, Eleanor. I said some stupid-ass shit because I was drunk and sad, and that night, I went home and overthought the situation in tenfold.

The second time I saw her, I'd only had one drink, and I watched her in the distance, laughing with Eric. She looked so happy and content without me.

I went home and fell apart in my bedroom.

My mind mocked me. *See? She doesn't need you. She's better without you. Move on. You're worthless.*

Who knew the hardest war would end up being me against my mind?

I was losing, too. I was completely slipping away from reality, day by day.

Just when I didn't think things could have gotten any worse for me, I received text messages from my friends that made me want to vomit.

Hank: Did you hear about Monica?

Eric: Dude, it's crazy!

Me: What happened?

Greyson: She overdosed last night when she was with Reggie. She's in the hospital now.

My head felt like exploding as I kept reading the word *overdose*.

Flashes of Lance came back to me. How he overdosed, how he lost his life, and how I couldn't save him. Then, I thought about my last conversation with Monica when she asked who was going to choose her. She questioned who was going to stand by her side, and I straight up told her it wasn't going to be me.

Fuck, Monica. Why?

I didn't know what to do. I couldn't breathe. But somehow, I managed to stand and grab my keys. I headed out to the hospital to sit with her, because I was almost certain she wouldn't have had anyone else coming out to be by her side.

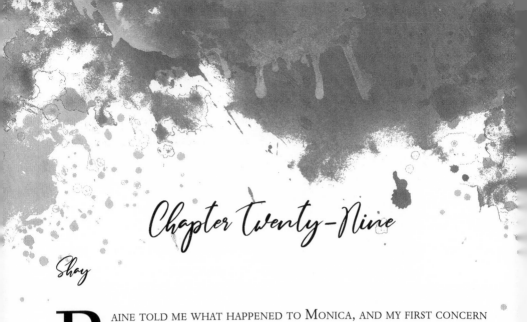

Chapter Twenty-Nine

Shay

RAINE TOLD ME WHAT HAPPENED TO MONICA, AND MY FIRST CONCERN was Landon.

I knew I shouldn't have been thinking about him after what he'd done to me during the opening weekend of our show. I shouldn't have cared about his well-being, but I couldn't help it. When love arrived, you couldn't shut it off like a faucet. It kept pouring out of you, uncontrollably, even when you wanted the pressure of it to stop.

I loved Landon, even though I knew I shouldn't have. I loved his light and his shadows. I loved the way he wore a crooked grin. I loved his frowns. I loved his highs. I loved his lows.

I loved him. Even when he didn't deserve it. Even when he broke my spirit.

My heart?

My soul?

My love?

Still his.

I knew he had to be hurting from the fact that Monica had overdosed. You couldn't ignore the fact that the two of them had history. I knew his mind was probably taking him to the darkest corners of his soul, and even though I felt so much anger toward him, he couldn't be alone.

Not now.

I headed straight to the hospital and found Landon sitting alone in the waiting room. His head was down, and his hands were clasped together. His knuckles were red from his tight grip, and he looked as if every part of him was shattered. His shoulders were rounded forward, and his sleeves were pushed up, revealing the scars he'd worked so hard to hide from the world.

Oh, Landon.

Where is your mind tonight?

I walked over to him and placed a hand on his shoulder.

He looked up with bloodshot eyes and confusion in his baby blues.

"What are you doing here?" he whispered, sniffling as he tilted his head.

"This," I told him. I lifted my chair and sat it directly in front of him. I took a seat, and then unclenched his fists and took his hands into mine. I held onto him, feeling the trembles of his hands. "I'm doing this."

He parted his mouth to speak, but no sounds came out.

I held his hands even tighter as I watched the corner of his mouth twitch.

"Shay…" he started.

"It's okay. We don't have to talk. I just want to be here for you."

He grimaced and cleared his throat as a few tears rolled down his cheeks. "I hurt you."

"I'm okay. I'm stronger than I look."

"Why would you be here for me? Why would you do this after what I did to you?"

"Because no one deserves to be alone during the hard times. Not even you."

He muttered a thank you as he pulled a hand away and wiped at his eyes. He quickly returned his hand to mine, and I held onto him once more.

"How is she?" I asked.

"They pumped her stomach. She's not awake yet. They won't tell me anything else because I'm not family. Her parents haven't even arrived yet. How fucked up is that? Their daughter overdosed, and they didn't rush to the fucking hospital."

"That's awful. Is she not close with her parents?"

"As close as you can get to people like that. They are all about money and status. Her father is in politics. An overdose scandal would be terrible timing for her family, seeing how her father is hoping to run for a senate seat someday. It wouldn't look great for him."

"And her mother?"

"Her mother is probably off getting a facial or something. She's a real number." He released a weighted sigh. "Shay. Really…why are you here?"

"I told you. You don't deserve to be alone. I know for some reason you think you do, but you don't, Landon. No matter what."

Devastation sat in his eyes as he looked up to me. "I miss you," he whispered. "I miss you so fucking much it hurts every single day."

My heart tightened in my chest. "Was it just a bet, Landon?"

"Come on, Chick…" he muttered. "I think we both know the answer to that."

My hands were trembling, or maybe it was his hands that shook. Who knew? Either way, I kept holding his hands.

"Why did you push me?" I questioned. "Why did you push me away?"

"Because I need to keep people at a distance," he confessed. "When people come near me, they get hurt. Monica, for example."

"What happened to Monica isn't your fault."

"Of course, it's my fault. It's all my fault."

"How so?"

"She asked me to stay with her, and I said no. I told her I wouldn't choose her. And then, she overdosed because I wasn't there."

"No," I said sternly. "She overdosed because she made a choice to use drugs. That's not your fault. None of this is your fault."

He flinched a little and lowered his head to stare at the floor.

"I didn't kiss that girl."

The words rolled off his tongue so gently that I wasn't sure he even spoke them. For a split second, I thought I'd lost my mind and was hoping he'd said it.

But then, his head rose back up, and his blues locked with my browns, and he gave me that broken smile of his.

"Why did you lie?"

"Because you deserve more than me. I did it so you wouldn't love me anymore."

"Well," I gently laughed and tried to keep my emotions in check. "It didn't work."

He scooted his chair closer to me and placed his forehead against mine as he closed his eyes, too. We were so close that I could have moved my lips an inch higher, and I'd had been kissing those lips of his. His breaths were brushing against my cheeks, and my heart was pounding wildly against my chest.

"Chick," he muttered.

"Satan," I replied.

"Tell me you don't love me."

"I can't do that."

"Yes, you can. Tell me you don't love me. Please," he begged. His lips brushed against mine as shivers raced through me.

"No."

"Then tell me a lie," he pleaded.

"I hate you." I breathed the words against his lips, and he swallowed them whole, as if they were the way to his existence.

"I hate you, too," he lied back to me, making a tear roll down my cheek.

"But I hate you the most," I swore.

"I love you," he told me, gently kissing my lips. It was so gentle that it almost felt like fiction. Like something I'd written about in my stories. Like a dream that finally came true.

"I love you, too."

"But I love you the most," he promised, and I felt it. I felt his love all throughout me. In my heart, in my soul, in my spirit. I also knew how hard it was for him to admit that. I knew Landon was sad. So, so sad, and so, so broken. And still, he loved me. That probably terrified the hell out of him.

"What are you doing here?!" a voice hissed, this time toward Landon.

He quickly stood and cleared his throat. "Mr. and Mrs. Cole, hi." He brushed his hand against his forehead and didn't make eye contact with them. "I heard about your daughter and wanted to make sure she was okay."

Monica's parents.

That made sense. She didn't look like them at all, but that wasn't shocking. I was sure she looked more like her mother at some point in time before all of the plastic surgery.

"That is none of your business," Mrs. Cole barked. "It's probably because of you that she's in the state she is! You've always been dragging our daughter into troubled waters, and now it finally reached the limit. Our poor Monica is here because of you and your bad influence."

"You're probably the one who gave her the drugs she overdosed on. This is your fault," Mr. Cole hissed. His words were coated in hate, which only made me despise him more.

"What? No, it's not!" I started, but Landon placed a hand in front of me to stop my words. It wasn't fair, though. He was being attacked left and right for things he had no part in. He wasn't the villain of this story; he was the hero. Yet, everyone was showing up with pitchforks, chasing after him while shouting, "Kill the beast!"

Their hatred was misguided and misdirected. They should've been calling themselves out for being crappy parents.

"You need to leave this place," Mr. Cole ordered Landon. "And you need to stay the hell away from our daughter. If I ever see you near her again, I will have the cops so far up your ass that you'll never be able to come back to this town. Now go."

"What's the matter with you people?" I cried, feeling so angry for Landon. I couldn't imagine what my brain would do if I had full-grown adults hollering at me about how terrible I was as a person. I wanted to rage for him. I wanted to defend him time and time again, every single second that a nasty comment was made toward him.

But he wouldn't let me.

He refused to allow me into the murky waters to fight his battle.

"It's okay, Shay. I'm fine. I'm going to go," he whispered before turning toward Monica's parents. "Mr. and Mrs. Cole, I am sorry for what you're going through. I hope your daughter is okay. Again, I'm sorry...for everything."

His voice cracked before he headed off toward the exit.

I went to hurry after him, and his mother gripped my arm, stopping me. "Let him go, girl. Isn't it clear to you yet that he's troubled? Don't you see the damage he's done?"

I ripped my arm away from her. "Don't you see the damage you've done, Mrs. Cole?" I turned to the two adults who were acting more like children. "You're all wrong about him. He's not a monster; he's not damaged...he's good. He's so good, kind, and gentle. Yet you all are so wrapped up in your fictional stories of who he is that you won't even open your eyes to the truth."

I hurried off in Landon's direction, and when I spotted him, I was quick to call out to him.

He turned around slowly with his hands stuffed in his jeans pockets. "What are you doing?" he asked.

"I'm coming with you."

"No, Shay. You can't. Didn't you hear them? I'm no good for you. I'm no good for anyone."

"Stop it. Don't let that crap get in your head, Landon. They are wrong. They are beyond wrong. Don't let them allow your mind to start spiraling. Let me come with you. Let me stay by your side."

He cringed and rubbed the back of his neck. "I can't, Shay. But can you do one thing for me?"

"What's that?"

"Stay here and let me know if Monica makes it out okay? I know her parents probably won't stick around too long if they have other places to be. But if you could just let me know? Keep me posted."

"But what about you?"

"Don't worry about me, Chick." He smirked a little. "I'm always okay."

Liar.

"Landon—"

"Please, Shay. *Please.*"

The way his mouth pleaded for my help was nothing compared to the way his eyes begged me to stay.

"She won't want me here," I warned.

"Trust me, I've been as low as Monica before. You'll want anyone there over the idea of being alone. You don't have to, though. If you don't want."

"I will for you. I'll do anything for you."

He smiled, and I thought it was a real one.

I moved in without permission and wrapped my arms around Landon's body. I held on tighter than ever, needing him to feel me. To feel close. To feel wanted.

"I love you," I whispered against his neck as he pulled me in closer. I loved how we fit together. As if we were two puzzle pieces who finally found their way home.

"I love you," he replied, his voice so low and drawn out.

He let me go and thanked me for watching after Monica. As he walked away, I wanted to follow after him, but I knew I couldn't. I made him a promise, and I knew I couldn't let him down.

As I walked back toward the waiting room, I thought back to Mima's words from a few weeks ago.

Sé valiente, sé fuerte, sé amable, y quédate.

Be brave, be strong, be kind, and stay.

I did exactly that.

Monica's parents left the moment they learned she was okay. They went back to their lives, leaving their daughter still in her hospital bed with no one around her.

When the nurses weren't looking, I went ahead and snuck into her room, knocking lightly on the door.

"Come in," she grumbled.

The moment I rounded the curtain, I felt the biggest knot in my stomach. She looked awful. Broken down in ways unknown to most people. She was pale, heavy bags sat under her eyes, and she looked as if her body had been drained of every ounce of energy she stored.

She sat up a little and combed her hair behind her ear, looking a bit embarrassed. "What are you doing here?" she asked, dodging clear eye contact with me.

"I came with Landon to make sure you were okay. Your parents sent him away the moment they saw him, and he asked me to stay to make sure you were okay."

She snickered but then began coughing. "Why would he do that? It's clear that he doesn't give a damn about me."

"I think we both know that's not true, Monica. Just because Landon isn't in love with you, doesn't mean he doesn't have love for you."

She huffed and rolled her eyes. "This must make you happy, huh? Seeing me like this."

I frowned. Did she really think that? That her pain was my glory?

"Never," I told her. "I'm just glad you're okay."

She turned her head away from me and wiped a few fallen tears from her eyes. "I hate you. You know that, right?"

"Yes. I know."

"Do you know why, though?"

"No…"

She looked at me with tears still streaming down her face. "Because you make him better. I see it when he looks at you. There's a light I could've never pulled out of him. You're fixing him. You're turning him back on after he's been shut down for so long, and I hate you for that. I hate you for being able to do what I never could."

"Monica—"

"I love you for that, too," she cut in. "I love you for giving him that light. His life has been dark for so long. Both of ours have. We've had some pretty shitty days together. But you're making it easier for him. At least one of us deserves that."

"Both of you deserve that." I looked down at the brochures on her table and picked them up. "Rehab?" I asked.

She rolled her eyes and shrugged. "I guess that's the next step after an overdose. Some hippie mumbo jumbo about how my life matters and a step program to help me get clean."

"That's good, Monica. That's really good." I shifted around in my sneakers. "If you want someone to come visit you while you're there—"

"Don't get it twisted, Gable," she snapped. "We aren't friends or anything."

I laughed a little. Fair enough.

"Okay, well, I'll let you rest. I just wanted to stop in and let you know we've been thinking about you, Landon and I."

"Yeah, okay."

She turned back to face the window, and I started walking away but paused when she spoke.

"Is he okay?" she asked.

"Honestly? I'm not sure. I feel like he's slipping away again."

She nodded but still kept her back toward me. "There's a key to my house under the plant in my backyard. The one near the backdoor. Go get it, then go into my room and grab the papers on my desk. Give those to him. I think they might help."

"Okay. I'll do that."

"Thank you," she muttered. Then, she turned my way with the sincerest stare I'd ever seen Monica give. "Really, Shay. Thank you."

I nodded once.

"And whatever," she mumbled, "if you happen to stop by the rehab clinic at some point this summer, I guess I wouldn't tell you to piss off."

"Sounds like a deal."

"And Shay? I still hate you."

"Don't worry, Monica." I smiled. "I still hate you, too."

After I left the hospital, I headed straight for Monica's house to grab the paperwork from her bedroom. When I saw the ripped-out pages from my notebook, I had a split second of anger push through me, knowing she stole something from me, but then again, she was trying to do right in that very moment. Plus, my biggest concern was Landon.

Before going to his place, I went back to Mima's and picked up a few more notebooks to give to him. I didn't know how much the words would mean to him, but I knew he had to fill his head with more love than hate that evening.

I knocked on Landon's door with nerves skyrocketing through my stomach as I waited for him to answer. A sigh of relief rolled through my system when the door opened and he stood there.

"Hey, you." I grinned. "Can I come in?"

He stepped to the side and cleared a pathway for me.

"Monica's doing okay. She's staying in the hospital for forty-eight hours before being transferred to a rehab clinic."

"Rehab?" he questioned, arching an eyebrow. "Good. That's good."

"She asked me to give these to you," I said, handing him the ripped-out pages of the notebook. "And I figured I should give you these, too, to go with it." I gave him three more notebooks.

"What are these?"

"The most in-depth character portfolio I've ever created. I get a feeling you've already read the first part, but in my head, there's nothing worse than an incomplete story, so you should finish reading until the very end."

He brushed a finger under his nose. "Will you stay with me as I read through it? I just...my mind is doing crazy shit right now, and I don't want to be alone tonight."

"I'm not going anywhere, Landon. I'm here. I'm always here."

We moved to the couch and sat down. I pulled my knees into my chest and chewed on the collar of my shirt as he read the words I'd written about him. There were a few paragraphs that made him laugh out loud, and others that made him almost tear up. Every word was filled with love. With want. With desire.

With respect.

"You think I'm all these good things?" he asked, his voice shaky as he placed the notebooks down on the coffee table.

"No. I think you're more." I moved closer to him and wrapped my arms around his body. He put his hands on my lower back, holding me in place. "I'm sorry you're so sad, Landon."

"Too sad. It's too much for you."

"You're never too much. I love your happy, and I love your sad. I love your light, and I love your dark. I love you. Every script, every page, every revision, every draft."

He brushed his lips against mine and closed his eyes. "I needed you today, and you were there. I cannot thank you for being there for me, for being here for me. For being…you. You make the darkest nights feel like the sun. I love you," he breathed out, "I love you. I…love… you…"

We were just two kids who made a stupid bet a few months ago. Two kids who pushed one another. Two kids who pissed each other off, who made rude remarks, who battled each other tooth and nail. And then, somewhere in the midst of our hate, we accidentally fell in love.

"Can I have you tonight, Shay? Can I take you to my room and taste every single inch of you?" he muttered as his lips slowly nibbled at mine. "Can I be yours tonight?"

"Yes. Every inch of me is all yours."

He carried me to his room and then undressed me slowly.

We made love twice that night. The first time was delicate and controlled; he went slow and worshipped every single inch of me. The second time, I asked him to show me his scars, and he did exactly that. It was a messy kind of love. His kisses were deeper, his thrusts were harder, and his love was loud. He rocked his hips against mine, pinning me against the dresser, against the bed, against his heartbeats. He made love like the wild beast that lived within him. He moaned and grunted as he pounded into me, showing me his pain, his heartache, his scars.

And that heartbroken boy? He was mine.

Damaged.

Broken.

Disheveled.

And mine.

When Sunday morning came, he walked me to the front door and wrapped me into a hug. "Thank you for staying."

"I'll always stay."

He gave me a lopsided smile. "You're everything good in this world. Do you know that?"

"Ditto."

He looked my way, and I began to read him. There was something he wasn't saying, something he was holding back to himself, and I hated that I couldn't tap into it. I hated that I couldn't tap into that part of him. It was as if he'd put up a wall to keep me from reading his current chapter.

"What is it?" I asked.

"What is what?"

"What's going on in your head?"

He snickered and tapped his temple. "Not much goes on in here," he joked.

"Landon, really. What is it?"

"Don't worry so much, Chick. I'm okay. I'll talk to you later, all right?" He pulled me into a hug and kissed my forehead. "I love you."

"I love you, too."

I couldn't get the knot out of my stomach, though, based on how he said his words. Why did his "I love you" feel like he was saying goodbye?

Chapter Thirty

Landon

SHAY LEFT SUNDAY MORNING, AND I WAS THANKFUL TO HAVE MARIA come that afternoon.

I knew I shouldn't have been alone. Even with Shay staying with me last night, I felt a heaviness on me that I couldn't shake away. I was afraid to be alone with my thoughts. I was afraid to be left with only myself and my mind.

"You are quiet tonight, which means you're probably thinking too much," Maria commented as we ate our dinner together.

"Just a lot going on in my mind," I commented, swirling my spoon around in the mashed potatoes.

"By all means, share your thoughts."

I wanted to talk to her about it. I wanted to open up and show her the messiness of my brain, but it didn't work that way. Even if I talked about it, my thoughts would leave my head jumbled and flustered. They wouldn't make sense to her, because they hardly made sense to me.

All I knew was that I was tired. Each day felt more like a burden, and I was being weighed down.

She clasped her hands together and leaned toward me. "Slow it down, Landon. Your brain is running on overdrive, so you must slow it down. Go slow. Take your time to process through your feelings."

I wished it were that easy. I wished depression was like a car, and I could simply push the brakes to slow down my mind whenever I needed a rest. I wished I could shut off the engine and be still for a small amount of time. But depression, for me, was the complete opposite of that. When my mind started driving, it hit the accelerator and took off at full speed toward a brick wall.

Any day now, I was going to crash.

Any day now, I was going to fall completely apart.

I gave Maria a sloppy grin. "It's okay. I'm okay."

She narrowed her eyes and placed a hand on top of mine. "You're not okay, and that's fine. But don't spiral too far away from home that you can't pull yourself out of it. I know that feeling. I've been living with depression for a very long time. I know how your mind can swallow you whole."

I raised a shocked eyebrow. There was no way Maria had depression. She was the happiest woman I'd ever crossed paths with. She was just like her granddaughter—the definition of joy.

"There's no way..." I started.

She smiled, and dammit her grin looked like Shay's, and dammit, dammit, dammit, I missed Shay's smile the most. And her laugh. And her eyes. And her small nibbling of candy.

"I've been working my whole life to make peace with my depression. It was a long battle of finding the right medication for my system and talking to the right people. I still see my therapist once a week. There seems to be this idea that if you have depression, you don't deserve certain things in this world, and Landon Scott, that is a lie. You deserve more. More than your thoughts that lie to you. More than your doubts that you keep feeding yourself. More than your fears that you'll never have a normal life. You deserve more."

I lowered my head and fiddled with my fingers. "I'm scared," I confessed.

"What's your biggest fear?"

"Being alone. Not being able to let people in because of the mess that is my brain."

"What about my granddaughter? You let her in. I know you did. I'd never seen you happier than when you two were getting close."

I nodded. "Shay's amazing. She's the best thing that's ever happened to me. But I don't deserve her. I honestly wish I could be more for her, but I can't. I'm just me."

"And that is enough," Maria whispered, squeezing my hand.

"That's not what your daughter told me."

Maria raised an eyebrow. "Camila said something to you?"

"Yes. She came to me and asked me to stay away from Shay because I was too damaged. She told me I wasn't good enough. That I wasn't worthy of loving your granddaughter."

"No..." Maria shook her head in shock, sitting back a bit in her chair. "No. No. No."

I shrugged. "It's okay. She wasn't wrong."

"Yes, Landon. She was. I love my daughter, but she was way out of line for ever saying those words to you. Camila is going through her own storm at this moment. Her life is upside down, and I'm certain her world is spinning just as fast as your mind. But she went toward the wrong target when she came to you. Instead of talking to you, she should've been having a conversation with her own heart. She should've gone internal and done some soul searching, but she didn't. Hurt people have a way of hurting others. Not even on purpose, but it happens. That's the problem with making decisions during stretches of temporary sadness or struggle. You sometimes shoot bullets at people who didn't deserve to be shot. You didn't deserve that, Landon.

"Any woman would be lucky to be loved by a heart like yours—including my granddaughter. You don't see what a gift you are to this world, to the people around you. But we want you in our lives. We need you in our lives. So, please, stop running. Place your feet on the ground and make peace with your demons. Stop fighting them and hold them. You're not broken; you're just complex. And the most beautiful things in the world have the most complex heartbeats."

I didn't reply, because I hadn't a clue what to say.

I was sad.

The kind of sad I didn't think I could get over.

"Do me a favor, son?" Maria asked me.

"Yeah?"

"Promise me one thing. Promise me that when you are feeling at your lowest, like you have nothing left to give...like your mind is slipping and swallowing you whole...that you'll reach out to someone. It doesn't have to be me, but just someone you trust wholeheartedly. Don't drown in your head, Landon. Reach out. Because this world? It needs you. We need you. I need you here. So, don't you dare think that you're not important. Don't you dare let those thoughts drown you. Promise me this."

I brushed my hand against my nose and sniffled as I nodded. "I promise."

"Again, please," she begged, her eyes piercing through me.

"I promise."

After we finished eating dinner, we cleaned everything up. I headed to my room and grabbed a letter I'd written before she came over.

"Can you do me a favor?" I asked. "Do you think you can give this letter to Shay for me?"

"Of course, sweetheart. Anything you need, I'll do for you."

"Thank you."

She gathered her things, and when she was about to leave, I walked her to my front door. "Thanks for today, Maria."

"Thanks for every day, Landon," she replied. She shifted around in her shoes, then held her hands out toward me. "Do you think I can pray over you before I go?" she asked.

I grimaced a little but nodded. I took her hands into mine and felt her warmth. The same warmth that raced through Shay's spirit. As Maria began praying, I prayed a little, too. I didn't know if I was doing it right, or if it would really make a difference at all. This time, I did something different than all the other times she prayed for me, though.

This time, I closed my eyes.

I headed to the swimming pool after Maria left and climbed up the diving board ladder. I sat on the edge of it, gripping the sides with both hands. I looked down at the gleaming water as it waved ever so slightly back and forth.

The past few weeks had been hard. Harder than I thought they could've been. I wondered if that was how Lance had felt before he took his life. I wondered how far his mind was gone before he took that plunge.

There was a heavy fear in my stomach as I sat on the diving board. I hadn't climbed it since Lance had taken his life. On that very board was where my uncle held his last thoughts. Where he took his last breaths. Where he let go.

I didn't want to be like him.

I didn't want to let go.

But I was so fucking sad that my heart felt as if it was trying to claw its way out of my damn chest.

Still, I didn't want to let go.

Tears started falling down my cheeks as I sat there, thinking about Lance, thinking about me, and thinking about the parallels that we shared in our lives. Then, I thought of Shay's words in those notebooks. How she called me my own person. How she swore I was unique, how she said I didn't have to walk in the footsteps of my past loved ones.

Then, I thought of Maria and the promise she had me make to her.

"I'm not him," I told myself. "I'm not Lance. I'm not him. I'm not him...I'm...not...him..."

I blinked my eyes shut and took a few deep inhalations.

Then, I opened my eyes, reached into my pocket, and pulled out my cell phone. I dialed a number rapidly, and when it started ringing, I let out a breath.

"Hey, Mom."

"Hey, Landon. You okay?" Mom asked quickly. There must've been something off in my voice based on how quick she was to ask me if I was okay.

"I, um..." I cleared my throat and scratched the back of my neck. "No. I'm not okay. I...I need you."

Her voice became alarmed, and I heard her start ruffling around. "Okay, okay. I'm coming, honey. I'm coming. Are you at home?"

"Yes."

"Stay there, sweetheart. I'm booking a plane ticket now. I'm on my way to you."

"Thanks, Mom."

"Always, baby. Always, always, always. I love you, I love you," she told me.

"I love you, I love you," I replied.

Mom called Greyson to come sit with me until she made it home. Greyson called Eric. Eric called Hank. Hank came with Raine.

I climbed down the diving board, and the four of them wrapped their arms around me and held onto me so tight. I cried into their arms like a fucking child, but they didn't mock me or laugh at my weakness.

They simply held on stronger.

It blew my mind how people unrelated to me could still be my brothers and sisters. Maybe not by blood, but by heart. Something had to be said about friends who never left your side, even when your storm was wild enough to strike their souls, too.

"I'm sorry I'm so fucked up, you guys," I sniffled, feeling embarrassed by my breakdown.

"Hey, man." Eric patted me on the back and shrugged. Then, he offered me the words I'd given him a few weeks back. "Whatever you are is good enough for us."

I didn't deserve them. I didn't deserve their love.

But still, they gave it freely.

Chapter Thirty-One

Shay

"L ANDON ASKED ME TO GIVE YOU THIS LETTER," MIMA SAID after she returned from his place. I was glad that my grandmother checked in on him every Sunday. I had a feeling he needed it a lot that afternoon.

She handed me over a folded piece of paper. "Now, just to be clear, I read the letter, because I am a nosy grandmother and I worry about the two of your hearts. You mean the world to me, sweetheart, and so does Landon. He's a good boy. A little banged up around the edges, but still worth loving."

"He's really broken, isn't he, Mima?"

"Oh, honey…we're all a little broken. If you think anyone in this world doesn't have cracks, scars, and a story, then you're not looking close enough. We weren't brought into this world to be perfect; we were brought here to be human. To live. To feel. To hurt. To love. To cry. To exist. And with that, comes a few broken parts. You don't have to be perfect to love or be loved. You just have to be brave enough to show the world your scars and call them beautiful."

"I love him."

"Yes, and once you read that letter, I think it will be pretty clear that he loves you, too. I want to warn you. Some of those words are hard, but I beg you to keep reading. The ending will always be worth the hard middle."

She left me alone with the pages. I walked over to the couch, sat down, and as I crossed my legs, I began reading Landon's mind.

Chick,

Reading that word was enough to make my chest tighten with nerves. I pushed myself to continue, even though I was afraid of what was coming next. Afraid of what his words would tell me, afraid of what his truths would reveal.

I hate myself, and that's my truth.

Each day, I wake up and wonder why I'm here. Why I'm fighting each day when everything feels hopeless. I wonder what the point is, and that scares me. I struggle to get out of bed, to exist in a way that looks normal to others. When we first began our bet, you told me that I was fake, and that's the truest thing I've ever been called.

I am fake.

I fake being popular.

I fake loving parties.

I fake being content with life.

I fake fitting in.

I am fake through every fiber of my soul, except for a small corner that's real solely for you.

I love myself when I'm with you. Each day I wake up and think of you, and I know why I'm here. I know why I'm fighting each day when everything feels hopeless. I know what the point is and that scares me. It scares me how much I love myself when I'm with you, because what will happen when you're gone? Will I struggle to get out of bed? Will I struggle to exist in a way that looks normal to others? Will I be okay without you around?

It kills me, Shay. It kills me how I break down, how I crumble under the smallest ounce of pressure. It kills me that I snap so easily and have all this rage inside of me that I'm not sure how to control. It kills me that I hurt you.

I hate me for hurting you.

You are the realest thing in my life, and I had to push you away, because I don't think I'm what you need. What you deserve.

I never kissed that girl, and I hope you believe me. I knew I'd have to make it seem that way for you to really not want to have anything to do with me. Still, you showed up at the hospital with arms wide open. Still, you love me. So, I figured I should tell you my hardest truths.

When I was younger, I thought about ending my life. I don't know if you recall, but I went through a pretty ugly duckling season. In sixth grade, I was bullied pretty badly, and I would come home crying every night. My mom was so worried about me, which was why she quit her traveling job in order to be home with me. The bullying was bad, though, and I didn't know how to deal with my thoughts and emotions in an appropriate way. Everything felt so wild and intense in my head that I'd get panic attacks.

That was the first time I cut myself.

That was the first time I told my mom I thought about ending my life.

It never really got easier; I just got stronger. Physically, at least. Emotionally and mentally, I was still a wreck. Working out became my outlet, and my parents got me on some anti-depression medications. They work a little. Not as much as I would like, but thankfully I don't have those urges to hurt myself anymore.

I picked up drinking and drugs to quiet my mind a little more. I tried to push the bad thoughts so far down that I'd almost forget they were there. It worked until it didn't. Then, after losing Lance to an overdose, I knew I couldn't keep down that line. Even though I loved my uncle, I didn't want to end up like his story. I didn't want to follow his path.

I went cold turkey, and then came you.

You threw me for a loop. You brought light into a world that I thought would always be encompassed with shadows. You made me wish and hope and dream of a future I never really thought about.

I don't want to die, Shay.

For the first time in my life, I want to live. I want to find a way to feel alive on my own. The way I feel when I'm around you is how I want to feel when I am alone. I want to sit in the darkness and be okay with the sound of my own heartbeats. I want to not struggle to get out of bed. I want to be okay with being by myself.

And then, I want to have you.

I want all of you, Shay, but not like this.

I want to get my mind right first, fix myself, so I can be yours.

So, this is my formal letter to let you know that I'm working to never be fake again.

I won't fake being popular.

I won't fake loving parties.

I won't fake being content with life.

I won't fake fitting in.

It will be real. I'll be real first for me, and then for you.

After I'm done with this, I'm planning on reaching out to my mom for help. I'm going to get help. I want to get better. I want this life more than I ever thought I could, and that's because of you.

You awakened my spirit after so many nightmares, and for that, I owe you the world.

I love you.

-Landon.

P.S.

I love you.

I said it once so you could hear me.

Twice to leave an imprint.

I sat back on the couch, feeling a rush of emotions racing through me. Yet, the one that stood out the most was the fact that he said he was going to get help. That alone made me cry. It took a strong man to admit to needing a hand.

I pulled out my phone and sent him a message.

Me: How's your heart tonight?

It took him a few hours to answer, but relief swept through me as my phone dinged later that night.

Landon: Still beating.

Chapter Thirty-Two

Landon

Shay: Meet me at the willows.

I read her text over and over again. Mom had been home for a few days, sorting things out for me. I was going to take a year off from college and work on my mental health. Dad flipped out when he heard the news, but Mom stood by my side through and through.

"Hey, I'm going to go see someone really quick if that's okay," I told Mom as she sat at the dining room table, fumbling through paperwork. She'd been very protective of me since she got back, not allowing me to be alone for too long. She even went as far as trying to pull her mattress into my bedroom to sleep on in order to keep me from being on my own.

"Where to? Who are you seeing?"

"Just to the park to see Shay."

She raised an eyebrow, and a small smirk appeared on her lips. "Shay? That's the girl?"

I nodded.

She bit her bottom lip and narrowed her eyes. "Are you sure you're okay to be going off on your own? I can come with you and wait in the car…"

"Mom. I'm good. I swear." I understood why she was worried, though. The last few days had been hard. I couldn't imagine being a parent dealing with a sad child. The blame I would've placed on myself would've been so heavy. But the truth of the matter was, just having her near was enough to quiet the loudest parts of me sometimes. I was lucky to have Mom at my side.

Though, still, she probably thought the worst of the worst about my mental state.

So, to give her a bit of ease, I shrugged. "But if you drove me, that would be fine, too."

A small breath slipped through her lips. "Okay, yes. I can do that. Of course."

She grabbed her keys, and we headed out of the house.

Me: On my way.

The first time I came to the two willows with Shay, it was still wintertime. All of the flowers were now fully bloomed, the trees were covered in vibrant green leaves, and the sun kissed everything around it. Everything looked so alive.

I headed down the pathway toward the two trees and smiled when I saw Shay standing there.

"Hey, Chick." I grinned.

"Hey, Satan."

Seconds later, we were in each other's embrace. I breathed her in, never wanting to let her go. Her head was nestled in my neck, and her gentle breaths brushed against my skin.

I was almost certain I'd spend the rest of my life smiling whenever I was near her. She had a way of pulling them out of me.

We sat right in front of the willows, staring up at people's love stories, wondering what to make of our own. Truth was, there was still so much to discover about ourselves. About who we were as individuals, and who we were as a couple.

"I've read your letter a million times so far," she explained. "I still cry each time."

I snickered. "That's funny, because I've read your notebooks a million times, too." I sat up straighter. "Didn't cry, because I'm a manly man," I joked, even though I cried like a fucking baby getting booster shots.

"Mima told me your mom is back in town," she said.

"Yeah. She's actually waiting for me in the car right now. She doesn't let me too far out of her viewpoint anymore."

"She sounds like a good mama."

"Only the best."

I looked up at the two willows as the leaves danced back and forth. I clasped my hands together. "A few years ago, I was on one of those stupid field trips to a farm. I was probably high as a kite, and my mind wasn't the most stable in the world, but I remember seeing this chicken with a bunch of baby chicks running around with her. They were so little. Pure and beautiful. There was something about them that stood out to me. Something that reminded me of you. The next day at school, I called you Chick, and you hated every second of it, but I loved it, because whenever I called you that nickname, I knew a part of me was calling you pure and beautiful."

Her cheeks reddened a little as she tilted her head toward me. "Do you know why I called you Satan?" she asked.

"No. Why?"

"Because I thought you were the freaking devil."

I laughed out loud. "Fair enough."

"So, what's the plan? What's going on with you?"

This was the part of the conversation I was dreading the most. "My mom's making plans for me to get better treatment. We are going to switch around my medications, too, to see what works best with me."

"That's good, Landon. That's great."

"Yeah. She even found this amazing therapist that I'm going to start going to maybe. I mean, she's no Mrs. Levi, but she will do."

Shay smiled ear to ear. "I'm so proud of you for reaching out for help. For being open to that avenue. A lot of people are afraid to even speak up."

"Yeah. It's hard, but I'm trying." I grimaced and lowered my head as I fiddled with my fingers. "There's just one problem."

"What's that?"

"Everything my mom is planning is out in California." Her jaw dropped slightly, and I cringed, seeing the disappointment hit her. I turned her way even more and took her hands into mine. "She has a friend who said we could stay with them out there, but we can look here if need be. We can find doctors out this way. I can figure out a way to get better and still be near you, Shay. Just tell me to stay, and I'll stay."

Her lips parted, and she shook her head. "I want to say those words. I want to be selfish and tell you to stay here with me so we can be an us, but I can't do that. Truth is, if you stay, I'll love you. If you go, I'll love you even more. Because that would be you doing something for yourself. Your healing is of the utmost importance here, Landon. And if the best doctors are out there in California, then that's where you should go. And also, you'll be able to be with your mom more often."

I lowered my head, because I knew she was right. I needed my mom right now. Maybe more than I ever needed her before. And in order for me to be the person I wanted to be for Shay, I needed to figure out this head of mine. I needed to learn how I worked.

Shay raised my hands to her mouth and kissed my palms. "This is a good thing, even though it feels a little sad."

"I didn't know good things could be sad."

"Yes..." She gave me a halfway grin. "But I always knew that sad things could be good. You're living proof of that. Let's make a promise to each other. When you find you, come back here," she said, placing her hand over her heart. "Come back to me. But please, by all means, take your time. I'll be here, I swear. I want you to find me, but not at the chance of you losing yourself. Take your time. Heal.

"Find yourself, lose yourself, then find yourself again. Do some soul searching, Landon. Go deep. Laugh, cry, discover. Do some digging, but don't you dare rush this. Don't you dare try to skip a few steps in your healing to just get back to me. I'm here. I'm here today, I'll be here tomorrow. But, Landon, please..." she whispered, placing a hand on my cheek. Her forehead fell against mine, and my lips brushed against hers as she spoke the most important words into my soul. "*Go slow.*"

Chapter Thirty-Three

Shay

GREYSON DECIDED TO THROW LANDON A GOING AWAY PARTY, WHICH was pretty intimate. Only Landon's core group—the fantastic four (+Raine) and I came. Along with Mima and Landon's mother. Somehow, that was enough love to fill a stadium.

The party was lighthearted, filled with a lot of laughter and smiling.

Mima cooked the food for the party and said a prayer over the meal. Then, during dinner, Raine stood to give a speech.

"Okay, okay, I will keep this short and sweet, because I did my makeup and I don't feel like crying off my mascara. But I wanted to raise a glass to Landon Scott Harrison—one of the most complex, intriguing boys I'd ever come across. I know we aren't family, but I look at you as a little brother to me."

"I'm older than you, Raine," Landon said.

"Yeah, but you've always acted like a little shit," she replied. She turned toward Mima and Landon's Mom to offer an apology for her language. "But anywho, I wanted to say I'm proud of you. We all are. And now, I'm not one to ever get involved in anyone else's lives—"

"CoughLIEScough," Hank hacked up a lung, making everyone chuckle.

Raine rolled her eyes. "Anyway. I just wanted to give you a few tips on your journey in California that will help you along the way. Number one: don't get plastic surgery, you already have a solid jawline. Number two: if you run into George Clooney, give him my number. He's my freebie in mine and Hank's relationship. Number three: Don't become a beach bum. I've seen you in the sun before. You'll burn. Number four..." Raine cleared her throat and her eyes watered over as she grew a little somber. "Call your sister and your brothers whenever you need us. Day or night. We'll answer. Well, maybe not Eric at night because he's a heavy sleeper. Number five—don't lose your asshole charm. It's what makes you...you. Number six—and this one is the most important one of them all—don't forget we love you. I know life can get crazy, and we'll all be busy with crap, but know that no matter what, the love is always there. We're always here. Even if we are miles apart." She wiped a few tears from her eyes and held her glass up. "Here's to you, Land. We love you, we're proud of you, and you're going to do great things in this world."

We all cheered and wiped the falling tears from our own eyes.

After everyone left, Landon and I headed over to his house for our final goodbye. My mind had been spinning all afternoon knowing that this moment was growing close. Before heading into his house, I went and grabbed a wrapped gift from my car. Then, I met him in his living room.

We sat on the couch, and stare at one another for a while. Unsure what to say, unsure how to start.

"I don't want to sit here crying all night," I joked, nudging him in the arm. "So, let's just make this a happy moment, okay?"

"Okay."

"Here." I handed him the gift and he raised an eyebrow.

"You didn't have to get me anything."

"Yes, I did. Open it."

He ripped the paper open to find ten new notebooks.

"There's about twenty different questions in every notebook. I figured it could help you figure out some of your thoughts when you're struggling."

"It's perfect," he said with a genuine smile. "You're perfect."

He kissed me and I loved it.

I loved him.

"You know what I want to do right now?" he asked.

"What's that?"

"Watch a few episodes of *Friends* with you in my arms."

I smiled. "Perfect."

As we lay against one another, Landon pulled out two pieces of Laffy Taffy from his pocket and handed me one.

Banana-flavored—obviously.

We watched the show, we fell deeper in love, and when it was time for me to go, I held on a little longer.

He walked me to my car and held the door open for me.

"I don't want to say goodbye," I told him. "I never want to say goodbye."

"Then let's just say goodnight." A small smirk fell to his lips as he spoke to me. "Good night, good night. Parting is such sweet sorrow."

My smile grew, and the butterflies he'd always delivered me came back in full force. "That I shall say good night till it be tomorrow," I finished the Romeo and Juliet line.

He leaned in and kissed me. "No regrets?" he whispered against my lips.

"No regrets," I replied.

I drove home with tears rolling down my cheeks, but they weren't sad tears. They were tears filled with hope for Landon. He was going to be okay.

Then, he'd come back to me.

Landon left a few days ago to head to California. He and his mother packed their bags and headed toward his future of healing. While he was gone, I was working on my own healing, too. Mom and I had some damage to our relationship that needed to be talked about. We had to go deep with one another in order to heal from what my father had done to the two of our lives.

But we were both willing to try to repair our connection, because our love was stronger than our struggles.

Landon made me promise him that I'd continue on with my life, too. So, I did exactly that. I made an attempt every single day to write new words toward my manuscripts. I began applying for scholarships, too, with the help of Eleanor. And each day, I found a reason to smile.

If the past few months had taught me anything about life, it was that it wasn't always easy, but there was something beautiful to be seen in every situation.

Every now and then, I'd receive a message from Landon, asking me about my heartbeats, and I'd shoot him my reply. Then, he'd do the same.

I tried my best to not dread the fact that he was gone. I tried to not overthink when—if ever—he'd come back to me. A part of me knew our story wasn't over. A part of me knew we'd only tapped into the beginning of the Landon and Shay story.

So, I could only do one thing. I was forced to take the same advice I'd given Landon when we sat near those two willows. I went slow with life, taking it all in and never rushing through my personal growth. Still, the thought of Landon and I together as one always seemed to cross my mind.

Even though we didn't carve our names into the willow trees, I knew his initials were forever imprinted against my heart. And whenever it beat, it was beating for him.

Made in the USA
Las Vegas, NV
06 February 2023

66975145R00182